LOOK THE PART

LOOK THE PART

by Jewel E. Ann

Copyright © 2018 by Jewel E. Ann
ISBN: 978-0-9990482-8-3
Print Edition

Cover Designer: ©Sarah Hansen, Okay Creations
Photo: ©MaelDesign and Photography
Formatting: BB eBooks

DEDICATION

To everyone in search of a second chance.

AUTHOR'S NOTE

This is not a story about autism. This is a story about life. And in life there are children with autism and parents navigating unchartered territory to give these children a voice and a future. Every child is unique. Every journey requires a different map. This is *one* story. *One* journey. Harrison was inspired by the children I have personally had the pleasure to know and love.

PROLOGUE

HEIDI GAVE ME a son and then I killed her. Lucky were the bastards who learned life lessons from close calls. I envied those lucky bastards.

"DON'T DRINK TONIGHT. I want you to put another baby inside of me," my wife whispered as her hand slid up my leg under the table surrounded by twelve of our closest family and friends. Heidi picked my favorite steak house in Omaha and reserved the party room for my special day. I had no idea until everyone yelled surprise.

I loved her beyond words.

"And for the birthday boy?" The brunette waitress winked at me, readying her pen against the pad of paper in her hand.

"Whisky neat."

Heidi frowned.

I grabbed her hand and pressed it to my erection. "I'm not going to have any issues granting your request."

"We'll see." Her curt response held little confidence.

My parents drove in from Denver to surprise me, but my two-year-old son, Harrison, stole the show. They took turns gushing over him with Heidi's mom. I didn't anticipate being a father before I graduated college; I also didn't anticipate meeting the woman I couldn't live without at the exact moment I needed her the most.

She was a nursing student at the hospital they sent me to the day an ACL injury shattered my football career. I called her an angel. Heidi insisted it was the drugs they gave me for the pain.

"Monaghan said you're going to be his agent when he goes Pro." My dad gave me a curious look.

"Monaghan is full of shit. No team in their right mind will draft Pretty Boy. He's going to be a teacher. That right there shows you he's too much of a pussy to have a serious chance in the NFL."

The Cornhusker's young quarterback shot me a smirk from the other end of the table. We both knew he'd go Pro, but I wasn't going to inflate his ego on my birthday.

"Language, Hopkins," Heidi warned.

When she called me by my last name, I squirmed in my chair. It always meant a punishment would follow—and all of her punishments were doled out in the bedroom.

I loved her beyond words.

The night marched on without missing one perfect beat.

Dinner. Friends. Family. Food. Drinks.

My wife outdid herself. She excelled in making every day perfect. She also excelled in making me feel irresponsible for drinking. Every time the waitress placed another drink in front of me, Heidi's lips pursed into a disapproving frown.

I let it slide without argument. Before he died, her father drank a lot of alcohol and was abusive. When we met, she thought I didn't drink. At the time, it was true. Football was my life. I treated my body like a temple. But after my injury, I settled into a life where my body was no longer a temple and the occasional drink was exactly what I needed to ease the pain of lost dreams.

Heidi thought every guy who drank was an abusive alcoholic. I made it my mission to prove her wrong so maybe someday she, too, would relax a little and have a drink on special occasions.

"Happy birthday, Flint. Take care of my babies." My mother-in-law, Sandy, hugged me as everyone said their final birthday wishes and goodnights.

"That's code for hand the keys to your wife." Heidi nudged me with a playful smile that I knew was not at all meant to be playful.

Sandy squeezed my cheeks and looked into my eyes. "I think he's fine, sweetie. Nothing like your father was so give him some slack."

I shot Heidi an I-told-you-so look. Her mother loved me. I was everything her father hadn't been. Heidi hated that I could do no wrong in Sandy's eyes, but I loved it. A dangerous pride came with so much confidence.

After she fastened Harrison into his car seat, Heidi held out her hand.

"I'm fine." I opened the driver's door.

"You're not. You drank a lot tonight."

"I weigh a lot."

"Flint."

I slipped into the driver's seat. "Call me Hopkins, baby. I like where that leads."

"Flint, I'm serious. Our child is in the backseat." She stood between me and the door so I couldn't shut it.

"I want to be in my birthday suit with you. Get in so we can get Harrison to bed."

She crossed her arms over her chest, raven hair flowing in all directions, blue eyes piercing mine.

"I'm. Fine."

Heidi shrugged. "Great. Then don't be a chauvinistic pig. Just let me drive."

Thunder rumbled in the distance as a few drops of rain fell from the night sky.

"You're going to get wet."

She huffed and stomped to the other side of the car. "Stubborn ass," she mumbled as she buckled up.

"Language, Mommy." I chuckled as I started the car.

"There will be a special place in Hell for you, Flint Hopkins, if you kill us or anyone else with your drunk driving."

I put the car in drive and cupped the back of her head, pulling her forehead to mine before letting up on the brake. "You're my world. I would never hurt you. I love you beyond words."

"Jesus, Flint ..." she whispered. "Your breath reeks of whisky. I'm begging you. Let me drive."

I released her and let up on the brake. As much as I loved my wife, I also loved being a man. And a strong man knew his limits and didn't have to be told when he was or wasn't capable of doing something.

THREE DAYS LATER I buried my wife in a cemetery two blocks from our house.

CHAPTER ONE

A Special Place in Hell—10 years later

HAPPY PEOPLE SHOULD come with a warning.

"Hello, Attorney Flint Hopkin's office. Amanda speaking ... Yes ... Okay ... I'll let him know. Thank you for calling. Have a fantastic day."

Who says fantastic? The word comes from fantasy which means not real. My secretary, who did not come with a proper warning, tells everyone who calls here to have a "not real" day. She should work at Disney World.

The intercom on my office phone buzzes. I sigh. "Amanda, my door is open and no one else is here. You don't have to use the intercom. I can hear you just fine."

"How am I supposed to know if you're on the phone?"

"Turn around."

She rotates in her chair. I glance up from my computer, meeting her gaze.

"I don't like to spy on you. When I do, the look you give me creeps me out."

I scratch my chin. "I give you a look?"

She curls her blond hair behind her ears and gives me a sour face. "Yes. You never smile. It's creepy."

"Never?" I cock my head to the side.

"Well, except when Harrison shows up after school. The corners of your mouth turn up like..." her lips twist "...an eighth of an inch. And most people would miss it if they weren't actively watching for it."

Smiling is overrated. And she's right; my son gets the best parts of me. What little remains.

"Who was on the phone?"

"What?"

"Before you informed me of my creepiness, you paged me."

"Oh, yes, Ellen Rodgers will be fifteen minutes late. She got held up at work."

"Running late. Not a good sign. Probably means she'll be late with rent each month."

"Yes, Flint. You're probably right. She got held up at *work*, a place she goes to make money. That's definitely a sign that she'll be late with rent." Amanda swings back around to her desk.

"You're rolling your eyes at me." I return my attention to my computer screen.

"I would never do that, Boss."

Twenty-five minutes later, there's chatter in the waiting room. My focus stays on my computer. There's no reason to give Ms. Rodgers the impression I have nothing better to do than wait for her.

My phone vibrates on my desk.

AMANDA: *Ellen Rodgers is here. I imagine you know this. She's not a client, so I wasn't sure if her arrival warranted an intercom announcement or a verbal announcement since your door is open. How do you want me to proceed with this delicate situation?*

ME: *You're fired.*

AMANDA: *For real!!!! Gosh, I have so much laundry to catch up on at home. Thank you!*

Note to self: Never hire a female secretary again.

> **ME:** *Not for real. Send her back and get me that research I requested three days ago.*
>
> **AMANDA:** *I'll send her back. And I put that research on the bookshelf behind your desk 2 days ago. :)*

"Women," I mumble.

"Hello." The woman applying to rent the space above my office charges toward me with her hand held out. "I'm Ellen Rodgers. I apologize for my tardiness."

I stand and shake her hand. She's *unexpected*. Cheerful—in need of a warning label. I let her enthusiasm for life slide this time because she's easy on the eyes.

"Flint Hopkins. And it's fine." I glance over her shoulder to our audience of one. Amanda shoots me a sly grin. I narrow my eyes until she turns back around.

"Please, have a seat," I point to the chair by my desk.

Ellen drops her handbag on the floor with an ungraceful *thump*. She must live out of her purse.

I home in on her shaky hands unbuttoning her gray wool coat that's overkill for the sixty-degree day. "Forgive my appearance. I had lunch with a four-year-old girl who has a few coordination issues."

Ironic. She appears to have a few of her own.

Long auburn hair stops short of covering the blotchy red stain on her fitted white sweater.

My gaze snaps to hers after it dawns on me that I'm staring at the stain, which happens to be over her breast. "Did you get the contract from Amanda the other day when she showed you the space?"

"Yes. Thank you." Ellen drapes her coat over the back of

the chair and takes a seat.

"Do you have any questions about it?"

"Nope. Looks pretty standard. I love this location, but it's impossible to find available spaces. So I was really excited when I found your ad the same day you posted it."

I scan her application even though I've read it over a dozen times. "You're a music therapist?"

"Yes."

"Music is considered therapy?"

Ellen chuckles. It's childlike. Her face is childlike too. Must be the freckles and light blue eyes.

"Yes. Think of it as an alternative therapy. But it's a legit job. I have a degree for my speciality like any other healthcare professional." She points at my hands folded on my desk. "Nice cufflinks, by the way."

I glance down and adjust each one. "Thank you."

Her teeth trap her glossed lips as if she wants to grin, but something inside vetoes the idea. "Sorry. That was sort of left field of me. I'm a little nervous."

"Why is that?" I ask while opening an email from a client.

She's humming. Why is she humming?

"Because I want the space."

"References?"

"Uh, yes. I sent them to your secretary."

I press the intercom button. "Amanda, I need those references."

"On the shelf next to the research you requested," she calls from her desk. Then the intercom buzzes. "You're welcome, Mr. Hopkins."

Ellen stifles a laugh as I draw in a slow breath of control.

"Well, then. I'll check your reference—"

"I checked them," Amanda says sans intercom.

"You're fired."

Amanda stands and slings her purse over her shoulder. "I'll file for unemployment in the morning."

"Have a good evening," I mumble, giving her a look— maybe *the* look.

"Night, Flint." She winks.

When the lock clicks, I return my attention to big, blue, unblinking eyes. Even her cheeks, which had been a bit rosy when she arrived, are now void of all color except her freckles.

"I fire her on a daily basis. She has no respect for authority."

Ellen's body remains statuesque, eyes shifting in tiny increments searching mine.

I turn and grab the references off the shelf behind me. On the papers in my hands there are a fair amount of good references. There's really no reason not to rent her the space other than my obsession with crossing more t's and dotting more i's than exist on the proverbial paper. Absolute control is my life.

A cautious smile rides up her face. "You're a hard man to read, Mr. Hopkins."

A dark read.

"And you're my newest tenant. Welcome. I'll need two months' rent and your signature on these papers." I slide the rental agreement that Amanda clipped to Ellen's references across my desk along with a pen.

There's a certain amount of envy I feel toward her. I can't remember the last time I smiled like that over *anything*. And she's lit up like a night in July over something as insignificant as a second-story space outside of downtown Minneapolis.

"Thank you. You've made my day. Heck, you've made my

week." She scribbles her name and initials by all the sticky arrows Amanda attached to the agreement, and she writes out a check with music notes on it.

"You're welcome." I unlock my side desk drawer and retrieve the keys. "Here are two sets of keys. One is to the building and the other is to your office space. Everything is secured with an alarm system, so I'll show you how to set your own code for that. From six at night to seven in the morning, the main doors to the building are locked. If you see clients during those hours, you will need to escort them in and out of the building. If you have issues with anything, you first try Amanda and then you call me if she is unavailable."

"Amanda? The woman you just fired?"

I stand and slip on my suit jacket, buttoning it and adjusting my tie. Ellen holds her smile like she's waiting for my reaction to her comment. "Yes." To the point. That's all she will get from me.

It took Amanda five years to worm her way into my existence to the point where I need her—but only professionally. She could piss in my coffee and I still wouldn't fire her because she's the woman behind one of the best attorneys in Minneapolis—me. And the only thing that makes me happier than her anticipating my every move twenty-four hours before I make it is her husband and three children. I am her job. Period.

"Follow me." I walk past Ellen, dodging the waves of happiness that flow from her all-too-giddy smile.

"It seems really cold outside. It wasn't this cold last year at this time." Ellen rubs her hands together and blows on them as we ride up the elevator.

I narrow one eye at her. "Sixty degrees is not cold in Minnesota. This time last year it was unusually warm. This is normal."

"I moved here from California." She lifts her shoulders to shrug and blows on her hands some more.

"I know." I nod toward the elevator doors as they open.

"Of course." She smiles as she steps off the elevator. "My references."

I steal a second to glance at her from behind. As much as I don't want to notice her subtle curves and her perky ass, I can't help it.

"You coming?" She tosses a flirty look over her shoulder at me.

I don't think she's trying to be flirty; it's just a familiar look. It's the way my wife used to look at me. "Yes." I mentally shake it off and follow her two doors to the left.

"Four offices total, right?"

I use my key to open the door to her space and shut off the alarm. "Yes. Mine, an optometrist across the lobby from me, and on the other side of you is an accounting firm. Here..." I step aside "...it's ready for you to type in a six-digit code."

She types in two numbers and then peers over at me. "You're watching me type in my personal code?"

"My code is the master code. I can get into any of the offices. You're not keeping *me* out."

"I reuse codes." Her lips pull into a tight grin.

On a sigh, I turn my back to her.

"Thank you." The keypad beeps four more times.

I turn back around and push the pound key. "That code will get you in the building as well."

She nods and roams around the empty room with nothing more than a bathroom in the far corner. A familiar hum fills the room. It's "You Are My Sunshine." I know it because Heidi sang it to Harrison a million times. Why is she humming that song?

"I love having a full wall of windows."

After catching myself watching her too intently again, I clear my throat. "Any more questions before I take off?"

She turns and resumes her humming. I glance out the window over her shoulder because I can't look at her without *staring* at her. Something about her has triggered something in me, throwing my control off kilter. I pump my fists a few times then glance at my watch. Maybe I can hit the gym before it's time to get Harrison from his after-school robotics class.

"I'm good. I'll move my stuff in this weekend if that's okay?"

"The space is yours now. You don't need my permission."

"And paint?"

"Paint away."

"Thank you." She grins and then spins in several circles.

What the fuck?

"I love it!" She stops and hugs her hands to her chest, blue eyes alive with gratitude like I just gave her a new car or something much more exciting than five hundred square feet of space—which she's paying *a lot* to rent from me.

"Okay, then." I slowly back my way toward the door. "You have Amanda's number, so we're good?" This is my code for *I don't have to see you again unless there's a catastrophic emergency.*

"One hundred percent good." She presses her thumb and index finger together in an A-Okay sign.

CHAPTER TWO

THE HARDEST PART of taking the life of another person is knowing nothing can ever make it right again.

Not a million "sorrys."

Not the strongest glue.

Not an infinity of good deeds.

Most days I manage to fool myself into believing that my son is a gift, and that I'm worthy of raising him. But on days of complete clarity, I see that having him and loving him is my greatest punishment. When he's old enough to make total sense of what happened to his mother, he will hate me—almost as much as I hate myself.

"I'm the only kid who eats weird stuff like this for lunch." Harrison sips his dairy-free smoothie at the counter as I make his allergen-free lunch.

"I spent a lot of money to have you tested for allergens. Not to mention endless hours of research. You're doing better in school, and we're getting along better as well. So I don't care if you're the only kid eating *healthy* stuff for lunch."

"Kids make fun of me."

"Kids are idiots."

"I'm a kid."

"You're the exception. That's why they're making fun of you."

"They're jealous that I'm not an idiot?"

"Precisely." I add a cold pack to his lunch bag.

He rolls his eyes. The kid's too smart for his own good.

"Your science teacher emailed me. She said you haven't handed in your research paper."

Harrison slips on his winter coat and grabs his lunch bag from the counter. "It's stupid."

"Why?" I shut my briefcase and check to make sure the lights are turned off before we leave the house and start a new workweek.

"The textbooks are outdated. Everything they're teaching is outdated. We have a mandatory resource list, and we can't use information from outside sources. So basically she wants me to write about incorrect science and cite it from ancient research. It's a waste of my time."

I shoo him out the door and into the vehicle. "You're twelve. No job. No major responsibilities. You have all the time in the world. I've told you a million times, you need to think of school as your job."

He fastens his seat belt as I pull out of the garage. "Fine. I have the time. But I'm not going to do it because it's an insult to my intelligence."

I have a "mildly" autistic child. Doctors don't seem to know their head from their ass when it comes to the epidemic that has devoured this generation of children. There's no clear way to diagnose it. Or a shot to prevent it. Or a pill to mask the symptoms.

Harrison is an information junkie. It's rare to see him without earbuds shoved in his ears listening to podcasts on everything from modern art to the theory of evolution. He has issues keeping his emotions in check, his social interactions are a little rough, and he has an odd sense of humor, which is interesting because he so rarely gets other people's humor. Other than that, he's a fairly "normal" and well-adjusted twelve-year-old.

"Play the game, Harrison."

"It's a stupid game." As if on cue, he slips in his earbuds, ending our conversation.

"She's going to fail you if you don't do the work. I think that's an even bigger insult to your intelligence." I glance over. He's zoned out.

I SPEND MY morning in court and grab lunch before heading back to my office.

"Hey, how'd it go?" Amanda asks as I toss my briefcase on my desk and unbutton my jacket.

"We won."

"Congrats. When's the last time you lost a case? I can't re-member." Her lips twist to the side.

She doesn't have to remember. My memory is just fine. And I remember every case I lose, replaying it over and over in my head, wondering what I could have done differently. And then my mind always goes back to Heidi, my biggest loss and the only one that didn't come with a chance to appeal.

"What's that sound?" I ease into my chair and pull a sand-wich out of the brown bag, glancing up at the ceiling.

"Ellen. She moved her stuff in over the weekend. Painted too."

"And?" I squint at the ceiling as the *bang bang bang* contin-ues.

"And she's seeing clients today. Drums now. But it was guitar and singing about an hour ago. *Wheels on the Bus*."

"Explain." I unwrap my sandwich, cringing at the racket.

Amanda flips her blond hair over her shoulder. "Well, it's about a bus and the wheels going round and round, people going up and down, the horn beep—"

I cut her off with a look—maybe *the* look. This is why I have to fire her every day.

She grins. Her smart-ass attitude keeps growing, just like her confidence. Working for me has allowed her the extra money to get a tummy tuck after three C-sections, a gym membership, and I think something with her varicose veins. I'm certain she'll leave her husband once she hits her goal weight. I see it all the time. Hell, I make a living off it.

"She's a music therapist, Flint. Please tell me you assumed music would be involved? Otherwise, I'm embarrassed for you."

bang bang … bang … bang bang bang

I glance up again, slowly chewing my food. "This isn't going to work."

"It's a year lease."

"I can get out of it."

Amanda laughs. "What rule is she breaking? You don't have noise restrictions in the contract. She gave you full disclosure as to her profession. But seriously … you have to tell me what you thought a music therapist does."

"Comfy sofas and relaxing music played through noise-cancelling headphones."

She smirks. "You should have done an internet search. Lots of videos showing exactly what happens at a music therapist's office. I'm a little surprised this one slid by you."

"You knew?" I toss the rest of my sandwich in the bag. The unsettling beat above me has ruined my appetite.

"Yep. How do you think I know about the videos?"

"But you didn't think I needed to know this before you allowed me to offer her the space?"

"I assumed you knew. You're the smartest guy I know. It's like my idol has fallen today. I no longer see you as an all-knowing god, but just a mortal of average intelligence like the rest of us."

Note to self: Never hire a female secretary again.

"I'll be back." In less than five strides, my feet eat up the floor between my desk and the front door to my office. My fingers drum the railing in the elevator. When it dings open, a young girl and her mom step on as I step out.

"Flint. Happy Monday." Ellen smiles, kneeling on the floor while she piles various percussion instruments into a basket.

Who says *happy Monday*?

She stands and brushes the carpet lint from her cream pants that hug her curves in a way that pisses me off, almost as much as the tight, blue turtleneck sweater hugging her perky breasts. The woman played me, distracted me with her body and happy dance for her new space, then *wham!* Bongos all day long.

"It *was* a 'happy Monday.' I won a case this morning and grabbed lunch from my favorite sandwich shop. But then I sat at my desk to eat it and heard this awful banging sound coming from above me."

"Not awful." She shakes her head. "That particular young girl has made great strides with her rhythm. She couldn't keep a simple beat when I first met her. Now she can play six different songs with complex rhythms. She's more focused in school and her speech has improved dramatically."

Ellen

THERE'S SOMETHING THRILLING, even a little forbidden, about a man in a perfectly-tailored suit. Flint Hopkins wears the hell out of a three-piece suit.

Not a single wrinkle.

Not a hair out of place.

Not a scuff mark on his shiny shoes.

His lips move, but all I hear is "I wore this suit for you today" as his hands make their rounds: caressing the buttons on his jacket, twisting his cufflinks, and adjusting his tie. It's sophisticated fidgeting.

"You said you're a therapist, not a music teacher."

Observant men are sexy too.

"I did. And I am. Specifically, I'm a music therapist. Do you want me to explain what a music therapist does?"

"No. I just want you to look for a different space to rent. I'll give you two weeks." He turns and makes it out the door in three long strides.

My toes are on his heels in seconds, chasing him down the stairs. "Wait? You're evicting me?"

"I'm giving you notice."

"Notice? You're kicking me out for what? Doing my job?"

"Preventing me from doing mine." He pushes through the door at the bottom of the stairs and makes a sharp right.

"Hey, Boss, how'd it—" Amanda's gaze moves from Flint to me as I follow him into his office.

"Hi, Amanda. Would you happen to have the name of a good real estate attorney? I may need to sue my landlord for wrongful eviction."

"Um …"

Flint turns, halting my forward momentum a second shy of slamming into his chest. "Shut my door, Amanda." His eyes narrow.

I don't care how hot this guy looks in a suit. I won't recoil under his glower. "Please leave it open, Amanda. I may need you to be my witness."

Arrogance tugs at his mouth. "A witness?"

"For when you threaten me."

He unbuttons his jacket and takes a step back. A whoosh of oxygen leaves my chest like it's attached to him. The man has an air of confidence and mystery about him that commands attention.

When he turned around to face me a few seconds ago, I sensed the slightest agitation in his narrowed eyes and flared nostrils, but not anymore. It's not hard to imagine Flint Hopkins in a courtroom—cool, calculated, ruthless.

"You seem to be an intelligent person, so surely you can see how the noise level of your profession could distract me from doing mine. I think sharing space with other businesses is not a good idea. You need a building of your own or maybe you should work out of your house."

"I live in an apartment. And I'm sorry, Mr. Money Bags, but I don't have the cash flow to buy or rent a building all to myself. You're an attorney. How often are you even in your office? And when you are, what are you doing that requires complete silence? Charming snakes? Narrating audio books?"

He adjusts his tie and fiddles with his cufflinks while pinning me with a cold glare. "I'm thinking. That's what I do when I'm here. Thinking is what wins cases. My job requires concentration."

"If you're having issues with concentration, I can help you with that. I'll even give you a discount on our sessions."

Flint takes a seat at his desk, flipping open the lid to his computer. "Yes. I'm having issues with concentration, but therapy won't help. You moving out will solve the whole problem. Two weeks. Amanda will help you find a new place to rent or maybe an old building space to purchase. Amanda? Can you give Philip's business card to Ms. Rodgers?"

My hands grip the edge of his dark wood desk. It's smooth like every subtle gesture the infuriatingly handsome man before me makes. Mr. Intimidator's thick, perfectly-shaped eyebrows jump up his forehead as I lean in closer to him. "I improve people's lives. Some have used the word miraculous to describe what I do and how it's changing the world for those who thought there was no hope. You are a bottom-dweller who makes money when humans behave badly. But you *seem to be an intelligent person*, surely you can see that a jury of my peers will be sympathetic to my situation, and you will have nothing but my music to soothe your bruised ego when it's all over."

The barely detectable twitch of his lips reminds me of the way my mom used to look at me when I'd throw a tantrum and she didn't want to make it worse by laughing but holding it in was almost too painful.

"You're stubborn." His gaze averts from mine to his phone screen.

"Is that the best you've got? I'm stubborn? Do you win a lot of cases with that defense? 'Ladies and gentlemen of the jury, the plaintiff is clearly suffering from a case of stubborn-ness.'" My voice lowers and my chin tucks low to my chest as I attempt to imitate Flint for no good reason other than he's a dark cloud blocking my sun on what *was* a really great day.

"Hey, Harrison, how was school?"

Flint leans to the side to see past me, and I glance over my shoulder to follow his gaze. The boy, a younger version of my unreasonable landlord, brushes his inky hair away from his unexpected blue eyes.

"A waste of a perfectly good day." The boy shrugs without so much as a tiny grin.

Amanda chuckles. "You're twelve. What else do you have to do with your time?"

"House the homeless. Feed the hungry. Cure cancer. The possibilities are endless."

"Your dad's in a meeting." Amanda lowers her voice. "I think he's met his match."

I smirk at Flint.

His gaze shifts from Harrison to me. "Sorry to disappoint, Ms. Rodgers, but you're no match for me. Two weeks. Now if you'll excuse me." He leans to the side again. "Why are you out of school, Harrison?"

"Early out. Nancy almost forgot to pick me and Troy up. She was still in her pajamas. She called them lounge pants, but I'm not stupid. They were pink with white bunnies on them." The boy shuffles past me and deposits his backpack on his dad's desk.

Flint frowns at him and sets it on the floor. "Early out for what?"

"I don't know."

"Teacher in-service?"

His son shrugs, making brief eye contact with me while sitting on the deep window ledge lined with signed footballs. "I don't know."

"How can you know so much and so little at the same

time?"

"I don't know."

I grin, but it fades when Flint shoots me a stern look. "Two weeks. Have a good evening."

My eyes narrow.

"Dad, this kid in my class is selling his electric guitar. I think I'm going to buy it."

Flint redirects his scowl from me to his son. "No."

"Do you play the guitar?" I smile at the boy.

"No," Flint says.

"Hence the reason I'm going to buy one." Harrison rolls his eyes.

I like this kid. "I have several acoustic guitars. If you've never played, you might want to start with nylon strings so you don't tear up your fingers like you could do with metal strings. I'd happily loan one to you." I turn my back on Flint and sit on the edge of his desk, facing Harrison. I think Mr. Attorney grumbles something that starts with an F and ends with a K, but I can't decipher it with certainty.

Harrison shrugs. "Sure."

"No." Flint's tone drops an octave.

"I have one upstairs. I can show you a few chords while your dad meditates or does whatever he needs to do in complete silence."

"Okay." Harrison stands, brushing his shaggy hair away from his eyes. He pays no attention to the silent battle that started before he arrived.

"Harrison, take a seat in the waiting room. I need to have a few words with Ms. Rodgers."

"Harry, I'll meet you upstairs. I'm renting the office space on the second floor, in case your dad didn't mention it. There are two guitars in their cases along the far wall. Try them out and see which one you like better. I'll be up after I have a few words with your dad."

Harry nods. I still don't sense that he detects an ounce of tension in the room.

After he's out of sight and Amanda swivels her back to us, I stand and face Sex in a Suit.

Flint comes to his full, something-way-over-six-feet height, leaning forward and balancing his weight with his fingertips pressed to the desk. "It's Harrison, not Harry."

I mirror his stance, willing my knees to stay where they are because he smells so good I want to crawl onto the desk and sink my teeth into his neck—in a non-vampire, non-cannibalistic way, of course. "Your tie is crooked."

"It's not." He doesn't blink.

The man makes minor adjustments to his wardrobe every ten seconds. He knows his tie is straight. His hair is perfect. And his attitude is infuriating. I may be a little turned on at the moment.

"It's crazy. I never thought about law school, but right now I'd love to duke it out with you in a courtroom. Shove you into the ropes a few times just to watch you spring back, fists jabbing, teeth clenched. But..." I push off his desk and pull back my shoulders as I whistle *do, re, mi, fa, so, la, ti, do* ending with a smile "...I need to get upstairs and teach a few chords. Maybe Harry's mom will appreciate his interest in music more than his father."

Turning on my heel, I wink at Amanda. Her ghosted complexion gives me a second of pause. I took her for a feisty one too. Why the look of horror?

"Harrison's mother is dead. So that leaves me with the final word on his musical endeavor, and the word is no," Flint says with a finality that shatters my confidence.

Amanda cringes. I die on the spot.

Death trumps everything else in life. He's left me without an argument.

"I'm sorry." I can't look at him. I don't want to know what death looks like on the face of Flint Hopkins. We should remember people in their most beautiful moments, but we don't. It's the etching of ugly and pain that leaves a lasting impression.

"So you'll be out in two weeks?"

Amanda's gaze flits between us like we really are in a boxing ring.

"I'm kind, Mr. Hopkins. Not weak."

CHAPTER THREE

Flint

T WO WEEKS SLIDE by and Ms. Rodgers still plays her crap all day. There's a loophole. I could evict her. There's always a loophole. Right now Harrison is guarding the loophole. His obsession with the guitar—his obsession with her—has me twiddling my thumbs when I should be booting her out.

I've learned the hard way that I can't take away his fixations. This is all he talks about right now. On the days when he doesn't have his robotics class, he drops his bag off at my office and goes upstairs to wait for Ellen to finish so they can play the guitar together. And she's even worse. She acts like I didn't give her two weeks to get out. I will need to have her physically removed from the premises when the time comes.

"Are you helping them move?" Amanda is the master of random questions. She doesn't face me. For all I know she could be on the phone, but I know she's not. This is her thing: hours of silence and then a question I can't answer.

"Who?"

"Cage. I know you're holding all the emotions inside, but your best friend is leaving you and you haven't said more than two words about it. You haven't requested I mark time off for you to help them move or anything like that."

"He's moving, not 'leaving' me. He's hired a moving company. His life. Not mine. It is what it is. Did you pull the Peterson files for me?"

"On your desk, three inches from your hand. If you move, the file will bite you because you're preoccupied with your best friend moving away and your fantastic new tenant who has stolen Harrison's music-loving heart."

Fantastic. She's got that right. Ellen Rodgers is *not real.* Women that strange only exist in fantasy. Her perfect tits are the only *real* part of her, an anomaly of their own because perfect tits are usually a fantasy.

I need to stop thinking about her tits.

"Go tell Harrison that I'm leaving in five minutes."

Amanda stands and slips on her jacket.

I sigh. "Please."

"Sorry. I'm off the clock. You'll have to go up there and tell him yourself. Say hi to Elle for me."

"L?"

"Short for Ellen."

"You're too lazy to add the N?"

"Stop being so …" She purses her lips to the side. "You."

"Me?"

"Elle is short for Ellen. Just like Flint is short for Flinton."

I return my attention to my computer. She knows damn well my name is not Flinton. I'm tired of acknowledging her lunacy. "You're fired."

"Yay me! I was worried you were about to let me squeak by today without firing me. See you Monday."

"Monday." I give her a parting glance and a slight grin in spite of how much she tortures me with her antics.

I've managed to avoid the second floor of the building since the day I failed at evicting Ms. Rodgers. As the elevator makes its short ascent, my clothes feel too warm, my tie too tight, and my skin too sweaty. I think my neck itches too. It's an Ellen allergy. Surely Harrison will understand why I have to get rid of her if I can show proof of an actual allergy to her. On second thought, he won't. His level of empathy has improved a little, but he's far from putting himself in anyone else's shoes.

"Do you still dance?" she asks Harrison as I stay behind the door, just out of sight.

"No."

"Do you do any other activities?"

"Football."

"Really?"

"No. That's what my dad told me to say. Ha! He'll be happy when I tell him I remembered to say it on cue."

I close my eyes and shake my head. That's not how it went down. This kid of mine thinks he can condense a fifteen minute discussion into eight words that are not on cue at all.

Ellen laughs. It's grating. Her happiness is grating. And itchy. I tug at my tie, tip up my chin, and scratch my neck.

"Your dad has a lot of footballs in his office. I can see why he might want you to play it."

"He played."

"Oh yeah? In college?"

"I think so."

Unbelievable. He remembers random shit he reads once, but he can't remember the details of my football years—something I've told him hundreds of times.

"Where?" Of course that's her follow-up question.

Here we go …

"I don't remember."

Bingo.

"He's always watching it on TV with his friend."

"Your dad has a friend?"

I clear my throat and walk around the corner. "Don't sound so surprised, Ms. Rodgers. I might have more than one friend."

"No." Harrison shakes his head. "Just the one."

I'm ready to shake him. Ellen bites back her grin but her lips get stuck on her teeth, so she wets them. And I stare at her wetting her lips because she's distracting—and itchy.

"Get your things and wait in the car for me." I hand him the key fob.

Lively blue eyes follow him. They remind me of Heidi's, only lighter, almost translucent. "Bye, Harry."

"Bye, Elle."

"He lets you call him Harry?"

She hums and smiles. I tug at my tie. It's strangling me.

"Apparently." Her shoulders lift into a slight shrug.

"And Elle?"

She steps closer. Why the hell is she stepping closer?

"My friends call me Elle. I could be your *second* friend and you could call me Elle too. But …" She whistles the tune from Jeopardy, flips her red mane behind her shoulders, and grabs my tie, giving it a yank in one direction and then the other until it's where it was before I started fidgeting with it on my way up here. "You're going to have to stop all this eviction nonsense. Friends don't kick friends out of the building."

I sniff. "You smell like pineapple."

She smirks. "Piña colada lip balm."

I hate piña colada.

"Are you going to let go of my tie?" My gaze shifts from her piña colada lips to her hands grasping my tie like it's tethering her.

"Do you *want* me to let go of you?" She rubs her smelly lips together.

My dick hardens, such betrayal. Stupid thing didn't get the memo that we don't get aroused over tropical drinks.

"I'm kidding." Releasing my tie, she takes a step back. "I'm a feather ruffler. And I've come to enjoy ruffling yours."

"And why is that?" I tug at the cuffs to my shirt and adjust the buttons of my jacket. There's no reason for me to ask follow-up questions to her ridiculous statements, but I can't stop staring at her. She's ... I don't know ... irritatingly beautiful.

"It's the suit. My father was a tailor. His father was a tailor. And his father ..." She grins. "You get where I'm going with this. A long line of tailors in my family. My mother used to smile and grab the lapels to my father's suit jacket and say, 'Jonathan Samuel Anderson, you sure do look the part.'

"Then she'd pull him in for a kiss. I'd wrinkle my nose in disgust, but I never turned away. Then he'd say, 'What part is that, my dear?'

"She replied, 'My man, of course.'"

"I remind you of your father?"

"Just the perfectly-tailored suit." She laughs while putting her guitar in its case. "My father is an unassuming man. Kind. Generous to a fault. He never looked at anyone the way you look at me."

I slip my hands in my pockets and sigh. Why am I still standing here? "How do I look at you?"

Bent over the case on the floor, she cocks her head toward

me, squinting one eye. "Like I'm the bane of your existence."

Fair assessment.

"I've given you a grace period because I'm not ready to deal with Harrison's reaction to you leaving. But you *will* have to leave this building. Not because you're the bane of my existence. This is just business. Nothing personal."

She straightens her back, blowing out a slow breath before that bright, she-fucking-looks-like-a-teenager smile graces her face. "I find that people who say something is business, not personal, usually lack personality. We are people, not machines. Everything we do is personal to someone."

She needs thicker skin. I give her a tight smile. "Good evening, Ms. Rodgers." I turn toward the door.

"Good evening, Flint."

"You can call me Mr. Hopkins." I push the button to the elevator.

"Mmm, my landlord likes to role play. Me too."

I stiffen—everywhere—turning my gaze back over my shoulder. Ellen peeks her head around the corner and winks.

I resist the urge to tug at my tie and scratch my neck. She's flirting with me. Messing with me. Fucking with my head.

HARRISON POPS IN his earbuds the moment I get in the car and ignores me the whole way home. We walk in the back door, and I flip one of the earbuds out of his ear.

"What?" He frowns, pausing whatever is playing from his phone.

I set my briefcase on the counter and grab an iced coffee from the fridge. "Why do you let her call you Harry?"

"I don't know."

"I've called you Harry over the years and you've had a conniption fit. Teachers and kids in school call you Harry and you lose it over a name that *is* in fact your nickname. But some stranger loans you a guitar and plays a few tunes with you and you submit to a name you've disliked for years? Help me understand this."

"I don't know."

"You're too smart to let 'I don't know' be your default for everything you're asked."

He shrugs, shaking his head to brush the hair from his eyes. "When she says it, it sounds cool. Not like when everyone else says it."

"Harry."

"Nice try. You don't say it right."

I chuckle. "It's not how she says it. She's an attractive woman and that's why you're okay with her calling you Harry."

"You're such an idiot." He rolls his eyes. "Don't say attractive."

I twist the cap back onto the glass bottle of coffee. "And what do young, totally cool kids like yourself say?"

Another eye roll. My son is a bobble-head with googly eyes.

"Hot. She's hot, Dad. Not that you would notice." He slips his earbuds back into his ears.

I yank them back out, and he grumbles.

"Why wouldn't I notice a hot woman?"

"Because you don't have sex with them."

Just when I think he can't say anything that can surprise me ... he surprises me. "You think the only way to acknowledge a 'hot' woman is to have sex with her? I fear you haven't listened to the conversations we've had about sex."

"Simon's dad has women over for sex. It's the only time he lets Simon watch TV for more than two hours at a time."

"More than two hours, huh?" *Simon's dad is a lucky fucker.*

"Gina is Simon's favorite. After he hears her upstairs thanking baby Jesus over and over, she comes down to the kitchen and bakes several dozen chocolate chip cookies. Last time I was there, she promised to make them dairy and gluten-free in the future so I can have some too."

Twelve is the new twenty. I didn't have these conversations with my parents when I was twelve. We discussed football and whose turn it was to mow the lawn. I think there may have been a few conversations about drugs and getting in cars with strangers, but that was it.

"I think you should take a break from hanging out at Simon's house."

"Whatever," says the kid who doesn't have any true close friends.

Then again, according to him, I only have one friend, and he's moving halfway across the country.

"Get me your lunch bag to clean out then go do your homework while I make dinner."

He mumbles something under his breath. I'm sure it has to do with how we never go out to eat. As I unzip his lunch bag, a rodent runs across the counter.

"What the hell?" I grab a pan from the hanging rack above the island and cock my arm back to kill it.

"Stop!" Harrison dives for the rat.

There's a *rat* in my house. How the hell did it get in here? "Don't touch—" Before I can stop him, Harrison picks it up. I cringe, still fisting the handle to the pan.

"Drop it before it bites you!" I warn.

He hugs it to his chest, stroking its head. "What the heck? You almost killed Mozart."

"Mozart?" I toss the pan on the counter with a *clang*. "Explain. Now!"

Harrison scowls at me for the loud noise.

"Where the hell did you get that thing?"

"Wolfgang Amadeus Mozart is a Dumbo rat not a *thing*. See his ears are bigger and round? Like Dumbo. I really like his gray head and white body. Elle says he's very kind and has a great personality."

I've had saintly patience with him. I love him. I listen to all of his in-depth descriptions of his latest obsessions. Thanks to him, I'm an expert in areas I never wanted to gain any sort of expertise. But this is not happening. I said no to a fish. There's no fucking way I'm letting him have a rat.

I rescind my earlier statement to Ellen; she *is* the bane of my existence.

"You can have a meltdown right here and now, but the answer is no. You are not keeping it."

"Him." There's the eye roll. "And I never said I was keeping him. Elle had him with her today and said maybe sometime I could bring him home for a night."

"Maybe? Sometime?" With my hands on my hips, I lean forward until we're at eye level. "Did she say you could bring him home tonight?"

He shrugs, petting the squirmy little critter.

"It's a simple question."

"I don't know. She said maybe sometime I could bring him home for the night, and I said I'd like that, so I put him in my guitar case and then you showed up. I played with him in the car while waiting on you, then I put him in my backpack when you came outside."

"Does she know you have him?"

Another shrug.

I yank my tie several times to loosen it. My fingers jerk open the top button of my shirt. I'm not in the mood for this shit tonight. "Put it in a bag. I'll return it to Ms. Rodgers while you do your homework."

"It will die in a plastic bag."

I retrieve a paper grocery sack from the pantry and hold it open. Harrison stares at it a few seconds before meeting my impatient expression. He eases it into the sack, and I roll the top down.

"What if there's not enough air? I kept the zipper to my backpack cracked a bit."

With a fork from his lunch bag, I stab the top of the sack several times.

"Jeez! You could kill it."

"I'm not having that kind of luck today, Harrison. Now … don't answer the door. Stay in your room, and get your homework done. I'll be back in a bit."

After we have our customary stare off, he pivots and drags his feet to his room.

I contemplate shaking the sack until the spastic scratching at the bottom ceases, but I'm not a total monster—at least not anymore.

CHAPTER FOUR

Ellen

STAY CALM. HE'S here somewhere. It doesn't matter that I've spent the past hour searching the building for Mozart. It doesn't matter that there are a gazillion places he could have squeezed his tiny body into. Don't think about mouse traps or poison. He will show up.

Stay calm.

"Mozart?" I call again in the lobby after the last person leaves the building while giving me a final cringe of disgust and a less-than-sincere "good luck." People are so weird about pet rats—such misunderstood creatures.

Stay calm. Don't cry.

My phone rings.

"This is Ellen." I feign happiness despite the tears burning my eyes.

"Ms. Rodgers."

I hold out my phone and stare at the unknown number before returning it to my ear. "Yes."

"Where are you?"

Now it's just creepy. The voice is familiar—but creepy. "Who is this?"

"Mr. Hopkins."

I sigh in spite of the chill I get from his voice, in spite of the way it makes me smile when he refers to himself as Mr. Hopkins, and in spite of the fact that I'm seconds from having a complete breakdown because my baby has disappeared.

"Flint, can I call you back? I'm ... in the middle of something important."

"By all means, Ms. Rodgers, you finish up with your *important* stuff and I'll just drive around babysitting your *rat* since I have nothing of importance of my own to do."

"Mozart! You have Mozart?" My cover is blown. A big fat F for staying calm. Closing my eyes, I shake my head.

"Let's try this again because I don't have all night. Where are you?"

"My building ... uh ... your building," I say.

"I'll be there in five. I'm not getting out. I'm not even pulling my vehicle to a complete stop. Hope you have quick hands, Ms. Rodgers."

"Don't you dare—"

I look at the phone screen. He hung up. The bastard hung up on me after threatening to toss Mozart out the window of his car.

I sprint up the stairs, grab my bag and Mozart's travel carrier, lock up, and fly back down the stairwell. The cool evening air steals my breath as I push through the front door of the building, desperate to catch Flint the second he pulls into the parking lot. Within seconds, his fancy black SUV makes the corner. I sprint toward him because, true to his word, he rolls down his window and holds out a brown paper sack.

No way! He does not have my baby in a sack. As any good mom would do, I run in front of his vehicle, arms flailing. "STOP!"

He stops, an inch at best from running me over.

"Are you crazy?" He jumps out, inspecting the less-than-an-inch space between my legs and his bumper.

I snatch the brown sack from his hand and rescue Mozart, nuzzling my nose into his soft fur.

Flint shakes his head. "Never mind. I already know the answer." He makes his way back to the driver's side.

"Harry took him?"

Flint turns, shooting me a "duh" look.

"Don't be mad at him. I said he could. We just didn't discuss *when* he could take him."

"When? You think you needed to discuss with my son *when* would be a good time to send a rat to *my* house?"

Gah! This tall, dark-haired man is so sexy when he's ruffled up like this. "You're mad at me. That's fine. I'll take the blame as long as you don't get mad at Harry."

After a few indiscernible blinks, he shakes his head. "He took it and he shouldn't have. He and I will have words about this, but truthfully he didn't mean to steal him. He's mildly autistic. In his mind—"

"He didn't steal Mozart. I understand." I grin because I adore Harry. He may struggle with the finer details of social interaction, but he's my musical soulmate.

"You do?" Flint narrows his eyes.

I nod. "I work with a lot of autistic children. I get it. Really. I'm good. Mozart is good. You're a little miffed, but hey, two out of three ain't bad."

"I'm not *miffed*." His jaw works side to side, the opposite of *not miffed*. "I'm elated. Read your rental contract. The only animals allowed in the building are service animals. You broke your contract. Grounds for eviction. It's official. Your two weeks start tomorrow. Hope you and your rat have a lovely evening, Ms. Rodgers."

I return Mozart to his carrier and set it and my purse on the SUV. My disheveled landlord frowns as I scuff my shoes along the blacktop toward him. "Thank you ..." I tug at the collar to his shirt.

He grunts or groans. I can't tell which. He stiffens when I get close to him, because I *have* to get close to him. I button the top button and fix his tie, eliciting another grunt when I get it nice and tight around his neck. "I appreciate you calling me and taking such good care of Mozart." *Mr. Hopkins* emanates warmth and spice, maybe a high-end aftershave. I like it a little too much.

The dark look he gives me makes the cool night feel like hot July. I can't tell if he wants to devour me with his lips or his teeth. Flint is the fine line between lust and hate. I'm not ready to walk it—yet.

"I'm going to miss tidying you up, Mr. Hopkins. I like to think of myself as an expert on suits, and I can say with one hundred percent certainty that no man has ever looked this good in a suit."

His jaw clenches once and his lips part. I could lift onto my toes and taste them. But seriously, I think he would bite me. "You're out of line," he whispers with a deep tone of warning.

I slide his tie through my fingers, holding just the tip of it for a few seconds before letting it fall back to his chest. "Well, you know what they say—rules are made to be broken and lines are drawn to be crossed." I step back.

His gaze follows me—my breasts, my lips—before landing on my eyes. He's a beautiful, dark man. So dark. Why? I'll probably never know.

"See you tomorrow. We'll start planning my going-away party." I wink before turning and grabbing my bag and Mozart. "For my party..." I walk toward my car without another glance back "...think about wearing a three-piece suit. I love what you have on today." I whistle a cat call. "Mmm mmm ... but the addition of a vest like you wore the day we met could make my panties fall right off."

⦃⦌

Flint

I WATCH HER ass wave goodbye, and I imagine her panties falling right off.

"You need to get laid," I grumble, climbing into my seat and slamming the door shut.

It's not that I've been celibate since I lost Heidi; I just haven't brought a woman to my house since I got custody of Harrison again. Simon's dad divorced his cheating wife. I killed Heidi because I was an alcoholic. Maybe in terms of sex, that shouldn't matter, but it does.

I hook up with women for one night. Hotels. Their place. But never mine. I don't introduce them to Harrison. I don't make any connections beyond the sex. And I don't have sex that often. It's only when he's at a friend's house, Heidi's mom's place, or when my parents come to visit. Yes, I have parents who understand my *needs*.

It's been a while since I've been with a woman. Ellen Rodgers traipsing into my life is not good. Ellen Rodgers all but flat out asking me to fuck her is disastrous.

As if my father knows I need him, his name pops up on my

dash screen. I hit the answer button on my steering wheel.

"Hey, Dad."

"How's my boy?"

"Hard to say. Are you referring to me or Harrison?"

He chuckles. "Who do you think?"

"Harrison is fine."

"And my other boy?"

"I'm surviving."

"I'll sugarcoat it when your mom asks."

"Good plan. I'm on my way home now. When are you and Mom coming for a visit?"

"Actually, your mom has a companion ticket that expires soon. She booked us flights in two weeks. That work for you boys?"

"Sure. Harrison will be thrilled. Well … his version of thrilled."

"You going to get out while we're there?" And by "get out" he means get laid.

My father played football in college and two years in the NFL before an injury ended his career like it ended mine. He also had a problem with addiction. There's nothing I can't say to him. He gets me.

"I hope so. I told you I rented out the upstairs space to that music teacher. Remember?"

"Great tits?"

I chuckle. The Hopkins men have singular thoughts.

"Yeah."

"You think screwing your tenant is a good idea?"

"No. It's a terrible idea. Not what I was trying to say." It *is* a terrible idea, but an idea nonetheless—an idea that's stuck in my head where it will die. "She's irritating. Physically irritating.

My neck itches when I'm around her. But she's the reason I need to get away for a night. I've tried to evict her, but she's using Harrison's love of music to manipulate me. He's been playing guitar with her. And today he brought home her pet rat. A pet *rat*. Who the fuck has a rat for a pet? Ellen Rodgers. That's who."

My dad laughs some more. "She's under your skin. Maybe screwing your tenant is exactly what you need. Once she realizes you're a one-night-stand guy, she'll give you her notice instead of the other way around. Women don't like facing men who reject them after one night."

"Sage advice from the man who married his high school sweetheart and was a virgin on his wedding night."

"Hey, I live vicariously through you."

"You poor guy." I grunt a laugh.

"You know…" his tone turns more serious "…it's been ten years. I think a decade is long enough. Heidi would want you to move on."

"Heidi would want me to burn in Hell for killing her— taking away Harrison's mother. I think that every fucking time I feel any sort of happiness or pleasure. I gotta go." I can't have this conversation. The day may never come that I can have this conversation. A decade … that's nothing. I killed her. I got away with murder. I should have rotted in a prison cell for the rest of my life.

"I love you, Flint. Your mom does too. And so does Harrison. And we forgive you."

I pull into the garage and shift into *Park*, leaning my head back and closing my eyes. I don't deserve forgiveness. I did the unforgivable. I'm here for Harrison. That's it. Raising him is the debt I owe. I don't deserve a day past his eighteenth birthday. And he only loves me because he doesn't know the truth.

"I'll see you in two weeks. Message me your flight info, and I'll make sure there's someone at the airport if I can't be there."

"Goodnight, Son."

I disconnect.

I make dinner.

I do laundry.

I pull weeds in the yard and tend to the garden.

I stay up late going over my case that goes to court next week.

And then I wake up and prepare to do it all over again because people like me don't deserve anything more than monotony.

CHAPTER FIVE

Ellen

A S A MUSIC enthusiast it would seem natural for hearing to be my most cherished sense. But Beethoven continued to compose, and in some ways *hear* the music, long after he went deaf. I will forever cherish music and live in awe of the lives that it saves, but I know without a single shred of uncertainty that touch is the one sense I cannot live without. And I know this because I tried for two years to let that need—the feeling that comes only from another human—die. At the most basic level, humans need physical touch to thrive.

"Will you be available this afternoon?" Dr. Hamilton asks as I grab a coffee from the hospital cafeteria. "I have a patient I'd like you to meet. She's a rape victim."

"I can see her if it's before two. I'll be at my office after that." I frown, dumping sugar into my coffee. "If I still have one. My landlord is trying to evict me."

She slips her phone into her lab coat and smirks. "I've known you for almost a year. You can charm the pants off a snake. Everyone loves you. How are you getting evicted? Rent issues?"

I put the lid on my cup and shake my head. "Noise issues." I smirk over the steam seeping from the hole in my lid. "My landlord didn't understand what my profession entails."

"Sounds like an idiot. You should hire an attorney to fight it. I know a really good one."

I laugh. "Funny thing ... my landlord is an attorney."

"Oh ..." She cringes, taking a sip of her coffee. "Well, all the more reason to have your own attorney."

"It's complicated. I've been teaching his son to play the guitar. This boy is amazing. I show him something once and he gets it and builds on it without my guidance. He's gifted—as in *really gifted.* And I like him and I think he likes me."

"So the dad hired you to teach his son guitar lessons, yet he's evicting you?"

I shake my head as we step onto the elevator. "I offered to teach him for free—sort of. Sex in a Suit was not happy about it."

"Sex in a Suit?" Dr. Hamilton grins.

Sipping my coffee, I shrug. "Yeah. Sex in a Suit. Tall, dark, and handsome. Every woman's fantasy. Check. Check. Check. The hot ones are always jerks or gay."

"Maybe he's gay."

The doors open to my floor. "His eyes wander too much. He's not gay, just a jerk."

"Bummer. Hey ..."

I turn as she pushes the button to hold open the elevator doors.

"Did you get my invite to the wine tasting at my house tonight?"

"Yes. Sorry, I forgot to respond."

"No big deal. Just stop by if you can."

"Thanks."

"GOOD AFTERNOON, AMANDA." I pop my head in Flint's office on my way to the elevator.

"Elle, don't you look cute." She grins.

I glance down at my sheer black leggings, ankle boots, mini skirt, and white boyfriend shirt. "Oh ... thanks. I have a wine tasting after work, so I stopped by home on my way here to change into something less boring than my usual pants and sweater."

"Pfft ... less boring? You always look stylish. I envy how easily you make simple look trendy."

"Boy, I have you fooled. But ... thanks."

The glass wall between Amanda's desk and Flint's office reveals an empty desk chair, lights off.

"Where's your boss man?"

"Court. You just missed him."

"Lucky me." I wink.

"He's out for the day, so Harrison won't be coming by either."

"Well, that *is* a true bummer."

"Harrison likes you." Amanda taps the end of her pen against her chin. "You should cultivate that relationship. I don't think Flint will evict you as long as Harrison is so enamored with you."

My nose wrinkles. "I'm not so sure. Did he mention the rat incident?"

Lines form on her forehead. "No."

"I see." I glance at my watch. "It's a long story. I'll share it with you later. I have an appointment soon, but let's just say my two-weeks' notice officially started again yesterday."

I grin just as Amanda answers the phone, giving me a wave back. A tiny part of me is not only disappointed I won't see

Harrison but Flint too. Over the past weeks, I've enjoyed our banter and flirting. Maybe just flirting on my part, but he hasn't exactly asked me to stop. I think he likes it, but it pisses him off that he does.

DR. HAMILTON LIVES in an older neighborhood filled with trees and enchanting houses that have been restored over time. It doesn't feel pretentious, but I have no doubt that these homes nestled off the main road are worth more than my salary could afford.

"Elle! I'm so glad you made it." Dr. Hamilton—Abigail— answers the door with a wine glass in one hand, dangly bracelets hanging from her wrist. Her blond hair flows at least fifteen inches down her back. I've never seen it down. She always wears it in a tight bun. I think she's around fifty, but with her hair down, it takes a good ten years off her age.

"Thank you. I love your home." I step inside and slip off my coat.

"It's almost a century old. Martin has been itching to sell it for years. He's sick of raking the leaves and mowing the lawn, but I can't sell it. This is my happy place."

"I can see why. Is Martin here or did you kick him out?"

"Yes. He's out back with the rest of the men. I'll introduce you in a bit."

A group of three ladies walk up the porch steps behind me.

Abigail gestures with her hand. "Nothing's off limits. Feel free to look around. We'll get started in the great room in about a half hour. Food is in the kitchen. Help yourself."

I wander around, falling in love with this house one room at a time. Every bedroom has a large window seat overlooking lush grass beneath full trees raining down autumn leaves. I can imagine curling up with a good book, a fluffy robe, hot drink, and Chopin playing from my vintage turntable.

After loading a plate full of finger food, I make my way to the terrace.

"Ellen ... Ellen ... Ellen ..." Dr. Pearce raises his glass of sparkling water and gives me a nod of approval. The old guy has been sober for two decades. He's by far the most popular pediatrician on staff at the hospital. I've consulted more with his patients than any other doctor's.

"Sparkling water at a wine tasting. How drab." I pop a red grape into my mouth and grin around it.

He's very open about his past and pokes fun at himself more than anyone else. I like that there are no eggshells on the ground when he's around.

"So drab, as you say." He winks. "I used to be the life of the party, but now I fear, being the oldest one here, I could be the death of it. However, Miller and Gibson are on call, so they're enjoying the kiddie drinks as well. I think Martin mixed them up Shirley Temples."

"Nothing wrong with a good Shirley Temple. Extra cherries of course."

Dr. Pearce steals a cheese cube from my plate. "Girl after my own heart."

"I love this house." I sigh, looking toward the bird feeders near the white fence.

"Indeed. It's arguably the best neighborhood in the city. I used to live right over there." He points toward the slate blue house on the other side of the picket fence.

"You were neighbors?"

"Yes, until my wife died. Then it became too much upkeep. Sold it in less than a day. The guy offered to buy it before he even looked at the inside."

"Really? That's crazy."

"I thought so too. He saw my wife's garden—rows and rows of rich black soil—and the greenhouse at the far end of the property. That's all he needed to see."

"A gardener's dream." I pop another grape into my mouth.

"There he is now."

I lean to see past the row of bird feeders.

"Martin says he spends hours out there every night. My wife did too. She thought it was therapeutic. Digging in the dirt seemed to clear her mind. In her words, it grounded her."

"I can see that. Music does that for me." I squint at the backside of the man in dark jeans and a gray long-sleeved shirt rolled up to his elbows, and green gardening gloves.

He bends down and pulls a few weeds.

I can't hide my grin as the man with inky hair turns and tosses the weeds in a white bucket, giving me a partial view of his face. "Mr. Hopkins," I whisper.

"Pardon?" Dr. Pearce says.

I slowly shake my head. "Nothing. I'm going to walk the grounds. I'll be back."

"They'll be starting soon."

I nod. "If I'm not back, tell Abigail to start without me. I'm not really a wine connoisseur anyway." Setting my plate on a high top table, I make my way to the white fence gate by the bird feeders.

Flint continues to pull weeds with his back to me. These are amazing gardens. A lot of rows are empty, probably from summer crops, but there are still rows of things like pumpkins, squash, and fall greens.

"Do you ever stop humming?"

I freeze. He still doesn't turn, hands busy yanking weeds.

"I didn't realize I was."

"Why doesn't that surprise me?" He grunts a laugh.

"Why are you not surprised that I'm standing in your garden?"

"You work at the same hospital as Abigail Hamilton. You probably drink wine. They're having a wine tasting tonight."

"You weren't invited?"

"I don't drink wine."

"Not everyone there is drinking wine. It's really more of a social event."

He still doesn't turn to acknowledge me. "I'm not that social."

Now I grunt a laugh. "Why doesn't *that* surprise me?" It doesn't. However, Flint Hopkins not wearing a suit is quite the surprise. "I don't know what to do with this image of you in jeans and a tee. In my mind I imagined you wearing a suit to bed."

He sits back on his heels and turns toward me, dark eyes making a full-length inspection. "I don't know what to do with the image of you imagining me in bed."

I shiver. It's cold … and surprisingly hot at the same time.

We share an intense look for a few seconds. I lose the stare off, letting my gaze follow the gravel path between the rows of plants. "What's Harrison doing?"

"He's at a movie with a friend."

"I missed seeing him today."

No response.

I can't wrap my head around this. Flint is a gardener. It takes a lot to really surprise me, but this knocks me back a few paces. Beneath the suit lies a well-defined body that's more visible in his jeans and tee. And beneath the suit lies a softer man, a glimpse of who he really is. There's something extraordinary about seeing the familiar in a new light. I've always thought that about music too. There are twenty-four tonally unique keys, and I'm certain they have the power to bestow enlightenment beyond the twenty-six letter alphabet.

"You're humming again."

My attention snaps back to him.

"Sorry. Are you anti-humming?"

He stands, tossing more weeds into the bucket. "They're going to be looking for you."

I smile at his attempt to dismiss me. With slow steps, I move toward him. He stiffens like I've come to expect. His nostrils flare a bit and his breaths deepen, but he doesn't move away.

"I told them to start without me."

His eyes follow my hands. I roll up his right sleeve that hangs down lower than his left sleeve. My fingertips brush his warm skin.

"What are you doing?" he whispers as if it pains him.

"Rolling up your sleeve."

"If I were you, I'd keep my distance."

I peer up at him. "Do you bite?"

His jaw clenches a few times before he relaxes, easing his tongue across his bottom lip. "Your shirt is white."

I grin, taking a step back. "Harrison is gifted with music. Did you know that?"

He nods once.

"Yet he said he's not taking any sort of music lessons."

"He took piano and ..." His words die off mid-sentence as

if his mind skips a track.

"And?" I tilt my head to the side.

Flint averts his gaze and sighs. "Dance."

"Was he a good dancer?"

"I suppose."

"You want him to play football."

"No."

"No?" My head pulls back a fraction. "Really? He said you played in college."

He grabs the bucket and heads toward the greenhouse. "He did, did he?"

"Yes." I chase after his long strides.

"What else did he say?"

"Nothing that I would share with you."

Flint grunts. "He's not your patient. I don't think confidentiality applies to after-school riffs."

I follow him into the greenhouse. Holy cow! This place is packed with plants. It's deceiving from the outside. He could feed a small village.

Flint drops the bucket and turns. I almost bump into his chest.

"What's wrong with you?"

I purse my lips to the side. "What makes you think something is wrong with me? Is this about Mozart?"

"It's about this." He nudges the toe of his shoe against the toe of my boot. "I'm evicting you, yet you like to stand so close to me I feel like I'm breathing in the breath you exhale. And you have this need to touch me—my ties, my collars, my sleeves." His brows knit together.

My heart pounds, pulsing in my ears.

"You're humming again."

I swallow hard and silence the noise I didn't realize I was making. "Do you not like to be touched?"

The crease between his eyebrows deepens. "Not by strangers."

Thump. Thump. Thump.

I like *feeling* so deeply that I can actually hear the rhythm of my heart. It's excited and happy. A feeling so much better than the crushing pain I felt for so long.

"When people touch, they no longer feel like strangers. It's a feeling. When humans share feelings, they connect on an intimate level. It's why I love music. It can go deeper than words. Rhythm is the heartbeat of your soul."

"What about those who don't have a soul?"

Ouch! That's hard to hear.

"Well..." I shrug and grin "...those are the bad dancers. Soulless, rhythmless, terrible dancers." My gaze meets his. "Are you a bad dancer, Flint?"

Something indescribable about this man calls to me. I want to help him. Help him do what? I don't know yet. I need to feel him—hear him—and then I'll know.

"You should go."

My chin drops, gaze fixing to the toes of our shoes touching. "Why?" I whisper.

"Because your shirt is white."

I look up. He tugs at the fingers to his gloves, dropping one to the ground and then the other.

"You have thirteen days." He's counting down the days until he kicks me out of the building.

"Thirteen days," I say.

"Now get going before I fuck up your white shirt." His gaze engulfs my whole body.

My pulse thrums along my skin. Flint embodies the opposite of every man I've known.

I don't want the familiar—because it broke me.

I don't want the predictable—because it's nothing more than a heartbreaking illusion.

Reasoning hurts too much. I just want to exist in a purely physical state.

"It's just a shirt," I whisper.

He grabs my head and kisses me.

It's rough.

It's wrong.

It's the best thing that's happened to me in years.

Touch. I die a little inside. No need has ever felt this painful—this necessary.

Flint deepens the kiss, pushing me back into a metal table of plants. One of them falls to the floor. I can't get enough of his body pressed to mine. My eagerness might be more embarrassing if his body didn't feel just as desperate. Consuming my mouth, he works the buttons to my shirt, ripping a few off with his impatience.

I jerk the button and zipper to his jeans, humming against his mouth. He shoves my shirt off my shoulders and yanks my bra down, palming my breasts as my hand slides down the inside of his briefs.

A low growl vibrates his chest. When was the last time I unraveled a guy with the touch of my hand? I don't remember and that's just sad.

He doesn't slow down the kiss one bit when his hands move down my body, grabbing the hem of my skirt and shoving it up over my waist. As if we've acted out this scene a hundred times before, my hands work his jeans and briefs down his hips just enough to release his cock. Flint lifts me onto the metal bench, spreads my legs, and rips my nylon leggings at the crotch.

Emotion tightens like a noose around my throat. No amount of therapy can fill this physical void—this dark hole carved out by years of rejection.

He breaks the kiss.

A small breath.

A heartbeat long enough to let our brains catch up.

I don't want my brain to catch up. Stupidity. Impulsivity. They have a place and a time.

Now. I need them *now* more than a million years of wisdom. No one on their deathbed says, "Remember how incredible it felt to make wise decisions?" I want to remember how it feels to physically drown in desire. I want to remember warm lips on mine, moans of pleasure, and the blinding, mind-numbing sensation of coming apart beneath the touch of this man.

Flint's lips part and I wait for it, the words that feel like someone ripping the TV cord from the wall in the middle of my favorite show. But they never come. Those parted lips land on my neck, biting and sucking before mumbling, "Move your panties out of the way."

My brain shuts down as I fist his hair with one hand and slide the crotch of my panties to the side with my other hand. To hell with death. I refuse to die until I've truly lived. I lean into his body, searching for the ultimate connection.

"Fuck ... I can't." He steps back, like he's suddenly afraid of me.

Before I can get my feet beneath me, my hand slips on the edge of the metal bench and my ass lands on the hard dirt floor. "Ouch!" I hug my arm to my chest. It scraped along something sharp on my way to the ground.

"Shit! Ellen ..." Flint pulls up his pants.

The long cut on my arm bleeds through the sleeve of my white shirt.

"Let me see." He squats down and pulls my arm away from me.

Crimson continues to spread.

I seethe as he unbuttons the cuff of my sleeve and eases it up, revealing the deep cut on my forearm.

"Fuck ..." He grumbles. "You're going to need stitches."

Biting my lip to fight back my reaction to the pain, I nod.

Standing, he rakes his fingers through his hair. "I'll be right back."

"Where are you going?" I grimace, leaning a little to the side to ease the pressure on my bruised ass.

He doesn't answer. Five or so minutes later he returns with help. I figured he'd load me in his car and take me to urgent care. I'm a little surprised by his choice.

Abigail fails to completely hide her surprise as her gaze lands on me for a few seconds before giving a disapproving scowl to Flint. Had I known he was going to bring back company, I would have made some effort to pull my skirt back down over my ass, or button what few buttons are left to my shirt, or remove my ripped nylon leggings.

She lowers to her haunches. "Ellen, are you okay—"

"We agreed no questions." Flint's jaw clenches.

Abigail shoots him another warning look. He sighs and glances away.

"My arm is cut." I ease it from my chest to show her.

She looks at it briefly before meeting my eyes with concern.

"Did he…" biting her lips together, her inspecting gaze studies my ripped clothes "…hurt you?"

The pain from the cut takes a backseat to the knot in my stomach as it hits me that she's questioning if he sexually assaulted me.

Flint takes a small step back, the pain on his face intensifying into something between confusion and regret.

"No." I shake my head, willing him to look at me, but he doesn't.

Abigail grabs the first aid kit she carried in with her and tends to my arm. "Let's run to the hospital and get this stitched up for you and make sure you don't have any other injuries." She gives Flint another look.

He keeps his eyes turned to the ground.

With gauze pressed to my wound, Abigail helps me to my feet, pulls my skirt down over my hips, and buttons the three buttons left on my shirt.

"Dr. Hamilton?"

Her jaw clenches as she realizes my shirt won't cover much with only three buttons left.

"Abigail?" I say a little louder.

She snaps her head up.

"This is embarrassing, not tragic. Okay?"

The worry glued to her forehead tells me she's not following.

"I left your party because I saw Flint in his garden. I didn't know he was your neighbor."

She nods slowly, but I still don't think she's following.

I sigh. "Sex. *Consensual* sex, Abigail. Or at least …" I meet Flint's gaze as he allows his eyes to focus on me instead of whatever the hell is so interesting about the dirt floor. "It was headed in that direction."

Why does he look so pained? I'm the one bleeding. I'm the one feeling rejected.

"How do you know Flint?"

I can't hold back my grin. "He's my landlord."

"Sex in a Suit?" She whips her head back toward him.

Flint's eyebrows shoot up his forehead.

I chuckle. Alone. Why am I the only one who sees the humor in this? "I'm going with Seduction in a Suit from now on. He fumbled the ball at the last second, which is a little surprising given his college football experience."

Again, I'm the only one searching for a shred of humor in this most embarrassing situation.

"Keep pressure on the gauze. I'm going to get a sweatshirt for you and let Martin know I have to leave."

"You have guests. Don't be silly. There are other doctors at the hospital who can stitch me up. Besides, my guess is you've been drinking."

Her lips twist as her gaze shifts from me to Flint several times. "Drive her. Stay with her. Don't lie to the doctor who examines her. And *please* consider using a bed next time."

He flinches. I don't think there will be a next time.

"I'll be back with a sweatshirt."

"I'll get her one of mine." Flint finally finds words.

Abigail nods. Rolls her eyes. Shakes her head. Then leaves.

"Let's go." He catches the door behind her and holds it open for me.

"Do you really own a sweatshirt? I feel like you're more of a white tee and V-neck sweater kind of guy."

No response. No surprise.

I WAS WRONG. He has a Nebraska hoodie, and it smells like his rich woodsy scent. I might not give it back.

"I need a favor," I say when he opens the car door for me at the entrance to the ER. It's the first words that have been spoken since we left his house. "Help me remove my leggings. The cut on my arm and bruised ass will be easy to explain. The ripped crotch to these will not be quite as easy to pass off as consensual sex."

Flint makes frowns look sexy. That's a special talent, but it's not going to help me out of these leggings.

I shake my head. "Never mind, Mr. Helpful." Holding my injured arm to my chest, I try to snake my other arm up my skirt to grab the waist of my leggings.

"Just …" He sighs, bending his long torso into the car over mine. "Move your arm."

I suck in a breath as his hands slide up my skirt.

He gives me a different kind of frown. How many does he have?

"Sorry." My teeth dig into my bottom lip. Despite my arm and bruised ass, his close proximity and hands sliding up my thighs turn me on.

It's possible I've imagined him easing nylons off my legs, but in that fantasy we weren't parked in a car at the entrance to the emergency room.

When he gets them to my knees, he slides off my boots, pulls them the rest of the way off, and slips my boots back on my bare feet. "Jesus …" He shakes his head. "You're bleeding *and* humming?"

I hum to keep my mind off the way his hands feel along my skin.

I hum to forget the first man who laid his hands on me. I hum to forget the pain that comes with knowing he will never touch me again.

Flint waits in the waiting room for me while the doctor stitches my arm, examines my bruised ass and hip, and updates my tetanus. I tell the young intern that I slipped off a dirty metal bench in a greenhouse onto a hard dirt floor. The truth.

"Five stitches." I hold up my bandaged arm.

"Ellen ..." Another original Flint frown.

I nod toward the exit. "Let's go. Life's too short for tripping over unnecessary apologies."

CHAPTER SIX

Flint

L IFE SERVES UP small doses of revenge at the most unex-pected moments. Tonight was no exception. Everything seems to get fucked up when my confidence wars with my fears.

"Thanks for the ride." Ellen digs her keys out of her purse as I pull into my driveway.

"Are you okay to drive?"

"It's my arm, not my hand. Yes, I'm good."

I nod, feeling the same bobble-head syndrome that Harrison always has with me.

"Ellen …"

"I know. Thirteen days."

"That's not what I was going to say."

She grips the door handle and rubs her lips together, that irritatingly familiar hum filling the space around us.

"It's just …" To tell her the truth or not? That might be hard since the truth isn't clear in my mind. "I'm good at reading people. Juries. Witnesses. My clients. But I can't figure you out. I screwed up. I'm sorry."

"Sorry that you can't figure me out? Sorry that I got hurt? Or sorry that you stopped?"

I miss my wife. Ten years later and I still can't breathe. Random women. That I can do. Women who don't really know my life. Women who don't know Harrison.

Ellen Rodgers has captured the attention of my son—a boy who rarely gives anyone his full attention. This situation surpassed messy some time ago. I can't take her away from Harrison, evict her, *and* stick my dick in her.

It's hard to decipher if my attraction to her is physical or if it's how she makes my son's day whenever he sees her. It seems ridiculous to be attracted to someone because of how they interact with a child, but fuck it anyway, I think that's part of it.

"Yes." I give her a tight grin and resolute nod.

"It was a multiple choice question, not a yes or no question."

"Thirteen days."

She bites her lower lip, shaking her head a half dozen times while opening the door. Her thoughts—her motives—remain a mystery I have no business trying to solve.

"For the record…" she ducks her head back in the car "…I didn't want you to stop."

Ellen

I WILL NEVER take human touch for granted again.

A handshake.

A hug.

A pat on the shoulder.

One body connected to another in search of the most basic

human pleasure.

I will not be ashamed of my needs.

"Should we talk?" Dr. Hamilton traps me in the lounge before I get a full cup of coffee filtering into my veins. "How's the arm?"

"Fine. Sore. But fine." I focus on the steam swirling from my favorite morning drug.

"So you're having sex with your landlord. Surely that solves the eviction issue." She leans her shoulder against the wall by the water cooler, cupping her coffee mug with both hands.

I chuckle, keeping my gaze on the fascinating coffee steam. "We didn't get to the actual sex part. And while you'd think the events of last night might change my rental circumstances, they don't. I'm down to twelve days."

"How uh …" She drums her fingers on the outside of the mug. "How did 'feel free to look around the house' turn into sex in my neighbor's greenhouse? I'm just trying to piece all of this together."

I can't help the grin that sneaks up my face as I look at her. "You know, just the usual banter, heated looks, inappropriate comments, and idle threats of dirtying up my shirt, all of which kinda, sorta led to a kiss, some quick ripping of clothes, and then an unexpected nothingness that left me physically off balance and dropping to the ground like a sack of potatoes."

"You said no?"

I shake my head. "He did. Actually, he didn't say no. It was more like a carpenter holding a nail in one hand and the hammer in his other hand, and at the last second he stops the forward motion of the hammer and lets the nail slip through his fingers."

"He was just about to nail you but stopped at the last second?"

I laugh. "Exactly."

"And then you cut your arm?"

"Well..." I shrug "...I was the board that fell because I didn't get properly nailed."

Dr. Hamilton grins before finishing the rest of her coffee. "Thank you, Elle. I haven't had a conversation this entertaining in a long time."

"Glad I could be of service this morning." I grab my iPad and head toward the door. "See ya later."

By the time I get to my office in the afternoon, my nerves won't stop vibrating with equal parts fear and excitement.

Will he be in today?

Will he be a jerk?

Will Amanda sense something?

"Hey, Elle! Want some cake?" Amanda's voice beckons me into Flint's office space.

I peek around the door. Streamers and balloons line the entry to his office. "Birthday?"

"He's thirty-five today. And I've already been fired for acknowledging it, so you might as well come have a piece of this fantastic birthday slash farewell party cake."

Flint glances up from his desk, giving me an indiscernible expression.

I smile.

He looks back down at his computer.

"Wow. You're getting the boot before me. Who will bring cake to my going-away party?"

"That's why you'd better have a piece now. I fear there will be no party. But call me, I'll meet you for drinks and help you find a new place."

My gut draws tight. Amanda is serious, not about him firing her, but she's serious about me. He's made it clear that I'm out in twelve days.

Amanda doesn't give me the you-two-almost-had-sex-yesterday look, so I assume it's safe to act normal. Whatever our normal might be.

"Thank you." I take the small plate of cake.

"It's gluten and dairy free—for Harrison."

I take a bite.

Flint gives me another quick glance.

"Harry has a lactose and gluten intolerance, huh?"

"Flint has him on a strict diet for his—"

"Amanda, I fired you. Why are you still here?"

She shakes her head and slings her purse over her shoulder.

My eyes widen. Holy shit. He really did fire her.

"I have a doctor's appointment," she whispers. "Don't worry, I'll be back tomorrow. He wouldn't function without me."

I nod slowly. "Thanks for the cake."

"Oh ..." Her eyes affix to my arm where the bandages peek out at the cuff of my sleeve. "What happened?"

"I ..."

Flint eyes me like pressing the tip of a sword to my carotid artery.

"Rough sex." I grin at Amanda. "Roleplaying taken a little too far."

Her face flushes around her cow eyes. "You're joking," she whispers.

I give her a noncommittal wink.

"Okay then ... fantastic. I'll see you later."

After the door closes behind her, I set my cake on her desk and lean against the doorframe to his office. "Happy birthday."

"We didn't have sex." He keeps his focus on the contents of the file folder in front of him, thumbing through the pages.

"We did. I finished out the scenario in my head when I got home last night. I was amazing. You were just okay. I have to say ... you're the first guy I've been with who cried during your orgasm. What you lacked in manliness, you made up for with complete tenderness. I will always remember the soft caress of your tears falling onto my cheeks."

Flint eases his squinted gaze up so slowly it's torturous. I nibble at the inside of my cheek to keep from grinning. Dang! He looks so sexy with ruffled feathers.

"I don't need this today."

"Because it's your birthday?"

Flint swallows hard as something unpleasant or painful ghosts across his face, disappearing in a blink. "It's my fucking birthday all right," he mumbles, returning his attention to his work.

"Had I known it was your birthday, I would have gotten you a gift or at least a card."

"Don't sweat it."

"I won't."

He looks up again, expelling a heavy sigh like he couldn't possibly be more irritated with me.

I smile a toothy grin. "Consider stroking your dick yesterday your birthday gift from me. No need to send a thank you card. I'm sure you'd outsource it to Amanda and that would rob all sincerity."

"Twelve days. Now go."

He felt me up. Tasted every inch of my mouth. Let me stroke his dick. And yet ... *twelve days*. "Abigail Hamilton said I should get an attorney to fight you on this. She said she knows a good one." I bring my shoulders back, straightening my spine because two can play this game.

Even with his chin tipped down, I can see the twitch of a smirk flirting with his lips. "Does she now? I wonder who that attorney might be. Do you have any educated guesses, Ms. Rodgers?"

Of course. Dammit all to hell anyway. "You," I whisper on a defeated sigh.

"To be honest, you had a case before you brought your rat to work."

"I brought him because I thought Harry would like him."

"Not a good defense, Ms. Rodgers."

Ms. Rodgers. Ms. Rodgers. MS. RODGERS! *Gah!* He can't address me like a school teacher after telling me—in the gruffest, sexiest voice ever—to *move my panties out of the way.*

I fish a pen out of my bag and pop all of his balloons.

Pop. Pop. Pop. Pop. Pop.

Childish? Absolutely. Do I regret it? No way. "I have to go. My next appointment likes to use drums and cymbals for therapy. Enjoy!"

It's not a lie. Landon finds loud beats therapeutic. He was abused by his father for years. Banging on a drum or clashing cymbals gives him a sense of power and control. In our hour session he goes from a timid child to a confident nine-year-old wearing a huge smile. My smile is for his progress and also because I know Flint is downstairs with his fingers in his ears, chanting, "Twelve days."

"Hey, Elle."

"Harry, how was your day?" I ask, closing my computer

and leaning back in my desk chair as he gets out his guitar. I'm not entirely sure how this happened, how offering to teach him a few chords has turned into a regular thing. I'm not a music teacher, but I can't turn this kid away, even if his dad is the world's biggest jerk. I'm certain I like Harrison more than Flint, but he's also the reason I *do* like Flint. It's complicated.

"There was a fire drill at school. I think the loud alarm punctured my eardrum."

"Well, I hope not. Did you get a piece of your dad's birthday cake?"

"Yeah, it was dry."

It was. I smile.

"What are you going to do for his birthday tonight?"

"Same thing we do every year—watch videos of our family before my mom died."

"Oh. That's ..." Depressing?

He sits on the floor and picks the strings a few times. "Yeah. She died on his birthday."

The floor disappears beneath me as his words suck all the oxygen from the room. I'm a terrible person. How the hell can I make this right?

"You warm up. I'll be right back."

I take the stairs since my body won't hold still long enough to ride the elevator to the first floor. Flint's still at his desk. It's hard to walk with my tail stuck so far between my legs. I cringe at the dead balloons.

He glances up as I slither my way into his office. I take calculated steps toward his desk, and his eyes narrow while mine hold his gaze the entire time. What do I say? What can I say? As I slide beside him with my butt rubbing the edge of his desk, he inches his chair back until I'm standing between his legs.

After a few more seconds of silence, he lifts his hand and takes my arm gently in it, ghosting his thumb over the bandaged cut. "He told you."

I nod, grimacing. "I popped your balloons on the anniversary of your wife's death. And I said stroking your dick was my present to you. I may be the worst person ever."

He stares at my arm, brow drawn tightly, as his thumb continues to trace the path of my cut. "*I'm* the worst person ever, so you're off the hook."

"What is that supposed to mean?" I want to hug him, kiss that frown from his face. *Touch* him in a way that takes away the pain. But … it's not right. Not the circumstances. Not the place. Not the day. Everything's off. So I let it go.

I ease my arm from his hold, feathering my fingers over his palm just before releasing my arm back to my side. "I'm truly sorry for what I said and for your grief."

Flint nods once, gaze affixed to my arm.

CHAPTER SEVEN

N EARLY TWO WEEKS drift by without any more mention of my eviction countdown. I've looked for new places, but I can't find any that will work, so I'm grateful for each day that I squeak by without Flint saying anything. He's been distant but polite. I'm not sure if it's the anniversary of his wife's death, my willingness to give Harry my time without asking for any compensation in return, or if he's still thinking about what almost happened.

When we see each other in passing or he comes upstairs to get Harry, his gaze always goes straight to my arm. The stitches are out. The wound is healing nicely. He doesn't need to hold such anguish in his expressions. But maybe it's not the arm. Maybe it's what the arm represents—what almost happened.

Today should be an anguish-free day since it's the weekend—my favorite time to be at the office with no one else in the other offices, no guilt over the noise. By six thirty, I grab my bag and escort my last client out of the secured building.

"Elle!"

I look over my shoulder as Harry waves, jogging toward me with Flint a few steps behind him.

"See you next week," I say to my client as she digs out her keys and heads toward her car.

"My grandparents are in the car. Can we play our song for them?" Harry asks.

"Harrison, can't you see Ms. Rodgers is leaving for the night?" Flint puts on a fake smile.

"Please. It won't take long."

I look at Flint.

"We have dinner reservations. Maybe some other time. I just need to grab the files I left here. Get back to the car."

Words linger on the tip of my tongue, uncertain if it's okay for them to be heard. I don't get the feeling Flint wants my opinion.

"I want to play it. There won't be another time before they leave."

"Harrison—"

"Dad! I want to play it." He starts to lose his cool.

Flint stiffens, frustration lining his face.

"It won't take more than five minutes to play." I shrug. "If you have five minutes to spare?"

Flint frowns. "Go get set up and I'll bring them up. But one song, Harrison. That's it."

He runs past me and tugs at the door to the building. "Dad, open the freaking door."

I shove my keys in the lock and enter my code.

"I'm sorry—"

I shake off Flint's attempt to apologize to me. "It's fine. We'll meet you upstairs. I can't wait to meet your parents." I bite my bottom lip to contain my smile.

Flint grimaces just before he turns back toward the parking lot. He doesn't seem as excited about me meeting them.

We get out the guitars and warm up while waiting for Flint and his parents.

"Where do your grandparents live?"

"Colorado."

"Where in Colorado?"

Harry focuses on his fingers strumming the guitar. "I don't know."

I grin. Of course he doesn't know, not because he hasn't been told; he just doesn't deem that particular detail worthy of his memory.

"What took you so long?" Harry rolls his eyes as Flint and his parents come in the room. "One. Two. Ready. Go." He doesn't wait for introductions or so much as a quick hello. I follow his lead, making the occasional glance over at Flint and his parents, who are grinning in spite of the straight line affixed to Flint's face.

When we finish, they clap, even Flint.

"That was amazing, Harrison!" His grandma gives him a hug which he stiffly accepts.

"Ellen, I'd like you to meet my parents, Gene and Camilla. This is Ellen Rodgers."

They both shake my hand.

"Harrison has talked about you nonstop." Camilla smiles.

"So this is the renter you said has nice..." Gene smirks at Flint for a brief moment like they have some inside joke "...teeth."

Flint narrows his eyes at his dad. I'm not following.

I grin, showing them my teeth.

The older Hopkins men give each other another look. They weren't talking about my teeth.

"Well, your five minutes are up, Harrison. We need to get to dinner."

"I know, I know ..." He puts the guitar back in its case. "We need to get to dinner so I can go home with Grandma and Grandpa while you go on a date."

Flint's back snaps ramrod straight, his gaze ping-ponging between his parents and Harrison.

Camilla gives him an impish grin. "It's silly for you to sneak around. The last time we were here, I simply explained that you are an adult and you need—"

"Female companionship," Harrison says flatly. "It's fine. I get it. Let's just go. Bye, Elle."

"It was nice to meet you." Gene and Camilla nod politely and follow Harrison to the elevator.

"I'll be right down," Flint calls to them, keeping his eyes on me.

"Smart kid." I bite my lips together, eyebrows raised a fraction.

"I don't bring women to my house. I don't know how to navigate this part of single parenting."

"None of my business, Flint." I slide my guitar in its case. "I think we've established the fact that you don't owe me anything. Least of all any sort of explanation to the hows and whys of where you meet women and what you do with them."

"Thanks for not saying anything to Harrison or my parents about ..."

I cock my head, eyes wide. "About? My arm?" I hold it up. A grunted laugh escapes in a short burst of air though my nose. "It's fine. I'm mature enough to keep a secret. I'm not twelve."

"You popped my balloons on my birthday." He gives me the closest thing to a grin that I've seen in weeks from him.

Yeah, there was that. "Don't you have a reservation? A date? Female companionship awaiting you?"

"Ellen ..."

Resting a hand on my hip, I stare at the floor, shaking my head. "I liked it." I look up. "You touching me. Me touching you. I liked it. It meant something to me, but … not what you think. Not love. Not any sort of commitment. The physical experience mattered to me. I don't want to taint it with words. When I leave, I don't want to remember what I said to you or what you said to me. I only want to remember your touch in that moment."

Yep. I've lost him. His eyebrows knit together.

I laugh. "Go. They're waiting on you. Don't read into anything. Don't let what happened the other day deter you from your post-dinner plans. I'm good. There was never a hook to begin with, but if you felt there was, then rest assured you're off it."

He nods several times, his signature contemplative thought stuck to his face as he turns and walks toward the elevator. I shut off the lights and close the door behind me. Flint waits for me to step onto the elevator first. A few seconds later when we step off, I ease my hand around his wrist. He looks down at my hand and then at me.

I release him and straighten his tie. "I like this suit. Nothing beats classic black with a red silk tie." My hand smooths his tie under his jacket.

"You're humming."

"Mmm …" Glancing up, I smile. "Go make some lucky lady's day. Just don't let her fall as hard as I did." I turn and don't look back.

Flint

THERE'S A PACK of peppermint gum in one of the inside

pockets to my suit jacket and three condoms in the other pocket. My parents are in town to stay with Harrison. He's given me his blessing to enjoy "female companionship." I have five numbers in my phone that would be a sure thing tonight—an easy, uncomplicated hookup.

Yet, I crave *her*. I still taste her. How can she make me irritable, itchy, and so fucking needy at the same time? She looks at me the way Heidi used to look at me. It's unsettling.

Sitting in my car, parked a few blocks away from my house after dropping off Harrison and my parents, I bring up *her* number on my phone and stare at it. My thumb hovers over the send button. I cancel out of that screen and bring up one of the five less complicated numbers. I go back and forth from one screen to the next until my thumb hits send of its own accord.

She picks up on the third ring. "Hello?"

"Hi."

"Flint?"

"Do you like Jazz?"

"Uh …" She softly laughs. "Yes, I do."

"I'll pick you up in ten."

I press end and dial her address into my navigation. When I park on the street in front of her apartment building, Ellen steps out the door and hurries to my vehicle, tugging the collar of her trench coat close to her neck. So much for showing my gentlemanly skills. I pull my door shut again since she was too quick.

"Brr …" She shivers while sliding into the seat and shooting me a teeth-chattering grin. "You know, I don't require a fancy night out. I'm good with sex if that's what you need."

I put it in *Drive* and shake my head, pulling away from the curb. "You really should make guys work a little harder for it."

She denies me a response, but out of the corner of my eye I see her smiling. I don't know what we're doing—what I'm doing—but it feels like something I need for whatever reason.

"How's your arm?"

"It's fine. Would you forget about it already?" She sighs with a soft hum. "You're your mom. Anyone ever tell you that?"

I chuckle. I look nothing like my mom. "Did you miss that the tall guy with dark hair was my dad and the short *blonde* was my mom?"

"Probably to most, you look like your dad. I notice the shape of your eyes—her eyes—earlobes, how you both roll your r's the same, the shape of your mouth when you smile, and the tone of your laugh. It's all your mom."

With each passing second she sucks me into this unfamiliar world of hers. She's smart and so damn sexy. That's enough to get my attention. But then I blink and she shines light onto my world in a way I've never seen it before.

As soon as I pull into the parking spot along the street, she hops out. I would have opened her door.

"Brr ..."

I laugh at her low tolerance for fifty-degree weather. She hugs her arms across her chest, and I rest my hand on her lower back, guiding her to the neon sign above the little dive that's one of the best kept secrets in the city.

"Elle!" The bouncer at the door hugs Ellen.

I didn't see that coming.

"Cam, how the hell are you?" She hugs him back.

"It's all good, girl. Haven't seen you around here in a while."

"I moved to a different apartment. It's not in walking distance."

"You ever heard of a car or public transportation?"

She laughs. "Yeah, yeah … Cam, this is Flint."

"I know Hopkins." Cam gives me a fist bump. "Everyone knows Hopkins."

"Oh?" Ellen's eyes widen and her head moves back as her gaze makes an exaggerated inspection of me.

"Clearly you don't follow football," Cam says.

"Clearly not as well as I should." Ellen twists her lips to the side like she's trying to figure me out.

"How do you two know each other?" Cam asks, crossing his thick arms over his black T-shirt clad chest.

"Flint is my landlord who's trying to evict me because he doesn't understand my job or the fact that rats are some of the cleanliest and most intelligent pets."

"Wow!" I tug at the cuffs to my shirt. "You just threw me under the bus."

Cam barks a hearty laugh over the smooth music, buzzing chatter, and glasses clinking against tables.

Ellen shrugs. "Saying those words to your parents would have been throwing you under the bus. Saying them to Cam is just nudging you into the bumper."

Cam nods toward the stage. "The corner booth is vacant."

"Thanks," Ellen and I say in unison.

"What happened to 'I'm not twelve?'" I whisper in her ear as we weave our way through a sea of people huddled into small groupings of round tables and chairs.

"I changed my mind." She slides into the low-back, curved booth and slips off her jacket, revealing a tight-fitting turtleneck sweater that hugs the curves of her breasts almost as nicely as the light denim jeans hugging her legs and ass. The dark red hair, soft blue eyes ... the whole damn package is going to be my ruination. I can just feel it.

I slide in next to her so we both have a good view of the stage. "Mr. Hopkins, the usual?" the waitress asks.

I nod.

"And for you?"

"Chardonnay please."

"So you used to live downtown?" I watch the performer on stage, going for small talk because I still don't know what possessed me to call her.

"For six months when I moved here. Couldn't find anything closer to the hospital that fit my budget. I had a roommate."

"And she agreed to a six month lease?"

"He."

I loosen my tie and slip off my jacket. "He? You moved in with a random guy you didn't know?"

"Sort of. He owns the building but spends most of his time in Florida where he owns other rentals. His sister is a nurse at the hospital. I met her when I came to town for an interview, and she gave me his name. I know, I know, it was a crazy leap of faith that he wasn't a serial killer."

"That's when you found this place?"

"Yep. Nick, landlord slash roommate slash non-serial killer, brought me here once, and I just kept coming back on my own when he wasn't in town."

The waitress sets our drinks on the table.

"Is that water?"

I nod. "With lime. I'm driving."

"You're quite cautious."

"I am." I return my attention to the sax player on the stage, feeling Ellen's gaze on me, but I don't give her a chance to take this topic any further. "What were you doing when I called?"

"Masturbating." She grins, keeping her eyes on the stage.

"I'm serious."

She shrugs. "Me too." Her head turns toward me and she sips her wine. "But ..." She sets the glass on the table. "If that's too much honesty for tonight, then..." her eyes roll to the ceiling "...let's say I was polishing my silver. Or maybe washing my hair. Writing a concerto. Studying theory and composition. Knitting. Take your pick."

I scratch my neck. There's something about her that my body rejects. Maybe it's not her. Maybe it's me and my need to understand her motives. I don't think she has any—and that makes me uneasy. "Why a music therapist?"

"Ha! Really? Now you want to know this? Where were these questions at my interview? No way. You go first."

I lean back, resting my arm on the back of the booth behind her. "Fine. What do you want to know?"

"Why does Cam act like you're famous?"

I smirk. "I'm not famous."

She turns her body toward mine, bringing one knee close to her chest, her foot resting on the seat of the booth. "Maybe not, but Cam thinks you're a big deal at least in the world of football."

I sip my water, staring at the lime trapped beneath the ice. "I played in college and would have gone Pro as wide receiver had I not fucked up my knee. Instead of finishing law school, I became an agent for a very promising quarterback. That's how people around here know me. The man behind the player who gave Minnesota their first Super Bowl win. He took early retirement. I went back to finish law school and the rest is history."

"That's a good story."

It's not a good story. It's so fucking tragic I can barely find the will to crawl out of bed every morning.

"You don't look happy. Your wife died somewhere in that story, didn't she?"

I nod.

She drops it. No how, why, or where. I omitted the most defining part of my life, and she doesn't ask anything else. Again, I can't figure out her motives.

We watch the band play for the next hour. She finishes one glass of wine but turns down the waitress's offer for a second glass. The dead wife topic always leads to nowhere. It's the ultimate conversation killer. Tonight is no exception.

"Let's go." She slides out of the booth.

I toss cash onto the table and follow her out the door, feeling guilty for the lack of any conversation over the past hour. "I'm sorry for not saying much—"

She whips around and grabs the lapels to my jacket, pulling me around the corner to the alley. She kisses me. Her hands take mine, and she guides them to her waist. "Touch me," she whispers over my mouth.

"Where?" I take a step forward until her back presses to the side of the brick building.

"Anywhere …" Her breath is labored and desperate as she licks and sucks the skin between my ear and the collar of my jacket. "Everywhere … just … touch me." The pain in her voice bleeds all around us as if she's dying and my hands are the only thing that can save her.

I touch her everywhere, making her moan into my mouth,

making her clench my arms to stay upright, making her beg, making her fall apart under my touch—in a dark alley just after midnight. Anyone who could see us would think we were simply making out. Her coat hides my hand up her sweater and the other down the front of her jeans.

"Jesus, Flint ..." My name rips from her chest as she tugs my tie to bring my mouth to hers. She hums like I'm the most delectable thing she's ever tasted. Her hips jerk and circle as I rub her off.

She sucks in a sharp breath, holds it, and releases it in small staccatos while my fingers slow down with her release. Her eyes blink open, searching my face. "Thank you," she whispers, resting her forehead against my shoulder as I zip and button her jeans before we draw attention to us.

I kiss the top of her head. "Let's go." She hugs my arm as I lead her to my car and open the door like the gentleman I'm clearly not after what I just did to her in the alley—what she asked me to do to her. Why? I'm not sure.

She drifts off to sleep on the way to her apartment. I try to figure out what just happened and what comes next.

"Ellen? We're here. Do you need me to carry you up?"

She stirs and rubs her eyes. "What? No." She shakes her head. "I'm good. Let me just get my keys out."

I go around and open her door.

"Thank you," she says in a sleepy voice.

"I'll walk you up to your door."

"Okay."

I follow her to the second floor and the door at the very end of the hallway. "This is me." She unlocks the door but doesn't open it. It's the first time I've sensed actual nerves on her part. "Do you want to come in for ..."

"No. I should get home."

Her shoulders sag with what looks like relief. I don't know what to take from that. And it's too late for my brain to make a good attempt at figuring her out.

Looking at her watch, she sighs. "It's late. Thank you for the call. It was definitely ... unexpected."

"Unexpected," I echo her. The word feels hollow and misplaced at the moment. Unplanned? Regrettable? I don't know how I feel.

"Goodnight." A small smile makes an attempt to stick to her face.

"Goodnight." Before I can even think about kissing her again, she cracks open her door, slides inside, and shuts it behind her.

When I hear her locks click, I take my blue balls, eternal erection, and completely fucked-up mind home for a cold shower and some much needed sleep.

CHAPTER EIGHT

Ellen

THOUGHTS OF AN impending eviction notice, no Plan B, and talented fingers giving me an alley orgasm bring me out of a restless sleep at four o'clock Sunday morning. Instead of wallowing around in bed, fighting sleep that I know will elude me for the rest of the day, I slip on old clothes and clean my apartment with The London Philharmonic Orchestra's "50 Greatest Pieces of Classical Music" floating through the air.

Two hours later I have nothing left to clean, but my mind still won't submit to sleep, so I power walk to my favorite coffee and bagel shop. Armed with caffeine and carbs, I head home to shower and look online for a new office space.

"It's not even seven. Your caffeine addiction must be worse than mine." Just as I reach for the door to my apartment building, Flint's uncharacteristically cheery voice calls from behind me.

I turn, not expecting or wanting to see anyone I know when I'm in desperate need of a shower. I have the hood to my sweatshirt pulled over my head.

"Hey …" I smile. "I'm incognito. How did you recognize me?"

"Ass and legs. They're unmistakable."

"Pervert."

"Sometimes." He saunters toward me holding two hot cups, no suit this morning, just jeans and a sweater.

"Did your parents give you permission to sneak out this morning? Or did you not go home? Was I not your only female companion last night?"

"Jealous?" His head cocks to the side.

"Nope." I open the door and head toward the stairs. "I risk feeding your ego by saying this, but you're what some women might call sex on a stick. As you know, I call you Sex in a Suit, but anyway, it would be a shame not to share you, so I hope whoever came after me enjoyed you as much as I did."

"I feel cheap."

I unlock my door and open it up to my clean apartment. "No." Shooting him a flirty look over my shoulder, I walk down my entry hall. "I've seen your suits, your car, and your house, Mr. Hopkins. You're far from cheap."

His gaze lands on the bucket of cleaning supplies by the door to the deck. "You cleaned up for me. It's like you knew I was coming."

I set my coffee on the kitchen counter and fish my bagel from its bag. "Ha! No ... you are quite the surprise this morning."

He removes the lid to his coffee cup, smirking while bringing it to his mouth. He sips it while keeping his eyes on me.

"Did you stop by just to bring me coffee? Early morning bootie call? Or to remind me that I need to find a new place to rent?"

Flint's smile fades as his eyes divert to everywhere in the room but me. "It's not person—"

"I know, I know ... it's business, not personal."

"Would you let me finish?" He gives me a stern look.

I blow out a slow breath and nod.

"I know you're pissed off that I didn't fully understand your job before signing our rental agreement, but the truth is I can't focus on my job when you're banging on drums and singing all afternoon. It's *not* personal. I didn't wake up one day and decide to be vindictive. When we met, I liked you and thought you would be a good renter. And whether you choose to believe it or not, I do need to concentrate to do my job properly."

I weigh his words, but they don't solve my problem. "You didn't answer my question. Why are you here?"

His chin dips as he shakes his head.

"Sex? You can say it. I won't judge you. Let me take a quick shower and we'll have sex."

"Jesus ..." he whispers. "You make it sound like a job, like I'm paying you for sex. That's not why ..."

"Fine. Do you want to sit down and talk? Do you want half of my bagel?"

He continues to shake his head.

"Then what? Why are you here?"

"I don't know!" He flinches at his own outburst when he looks up at me.

"Well, then we can play until you figure it out." I turn, re-treating to the bedroom next to mine. "Good morning, gentlemen and my lady." I open the door to the cage. "Come. We have company this morning. Come on."

Flint stands in the middle of my living room with complete confusion etched along his face. It morphs into disgust and his body goes rigid when he spots what's skittering down the hall behind me. "What the fuck?" he whispers.

"You've met Wolfgang Amadeus Mozart, but I'd like you to meet Johann Sebastian Bach, Ludwig Van Beethoven, Frédérick Chopin, and Stefani Joanne Angelina Germanotta, the only girl. But she prefers to go by the name Lady Gaga."

I can't describe the horror on his face as he watches my five pet rats roam around him and onto the furniture.

"Still thinking about having sex with me? My little classical composers won't bother us, but I'm not going to lie ... Gaga likes to watch."

I've never used my pets to ward off the attention of a man. Rats are misunderstood as pets. Feeding that misunderstanding by making them seem creepy is not my intention, but right now I don't know what to do with the man before me.

Our days are numbered, and I feel like he needs an easy out. I'll let my babies be his out. "I don't know if Harry told you, but Mozart is a Dumbo rat, hence the cute ears on the side of his head instead of the top, and Bach, Chopin, and Beethoven are Rex rats. They have soft, curly coats and curly whiskers. And Lady Gaga, as you can see, is a hairless rat. I have to keep a close eye on her so she doesn't get too cold."

Flint watches my babies for a few moments and looks at me.

"You're welcome to bring Harry by to see all of them. My landlord won't let me take them to the office building."

After a few slow blinks and a blank look, he watches for long tails as he walks to the door. "Goodbye."

"Bye," I whisper long after the door shuts behind him.

Plopping down in my recliner, I stare at my phone, needing some love, so I call my dad.

"What do you want?"

I grin at his grumpy façade. "Hey, Dad. I figured you

might still be out fishing."

"Been there. Done that. Did you just roll out of bed?"

"Yeah, like … three hours ago. Couldn't sleep."

"Nightmares?"

"No. Just a racing mind. You should come for a visit?"

"And leave my boat?"

"It would survive without you." I chuckle.

"I think you're the one who should come for a visit."

"I'm not ready."

"Can't stay in the middle forever."

I laugh. "I like Minnesota. It's cold here, but I like it."

"Goddamn! When did my New England girl turn into such a delicate little flower?"

"When I moved to Florida and then Southern California."

"That's a bunch of bull. Southern California is not Arizona. Are you sick?"

"I'm fine, Dad."

"You're calling *me*. That usually means you're not fine. What's going on?"

Lady Gaga crawls into the front pouch of my sweatshirt. Smart girl. "I just miss you. Can't I want to hear your voice without reason?"

"It's a gruff old voice, but if that's what you need, then I can talk all day."

"You seeing anyone?"

"Do you have a new mother?"

"Dad …"

"Well, you're suggesting I've replaced her. Why can't I ask if you've replaced her?"

"It's not the same thing and you know it."

"If you come for a visit, I'll let you fix me up with a hot, younger woman. You have any friends?"

I twist my lips. "I was thinking we'd hire a professional."

"Now you're talking."

We both laugh in spite of the underlying pain of losing my mom.

"You find yourself a worthy man? I bet you're breaking hearts especially if you still shamelessly flirt like your mom always did. God ... she was a ball-buster."

"I'm doing my best."

"And Alex?"

My hands clinch a few times. "Haven't talked to him."

"You miss him?"

Drawing in a shaky breath, I nod. "Sometimes." All the time. I miss him every day. In spite of how terrible he was to me. I remember the old Alex.

"Maybe he just needs more time."

We're divorced. Dad knows this, yet he acts like we're just separated, awaiting reconciliation.

"Maybe." Time can't heal everything. I know this. I also know my dad wants to keep hope alive.

"I got the pictures you sent me of your new office space. Looks perfect."

I grunt a laugh. He doesn't know about my recent eviction notice. "It's okay. I'd still like to find a main level place. I could potentially end up with a handicapped client who has a fear of elevators. Then what?"

"You go to their house. Years ago healthcare used to be more personalized. Doctors made house calls. It would probably be cheaper to drive to clients' homes than rent a space in the city."

"It's an idea." Not a perfect one, but I don't want to think about it right now. I really did just call to hear his voice.

"What are you doing for the holidays? Going to see Alex or coming to see me?"

Again with my *ex-husband*. My dad is such a dreamer.

"I thought you could come to me."

"Christmas in your dinky apartment?"

"You haven't seen my apartment. What makes you think it's dinky?" It's dinky.

"Just a hunch."

"Besides, I don't have anyone to watch my rats."

"Oh, Elle … don't tell me you still have those varmints."

"You haven't even met them yet. Don't be so judgmental."

"You said they have a short lifespan. Let me know when they die and you're between rats. I'll come for a visit."

"That's just mean. I'm going to be broken hearted when they die."

"I'll send flowers."

"Terrible. You're a terrible old man. I have to go shower and play with your grandbabies. I love you."

He grumbles at the grandbabies remark. "Love you too. Bye."

MONDAY. AN AWKWARD day. There's the lingering eviction notice. The getting me off in the alley. And the meet-my-rats incident. I have no idea what to expect this week. Flint and I are two pinballs bouncing into each other and shooting off in opposite directions until we're destined to collide again. Each crash feels more explosive.

I see patients at the hospital in the morning and take a long lunch at home since my first afternoon appointment had to cancel. By the time I arrive, Amanda is on her way out.

"You get fired again?"

She laughs. "Every day. He's in court most of the week, so I have flexible hours to chauffeur my kids around. Have you found a new place yet?" Her smile turns into a small frown.

"Not yet. I'm looking at a place tomorrow morning."

"Hope it works out. Harrison will be crushed when he finds out."

I nod. I don't know Harry well enough to know how crushed he will be, but I'll be a little crushed because I like him a lot.

"See you tomorrow."

"Yes. Bye." I smile as she passes me.

My new client suffers from early-onset Alzheimer's. The client after her is a seventeen-year-old girl with an eating disorder. After her, I sit at my small desk by the window and type up case notes on my laptop as the sun sets and my favorite Chopin Nocturne No. 2 in E-Flat Major drifts from the speakers.

"Hi."

I jump. "Jeepers! You startled me."

Harry frowns. "I didn't say boo."

"What are you doing here?" I close my laptop and swivel in my chair to face him.

"My dad said if I helped out around the house more, finished my homework without being asked to do it, and stopped complaining about the meals he makes, then I could play guitar with you."

"Oh, I see." My lips roll between my teeth as I sort out his explanation. "Well, it's getting late. How much longer will he be here?"

"Who?"

"Your dad."

"He's not here."

"He just dropped you off?"

"I rode my bike."

"You rode your bike? That has to be an hour ride."

"Eighty minutes." He sets the guitar case on the floor.

Holy crap. He rode eighty minutes on his bike with a guitar case that doesn't have a strap.

"I have two guitars here."

"I like this one. I have it tuned perfectly."

"Your dad let you ride your bike here?"

Harry shrugs. "Sort of. I mean he said I could come here if I helped out around the house, finished my homework without being asked to do it, and stopped complaining about the meals he makes. So I finished my homework as soon as I got home from school. Cleaned my bathroom and emptied the trash from the kitchen. And I didn't complain about the shitty lentil loaf and some squash thingy he made for dinner."

"Harrison, does he know you're here?"

He sighs. "He'll figure it out."

I watch him strum the guitar. He's good—incredible natural talent. But I can't get distracted by his abilities. He rode off without telling anyone where he was going.

I bring up Flint's number and press *send*. It eventually goes to voicemail.

"Hey, it's Ellen. Harry is with me. He rode his bike to the office. I'm about ready to leave, so I'll drop him off. Hope you get this message and know that he's safe with me."

"I thought we were going to play." Harry shoots me a frown that is totally Flint.

"Let's play in the car—carpool karaoke. You play and I'll sing."

After determining that his bike will have to stay since it's too big for my car, we get settled into the front seat, guitar hugged to his chest. My phone vibrates with a text from Flint.

Thank you

Harry plays and I make up songs on the way to his house. "I know some good music teachers. I could give your dad their names."

"I have you," he replies with such innocence.

"I'm more of a therapist. I could work with you too, but I'm not sure your dad wants you working with me as a client like that."

"So I'll just keep playing with you when I come to my dad's office after school or when I get my stuff done at home." He opens the door and hops out. "Come see my room."

"Uh ... I'm not sure tonight is a goodnight for that." I base my response on the steam flowing from Flint's nose as he waits on the front porch for his runaway son.

"Come on!" Harry waves me in his direction.

"What in the ever loving hell do you think you're doing running off without saying a word?"

I cringe as Flint yells at Harry.

"Not now, Dad. Okay? Come on, Elle."

Flint looks past Harry to me sinking low in the driver's seat. I should back out and let them bicker, but I feel a certain obligation to Harry. I don't want to just leave without saying goodbye.

I ease out, staying guarded behind the car door. "Another time, Harry. Okay?"

"Why?" He deflates.

"Get your butt inside." Flint grits his teeth.

"Elle, it won't take long." Harry ignores his father.

Camilla steps out onto the porch and pulls Harry in for a hug. He says something to her and she motions for me to come in. I cringe, glancing at Flint, who is not giving me any sort of welcoming look.

"Quickly. I have to get home soon." I climb the porch steps.

"Take the guitar with you when you leave." Flint's jaw works overtime as I pass him, giving him a slight nod of understanding. Taking away the guitar I loaned Harry is not the right kind of punishment, but he's not my son.

Not my house.

Not my rules.

Not my call.

Their home is just as magnificent and enchanting as the Hamiltons', but they have a grand piano in their great room. I gawk at it a few seconds before following Harry. Just as I suspected, Harry has a huge window seat in his bedroom. He shows me everything, including pictures from when he took dance lessons and his fishing lure collection.

"My dad loves to fish. He lives in Cape Cod," I say.

"Really? That'd be cool to fish in the ocean."

I nod while grinning. "My dad sure thinks so."

Flint's large frame fills the doorway. He's removed his suit jacket, loosened his tie, unbuttoned the top of his shirt, and rolled up his sleeves. I fight the internal struggle to want to piece him back together versus strip him the rest of the way because I still feel cheated that I've not seen him completely naked.

"Who's this?" I nod to a photo.

"My mom. She died in a car accident when I was two."

He hands me a framed picture of a woman breaking the finish line tape.

"Is this a marathon?"

"Chicago. I think. She was supposedly a runner."

And beautiful. I study the picture until Flint clears his throat.

"We need to have words, young man. And I don't think you want Ms. Rodgers here when we have them."

"I did everything you told me to do. Homework. Chores. Gagging down dinner without complaining."

"I'm going to walk Ms. Rodgers out and then we'll talk."

I give Harry a sympathetic smile and hand the photo of his mom back to him. "Do you have a phone?"

He nods and pulls it out of his pocket.

"Unlock it and I'll give you my phone number. I could have been gone earlier when you rode all that way to see me. Next time just give me a quick call or text me. Okay?"

"Okay." He unlocks his phone, and I add my name to his contacts. "Wait!"

I turn just as Flint moves out of my way.

"Smile." He shrugs. "Or don't." Harry takes my picture. "For your contact profile."

"Bye." I hold up a hand, hoping it's not the last time I see him, but, from the look on Flint's face, I fear it might be a final goodbye.

"Good to see you again." Camilla and Gene smile as I pass by them at the bottom of the stairs.

I think they were eavesdropping because they look awkward just standing at the bottom of the stairs.

"You too."

"Maybe you could come for dinner tomorrow."

Flint halts in front of me, turns, and scowls at his mom.

Dear god this is awkward.

"Flint, it's fine. Your dad and I will make dinner. I know you have a lot of work this week with your trial. It's better that she come here than Harrison ride his bike to see her."

"Mom—"

"Six thirty sound okay, Ellen?" Camilla waves off Gene as he nudges her, probably to warn her what a terrible idea it is to invite me to dinner. "Please, Harrison would love it."

"Um ... sure."

"Great. See you tomorrow."

I turn back to Flint and shoot him a sheepish smile. He grumbles something and stomps out the door.

"What was I supposed to do?" I jog to catch up to his long strides. He doesn't have to escort me to my car. I will leave the premises without being kicked off.

"Say no."

"Fine." I stop and pivot back toward the house. "I'll go back in and tell her no."

"Stop. Just ..."

I turn back to him.

He rubs his hands over his face. "It's fine. Just let it be."

I brush past him, too hungry and tired to deal with his family issues. Or maybe they're just Ellen Rodgers issues.

"Fine. I'll let it be." I get in my car.

Flint grabs the door before I can shut it. He leans down putting us at eye level. There's not room for oxygen *and* him in this vehicle. My heart pounds like a metal detector nearing a treasure.

If I lean in three inches, our lips will meet. I like his lips, and the way he's looking at mine leads me to believe the feeling is mutual.

"Thank you for bringing him home."

He smells like herbs, like I imagine a chef might smell. I'm hungry. I'd settle for him, but I don't think he's on the menu tonight. I don't know if he'll ever be on the menu. He's that dessert on the dessert tray that no one ever gets to eat because it's just a display.

"No problem. Did you notice how I returned him to you without bitching about my time? And I didn't put him in a brown paper bag and threaten to dump him out the window without stopping the car first."

His lips press together and he hums. "That was very kind of you." Those dark eyes shift to my mouth again, then lower.

I feel his gaze everywhere. It's warm and tingly. "Go easy on him."

"We'll see." He straightens to full height. "Goodnight."

The door shuts.

CHAPTER NINE

Flint

"I T'S NOT OKAY for you to leave without telling anyone where you're going."

Harrison, perched on his window seat, keeps his nose in a book while ignoring me.

"You said I could play guitar with her if I—"

"You take things too literally. I meant if you showed me a pattern, if you did it for a week or more. And then I would *take* you to the office. I would call to make sure it was okay with her. You're twelve. You can't ride your bike that far alone. It's not smart. It's not safe. Had she not given you a ride home, you would have had to ride home in the dark with no reflective clothing, no lights on your bike, and no sense of direction because I know damn well you rely on familiar things that would not look familiar at night."

"Fine."

I hold back my irritation to his *fine* remark. It's his version of sorry. I know this, but it still irritates the hell out of me when he says it so dismissively.

"Grandma invited Ellen to dinner tomorrow night, but after that, you're going to take a break from seeing her."

"That's not—"

I hold out my finger. "And if you argue with me, I'll send the borrowed guitar home with her like I should have done tonight."

He leaps up, stomps across the floor, and slams the door in my face.

I remind myself that raising him is a gift and a debt. Tonight it doesn't feel like a gift.

MY COURT CASE drags out. It should have ended by now, but opposing counsel sprung a new witness on me, and now I have the weekend to prepare a cross-examination. Harrison is giving me the silent treatment, which is better than him relentlessly pushing my buttons like he usually does. And my parents are cooking up a storm in my kitchen for Ellen, the woman I'm evicting as soon as I can squash my son's obsession with her.

I take my penance without complaining. Killing my wife shouldn't come with any sort of mercy.

"She's here!" Those are the first words I've heard out of Harrison since he slammed the door in my face last night.

I continue to comb over the evidence in this never-ending case as I listen to voices echo from my parents greeting Ellen.

"Flint? Dinner is almost ready. Come out of your office and join us," my mom calls.

"In a minute," I mumble to myself.

One minute turns into fifteen before I get another dinner call from my mom. I tug at my already loosened tie and stand with a sigh. This suit has to go, so I take the spiral staircase in the back corner that goes from my office directly to the master bedroom. It's one of the original design features I love most about this old house.

I untie my tie and return it to its drawer, remove my shirt, and unfasten my pants just as the toilet flushes in the en suite bathroom. "Harrison, how many times do I have to tell you to use your own—"

The pocket door slides open, and Ellen sucks in a quick breath, eyes wide. "I … the hall bathroom was …" Her gaze roams along my bare chest and down to my unfastened pants.

I picture her rats, imagine her with spinach stuck in her perfect teeth, anything to keep my dick in check.

"I'll be downstairs in a minute."

Ellen nods slowly but her gaze remains affixed to my chest. I don't get the sense that my words registered with her brain. She moves toward me, but the dresser at my back prevents me from retreating. Her warm breath along my bare chest sends an instant message to my dick. Not even rats can compete with the nearness of her body to mine.

"I think your mom is a great cook. It smells delicious downstairs."

There's nothing I love more than having my mom's cooking mentioned at the same time I'm imagining my cock in Ellen's mouth because she won't stop wetting her lips.

Rats. She owns rats. My dick needs to get that unsavory message.

Nope. Not even that thought can make this erection disappear.

"I'm evicting you," I whisper.

She steps back and nods, redirecting her gaze from my chest to her feet. I'm not trying to be a dick about it, I'm just trying to go to dinner without a hard-on. The reality of our professional relationship and her reaction to it is enough to abate the situation in my pants.

She looks up. "I signed a new lease this morning."

I open my mouth to speak, but I don't know what to say.

"See you downstairs." She smiles.

"NICE OF YOU to take a break and join us for dinner." My mom nods to the lone chair opposite Harrison and Ellen.

"Ellen was just telling us her father lives in Cape Cod."

I lay my napkin over one leg while inspecting the woman who is really still a mystery to me. "I didn't know that. I thought you were from California."

She dabs her mouth and swallows. "I moved here from California, but that's not where I grew up."

"And you think it's cold here?" I narrow my eyes.

"College in Florida and my first job in Southern California spoiled me." She shrugs.

"I'd never live in California. You'd have to be stupid to live near the San Andres fault. Eventually everyone will die." My uncensored son pipes up.

"Harrison—"

"It's fine." She chuckles. "Good thing I moved here."

"It's not safe anywhere. My mom died because it was raining."

Your mom died because I was drunk. More penance. I deserve this more than the oxygen in my lungs. It should have been me. This boy I love beyond all words is a walking reminder of who I am—a murderer.

"My mom died too. Life's not fair. Fate doesn't show favoritism." Ellen shrugs.

Harrison nods like he understands her, like he connects with her.

"I wonder what it would feel like to be on a boat in the Pacific if there were an earthquake in California."

I grin. Harrison is always three topics behind the conversation—fixating, obsessing over one thing.

My parents ask Ellen a million questions about her job. I hear a few of her answers, but my thoughts war between court tomorrow and the needy woman I brought to orgasm in a dark alley.

"Dinner was great, Mom. Thank you. But I have a few things left to do before morning." I wipe my mouth and push my chair back. "Help with the dishes, Harrison, and then get to bed. Okay?"

He doesn't acknowledge me. No surprise.

"We'll make sure he pitches in." My dad gives me a reassuring nod.

"Goodnight." I give Ellen a brief glance before retreating to my office.

For the next hour, I block out the chatter and clanking in the kitchen, giving my full attention to preparing for court tomorrow. As I shut off my computer and rub my tired eyes, the voices get closer.

"He won't mind if you say goodbye one more time," my dad says just outside of my office before knocking twice on the door.

"Come in."

"Ellen's leaving. She wanted to say goodbye," he says.

I nod.

"Harrison went to bed and your mom and I are turning in too. Be a gentleman and see her out. Okay?" He winks before stepping back to let her into my office.

"Thank you. Goodnight," she whispers to him before turning toward me.

I wait to hear him climbing the stairs, the third and eighth ones creak.

"Nice office."

I watch her like a wolf closing in on a lost sheep. After a long day, I'm not in the mood for idle chitchat.

"Dinner was exceptionally good. Your mom is a wonderful cook."

I nod slowly, my finger tracing my bottom lip—the same finger that rubbed circles on her clit in the alley.

She walks around my office, inspecting shelves filled with boring law books, making the occasional glance in my direction. I strip her without touching her, slowly fucking her with every look.

"Where do these stairs lead?" She grips the railing, blue eyes curious.

I like curious. In fact, I'm pretty damn curious right now too. Easing out of my chair, I walk up behind her. She glances up at me over her shoulder. I cock my head a fraction, twisting my mouth, waiting for her to do exactly what I want her to do without having to say one. Single. Fucking. Word.

Keeping her gaze locked to mine, she takes a cautious step and then another. My feet shadow hers; my body presses to the back of hers, heat radiating between us. As she circles the last part of the spiral staircase, my hands mold to her hips, causing her breath to hitch, halting her forward motion.

Every curve so perfect. My hands slide under her black sheer blouse, fingertips tracing the taut, silky skin and forging on until her bra is shoved up and out of my way.

A moan vibrates her sternum when my hands claim her breasts, kneading and teasing her nipples before pressing the pads of my fingers to her stomach, navigating my way back to her hips and along her outer thighs to the hem of her soft knitted skirt.

She wore this for me, just like she chose tall schoolgirl socks and boots instead of making me rip her hosiery. I ease her skirt up her legs. Tiny staccato breaths fall from her parted lips. It's the only sound in the room. The pad of my middle finger slides over the wet cotton and lace between her legs before gripping the waist of her panties and easing them down her toned, soft, and oh-so-sexy legs and over her boots before landing on the stair behind me.

My lips start at the skin just above the top of her right boot and ghost their way up the back of her leg.

"Flint ..."

"Shhh ..." I nip at the skin right below the perfect curve of her ass, warning her to be quiet. She smells like the forbidden and tastes like my newest addiction. My hands work her skirt up her torso and over her head. With a firm yank it releases her arms, taking her shirt with it. I discard them behind me as well.

She turns. I take a step up, putting my face level with her perky tits. Glancing up to meet her drunken gaze and parted lips, I grin, unfastening her bra and tossing it over my shoulder.

Fucking perfect.

Long auburn hair flowing down her back and over the top of her breasts makes her look like a goddess, something an artist would spend months sculpting to perfection. I don't want to sculpt her. I want to feel her beneath me, writhing, moaning, completely falling into a million tiny pieces of ecstasy.

"Sit," I command before shrugging off my shirt.

I swear I can hear her heart pounding against her chest. Her teeth scrape along her bottom lip as she grips the metal railing and sits on the edge of the narrow step.

I drop to my knees several steps down from the one she's sitting on. Our gazes lock for a long moment before I bring my index finger to my lips in a *shhh* warning. Her hands grip the railing tighter until her knuckles blanch. She bites her lips together when I lean forward and drape her right leg over my left shoulder and her left leg over my right one.

She gasps, stomach muscles contracting, followed by a throaty groan when my tongue makes its first swipe. One of her hands releases the railing and clenches my hair as her pelvis jerks, legs trembling a little more with every move I make. Some depraved part of me has wanted to do this since the first day she arrived for the interview.

When her hand tugs harder at my hair and her hips grind frantically, I pull back, letting my eyes drink up every inch of her flushed skin before dipping my head down. Trapping one nipple between my teeth, I give it a firm tug, flick my tongue over it twice, and pinch the hell out of her other nipple.

"Jesu—"

My hand covers her mouth as her body jerks, knees clamping my torso. Releasing her nipple, I lift my head and grin, keeping my hand over her mouth as she convulses, eyes rolling back for a few seconds before widening again to meet my gaze.

When I'm confident she can control her volume, I slide my hand from her mouth, hug her body to mine, and carry her the rest of the way up the stairs to my bed.

"How the hell did you make me com—"

I silence her with my mouth on hers while removing my pants and briefs. "I need you to be silent," I whisper next to her ear before retrieving a condom from the drawer, rolling it on, and pinning her to my bed with my cock buried inside of her.

Harrison is across the hall and my parents are in the room next to mine. We don't need to talk. I wasn't really in the mood for it anyway.

CHAPTER TEN

Ellen

I WAS FINE having sex with the same man for my whole life, but circumstances landed me in Flint Hopkins' bed, and now I feel guilty for feeling so grateful for this opportunity. Thank you, Alex, for literally kicking all of my belongings to the curb. It's possible I still have some residual anger.

Eyes closed, sated, and relishing the thread count of Flint's sheets against my naked body, something tickles my leg. I jerk, cracking open my eyes and tipping my chin to my chest.

"What are you—"

"Shhh ..." I've been hushed a million times in the past hour. Flint pulls my panties up my legs. "You have to go," he whispers.

Did I black out? I *just* orgasmed again. When did he get dressed?

I lift my ass like an obedient child letting someone dress me. He grabs my good arm and pulls me to sitting. Bra. Sweater. Skirt. Socks and boots. Flint Hopkins is an expert at dressing people.

He takes my hand and pulls me to the back stairs—where it all began tonight.

"I had three orgasms. That's—"

"Shhh …" He hushes me again as we circle down the stairs. "And you're welcome."

"Smug bastard," I mumble.

He glances over his shoulder while pulling me to the front door. The smirk on his face confirms my assessment, but it's replaced with a grimace as one of the stairs squeaks.

Before I can look back to see who's coming down the main staircase, Flint pulls me into the coat closet and eases the door shut behind us. His head presses against the wall next to the door so he doesn't have to duck under the bar of hanging coats. He covers my mouth with his hand.

Seriously? It's a little before midnight and we're hiding in a coat closet. I think I can deduce on my own that we need to be quiet. I nip at his hand until he pulls it away.

"Shhh …" he whispers.

"I'm being quiet," I whisper yell.

"Shhh …" Cupping the back of my head, he pulls my face to his chest like he wants to suffocate me into silence.

Jeez he smells good … but, seriously, I need some oxygen. I shove at his chest. "Stop—"

His strong hands palm my head like it's a basketball he's ready to pass, and his lips cover mine. I love the slide of his tongue against mine. It's a drug that makes my legs feel boneless. My hands grip his biceps the way they did earlier when he moved above me—inside me—naked, intense, and so sexy.

He's distracting me. Silencing me with his mouth. It's rude. And as soon as I get my fill, I will show him how offended I am. We are grown adults in our thirties. There is no reason for us to hide in this closet.

Flint bites my bottom lip and moves his mouth to my ear. "Stop. Humming."

Was I humming? Huh, I had no idea.

The door to the closet opens. I fist Flint's T-shirt and freeze.

"Heard a humming sound." Gene yawns while scratching his head covered in thick, salt and pepper hair.

"Sorry." I cringe, biting my lips together.

Gene's gaze moves up a few inches to Flint. "Forgot to take my pills. I just needed some water."

"Okay." I nod, still fisting Flint's shirt. What's Flint's deal? He has nothing to say?

"Okay." Gene cracks a tiny smile. "Enjoy the rest of your evening."

And then ... He. Shuts. The. Door.

We stand in the dark, listening to the creaking of one stair and a few seconds later another stair creaks before everything falls silent again.

Flint opens the door and guides me out of the closet with his hand on my lower back. I retrieve my coat from the coat tree and slide my arms into it as we walk out to my car. I can't stop smiling.

"You just can't stay quiet," he grumbles.

I open the car door and turn back to the broad-shouldered man looming above me. "I feel eighteen and so alive right now. Oh my gosh! Your *dad* caught us in the coat closet."

His barely detectable grin fades. "Ellen ..."

I start to speak, start to make up an excuse for tonight before he has to make up his own excuse for why this can't go beyond tonight. But I stop myself. I'm not his problem. I'll have a new office space next week. I don't regret tonight, so if he does, then he'll have to man up and say it.

"Harrison can't find out about this."

"Okay." I draw in a breath to elaborate but decide to let the words die in a silent exhale. Is that code for tonight never happened? Instead of coming across as needy or clingy, I simply smile. "Goodnight."

Flint nods once as I get in my car. He closes my door and watches me pull out of his driveway. It's possible I won't see Flint again after I move in five days. That makes me sad, but I still smile because tonight a man touched me, healed me, and erased a little bit of the hate from my past.

Flint

I CAN'T TELL which burns more, my legs or my lungs. Heidi would hate me for allowing a woman into my bed with our son in the room across the hall. Heidi would hate me for thinking I have the right to one second of pleasure. And she would be right.

"Good morning. How was your run?" my mom asks as I push through the back door and grab a green juice out of the fridge.

Harrison keeps his head down toward his bowl of fruit, earbuds blocking out the rest of the world, while my dad gives me a knowing smirk over the newspaper framed in his hands.

"It was good."

"Did Ellen ever find her coat?" Dad asks.

I narrow my eyes at him.

"I hung her coat up on the coat tree." Mom offers me a cup of coffee.

I shake my head at it.

"That's what I thought too…" my dad refocuses on the paper but continues to run his mouth "…but she and Flint were focusing their attention on the coat closet."

"I sure like her." My mom sips her coffee.

"I do too." Dad folds down the side of the paper to grab his mug of coffee. "What do you think of her, Flint?"

I think Ellen Rodgers is trouble. "She's nice enough."

He tips his chin and glances at me over the frames of his glasses, coffee mug paused a few inches from his mouth. "On a scale of one to ten, how *nice* do you think she is?"

"You're acting weird, Gene. Did you miscount your pills last night?" Mom eyes him with sincerity.

"I'm fine, Camilla. Answer the question, Son."

I scratch my chin with my middle finger. "A seven."

"Just a seven, huh?"

Tossing the bottle into the recycling bin, I nod. "Seven."

"She was more than a seven, sweetie. You just didn't hang around after dinner to get to know her like we did," Mom says.

"Exactly." My dad nods several times. "We saw a side of her you probably didn't get to see. Maybe you should get to know her better."

I want to strangle him.

"And she's so pretty, Flint. My goodness … that auburn hair makes her blue eyes pop. She looks like a living doll. I couldn't stop staring at her. I want to look like her in my next life. She's stunning."

"Stunning." My dad coughs, hiding his grin behind his fist. Such a smart-ass.

"I'm going to shower."

Ellen

FRIDAY. TWO DAYS and counting down …

I'm glad my new landlord is eighty and partially deaf. I don't have to worry about him hearing the instruments and singing. I also don't have to worry about having sex with him after being served an eviction notice. I don't have to explain to his son why I won't be able to play guitar with him after school anymore.

"My dad said you're leaving and I have to give the guitar back."

I turn in my desk chair toward the voice I will miss.

"Hey, Harry. Yes, I'm moving out, but you don't have to give me back the guitar. I want you to have it."

"Okay."

I smile at his somber enthusiasm.

He kneels on the floor to take the guitar out of its case.

"I'm surprised you're here. I haven't seen your dad today. I hope he knows where you are."

"My grandpa dropped me off. My dad is on his way. I'll ride home with him after he does whatever …" He dismissively waves his hand.

"It was fun having dinner with you."

"Yeah." Harry nods, strumming a few chords. "They were talking about it yesterday."

"Oh?"

"Everyone thinks you're nice. A seven."

"A seven?"

"Something like that. I don't know. Just something my grandpa asked my dad." He continues to play as he mumbles.

"What did your grandpa ask your dad?"

"I don't know. Something about a scale from one to ten. My dad said you're a seven. Which is weird. Seven's like seventy percent. That's a D at my school. Sixty-six to seventy is a D."

I hear everything—*everything* in my profession. It's part of therapy. But this eats at me. Flint called me a seven. Sure, it's been a while, but I'd hardly call Tuesday night a seven. What could I have done to up my game? I smile when Harry glances up at me, but it's a fake gritted-teeth smile. Inside I'm not smiling. I'm ready to tear someone apart.

As if the gods of revenge are granting extra wishes today, my phone vibrates with a text from Mr. Seven himself.

I'm finishing up some paperwork downstairs. Send him back down if you need to leave or have other things to do. Thanks.

"Harry, I'm going to run downstairs for a minute. I'll be right back."

"K."

I take the stairs, my heels clicking on each concrete step as I stomp my way to the first floor. I hum, trying to calm my anger, but it's not working.

"Hey, Elle." Amanda smiles, twisting off the cap to a glass bottle of flavored tea.

"Hey …" I hold up a finger as I breeze past her. "I just need a quick second to talk to your boss."

Flint looks up from his paperwork as I shut the door behind me. A slight smile curls his lips. It's not a stellar smile. I'd give it a seven out of ten at best.

"Ms. Rodgers." His slight grin twists into a smirk that I want to punch off his face.

"You can't bury your face between my legs and then call me Ms. Rodgers."

His smirk fades, his expression settling into discomfort as he glances past me toward Amanda. I wedge my way between him and his desk, forcing him to roll back a foot or so. His gaze makes a quick inspection of me as I sit on the edge.

I love the quick glances he makes to Amanda and the thoughts that must be going through his pretty little head. *What if she turns around? How must this look? Why doesn't "Ms. Rodgers" care what Amanda thinks?*

He clears his throat. "Sorry, what shall I call you? Ellen? Elle? Are we friends now?"

I ease my leg up, resting the toe of my shoe on his lower abdomen and pressing the pointy heel of it into his junk.

He grunts, grabbing my ankle.

"How about you call me Ten."

Flint's eyes narrow a fraction as he continues to tighten his grip on my ankle to fight the pressure I'm exerting on his cock. Within seconds, realization steals his expression.

"That little shit. He's so selective with what he acknowledges, but he hears everything."

"Don't pass the blame onto him. He only repeated what you said. I just came down here to let you know that I am not a seven. Not a D. So you can be an ass all you want. You can try to make me feel inferior and unwanted, but I am *not* that girl anymore. So go fuck your own hand. I'm sure it's the only thing you consider a ten, you egomaniac."

I jerk my foot out of his grip and push off his desk. That was not cool. I know it, but I'm suppressing the shame the same way I did after I popped his birthday balloons.

"Bye, Elle," Amanda says.

"Bye." I don't stop for small talk, instead I run to the lobby restroom and splash water on my face, closing my eyes and humming Chopin. After my pulse settles into a slow steady rhythm, I exhale a cleansing breath and make my way to the elevator. When the doors open on the second floor, Flint—leaning against the opposing wall with his hands resting in his pants pockets, one leg crossed over the other—twists his lips and makes a slow visual assessment.

It's quiet. The lights at the accounting office are off, and I don't hear Harrison on the guitar.

"Who made you feel less than perfect?"

I laugh a little, stepping off the elevator. "Where's Harry?"

"Doing his homework in my office."

Brushing past him, I continue humming Chopin.

"Answer my question."

Plopping down in my desk chair, I lean back and prop my feet on the desk, watching the sun begin to set behind a curtain of scattered clouds. "Besides you?"

He doesn't respond; I knew he wouldn't. I don't look at him. And I'm not going to have this conversation with him.

"Did you know that music and exercise are the only two activities that stimulate your whole brain? It also stimulates the release of dopamine. And it can heal … not just emotions. Music can repair brain damage. Parkinson's disease, stroke victims, gunshot wounds to the head. I've worked with so many people and they all think I'm responsible for this miraculous recovery, but … it's the music. I'm just a facilitator. It never stops amazing me. I know what could or even should happen over the course of treatment, but it still shocks the hell out of me every single time."

"Do you think it could help Harrison?"

I turn toward him. "Maybe. No two autistic children are the same. But, honestly, he's already helping himself. Every time he picks up that guitar, good things happen. It helps him focus on something that's truly good for his mind—not like hours in front of a screen. It's calming. And when he plays with me, or let's say you put him in band someday, it will help him build connections and learn to work well and collaborate with other people."

Flint blinks slowly. If thoughts made sounds, I'm certain his would sound like a marching band.

"I have plans with my parents this weekend."

"I'll be out by Sunday night." I ease my feet off the desk and stand, taking slow steps to him. "So is this goodbye?" I straighten his tie. Absolutely any excuse to touch him … even if I'm a seven in his mind. He's a ten in mine because he touched me when I needed it so desperately.

"Why are you humming?"

"Because," I whisper, keeping my eyes on his tie, "it calms my heart."

"What's wrong with your heart?"

"It gets a little out of control when I touch you—like it could explode."

"Then why touch me?"

I glance up to meet his softened gaze. "Because you never feel more alive than when you're flirting with death."

"Have you flirted with death?"

I smile. "Yes."

He drops his head into an easy nod. "Do you want me to tell you why this is goodbye?"

"I already know. You don't feel worthy."

"Of?"

I sigh. "Me. Something that's for you. A life beyond Harry and your work. Sex in your greenhouse. Wine with your neighbors. A second date. A pet rat ... or five. Pleasure without guilt. Puddle jumping when it's lightning outside. Driving with one hand on the steering wheel. Unprotected sex." I press my hand to his chest, smoothing his tie. "I don't know ... maybe you don't feel worthy of *life* because your wife's not here to share it with you."

His right hand cups my jaw. My eyes drift shut when the pad of his thumb traces the curve of my lips. "Maybe," he whispers.

Before I open my eyes, his lips replace his thumb, leaving me with a gentle kiss. I can't look at him because if this is goodbye, then I want to feel it. I want to remember this rhythm that my heart falls into only when he touches me.

His lips release mine and his hand vanishes from my face. All that's connecting us is my fingers feeling the soft silk of his tie one small increment at a time until it releases.

My closed eyes hold back all emotion.

The heat of his body fades along with his footsteps. My heartbeat slows, mourning the loss of his touch. I open my eyes to the empty space before me and pull in a slow, shaky breath.

"Bye," I whisper.

CHAPTER ELEVEN

Flint

"HEY, BOSS. DID you have a good weekend? I tried calling you last night. You must have been out with your parents." As I drag my tired ass into work just after noon, Amanda hands me a list of calls I need to make.

"Stenson no longer wants to make a deal. He said he'd rather live on the street than give his 'cheating bitch of a wife' the house he built 'with his own goddamn hands.'"

"Of course he did." I yawn, unbuttoning my jacket and easing into my leather desk chair.

bang bang bang

I glance up. "What's that?"

"Elle. She's a music therapist. We've been over this."

"It's Monday. She was supposed to be out yesterday."

"Oh, didn't you hear or see it on the news?"

bang bang bang

I roll my eyes to the ceiling again. "See what?"

"The Dickson building burned to the ground the other night. They still haven't determined the cause."

"Let me guess. That's where her office was located?"

"See there … you really are much smarter than you look. Had you answered your phone last night, you would have

known that I told Elle she could stay here until she found
another vacancy."

bang bang bang

"How kind of you."

"Yeah, I thought so too. Harrison will think it's pretty fantastic."

I glance up from my desk.

Amanda shrugs. "Okay, he'll be moderately happy in his
own way."

"Remind me to discuss the word fantastic with you."

She spins back around in her chair. "I'll do that. In fact, I'll
set a reminder on my phone right now. You have a gap tomorrow between 1:30 and 2:00, so I'm putting 'fantastic
discussion' in that spot."

In the world of football, people respected me. In the courtroom, people respect me. I think the broken link has to do
with women. It's revenge—karma. I killed my wife and now
the women around me are hell-bent on driving me crazy.

"Shut my blinds and my door, please."

Amanda sighs and rounds the corner into my office. "By all
means, don't you get up. I've got this."

No respect.

She closes the blinds to the glass wall separating my office
and her desk, and she shuts the door on her way out. "I know
you're going to take a nap while you're on the clock."

I slide off my jacket, loosen my tie, and recline back in my
chair with my feet propped up on my desk. Damn right I'm
going to take a nap.

bang bang bang

I groan and attempt to block out the noise above me.

"The wheels on the bus go round and—"

Oh for fuck's sake. I shoot to my feet, sending my chair back into the bookshelf.

"Short nap," Amanda says as I storm out of my office.

"You're fired for letting her stay."

"Sure thing, Boss. You know where to send my unemployment check."

When I get to Ellen's door, I wait outside. The noise has stopped and she's talking.

"You missed it. She sang today."

A woman chokes out a cry. I feel her pain. I wanted to cry when the singing started too.

"Thank you." The woman sniffles.

I give a polite nod as the teary-eyed woman and an older woman make their way past me to the elevator.

"Are you going to make me cry too?" I step into her office space.

Ellen turns, setting her phone down on her desk. My anger escalates because I'm tired, she's still here, and she felt the need to wear tight jeans, a fitted sweater, and high heels. I need to have words with her, but at the moment I'd like to have my way with her.

Her lips twist to the side. "I have another appointment. And since we both know you only cry when you orgasm, then I'd say ... no. Maybe a raincheck?"

"If a man talked to a woman the way you and Amanda talk to me, everyone would call him a jerk. But when women say similar things, they're labeled sassy. It's not right."

"Not true." She holds up her finger. "I think you're incredibly sassy."

"You think I'm sex in a suit."

Ellen bites her lips and her cheeks turn pink.

"What if I called you Sex in a Skirt? You'd scream sexual harassment."

Her eyes widen for a few seconds before she makes her way to me. She's going to mess with me—my tie, my jacket, my resolve—and I won't move because I like her hands on me, the fruity smell of her hair, and the view of her cleavage when she's right under my nose.

I'm fucked.

"Do you feel objectified?" Her hands go right to my tie. By this point she might as well grab my dick since it's now programmed to respond to her yanking my tie every which way. "I'm not wearing a skirt today, but after my last appointment I could change and we could role play your sex-in-a-suit and sex-in-a-skirt scenario. Or ..."

She lifts onto her toes and licks my neck from the top of my tie to my chin. "We could job shadow each other. I could let you play with my bongos and you could show me your briefs."

So fucked—and not just because my dick is jealous of my neck; it's her ridiculous, suggestive words that shouldn't turn on any guy in his right mind. *Bongos and briefs?*

"Do you even know what the words 'sexual harassment' mean?"

She laughs, releasing my tie and taking a step back while shoving her hands in her back pockets. "Hey, unrelated to you gawking at my boobs in spite of calling me a *seven,* I can't tell you how grateful I am that you're letting me stay until I find a new place."

She sighs and shakes her head. "It's scary to think had I moved in just two days earlier, I would have lost all of my stuff in the fire."

No drums or cymbals? Tragic.

"How's the search for a new place going? Anything look promising?"

She coughs a laugh. "I haven't started looking. I've been working. This fire was a little unexpected, so I need to regroup and start from the beginning again."

I glance at my watch. "What time are you done?"

"Four."

"Good. I'll wait for you downstairs."

Her head cocks to the side, exposing her neck. I like her neck, specifically when I can feel her pulse racing against my lips. "Are you asking me out on a date? If so, I think you need to work on your sales pitch."

"No. I'm taking you shopping for a new space to rent."

"Do you think I'm incapable of doing it on my own?"

"I know the area. And I know some places that might be available, but they're not advertising it to everyone."

"Oh, you're connected."

"Yes."

"And you can't stand having me here."

"I can't work with you here."

"Because I'm not a ten?"

"Because you're too loud." I turn and walk down the hall before this gets any crazier.

"On a scale of one to ten..." she pokes her head around the corner just as I push open the door to the stairwell "...how loud am I?"

"An eleven."

I MANAGE TO grab a nap before Amanda squeezes in a last

minute appointment at the end of the day.

"Your husband 'not looking at you the same way' does not prove that he's having an affair. I can't make a case out of that. I need more."

"He sends me chocolates at work every week. That proves he has a guilty conscience ... *and* that proves he's trying to make me fat because he knows I don't want to have sex when I feel bad about myself."

"Bernadette—"

"Bernie. Gordon calls me Bernadette. You're on my side, not his."

I set down my pen and lean back in my chair. "Bernie ... I get paid whether you win or lose. But I don't feel right about taking your money when I know you don't stand a chance of winning with nothing more than a look and chocolates. So either you stay and see if things get better or you file for divorce. But without proof of an affair, you won't get a dime since you signed the prenup against my advice."

She sighs as a sad smile pulls at her glossy lips. "He told me the prenup was just something stupid his attorney wanted. He told me I was his forever."

"All good attorneys want their wealthy clients to have prenups. And..." I stand and button my jacket so she gets the clue that our meeting is about over "...nothing lasts forever."

"Don't sugarcoat it." She stands, shimmying her tight dress down over her chocolate-indulged hips.

"Never have, never will."

"Hey, Elle."

I glance up as Ellen smiles at Amanda before making eye contact with me. I should have kept my blinds shut.

"I thought I was your last appointment today," Bernie says

while hoisting her fancy purse over her shoulder.

"You here to chat with me or see Flint?" Amanda asks.

Keeping those fucking seductive eyes on me, Ellen's grin intensifies. "Flint. We have a date."

My eyes narrow a fraction as I usher Bernie to the waiting room.

"A date?" Amanda whips around to me with wide eyes.

"Well…" Bernie huffs "…if he asks you to sign a prenup, I'd advise against it." She marches past Ellen, straight out the door.

Women. If I could convince my dick I didn't need them, my life would be a hell of a lot easier.

"Not a date. I'm finding a new space for Ms. Rodgers to rent."

I don't have to look at Amanda to know she has some knowing look on her face. She knows nothing. Ellen knows nothing either, but I get the feeling she thinks she does. I step back as she moves toward me.

Don't touch me. I warn her with a stern glare.

My next step ends with my legs backed into Amanda's desk and Ellen's body crossing every possible personal space boundary.

"But if I buy you dinner afterwards, it's a date." Ellen keeps her gaze locked to mine.

It's a miracle her hands remain idle at her sides instead of wrapped around my tie.

"It's not."

"Is it just me or is it warm in here?" Amanda asks behind me.

"It's Ms. Rodgers' fever, which would also explain her hallucinations." I take a step forward, forcing her to retreat a step, refusing to let her *ruffle* me. "Shall we go before you get any worse?"

"You mean like ... a seven?" Her head cocks to the side. "Right now I feel like a ten, but if this fever of mine persists, my condition could downgrade to a seven, and I have it on good authority that a seven is like getting a D in school."

"Yep," Amanda mumbles, "it is *definitely* hot in here."

"Let's. Go," I say.

Ellen tips her chin up as if she's readying another comeback. I narrow my eyes a bit more to let her know this conversation in front of my secretary is over. She can be so damn infuriating and stubborn.

Tilting her body to see past mine, she flashes Amanda a toothy grin. "Bye. See you tomorrow."

"You two kids have fun."

It's torture, not fun.

"My car or yours?" Ellen asks, slipping on her wool jacket just as we emerge from the building.

"Why did you have to say this is a date? Amanda's a dog with a bone when it comes to my personal life."

"What's Harry doing? I'd hoped he might stop by."

I grab her arm and turn her toward me. "Did you hear my question?"

Blue eyes scan my face before landing on mine as she scrapes her teeth across her bottom lip several times. "Do you think about what happened at your house? I'm not asking if you regret it or not, just ... do you think about it. Do you think about me?"

My mouth opens, but my brain vetoes the idea of acknowledging this. "We'll take my car." I nod to the right.

Her heels click behind my long strides. "You didn't answer

me. Where's Harry?"

"You didn't answer me either." I unlock my car, instinctively opening the passenger door. Heidi liked it when I opened the door for her. The night I killed her, she opened her own door.

Ellen tosses her handbag on the seat and turns toward me instead of getting in the car. "Your question? Why did I tell Amanda this is a date? Well, I'm struggling to figure out if what we've done makes me spontaneous or just cheap. And since you like to analyze the stereotypical male and female roles, I would guess that men never feel cheap. I bet you haven't lost a single second of sleep over wondering if what we did makes you cheap and easy. Correct?"

"Please tell me this isn't leading to a discussion about emotions and expectations. There's no place in my life for that right now."

She deflates on a slow sigh, staring at her feet for a few seconds before inching her gaze back up to meet mine. "But the sex was good, right?"

"Get in the car."

"Better than average?"

"Get in the car."

"Was the seven a rating of my appearance or my performance?"

"Fucking hell, woman, get in the car!"

She grins like the snake-charmer-to-my-dick that she is. What have I gotten myself into?

"THIS FEELS TOO residential for my business needs." Ellen stops humming long enough to speak.

I had her in my bed, but we didn't sleep. There's a good chance she snores classical music.

Pulling into a driveway, I slip off my sunglasses as the sun takes up residency beyond the horizon. "I have to pick up Harrison."

Harrison appears at the front door and hikes his backpack over his shoulder. He frowns at me as he walks down the porch steps, but as soon as he spots Ellen in the front seat, he grins.

Little shit.

"Hey, Harry." Ellen twists around to greet him as he gets in the back seat.

"What are you doing here? Please tell me this means we're going out for dinner."

Ellen says, "Yes," as I say, "No."

I shoot her a disgusted look that she ignores as we back out of the drive.

"Your dad offered to help me find a new office space before taking us to dinner."

I hate her.

"Why do you need a new office space?"

"My new one burned down."

"But why don't you just stay at my dad's office? I didn't understand why you were leaving anyway."

I haven't had a chance to discuss this with him in detail.

"Your dad finds me too distracting."

Nice of Ellen to do it for me. I clear my throat. "Did you and Drew get your science project finished?"

"Yes, but the supplies were cheap crap."

"Harrison," I warn.

"Why didn't you buy the ones I told you to buy?"

"Drew's mom said she'd get the supplies if I covered half

the cost."

"They were crap."

"Harrison ..."

Ellen bites her lips together, hiding her amusement. I'm sure her rats don't talk back to her like this.

"Where are Grandma and Grandpa?"

"Home packing. They leave in the morning."

"That sucks."

"You think everything sucks."

Ellen snickers.

I shoot her a sideways glance. She bites her lips together again. Harrison shoves in his earbuds and zones out. I'd like to escape for a while too.

"No," Ellen says as we pull into the parking lot of the building. One of my clients owns it and it has two vacant office spaces.

"No what?" I put the car in *Park*.

"This won't work." She shakes her head.

"You haven't even seen it yet."

"They're doing demolition to the building right next to it which means there will be lots of noise while they're tearing it down and just as much when they start construction on a new building. The noise will be too distracting to some of my clients."

I laugh, rubbing my temples. "You see the irony in this, right? It's okay for you to be the one distracting other people, but god forbid *you* have to deal with a little noise."

"Harry likes music."

My head jerks back and I shake it a few times. "What does that have to do with anything?"

"He likes music, but I bet you a hundred dollars he doesn't

like it when people chew too loudly, or the sound of a fountain, or the tick of a grandfather clock, or the constant beeping of construction equipment."

I process what she's saying and I'd lose a hundred dollars if I took the bet, but it still pisses me off. "I'm trying to be nice. I don't have to find you a new place. It's not my problem. I just—"

"Then don't." She shrugs and glances back at Harry.

I'd say he's not hearing a word we're saying, but after the seven incident, I don't trust him.

As if he knows we're watching him, he glances up from his phone screen. "What?"

"What sounds good to eat?" Ellen asks.

"We'll eat at home after we drop Ellen off to get her car."

"Pizza." Harry grins. "Lucé."

"I've never been. Sounds good to me." She winks at me.

Snake charmer.

CHAPTER TWELVE

Ellen

THERE'S A TWENTY minute wait at Harry's favorite pizza place in downtown Minneapolis. We wait in the bar. Harry gets a lemonade, I get a glass of wine, and Flint gets water.

"Not even one beer?" I ask.

He sips his water and shakes his head. "I'm driving."

I chuckle. "You must be a lightweight. But that's cool."

"He doesn't drink alcohol," Harry says, watching the TV in the corner.

I stare at my glass of wine and feel a pang of guilt. Flint doesn't say anything. When I look up, his dark eyes dare me to speak one word. He has his son on a strict diet for his autism symptoms. He grows everything imaginable. And he doesn't drink. Maybe he's an alcoholic, but I don't necessarily get that vibe. I think he's just health conscious.

I think.

I swivel the bar stool to face Flint. My knee rests along his inner thigh. He glances down to where our bodies touch. My pulse kicks up a notch. I love touching him. His body stiffens, eyes shifting to see if Harry's still watching the TV.

"I'm done with this," I tell the bartender as I slide my wine away from me. "Could you please get me a glass of water with lemon?"

"Don't," Flint says, sliding the wine glass back toward me.

It's not that he's a health nut. The look he gives me is more. That *more* saddens me.

"I'm done."

"You took one sip."

"I'm done."

"I paid for it."

I narrow my eyes at him.

"Your table is ready," a cheery brunette says, hugging menus to her chest.

Harry hops off his stool and follows the waitress while Flint and I stand toe to toe. His scowl intensifies. I roll my eyes and reach into my purse, pulling out a ten-dollar bill. He stiffens even more as I slide the money into the pocket of his pants.

"Take the wine."

"I'm. Done." I turn and follow Harry. "Do you want to sit by me or your dad?" I ask before sliding into the booth.

"You." He grins.

"Good choice." I wink and sit next to him as Flint sets *the wine glass* on the table and removes his suit jacket before sliding in across from us.

He grunts, squinting at me as I cross my legs making sure the toe of my shoe jabs his shin in the process.

"So what's good here?"

"What is it we get, Dad?"

Flint hides his gaze in the menu. "Pizza with chicken and veggies."

"Sounds good." I smile. "Just get a large and we'll all share it."

Flint glances up. "It's gluten-free crust."

I shrug. "That's fine."

"And non-dairy cheese."

Rolling my lips between my teeth, I nod a few times. "That's. Fine."

He sighs or grumbles. "It only comes in one size."

"We'll get two. I'm pretty hungry," Harrison says.

Why does sharing a pizza with me seem to upset him? We order three salads. Harry gets his with no dressing, Flint orders his with white balsamic vinaigrette, and I order the same. This seems to anger him as well.

"Drink your wine." He nods to my glass after the waitress leaves with our order.

Holy hell … why did I mention the beer? This is spiraling downward out of control.

"I'm good, but thank you."

Dinner follows the same theme. I don't drink my wine. That pisses him off. I say I like the dressing. That pisses him off. I like the gluten-free pizza with non-dairy cheese. That *really* pisses him off. The autistic twelve-year-old is the mature one out of the two *boys* at the table.

We slide out to leave, and Flint stares at the glass of wine as he slips on his jacket. On a defeated sigh, I grab the glass and chug every single ounce of it. "Happy?" I shoot him a cold look and turn, quickly finding my best smile to give Harry as we leave the restaurant.

"You wanna hear my new song when we get back to my house?" Harry asks as Flint pulls out into traffic.

"We're dropping Ms. Rodgers off at the office. That's where her car is. Besides, you have homework to do."

We're back to *Ms. Rodgers*. I stare out my window and

shake my head. Unbelievable.

"The science project was my homework. I don't have anything else to do tonight."

"Still ... it's not happening tonight."

Chugging a glass of wine in under ten seconds has made my brain a little too relaxed, blurring my thoughts a bit. "I'm a little dizzy after drinking that wine I was forced to drink. Maybe you should take me home and I'll take an Uber to get my car tomorrow."

Flint grumbles something under his breath as my phone rings. I fish it out of my bag and it slips through my hand between the seat and the console.

"Shoot ..." It continues to ring as I try to thread my hand between the seats.

"Here." Harry bends forward and grabs it. "Oh cool. Who's Alex?" He stares at the screen a few seconds before handing it to me.

My breath catches as the image illuminates.

"That dude was jumping from a plane."

I nod slowly, slipping the phone back into my purse. Flint gives me a curious look. I glance away.

"Have you gone skydiving?" Harry asks.

I nod.

"Really?"

I nod.

"You ever wonder what would happen if the parachute didn't release?"

I grunt a little laugh. Harry says absolutely whatever pops into his head.

"There's a backup."

"What if it didn't work? You'd die, right?"

"Harrison ..." Flint glances in his rearview mirror.

"That's the likely scenario," I say.

"Do you think you'd splatter like a bug or—"

"Harrison," Flint says with an edge to his voice.

"Jeez, what, Dad?"

I don't like being the cause of their fights. I also don't like talking about Alex. It's still something I can't find peace with in my life. But I choose to save Harry at the moment. "Alex did all kinds of cool things. Skydiving, scuba diving, and man could he surf. But he loved to journey up mountains more than anything. He was a passionate mountaineer."

"Like in the snow with ice picks?"

"Yep."

"Has he climbed Mount Everest?"

"He sure did."

"I want to do that someday."

Flint pulls into a spot in front of my apartment building and looks over his shoulder. "You do?"

Harry nods.

"That requires physical activity. You do realize that, right?" Flint says.

"Shut up." Harry rolls his eyes.

I open my door. "Thanks for dinner."

"Can I see your rats?"

I look at Flint.

"Another time."

"You always say that. I told you I don't have homework."

I shrug. "It's fine with me."

"Thanks." Harry jumps out.

Mr. Grumbly follows us up to my apartment.

"Cool place."

I laugh. This kid lives in a truly cool house, yet he finds my two-bedroom apartment "cool." I want to be twelve again. "Thanks." I toss my bag on the kitchen counter. "Follow me. We can let them out and feed them while your dad's skin crawls."

Flint leans his shoulder against the wall, messing with his phone. "Five minutes, Harrison."

"In here." I lead Harry to the bedroom and open the cage. "Come, babies." I make kissing sounds. "Mozart, come see Harry. You remember Harry don't you, baby."

Mozart waddles his chubby little rat ass out of the cage, and Harry picks him up.

"That one is a lot smaller." He nods to my shy girl staying in the cage as the rest of my musical geniuses make their way to freedom.

"That's Stefani Joanne Angelina Germanotta."

Harry gives me a funny look of confusion as Mozart squirms in his hands, trying to get onto his shoulder.

"Lady Gaga."

"That's her real name?"

I nod, nuzzling my nose into Beethoven. "Gaga might not come out to play today. We'll see. This is Beethoven, and this is Chopin, and this crazy guy here is Bach."

"I'm going to ask my grandparents for rats this Christmas. My dad would never buy them for me."

That's totally true. I set Beethoven down and stand. "Here's a banana. You can break off some pieces for them and they'll love you. Lady Gaga might even come out if you have food to share."

"Will they bite me?"

"No. They're very tame. They've always lived in a pack,

133

which usually makes rats less aggressive. But they'll all lick your hands. I think of it as giving you kisses. Anyway, I'll be out in the other room. It's okay if they wander out too, but that banana will keep their attention for a while."

Flint's still focused on his phone, one leg crossed over the other at his ankles. Even when he's an ass, he's over six feet of sex in a suit.

"Can I get you a glass of water?"

He shakes his head without looking up at me. "Who's Alex?"

I lean against my counter, crossing my arms over my chest. "Are you an alcoholic?"

"That's your assumption?" Still no eye contact.

"It wasn't until I realized how pissed off you were at that full glass of wine."

"Who's Alex?"

"My ex-husband. Are you an alcoholic?"

"I'm chronically sober. Why didn't you answer his call?" He still doesn't look at me.

"I wasn't in the mood to talk to him. Was alcohol your only addiction?"

"Yes. Why did you get a divorce?"

"Because he hated me for having two hands after part of his were amputated. Were you driving the car the night your wife died?"

Now he looks up and a complex expression of shock, confusion, and anger twists his face. "Harrison, we're leaving right this minute."

If I crossed some line by asking that, it was only because he crossed the same line, and in the middle our realities collided.

"Gaga came out." Harry brings my little lady out with him.

I fight past the pain to smile at him. I bet he has no idea that his father carries around such an unfathomable grief on his conscience.

"Want to hold her?" He tries to hand Lady Gaga to Flint.

"Put it down, we're leaving."

"*Her*, not it," Harry scolds.

I take her from him and set her on the sofa. "Thanks again for dinner."

Flint opens the door.

"Bye," Harry says.

As Flint turns to follow behind him, I grab his wrist. Flint looks over his shoulder at my hand on him.

"Sometimes the world ends and forgets to take you with it. I get it."

He pulls his arm from my grasp, giving me a quick glance of hollow, heartbreaking nothingness before following Harry.

CHAPTER THIRTEEN

Flint

"IF YOU'RE WONDERING what I want for Christmas, I want rats—at least three." Harrison interrupts the conversation I'm having with my parents—the one that has nothing to do with rats for Christmas presents.

My dad laughs. "I think that's doable."

"No." I shake my head. "It's not. If you want him to have rats, you're going to have to keep them at your house, and he'll come visit them."

"They carry less diseases than dogs." Harrison huffs out a sigh.

"I'll keep that in mind when we *don't* get a dog either."

"You're not even half as cool as Elle."

"You mean the rat lady who hums all day long? I'm really wounded." I press one hand over my heart and point to the stairs with my other hand. "Go to bed."

He wrinkles his nose at me and shifts his attention back to my parents wearing amused grins on the couch. "Elle has gone skydiving too, and she has a friend who climbed Mount Everest. There's a lot of dead bodies still on the mountain. It's too dangerous to try and retrieve them, so they're just there … some of them frozen in time with ropes still tied around their waists. Some climbers who come across these dead bodies on their way to the summit will try to bury them. Can you imagine coming across a dead body and just tossing your equipment aside to bury it like no big deal?"

"Wow!" my mom says. "That's ... I don't know. Seems like you'd have to be a little crazy to want to climb to the summit."

"Crazy?" Harrison shakes his head. "I'm going to do it someday."

"But for now..." I point to the stairs again "...you're going to go to bed."

"Yeah, yeah ..." He heads toward the stairs.

"Goodnight, Harrison," my parents say.

"Elle has made quite an impression on him." My dad gives me a grin that says he's thinking about finding us in the closet.

I run my hands through my hair and nod slowly. "Unfortunately."

"Having a positive female role model would be a good thing for him." My mom gives me a sad smile. "And you too."

"I thought you were our positive female role model."

"You only see me a few times a year. It's not enough. And Harrison clearly finds your friend Ellen much more intriguing than what he finds me."

"Who said Ellen is *my* friend?"

My dad's overly bushy eyebrows shoot up. "Oh? You're not friends? Or are you more than friends?"

"I should be in prison." I fight away the pain as my gaze drifts to the stairs. Thoughts of *our* son, and how little he knows about the past, hits me hard in the chest. "This isn't my life anymore, it's his."

My mom stands, tightening the sash to her robe as she walks toward me. She presses a finger under my chin like she did when I was a child and tips it up until I look at her. "If you truly mean that, then get the boy some rats." She smiles. "But if there's even the slightest part of you that feels deserving of a tiny bit of happiness, then get the girl. I think Harrison likes her more than rats."

My eyes slide to the side, catching my dad's shrug. He told her about the closet.

Mom keeps my chin tilted up and leans down, pressing a kiss to my cheek and the tip of my nose. "Goodnight, my lovely boy." She leaves me with my all-knowing father.

"We'll get Harrison breakfast. Be back in time to take him to school and drop us off at the airport." He rests his hand on my shoulder, giving it a firm squeeze.

Before he gets halfway up the stairs, I say, "What if I get him rats?"

He chuckles. "Then you're an idiot. Live or die, Flint … but don't sit in the fucking middle just … existing."

I KNOCK ON the door. It's almost ten. This is a bad idea. A weak moment. She doesn't answer. I turn.

"Giving up so easily?"

I turn back, taking in her tiny shorts, baggy nightshirt hanging off one bare shoulder, and fuzzy socks. Her hair is a wavy mess and … so fucking gorgeous.

"I was drunk." I swallow hard. I've never said those three words to anyone, even those who know. Not my parents. Not Heidi's mom. Not Harrison. And not to anyone at the hundreds of AA meetings I've attended.

Ellen nods slowly. "I know," she whispers.

I clear my throat. "It feels … unforgivable."

She nods again. I wait for her to tell me that nothing is unforgivable. I wait for her to tell me that I need to forgive myself. I wait for her to tell me that Heidi would forgive me. I wait and wait, but she just gives me a sad smile like there is nothing in the world to say to my confession. And the truth is ... there's not.

I killed my wife.

It's unforgivable.

But I'm alive. And this woman before me is so much better than rats.

She takes a step toward me and grabs my tie, pulling me into her apartment. The door shuts behind me, and she shoves me up against it. My lips twitch into a small grin as she jerks my tie side to side, loosening it before working the buttons to my shirt.

"He didn't let you touch him?"

She releases the last button and blue eyes meet mine. I see it in the glassy pools of tears filling her eyes.

Inching my tie around my collar, she releases it to the floor and pushes my shirt over my shoulders as her lips press to my chest.

I thread my fingers through her silky strands of hair and tilt her head up. "Because he couldn't touch you."

She blinks and fat tears bleed down her cheeks. I catch them with the pads of my thumbs and lower my head, brushing my lips over hers, relishing the warmth of her breath.

"Let me touch you," I whisper a second before kissing her.

She lets go of a soft sob before her lips respond to mine, our tongues seeking something deeper, her hands snaking around my back, fingers curling into my skin like she's never needed anything more than she needs this kiss.

My fucking heart feels like it could splinter into a million pieces, because in this very moment I feel like *I* deserve this, and I haven't felt deserving of anything in a decade.

She peels my shirt back more. I release her hand to let her pull the starched white fabric from my arms, adding it to the trail that we make as I back her toward the bedroom.

"Rats?" I mumble against the soft flesh of her neck while lifting her shirt up her body.

She lifts her arms for me to shrug it off her and grins, eyelashes still wet with emotion. Vulnerability has never looked so stunning.

"In their cage for the night."

I palm her butt and capture her mouth as I lift her up. She wraps her legs around my waist, grinding against the head of my erection.

"Condom?" she asks between kisses.

"Pocket."

She giggles against my mouth. "You planned on this?"

I kick her bedroom door shut behind us, still not entirely confident those rats are all caged up. "Ms. Rodgers ..."

Her lips grin against my skin as her tongue traces the hollow area above my collarbone.

"I may have planned on sex ... but I sure as hell never planned on you." I ease her to her feet, and she sits on the bed, unfastening my pants with way more patience than I have at the moment. My hands take over, discarding the rest of our clothes before claiming her mouth again, pressing my body against the soft, warm curves of hers.

She tastes like forgiveness and feels like freedom. And she sounds like a prayer, humming against my mouth—not a moan, an actual tune that I don't recognize. Her eyes drift shut, back arched and lips parted with her head turned to the side as I sink into her.

Since my wife died, I haven't been able to have sex with another woman without closing my eyes and wishing she were Heidi. But right now, I can't stop staring at Ellen Rodgers writhing beneath me, humming, smiling, and peeking open those breathtaking eyes to look at me with unmistakable want—need. All I can think is how ineffable she is through and through.

"Flint …" She jerks her hips against mine.

I dip my head down to taste her.

"Elle …" I whisper over her lips just before my tongue flicks hers.

Her lips curl into a smile. "*Elle...*" she breathes out "…does that mean we're friends?"

I lace our hands together, pressing them into the mattress just above her head, searching for deeper penetration because she feels so fucking good. "Yes, I think we're officially friends." As much as I want this to last all night, I can't stop. I can't slow down. And when she locks her ankles around my waist, and whispers "yes" over and over, I lose it.

Her relaxed gaze and sexy smile greet me when I open my eyes. "Don't cry," she whispers.

I shake my head. "Zip those pretty lips of yours."

"Or what?"

Releasing her hands, I grab her head and bite her lips together like a duck's.

"Ouch!"

I roll over onto my back and laugh. This unguarded moment of spontaneous laughter feels so foreign to me.

"Biting? Really? If that's how you're going to play." She

bites my bicep.

I roll to the side.

She bites my shoulder blade.

I laugh some more.

Then she presses her lips to the middle of my back for a few seconds and molds her naked body to mine. "Thank you," she whispers.

Rolling toward her, my grin fades at the solemn look on her face. "For what?"

Her fingertips float over my abs, one at a time, tracing the V below my navel before retracing their path, over my chest, up my neck, and along my jaw. "For letting me touch you … for touching me."

I press her hands together between mine. "I can't stay."

"I know." Her gaze focuses on our hands.

"Harrison has school, and I have to take my parents to the airport."

She looks at me and cranes her neck to kiss mine all the way to my chin. "Don't leave your condom on the floor where my rat babies could get a hold of it."

"I was just thinking about how incredibly sexy you look tangled in these sheets next to me and how hard it's going to be to leave your bed. But then you said 'rat babies,' and my erection died."

"Harry lights up around my rat babies. You should get him some rats."

I give her a small smile. *I chose you.* That's what's going through my mind. I chose to get *the girl* instead of rats. But if I'm honest with myself, I don't know what any of this means. I can't bring another woman into our lives until I tell Harrison the truth about his mom. The problem is I'm not sure he's mature enough to truly understand. And it's not just the Asperger's, it's that he's twelve and reason hasn't settled into something his mind can completely do.

"I know this woman who likes to play the guitar, and she has rats. In lieu of getting him his own, I might just check with her to see if she'd let him come visit them when he needs his rat fix."

Ellen rolls on top of me, straddling my waist, and sitting up straight. The view is fucking spectacular.

"I think I know this woman to whom you're referring. There's a good chance she'd be willing to barter with you."

"Barter, huh?" I grab her hips. "Sex?"

She rolls her eyes. "She's not that easy."

"No?" I lift a single eyebrow.

"She needs some legal help."

"Oh yeah?"

"Yeah." Her hands cover mine. "Her landlord has been trying to evict her, but she wants to stay."

"I'm sure he has a good reason for evicting her, and if he finds her a great place to rent, then it's a win-win situation."

Her jaw drops, I think. I'm too busy focusing on the curves of her breasts.

"I'm sitting astride you *naked*! How can you kick me out?"

"I'm relocating you, not kicking you out." I sit up, burying my face in her neck, thinking I should have brought more than one condom. "It's business, not—"

"I will break your dick off if you use that line on me one more time."

I chuckle, nipping at her neck while my hands explore the rest of her. "You're too loud. I'm sorry. It's just a fact. I have to work. I'll find you something just as good if not better."

"Ugh!" She shoves me back and climbs out of bed, leaving me with a dirty condom and a new erection. Slipping on her robe, she gives me a look—a look I don't trust. "You fire Amanda every day, but she's still there." Her voice fades a bit as she disappears out the door. "Can't you evict me without forcing me to physically leave the building?"

Glancing around her room, I shake my head. She's a messy creature. Stacks of books on the floor, clothes strewn all around and hanging out half-opened drawers, a guitar in the corner next to a basket of other instruments like she has at her office, and an old turntable on an equally old square table in the corner. I may be in over my head.

"You didn't answer my question." She brings in the half of my wardrobe that landed somewhere between the bedroom and the front door.

I slide out of bed, grabbing my briefs on the way to the bathroom. "While Amanda can be annoying at times, she doesn't prevent me from getting my work done."

Ellen hands me my pants when I come back into the bedroom. I slip them on, followed by my shirt. Her fingers go to work on the buttons. How could any man deny her touch?

Easing my tie around my neck, she grins. "Is it the noise or is it me?"

I don't need to wear a tie home at this late hour, but I don't say anything because I want her this close—touching me, making something as simple as buttoning a shirt and tying a tie feel like a slow seduction. It makes me want to strip down again just to let her dress me.

"Why do I get the feeling you've tied a lot of ties?"

Ellen shrugs. "Not really. But I've watched my dad do it a million times. He unknowingly taught me many things." She holds out my jacket for me to slide my arms into it and grabs the lapels, giving them a gentle tug, bringing her chest close to mine. "Flint Hopkins, you sure do look the part."

Threading my fingers through her hair, I bend down, pressing my lips just below her ear where I can feel her pulse. "What part is that?"

She leans into my touch, drawing in a shaky breath. I don't need to look at her to know vulnerability bleeds in her eyes like the ocean swelling at high tide. "I'm not sure yet," she whispers.

Savoring every inch of skin, I kiss my way to her jaw, over her cheek, stopping to hover over her lips. "No?"

She shakes her head.

"Let me know when you figure it out."

She lifts onto her toes until our lips lock. I kiss her as if I deserve this. I kiss her as if my past doesn't exist. I kiss her until reality crashes down.

"Goodnight."

She nods and whispers, "Night."

TO MY DISAPPOINTMENT, the kitchen light is on when I arrive home just after midnight.

"You'd sleep better if you drank coffee in the morning instead of at midnight," I say to my dad as I loosen my tie.

"Ah, the door to your bedroom was shut, but I had a feeling you snuck out. But I have to say, man to man, I'm a little disappointed you're already home. She turn you down? You're evicting her ... hell, I'd kick your ass to the curb too."

I fill a glass with water and sit across from him at the kitchen table.

"Your hair's a mess, so either she dragged your ass to the curb by your hair or she had her fingers in it for other reasons." He smirks.

"I'm going to call you 'Mom' if you keep making such investigatory statements."

He sips his coffee, eyeing me with an I-told-you-so look. "Your mom and I like her."

I nod a few times.

"Harrison likes her."

Another nod.

"You clearly like her ... or at least your hair does."

I give him my best fuck-you look.

"So what's the problem?"

"I haven't told Harrison the truth."

"So tell him."

"He's twelve."

"He's smart."

I shake my head. "He can't reason it out. Everything is so black and white with him. He won't forgive me, and I'll be stuck for the next six years raising a kid who hates me. Some days I'm at my fucking wit's end trying to keep us from killing each other as it is."

Dad unfolds from his chair with the grace of pulling an old wagon up a hill. "Maybe Ellen will wait a decade for Harrison to reach the age of reason."

His sarcasm doesn't help. When I'm with her, it's easy to pretend that I deserve her. It's easy to imagine allowing her into my life because Harrison likes her. That's the very reason this feels so wrong. If we don't work out, he loses her. I took one woman from him. I can't do it again.

"Stop overthinking it." He pours the rest of his coffee into the sink and rests his fatherly hand on my shoulder. "Just say fuck it and see what happens. We could all die tomorrow, so thank the big man upstairs that a sexy woman ran her hands through your hair tonight."

After the last stair whines beneath his weight, I close my eyes and wonder if people living in my special Hell are allowed a fuck-it pass in life.

CHAPTER FOURTEEN

Ellen

"YOU LOOK AWFUL, chipper. How's your arm?" Dr. Hamilton grins as the elevator doors close.

"It's all healed. And I'm always chipper." I watch the digital display as the numbers increase. I feel her eyes on me.

"You're humming a little louder than you normally do."

I glance over at her. "You notice me humming?"

She chuckles. "Everyone does. We grumble our way through the day, you hum. You need to tell me what you're putting in your morning coffee. I could use some."

I have a shot of Flint in my coffee this morning, but I don't know how I feel about sharing him.

"That smile is going to break your face. Would it have anything to do with a certain neighbor of mine?"

The elevator doors open and I step off. "You'll never know."

As I make my way to my first appointment, a cancer patient going through chemotherapy, I shoot off a text to Flint.

ME: *Good morning. :)*

Just as I go to open the door to the room, my phone vibrates.

FLINT: *Good morning.*

I grin, slipping my phone into my pocket. If he regretted last night, he would have ignored my text.

The high from those two words makes my morning breeze by with the exception of Alex calling me twice; both times I let it go to voicemail, but he doesn't leave a message. I gave him everything, and now I owe him nothing.

As I walk into the office building owned by Flint Hopkins, Attorney at Law, I slow up to see if he's in this afternoon. Amanda glances up and smiles, but his office is empty behind her. I give her a wave and continue to the elevator, feeling a pang of disappointment that I don't get to see him.

I unlock my door, disarm the alarm, and flip on the light. "Whoa ..." A huge bouquet of flowers sits atop my desk. Dropping my purse on the chair, I sift through the flowers looking for a card that's not there.

Flint? It has to be. No one else can get in here. I grin, feeling flushed from head to toe. I can't remember the last time someone sent me flowers. Alex was a lot of things, but he wasn't a flower-giving guy. At the time that was fine with me because I didn't think I was the girl who cared if she got flowers. But right now, with this colorful display on my desk, I'm certain flowers are officially my thing.

ME: *Thank you.*

I stare at the text before sending it, contemplating using a heart emoji or maybe an XO, but I'm not sure if we're there yet. The last thing I want to do is scare him off with an emoji. I used a lot of heart emojis with Alex; it feels weird using it with Flint. I go with a smiley face and press *send*.

FLINT: *You're welcome.*

It will take a hammer and chisel to remove this grin from my face today.

"Hey."

I look up from the floor, scattered with sheet music I've been organizing since my last client left. "Harry, how's it going?"

"Fine, I guess." He ambles in like Eeyore.

I grin.

He sighs, plopping down on the floor across from me with his backpack and guitar case. "Except my dad is being weird."

Stacking the music in several piles to finish sorting later, I grab my guitar and slide the strap over my head. "What makes him so weird?"

He strums a few chords, staring at his fingers. "I don't know. He was asking me weird questions."

"What made them weird?"

"He was talking about girls, and we never talk about girls."

My fingers mimic his on the strings. "Do you have a girlfriend?"

"No, but I think *he's* looking for one."

My fingers stumble, falling behind for a few beats. "Why do you say that?"

"He wanted to know how I would feel if he met a woman he liked and wanted to invite her to our house."

Now my heart skips a beat.

"And what did you say?"

He shrugs. "I said *whatever*." His nose scrunches as if he just swallowed something bitter. "Well, as long as it's not one of my teachers or you."

My heart stops completely as I exhale a nervous laugh. "Has he asked one of your teachers out on a date?"

"I hope not. Simon's dad has women over for 'adult time,' and one time it was one of Simon's teachers. She got mad at his dad and gave Simon a D in art, which is crazy because Simon had the best pottery design that year. Simon said the D was for his dad, not the art. Whatever that's supposed to mean."

"Well, I don't give you grades, so ..." I have no idea where I'm going with this. So what? So I can date your dad?

"Yeah, but you're too cool for him."

I laugh. "That's true. But your dad's cool too. He's a lawyer. He played football in college."

He's incredibly sexy and I can't stop thinking about him.

"His job is boring and he got hurt playing football, so he must not have been that great."

I change the song and wait for Harry to recognize it and catch up. He stops, stares at my hands while bobbing his head a few times, and follows my lead. The kid is so gifted.

"You know, Harry, everyone has greatness in them. Even your boring dad."

A deep rumble sounds from the door as I look up to Flint, clearing his throat, arms crossed over his suit-clad chest. My heart goes back into its arrhythmia.

I grin. "Hey."

"Don't let me interrupt. I'm just the *boring* dad."

My smile grows.

"Shhh!" Harry shoots Flint an evil look.

"Ten minutes, Harrison."

"Shhh!"

I bite my lips together as Flint shakes his head and leaves

the room. I reach for my phone and bring up an app that plays guitar accompaniments. "Find a good match for this."

He narrows his eyes at the phone, and in the next breath his head bobs and his fingers find the perfect chords.

"I'll be right back to hear what you come up with."

He nods or bobs, I'm not sure which one. I take the stairs down to Flint's office. He's by the front door to the building talking to someone, I think the optometrist from the office across from his.

I smile at the older gentleman. Flint's eyes make a slow inspection of me as I take a right turn into his office.

"Elle, I'm going out for dinner and drinks since my husband is taking the kids to a birthday party. I'm meeting a few other girlfriends at the restaurant. You should join us." Amanda slips on her red jacket.

Flint comes in behind me as Amanda bends over with her back to us to grab her purse out of a bottom file drawer. Goose bumps crest up my arms as his hand purposely brushes mine on his way to his office. "Ms. Rodgers." He comes close to making me orgasm just by saying my name.

Fiery embarrassment burns my cheeks.

Amanda turns, cocking an eyebrow at Flint and then at me. "It's warm in here again."

"Goodnight, Amanda," Flint calls from his office.

Her mouth twists into a knowing smile. "Night, Boss."

I risk a glance at her.

"Would it be correct to assume you have other plans tonight?"

I don't look at Flint, that would give us away, but I'm certain it's too late to act discreet. "I don't actually."

"No?" She stares at me for a few seconds before glancing

over her shoulder at Flint. His head is down, focused on his computer screen.

"So you want to join us?"

"Um … sure. I need to finish up a few things."

"Fantastic. I'll text you the address in about an hour when I find out where we're meeting."

"Sounds good." I wait until I hear the front door to the building close with a sharp click before moving one inch. "The flowers are beautiful." I take slow steps into his office.

Dark eyes track my moves as he leans back in his chair, interlacing his hands over his abdomen. "I'm glad you liked them. They're from my greenhouse."

My feet stop. I think my heart takes a brief pause as well. He didn't make a phone call and spew off his credit card number. He cut each flower and arranged them in a vase—for me.

Reality is a bitch. We're not untethered, young twenty-somethings with the world as our playground. We're a decade past that with jobs, responsibilities, pasts, and a child who doesn't want us to be together.

I smile—it feels painful—as I move past him to the window behind him. The last of the leaves rain down with a gust of wind. "Harry said you had a discussion about *girls*. He seems to be fine with you having a girlfriend as long as it's not one of his teachers…" I turn and lean against the window ledge "…or me."

He traces his finger over his bottom lip, eyes focused on some random point between us, as he nods slowly. "So it would seem. But he's twelve."

"With Asperger's."

"A mild case."

"Thanks to you?"

Flint shrugs. "I don't know. I've researched it all. He's so much better than he was even a few years ago. Maybe it's what I feed him—the strict diet, the herbs, the routine I give him. Maybe it's luck, and what little control I think I have is an illusion. Either way, I'm going to keep doing what I'm doing because the good days by far outnumber the bad days, and there was a period of time I felt certain the bad days would break me."

"You're a wonderful dad."

His brow draws tight as he looks at me like he wants to believe it too.

"I'm serious. I've seen it all. It's not really who does it the best, it's who survives. You're improving his life and you're doing it really well."

Flint shrugs. "I owe him."

"No more than any other parent owes their child."

He laughs a little. "*So* much more. I took everything. Who takes everything from their child?"

"You're here. You didn't take *everything*."

"It should have been me."

"Probably."

His head jerks up. I don't flinch one bit in regret, even with the pain on his face.

My hands slide into the front pockets of my black pants as my eyes focus on the scuff mark curled around the toe of my right shoe. "You drank. You got behind the wheel. You crashed the car. Your wife died as a result. I don't know the finer details, but had Karma been on her game that day, you would have died instead of your wife."

"Please, give it to me straight."

"I will. It's cause and effect. Did you accidentally drink? Did you accidentally get behind the wheel of the car? This is one defense you cannot win. There's no way to spin this. And everyone in the world including yourself can forgive you, but it doesn't fix it. And that sucks. But you can move on and be a good person who fights the good fights. It's extraordinarily hard to acknowledge our imperfections, especially when they cause something so devastating ... but you are in fact just like everyone else. You're human, Flint."

Flint

I'M NOT SURE when the thanks-for-the-flowers mood shifted into a humanity speech on drinking and driving, but it went from zero to one hundred in a blink. I can handle the guilt and accusations—they're true. I know this, and I have no good defense. But something in her words feels personal, not to me, but to her.

"Who?"

Her eyes narrow. "What?"

"Did Alex lose his hands in a drunk-driving accident?"

Her head jerks back. "What? No."

"Then who? Because that speech wasn't just about me."

"Hello? Are you coming?"

I swivel in my chair toward Harrison's voice.

"I'm ready to play it."

"Sorry. I'm coming," Ellen says, walking past me without making eye contact.

"Wait up," I say, shoving my foot onto the elevator to keep

the doors from closing.

"What are you doing?" Harrison asks.

Ellen keeps her eyes on her feet.

"Coming to hear you play."

"Why?"

I stand next to Harrison and nudge him. "Because you're my son, and I want to hear you play."

"Whatever."

I choose to take that as code for "I love you too, Dad."

The doors open and Harrison runs off first, I rest my hand on Ellen's lower back. She stiffens. It pisses me off that I've somehow offended her, but I don't know why. As she goes to step off, I curl my fingers under the waistband of her pants and pull her backward.

She sucks in an audible gasp as the doors close, leaving just the two of us on the elevator. "What are you doing?"

I back her up against the railing, pinning her hands behind her back. "I can't have you going out with Amanda and her friends tonight without knowing that we're good."

"Harry—"

I shake my head and tug at her arms, forcing her chest out a bit more. "Not Harrison. You and I. Are we good?"

I wish I could read the unspoken emotions in her eyes, but I can't, so I wait. Blink after blink …

"Yes," she whispers.

My mouth crashes onto hers. I swallow her breath and her moans that carry a distinct tune. As she leans into the kiss, I step back, grin, push the open doors button, and adjust my tie.

"What happened?" As expected, Harrison is right here, waiting for us.

I step off the elevator and shrug. "Ellen had a bit of gas that she didn't want to pass around you, so she locked me in the elevator with her, because just like you, she's out to get me."

Behind me I hear Ellen gasp and Harrison laugh, which is music to my ears because he doesn't full-on belly laugh very often. But he's a boy, and all boys find farts, burps, and all other bodily sounds quite funny. I take a seat at Ellen's desk and pluck one of the flowers from the vase, bringing it to my nose as she shoots me a death glare, face flush with embarrassment.

As if on cue, Harrison farts and strums his guitar with a huge grin on his face.

Ellen rolls her eyes at him before killing me with another evil glare. She starts a song on her phone and Harrison joins in. All laughter fades as he plays that guitar like a seasoned guitarist in a rock band. I'm speechless.

When he's done, there's no gloating or waiting for a standing ovation, which he deserves. Instead, he carefully puts the guitar back in its case and slings his backpack over his shoulder, guitar case in hand. "Let's go. I'm starving. Bye, Ellen." He turns and walks toward the elevator.

I'm not sure I've blinked since he finished playing. Ellen steals the flower from my hand and bops me on the nose with it. I flinch.

"You have something so rare and spectacular right in front of you, and you are clueless what to do with it."

I stand, tugging on the cuffs to my shirt. Ellen buttons my jacket and glances up at me, long auburn hair falling down her back.

"Are you talking about Harrison?"

Ellen grins. "He's not bad either. Now ..." She steps past me, clicking on her phone. "I have a girls' night out to get to, where I shall discover all of your secrets, including what made you accuse me of *farting*."

As she walks toward the door, I grab her wrist. She looks back at me.

"Terrible of me. But his laughter was—"

She nods. "Totally worth it."

I follow her to the elevator. Harrison is no doubt already waiting at the door to the building, tapping his foot impatiently. She steps on, turns, and I possess her lips again before she can catch her breath. When the ding of the elevator sounds, I pull away again, leaving her unbalanced and gasping.

I wink, straightening my tie. "After you, Ms. Rodgers."

"Jerk." She wipes her mouth and runs her fingers through her hair before pulling back her shoulders and stepping off the elevator into the lobby.

CHAPTER FIFTEEN

Flint

"WE'RE GOING OUT to eat? Twice in one month?" Harrison looks over at me with wide eyes.

"Sure. Why not?"

"Because I might die of a preservative overdose. You've said it yourself. Are you trying to kill me?"

"Not today."

We make our way into the only Mexican restaurant in town that has a decent gluten-free menu. Harrison orders nearly everything on it; the kid is insatiable and he doesn't move a muscle except to go from point A to point B. I don't know how he squeaks through life with his pants sagging—no gut and no ass.

"What you played earlier left me speechless."

"What do you mean?" He sips his water.

"I mean you're a pretty talented kid. If you want to take lessons or join the band or ... I don't know, something like that. I'd do whatever I could to make it happen."

He shrugs. "I just like to play. Ellen says I don't really need a teacher."

"You like Ellen?"

Another shrug. "Yeah."

"I do too."

He nods.

"What would you think of me asking her out on a date?"

"Sex?" His head snaps up as everyone in the restaurant turns toward us for a few awkward seconds.

I look around giving an apologetic cringe.

"A *date*, Harrison."

"People have sex on dates. You want to have sex with Ellen?"

"Shhh ..." I close my eyes and sigh. "People go to dinner and maybe a movie on a date."

"So, no sex?"

"Harrison ..."

He shakes his head. "Just promise no sex with Ellen and no sex with my teachers. I have straight A's right now."

"Ellen is not your teacher."

"She's my friend—*my* friend. Why do you have to have sex with her? Can't you find your own friends?"

The waiter sets down chips and salsa. I cringe. If Harrison could stop saying sex, this night would go much better.

"Dinner, Harrison. Did you hear me say dinner? Maybe a movie."

"And ..." Harrison leans toward me, eyes wide.

"And I take her home."

"No sex?"

The little shit. I'm ready to strangle him. I don't care what type of musical savant he may be. "No sex." I'm going to Hell anyway. What's a little lie on top of everything else?

"Are you going to kiss her?"

I loosen my tie and scratch my neck. I'm developing an allergy to Harrison too. "Maybe."

"Then no." He shakes his head a half dozen times. "Kissing leads to sex. They taught us that in school last year."

"Somehow I don't think that was the point of the lesson."

"I'm not lying. Call my health teacher and ask her."

"No kiss. No sex. Dinner and a movie."

"Can I come?"

"No."

"Why not?"

"Because children don't go on dates with adults."

"Well, if you're not having sex, then what's the big deal?"

"We want to have adult conversation."

"About what?"

"Jesus ... fucking kill me now," I mumble with my hands over my face.

"Did you say fuck?" The kid has no volume to his voice. Everything is megaphone volume.

"Harrison ..." I tilt my head and give him a last-warning look that he knows very well.

He stares at his straw, refusing to look at me. It's his usual reaction when he's pushed me to my limit. A year ago he would have kept going—always hell-bent on bringing me to my knees. But the past year has been better. I don't fear the meltdowns like we've had in the past.

We finish dinner in a much welcome silence. I'm sure the rest of the patrons appreciate it as well. By the time we get home, he holes up in his room while I applaud myself for making it this far in parenting a pre-teen without a single drop of alcohol in my blood. Had I not killed my wife, she would have been proud of my restraint too.

By midnight, I'm still wide awake, thinking about Ellen. I stare at my phone and decide to call her.

"It's past your bedtime, Mr. Hopkins."

I smile. "I didn't know if you'd be home yet."

"Just walked in the door fifteen minutes ago. I'm playing with my babies."

I try not to cringe, but my face automatically goes there when she mentions those rats. "Did Amanda spill all of my deep dark secrets?"

"Sadly ... no. She's loyal to a fault. I don't know why you insist on firing her every day. She didn't even ask about the 'heat' between us."

"She's snarky to a fault ... like someone else I know."

"How *is* Harry?"

I chuckle. "He's *challenging*. We went to dinner tonight. Unfortunately, I don't think we'll be able to return to that same restaurant ever again."

"Do tell."

I tell her about our conversation. She laughs and tries to reassure me it could have been worse. I'm not convinced of it. She tells me about her girls' night out. She wins. Harrison's display was not even close to how those women acted.

After the laughter dies down, a moment of silence settles on the line.

"So ..." she says. "About this date ..."

I laugh. "You mean the no-sex, no-physical-contact date?"

"Yeah, that one. Are you going to call me, text me, or pass me a note at work?"

"I'm offended you find me so unoriginal. I usually go for skywriting, but I'd bet you'd rather jump from the plane than have it write you a message, since you're so cool."

"Intrigued about my life, are you? Looks like we'll have plenty to discuss on our no-sex date. I want to know all about your brief football career. I like football. We should play sometime."

"Rats *and* football? You're full of surprises."

"Would you want me any other way?"

No. I wouldn't. She's shown me a glimpse of the tragedy in her past, but I know there's some good stuff too. I want to know everything, but I want to take my time.

"Who's your favorite football team?" I ask.

"Pro or College?"

"Both."

"Patriots and University of Miami."

"Ah … are you serious? How did this happen?"

She laughs. "I'm from New England, but I went to college in Miami. I'm sure you're a Minnesota fan."

"Of course."

"And college?"

"Nebraska."

She laughs again. "Harrison had no clue where you went to college."

"Of course he didn't."

"He's great. I love my time with him."

"He thinks you're his friend. He said I should find my own friends."

"Well, you only have *one*. He really should share me."

I lean back and run my hand through my hair. "Can't blame him. I don't want to share you."

"Sorry. If I end up having to choose between the two of you, I'm going to have to go with Harry because he loves music *and* he loves my rats."

"Rats." I shake my head. "At what point did you forego the obvious choice of a cat or dog and decide on rodents?"

"That's..." I can hear the yawn in her voice "...a story for another time."

"I'll let you go to sleep."

"What are you doing Saturday?"

"The usual. Exercise. Working in the yard and my greenhouse. Dragging my son out of his room to get fresh air."

"Let me make dinner at my place for you and Harrison."

"You cook?"

She giggles. "Yes. Don't act so surprised."

"Harrison has a strict diet."

"I know. Text me a list of things he can't have."

"I'll feel like a third wheel."

"Poor baby. We'll try to include you in the rat play."

"Maybe we should have dinner at my house."

"Harry likes to play with my rats. Do you want them at your house?"

"Good point. What time?"

"Six?"

"Six it is. Goodnight."

"Night, Flint."

I toss my phone on the bed beside me and grin like a fool. My face doesn't know how to handle the upward turn of my lips. For now ... I let myself believe I deserve this chance, this feeling, this woman. Nothing lasts, but I want to take this as far as I can because it feels so fucking incredible to *feel* again.

Ellen

I SPEND SATURDAY morning tidying up my apartment and

cleaning the rat cages, even though Flint's unexpected visit the other night happened to be when things were a bit messy. Hopefully the naked-and-willing woman distracted him from focusing on the clutter.

The place smells like apples and cinnamon from the crisp in the oven, and I made a pot of chicken noodle soup with gluten-free noodles. I also changed my outfit five times like a sixteen-year-old on her first date. There's no need to be nervous. Flint found me desirable in fuzzy socks and messy hair, but this no-sex thing makes me nervous. I want to make sure he continues to find me desirable until we can work something out with Harry.

God … I hope we can work something out with Harry.

Tonight is step one in my plan. If all three of us hang out enough, he might see how well Flint and I get along, and—fingers crossed, prayers said to any god willing to listen—he will change his mind about the no physical contact rule.

Long shot. I know. But a girl's gotta try.

"They're here!" I clench my fists and shake with way too much excitement from the knock on my door. I'm thirty-two. I should have mastered getting a grip by now.

"Hey, guys!"

"Hey." Harry gives me a half smile and brushes past me, guitar case in hand. "Can I let your rats out?"

I laugh. "Absolutely. Just tell them to 'come.'"

Stepping out into the hallway, I close the door behind me. Flint peaks an eyebrow, lips twisting into something too irresistible not to kiss.

"An untucked button-down and jeans? I feel cheated of my sex-in-a-suit fix." Fisting his shirt, I lean up on my tippy toes and kiss him. His hands palm my butt, eliciting a hum of pure pleasure—and torture.

I pull away and rub my lips together.

He makes a quick inspection of my white shirt with the sleeves rolled up, short skirt, knee-high socks, and ankle boots.

"Good lord, you're a tease. You can't do this to a man with a child-enforced vow of celibacy."

"I just don't want you to lose interest in what you can't have at the moment." I open the door and head inside.

"You do realize people desire most what they can't have."

"Mmm, I'm counting on it." I lead him down the hall to the kitchen.

"Smells good."

I shut off the oven, but leave the crisp in to stay warm until after dinner. "Don't sound so surprised."

"I'm not."

"Lady Gaga came out for me." Harry carries my naked rat into the living room.

"You're a rat whisperer." I wink at him.

"I didn't whisper. I just said 'come' in my regular voice."

Flint and I share grins.

"A whisperer is someone who is good with a specific kind of animal. Dog whisperer. Horse whisperer," I say.

"Huh …" Harry lets Lady Gaga climb up his chest to his shoulder. "I guess I could be a rat whisperer someday."

"I can already feel myself swelling with fatherly pride. 'What does your son do? He's a highly sought after rat whisperer.'"

"You know…" I plant my hands on my waist "…some rats can detect tuberculosis, and there's a specific breed of rats that can locate landmines. So basically, rats are saving lives."

"Really? That's cool." Harry continues to play with Lady

Gaga as my other babies make their way into the room.

Flint lifts his feet onto the rung of the barstool and gives me a poorly restrained smile. "I love the case you make for rats. If I ever have to defend the actions of one in court, you'll be my expert witness."

"Aw, that means a lot coming from my favorite shyster. I mean ... legal beagle."

This grin works its way up Flint's handsome face. It's different than any other grin he's given me ... not that he hands them out with any sort of generosity. Sometimes I wonder if his laughter, his smile, and his *life* died with Harry's mother. I wouldn't blame him one bit if they did.

I meant what I said to him the other day. *Sometimes the world ends and forgets to take you with it.*

Alex said it to me after he lost his hands. And those same words echoed in my mind when my mom died and when Alex served me with divorce papers.

But just now ... Flint grinned like someone told him there was in fact life after death—something magical, something good—and he gave *me* that look. I don't know where this journey will take us, but I will always remember this one look and how it made me feel physically touched while standing out of arm's reach.

"Harry, will you say 'cage' to my lady and gentlemen? We'll play more after dinner, and you can feed them theirs."

Harry calls their names—their full names—even Lady Gaga's, and he tells them "cage."

Flint eases off the kitchen stool and brushes his arm against mine as he makes his way to the stove. He pauses next to me long enough to run his finger along my bare outer thigh, just below the hem of my short skirt.

I nudge him away. "Now who's the tease?"

He chuckles and lifts the lid to the soup pot. "Harrison loves chicken noodle soup."

"All kids do." I grab three bowls and set them on the counter.

"Are you an expert on kids?" He stirs the soup.

I lean my back against the counter next to the stove and watch him. He makes stirring soup look sexy. How is that possible? "Well, I was a kid, so there's that eighteen years of experience. And I work with a lot of kids, so I'd say I have some degree of expertise."

Flint glances over his shoulder. "Wash your hands, Harrison."

"They didn't pee on me."

"I'm glad. Wash your hands."

I bite my lips together.

"I read that rats spend most of their waking hours cleaning themselves or each other. More so than cats." Harry rocks back and forth on his feet, wringing his hands together.

"It's good to know you're spending your spare time researching rats. Did you happen to see how they clean themselves? In a bathtub? In a shower with hot water and soap? Or do they lick themselves?" Flint asks.

"They lick themselves."

"So if I lick your hands, will you feel the need to wash them before you eat?"

"That's gross. Why would you lick my hands?"

"I wouldn't. Just go wash them."

I take the ladle, nudging Flint aside with my hip. "We swapped saliva in the hallway. Is that going to ruin your dinner?"

"Only if you tell Harrison and get me in trouble."

"I would never." I fill the bowls with soup, and Flint takes them to the table. "And for your information … I do bathe my rats."

He looks over his shoulder at me. "Why am I not surprised?"

"Is this gluten-free?" Harry asks, taking a seat at the table.

"Yes." I smile, sitting next to him, forcing Flint to sit across from us.

"No dairy?"

"No dairy."

"Nuts?"

"No nuts. It's all been approved by your dad."

"He thinks the things I eat affect my brain."

"What do you think?" I sip the steamy soup from my spoon.

"I don't know. Grandma said it's his job to be overprotective. Weird job."

Flint smirks, placing the napkin on his knee.

"I've met some parents who need to be *more* protective of their children, so it's a good thing that your dad cares about you so much."

Harry shrugs, blowing on his soup. "Are you going to ask Ellen on a date?"

Flint stirs his soup, a slight shake to his head. "Oh, Harrison, you're quite the wingman."

"What do you mean?" Harry asks.

"You're quite the helper when it comes to getting me a date."

I watch the commentary between them, amused with where this might be going.

"I'm not helping you get a date. I just asked if you were going to ask." Harry gives me a quick glance. "He wants to ask you on a date. No sex. No kissing. Dinner and a movie. And I can't go with you."

I cover my mouth with my napkin, but I can feel the red flush working up my face into my cheeks and nose.

Flint takes a spoonful of soup, eyes rolling up to glance at me.

"Sounds like fun. I haven't been to a movie in a long time."

"Just don't go see the new Spiderman movie because I want to see it."

"Well, your dad hasn't asked me on a date yet, so we don't have to worry about picking out a movie."

"Are you going to ask her?"

I tap the toe of my boot against Flint's shoe. He eyes me while taking a drink of water.

"Maybe," he says. "But let's talk about this new Spiderman movie."

And with that, the next half hour turns into a thorough comparison of all the superheroes. I confess my favorite superhero is Superman, specifically played by Henry Cavill. I don't mention that Flint's body and sexy smile bears an uncanny resemblance to Henry. Something tells me Harry would not like that comparison.

After dessert, which earns me two thumbs up from Flint and Harry, Flint shoos me off to play rat games with Harry while he washes the dishes. If it weren't for the seven rating and eviction notice, he'd be the perfect guy.

"Oh my god ... they play basketball."

I adore the excitement on Harry's face when I show him how Bach and Chopin play basketball with their tiny hoop and ball. Then I teach him how to set up an obstacle course they can do—except my diva Gaga—and hand him treats to give them as rewards.

"I'm going to go make sure your dad doesn't need help in the kitchen. He won't know where my dishes belong."

"K." Harry mumbles, too enthralled with my rat pack to even look up at me.

I slide up onto the kitchen counter next to my Superman. "I didn't think I could like you more than I do in a suit." I cross my legs, eliciting a quick glance from my dishwasher. "But when you roll up your sleeves and get all domestic on me, it's kinda hot. Like Gardener Flint, the dirtier you get, the dirtier my thoughts get."

He tips his chin down, staying focused on the pan and sink of sudsy water, his teeth digging gently into his lower lip.

"I have him set up with obstacle courses and snacks for my babies. I bet we don't see him for a while. What do you think about a quickie in the bathroom?"

He gives me the slightest chuckle, handing me the pan to dry. "You think this is fun?"

"Dishes?" I rub the towel over the pan. "No. I hate doing dishes. But I think a quickie in the bathroom could be quite fun." I hop off the counter and take the pan to the drawer under my stove top. "Ouch!" I drop the pan in the drawer with a *clunk* and straighten my back, my hand reaching for the back of my leg, just below my butt cheek. There's a stinging welt.

Flint holds the end of the twisted damp towel in his hand like a whip.

"Oh my gosh! Did you seriously just whip me with a towel?" I say in a loud whisper. "There's a welt. You marked me."

"Your skirt is too short. When you bent over to put that

pan in the drawer, I could see black lace."

"So you whipped me?"

He stalks toward me until I'm forced to crane my neck to maintain eye contact. "No," he whispers. "I whipped you because you're a fucking tease."

"You're a terrible role model. Would you want Harry whipping some poor unsuspecting woman on the ass?"

His eyes focus on my cleavage for a few seconds before returning to meet my gaze. No signs of apology that I just caught him staring at my boobs. "He's twelve. So I think that might not be a good idea at this point in his life, but if the day comes that he finds a feisty, sexy, playful woman in need of a little reprimanding, then I'd have to say the idea of him giving her a little nip on the backside would make me pretty proud. Much more proud than whispering to rats."

"You're stubborn and infuriating." I narrow my eyes.

He glances in the direction of the bedrooms and presses his lips to his middle and index fingers. Bending over, he slides his hand up my leg until the fingers he just kissed cover my welt. "And you're the first breath of oxygen that's touched my lungs in ten years," he whispers in my ear.

Tears instantly sting my eyes. I thought I'd forgiven Alex. But when Flint says things like this to me, I feel this surge of pain all over again, stirring the anger to life. I should have *always* been the oxygen in Alex's lungs.

Flint's hand slides out as slowly and seductively as it slid to my welted leg. His brows draw together. "It hurts that bad?"

I blink back the tears and smile. "Yes. But not my leg."

His dark eyes search mine.

"What's this?" Harry calls.

I wipe the corners of my eyes and follow his voice to my

bedroom.

"Harrison you can't snoop around in her bedroom without permission."

"I'm not snooping. I followed Mozart in here. What's this?" He points to my turntable.

"It's a record player, a turntable. My mom found it and bought it as a graduation gift for me along with a bunch of vinyl records."

"This is how you listened to music when you were my age?"

I laugh. "Not really. I used cassette tapes and eventually CDs. But my dad has a vinyl record player and he still uses it." I grab a record off the shelf below the turntable. "'Abbey Road.' The Beatles?"

Harry stares blankly at me. Flint takes a seat on the edge of my bed.

I grin, sliding the record out. "I'll play you my favorite song off this album. My mom and dad used to dance to it late at night when they thought I'd gone to sleep. I'd sneak halfway down the stairs and watch them dance." I wrinkle my nose. "And then they'd kiss and I'd run back up to my bed and bury my head under the covers."

Harry's cheeks turn a little pink. I've not seen him blush before. It's sweet.

"Something" starts to play.

"Show me your dance moves, Harrison Hopkins." I hold out my arms.

He shakes his head. "That's not the kind of dancing I know."

I take his hand. He stiffens as I place it on my lower back and bring his other hand out to his side, latched to mine.

"Have you had a school dance? Slow dancing with a girl?"

"No way." He shakes his head, stiffly letting me move him side to side.

"Well, if you go to homecoming or prom someday, I'll give you dance lessons on slow dancing. Girls like a guy who knows how to lead."

"It's too weird." He releases me, stepping back a few feet while shaking his head.

I laugh a little and twist my lips, focusing on the sexy guy perched on the edge of my bed. "Does your dad know how to dance?"

"Doubt it." Harry watches the turntable like he's trying to figure it out.

"Mr. Hopkins. You got any moves?" I hold out my hand and wink, knowing damn well he has some *moves*.

He glances at his preoccupied son in the corner of my bedroom. Standing, he takes my hand. I try to control my breathing as he slides his hand around my waist, pulling me close to him while bringing my other hand to his chest.

His gaze falls to my lips as he leads me around the small space between the end of my bed and the door. Something about this stolen—forbidden—moment feels more intimate than the last time we were in my bedroom together.

"Wh—" I stop to even out my voice. God, I sound so breathy.

Flint smirks, doing really inappropriate things to me with just a single look.

I try it again. "Who taught you to dance?"

"My mom."

"Really?"

"Really," he says like it's no big deal.

The song ends and he releases me with his hands, but damn! He has to stop looking at me like he's imagining me naked. I pull my top away from my chest a bit to hide my hard nipples.

Flint grins. Of course he saw them.

"We should go, buddy. Why don't you make sure Ellen's *rat babies* are all put back in their cage."

"K." He turns.

I smile, hoping he's too young to see how incredibly flushed I am because his dad has my body in a tizzy from one sexy look.

"You feeling okay?"

"Shut up," I whisper.

He takes a step toward me.

"Don't." I shake my head, taking a step back.

He watches me like he did in the office at his house, just minutes before he did wicked things to me on the spiral staircase.

My gaze falls to his hands. They're strong hands that hold a football and win fights, not delicate manicured hands of a stuffy guy with a desk job. That's what makes him so damn sexy in a suit. He's the perfect clash of sophistication and ruggedness. It accentuates his broad shoulders and defined chest. And when he sits down in a suit, I can see the delineation of his quadriceps.

"You're humming."

My gaze snaps from his hands to his face. "I'm nervous."

"Why?"

"Because you're too close, and I'm ..."

"Regretting wearing such a short skirt and flimsy lace panties?"

I swallow hard. "Maybe."

He works his teeth over his bottom lip, staring at my legs for a few seconds before meeting my eyes again. "Harry can be home alone for a few hours, but I only leave him by himself during the day. How about lunch and a matinee tomorrow?"

"A date?" My head cocks to the side.

"A date." He grins.

"No skywriting?"

His grin grows a fraction more.

I shrug. "I suppose. Where are we going to eat?"

As his grin morphs into something quite wolfish, his gaze drifts down my body, the tip of his tongue easing out to slide across his lower lip.

I cross my ankles. Yeah, wearing flimsy panties and a short skirt was a terrible idea.

"This place I recently tried. It's quite *delectable*."

Gulp.

"Ready?" Harry peeks his head in the room.

"Yeah, I'm ready."

I pull my shirt away from my chest again and clear my throat. "I'll walk you out." Taking in a deep breath, I hurry past him, praying he doesn't make some sly move to touch me. I'm one slide of a finger—any finger—away from convulsing. "Thanks for coming."

"I haven't ... yet." Flint says just above a whisper that only I can hear.

Fucking hell! Kill me. Just kill me now.

"What are you going to do with the rest of the apple crisp?" Harry asks, shoving his arms into his hoodie.

"Oh. Gosh ... I don't need it. You take it." I walk toward the counter.

"We don't need all of it," Flint says, shadowing me.

"No. Take it."

I pull out a sheet of foil and cover it.

"We don't—"

I shove the dish into Flint's chest.

"I want you to eat all of it."

A single brow slides up his forehead as one corner of his mouth twitches into a tiny grin.

I grimace. "The crisp."

"The crisp." He nods slowly. "Thank you. I look forward to it."

In thirty-two years, I have never *needed* to get off like I do right now. Pink balls are real.

"It was fun." I chomp down on the inside of my lip as I ease past Flint. So much blood has converged between my legs, waiting for a release of pleasure, even walking is a bit uncomfortable. "We'll have to do it again."

"Oh!" Harry almost runs into me as he stops and changes direction. "I forgot my guitar. We didn't get to play." He heads back to the rats' room.

"Next time," I say, keeping my gaze anywhere but on the man who has the superpower to make me squirm.

"Which finger or *fingers* of yours should I be jealous of tonight?" he says in a low, deep voice.

I hide my gasp, but it's there. Apparently shockingly crude remarks are the theme of the night. I can play this game. Making a quick glance over my shoulder for young ears coming, I turn back and hold up my index and middle finger. "These two up front..." I add my ring finger "...this one in the back."

And there it is ... Flint Hopkins expressionless and speechless. It's an oddly beautiful sight.

"Got it." Harry brushes by us and opens the front door.

I grin, batting my eyelashes like someone wearing contacts for the first time. "Goodnight, boys."

CHAPTER SIXTEEN

M Y ALARM RUINS my morning at seven, just like I set it to do. I like sleeping in, but the new man in my life inspires me to be the typical woman—self-conscious about my body image. All men should be forced to come back in another life as a woman.

I bring up my fourteen-minute kick-ass workout app and rotate through a series of jumping rope, burpees, squats, pushups, and tricep dips, followed by a long shower and thoughts of Flint Hopkins.

"Who's calling me before eight?" I wrap a towel around my head and slip into my robe as I run to answer my phone in the bedroom.

"Hey, Dad. It's Sunday. I'm not in your time zone. Do you keep forgetting?"

"Did I wake you?"

I sigh. "No, but—"

"Then stop making your old man feel bad."

"Sorry. How are you?"

"Old."

I laugh, plopping back onto my bed. "Aged like a fine wine."

"Find yourself a worthy man?"

"Well …" I grin. "He's definitely a man."

"A good man?"

Is Flint a good man?

"I think so. He has a son."

"Divorced?"

"Widowed."

"Oh …"

"Yeah. It's a little complicated. His name is Flint. He's actually my landlord."

"So he's into real estate?"

"He's an attorney."

"A good one?"

I laugh. "I don't know for sure. I haven't needed his legal services. Does it matter?"

"Of course it matters. You want to be with a guy who's on the right side."

"Republican?"

"I couldn't give a rat's ass if he's republican or democrat. And no offense to your baby varmints."

I shake with silent laughter while rolling my eyes.

"I mean does he have good morals? Is he defending the right people?"

"I think he's mostly family law, so I'm sure it could go either way."

My doorbell rings. Seriously, do people not respect the sacredness of sleeping in on Sundays?

I jackknife out of bed and answer the door.

"I'm sure if you think he's worthy to date, then he is," my dad says as I spot a guy holding a package outside my door.

"He's a good guy. I really believe so. Hang on a sec …" I slip the phone in my robe pocket. "Hi."

"Miss Rodgers?"

"Yes."

"Delivery."

"On a Sunday?"

He's not wearing a delivery uniform.

"Yes, ma'am."

"What company are you with?"

"I'm not with a company. Have a good day." He hands me the small box and turns without further explanation.

I fish my phone back out of my pocket. "Sorry. Delivery."

"On a Sunday?" my dad asks.

"Right? Yeah, I don't know what it is." I put my dad on speaker and set the box on the kitchen counter to open it.

"Chocolates? Flowers?"

I laugh. "The box is too small."

"Hurry up. The suspense is killing me."

"It's my delivery."

"But now you have me curious."

"Okay, okay ... just a sec ..." Inside the brown box is a blue box with a ribbon. "Oh my gosh ... it's a blue box."

"Is blue good luck?"

I roll my eyes. "It's from a luxury jewelry store."

"If this guy thinks he's proposing without asking my permission—"

"Down boy. It's too big for a ring. It might be a watch or bracelet." He sent me jewelry. I can't believe it. I remove the lid. "Oh my god ..."

"What is it?"

"Um ..." I take out the card next to the small bottle of *water-based personal lubricant*.

For my kinky lady. I'm a lot bigger than your ring finger. I'll pick you up at noon. ~Flint

"Elle, I'm old ... I want to know what's in the box before I die."

If I tell him what's in the box, it will kill him.

"A watch."

"Do you wear a watch?"

"Sometimes."

"Does it look expensive?"

"Not terribly."

"Well, that's good. It's never a good idea to purchase expensive gifts so early in a relationship. Does it fit?"

I clamp down on my lip to keep from giggling. "I ... uh ... think it's a one-size-fits-all."

"Is it engraved?"

My body vibrates with unleashed laughter, until tears fill my eyes. "No ..." I manage to squeak out.

"For crying out loud ... a luxury jewelry store that doesn't do free engraving? If that's the case, then they're just screwing you up the ass."

Oh. My. God ... I can't breathe. My stomach hurts from so much restrained laughter. I click mute on my phone to let it out. Howling laughter echoes in my apartment.

"You should teach your new guy a lesson on demanding good service, like I taught you. Never let someone screw you like that."

I could pee. I squeeze my legs together to keep from leaking. Forcing a few deep breaths, I turn off the mute button. "So how have you been feeling, Dad?"

"Good. Stiff. Soft in the middle. But good."

I'm drowning in gutter thoughts. I need to focus. "I miss you."

"Then get on a plane and come see me."

"Dad …"

"Live life, my lovely girl. Take chances—a new path—and find happiness. No fear."

I nod. He has a way of sobering the moment.

"I will."

"You'll come see me?"

"Yes."

"When?"

I smile. "Soon."

"Holiday soon?"

"Soon."

"Ah … fine. Love you. Tell that guy of yours to find a better place to buy jewelry."

"Will do, Dad."

Flint

"I CALLED THE Hamiltons. They'll be home all day if there's a non-9-1-1 emergency that requires assistance before I can get home."

Harrison plugs in his phone cord by the couch. "I don't think my charger cord works."

"Not an emergency." I check to make sure as many lights as possible are off. He's never figured out how or why it's important to flip the off switch. Someday he's going to be introduced to a little piece of paper called an electric bill. "Do you have any questions?"

"Will you pick me up a new charging cord?"

"No."

"You suck."

"I try my best. I'll see you in a few hours."

The last time I truly dated a woman, I didn't have a child or a guilty conscience. It wasn't a big deal if after a few dates things ended. No hard feelings ... I just moved on to someone else.

Things aren't so simple anymore. I'm scared out of my fucking mind of what may come from this. I'm equally as fearful of what may not come from this.

I fuck around with my son's "friend" and he hates me if he finds out. I break her heart and he hates me. Yet, here I am, ten feet from her apartment and unable to turn around and call it all off before anyone gets hurt or pissed off.

Ellen opens the door. I take a few seconds to admire the view. I fucking love that long red hair and those blue eyes. But more than that ... I love the way she looks at me, like she has one hundred ideas in her head of what she'd like to do to me but she can't decide where to start.

"You have some explaining to do, mister."

"Is that so?"

She nods for me to come in. I shake my head.

"Lunch and a movie."

"Yes. I need to grab my jacket and purse." She laughs.

"I'll wait for you. I'm trying to be a gentleman."

Her lips twist to the side. "Gentlemen wait in the hall, even when they're invited inside?"

"It's the only way for me to be a gentleman at the moment."

She blinks a few more times, with a contemplative expression stuck to her face.

"Ellen, you can grab your coat and purse so we can go to

lunch and a movie like I told Harrison we would be doing, or you can stare at me like that and we'll be forced to play my favorite game in lieu of lunch and a movie."

Her gaze meets mine. "What's your favorite game?"

"It's called Fuck Ellen."

Her lips part, eyes widening a bit more as a rosy color works its way into her cheeks. She eases the door shut and returns a minute later with her purse and coat. "Lunch and a movie it is." She smiles, locking the door behind her.

After she slips her keys into her purse, I take her hand. The last time I held a woman's hand in public, I was walking her out of a restaurant. Less than thirty minutes later, she was trapped in an overturned car, taking her last breath.

"You have two cars?" Ellen eyes me as I open the door to my black Jaguar Coupe.

"I do."

She shoots me a sly grin. I'm not sure what it means.

I cup both sides of her head and bend down. "You have to give me something," I whisper over her lips. "I'm dying a little here." I kiss her. She fists my jacket and kisses me back as if she, too, was dying a little before this moment. I don't want lunch. And I sure as hell don't want to watch a movie. I want to possess every inch of this woman, because when I'm with her, I feel deserving of *more*.

"Now, get in." I smack her ass. "Before I break any more promises."

Ellen

"WHO WAS THE gentleman who arrived at my door this morning?"

Keeping his eyes on the road, Flint smirks.

"He was handsome … and large. We used over half the bottle of lube before we got it to fit."

"Half a bottle, huh? Clearly he didn't know what he was doing."

"You're such an ass, Flint Hopkins. My *dad* was on the phone with me when it arrived. Seriously, who's your weekend gofer?"

He shrugs. "I can't reveal my sources."

"Fine. Then let's talk about my eviction notice. I want you to let me stay. I made you and Harrison dinner last night. He played with my rats. We danced to the Beatles. You gave me a welt just below my ass. And we're going on an official date. You can't kick me out."

"I can. And you can have a little tantrum if you must … but *it's business*."

"Ahhh! Why are you being so irrational about this? We've had sex. You said we're friends. You can't kick your friend out. You just can't."

He chuckles and I want to smack him.

"I go for the jugular in the courtroom against attorneys that I've known for years. I know their wives and kids. I've attended baptisms and graduations. We are friends, but inside the courtroom they are opposing counsel and I do whatever is in the best interest of my clients, even if it means tearing my *friend's* case apart and making them look unprepared and incompetent."

He pulls into a parking spot.

I get out before he has a chance to open my door. When he goes to take my hand, I slip it in my coat pocket, so he rests his hand on my lower back and guides me into the restaurant. It's a nice café with a bakery—I love the smell of fresh-baked bread. We're seated in a booth by the window. It's dreary out, almost like it could snow. I'm feeling a bit dreary as well.

"Wine?"

I glance up from my menu. "Fuck you. I'm pretty sure you've ruined wine for me."

"Fair." He nods slowly. "I acted childish at our last outing. I've gathered from your recent change in mood that it's your turn to act childish."

I slap my menu down on the table. "I'm sorry I'm having trouble with this, but I am. You can sleep with me or evict me. I just don't think you can do both."

He scratches his stubble-covered jaw. It's the first time I've really noticed that he hasn't shaven in a few days. "Hypothetically ... and please focus on the word *hypothetically* because this is not an actual option, I'm just curious ... would you rather stay and we never have sex again, or have sex again and find a new office space?"

"That scenario is too emotionally detached for me to even consider it."

"It's hypothetical."

Leaning back in the booth, I cross my arms over my chest. "What's not hypothetical is that you're not the only dick to ride. So if I had to choose between riding one dick and finding new office space or riding another dick and staying where I'm at ... I'd choose to find a new dick—hypothetically." I don't really mean it, but dang! I'm pissed off about this.

"You're being fucking ridiculous."

"I am not being ridiculous. You're being ridiculous. The way you make me feel special and wanted one minute and the next you're tossing my ass out like the trash."

"It's business."

"It's not business!"

Flint looks around as the handful of patrons in the restaurant look our way.

"I have one child to deal with, I don't need another." He tosses a twenty on the table and stands, slipping on his jacket.

We haven't ordered one thing. Is the money for my lunch? A cab? What the heck? Before I can shimmy out of the booth and grab my stuff, he's out the door.

"You're leaving me?!" I button my coat as the cool air takes my breath away.

"Yep." He unlocks his car.

I grab his arm and yank on it until he turns to face me. He pulls out of my grasp and bends over to get in my face.

"I deal with bickering idiots all week. I'm trying to raise a child who feels emotionally a world away from me. The last thing I need is a manipulative woman asking for favors that are not fair to ask and then treating me like a random 'dick to ride' just because I have the balls to stand up to her."

I shove him back so he's out of my face. "I signed a contract with you. I didn't ask for an unfair favor. I ordered business cards with my new office address. I painted the space. I had my name put on the door and I paid for my name to be added to the sign out front, all to the tune of over a thousand dollars. THEN ... my landlord gets out his calculator and adds two plus two and discovers a *music* therapist plays MUSIC!

Now I'm stuck looking for a new place because you were too damn stupid to use your brain before you took my money and signed on the dotted line."

Wow. I just said all of that. And I didn't have to think. The words have been waiting to come out, and I didn't realize it until now.

Here it is ... the silence. We've danced around this issue for weeks. I've tried to be playful and charming, he's tried to be polite and accommodating. But the truth is ... he's never going to let me stay, and I'm going to hold a grudge if he makes me leave. All the sex in the world won't change it. Not dinner. Not playing the guitar with Harry. Not lunch and a movie.

And this sucks because I genuinely like Flint Hopkins. But what sucks even more ... this rental agreement and the eviction notice are my proverbial glassful of wine left on the table. It's my trigger, and triggers hurt like hell.

"I'll drive you home and tomorrow I'll have Amanda cut you a check to cover the signage and business card expenses."

I stare at his chest. I can't even look him in the eye. "I don't want your money and I don't want a ride home."

"Ellen, it's cold. Just get in."

I shake my head as I walk back to the restaurant. I'll call a cab or I'll walk, but I won't get in his car because I just need a very long moment to find my balance again.

IT'S A BIT late for a clean break, but I catch a cab home, grab a few boxes, and drive to the office in search of something resembling closure. The parking lot is empty on this Sunday afternoon, so I park right in front of the door to make it easier to carry out my stuff.

After I get the boxes packed and my not-so-fancy desk disassembled, I call my clients for the week and reschedule them, letting them know I'll contact them soon with the new address. If I don't find a new place by the end of the week, I'll make house calls. Dad will be proud.

My phone rings. I don't recognize the number; it's out of area.

"Ellen Rodgers," I answer.

"Ellen, it's Lori Willet, your dad's neighbor."

"Hi." I tape up the last box.

"Forrest found your dad passed out in the yard. They just left with him in the ambulance. We're on our way there too. I'll let you know more as soon as we get there."

Tears prick my eyes as I cover my mouth.

"Sweetie, are you still there?"

"P-passed out or ..."

"Still breathing, just unresponsive."

"Okay ... um, I'll be there as soon as I can get there. Call me when you know more."

"We will. Safe travels. We're praying for him."

My phone drops from my shaky hands. I grab it and swat away more tears while bringing up Abigail Hamilton's number on my phone.

"Hello?"

"Abigail ..." I clear my throat and swallow back the flood of emotions. "It's Ellen. I need a huge favor."

"What is it, dear?"

"They're taking my dad to the hospital." I shake with silent sobs.

"I'm sorry. What happened?"

"I don't know. The neighbor found him unconscious in

the yard. I need to get on a plane."

"Oh … do you want me to book you a flight?"

I pinch the bridge of my nose. "No, I … I need you to give me something to be able to get on the plane."

"I don't under—oh dear, are you afraid of flying?"

I bite my quivering lips together and nod.

"Ellen?"

"Yes," I whisper past the knot in my throat. "My mom…" this hurts so bad "…she um … died in a plane crash."

"Ellen, I didn't know. I'm … I'll … where are you?"

"At my office. My car is here."

"Stay there. We'll come get you. I don't even want you trying to drive home. Just stay put. Okay."

I nod, unable to find another word before pressing *End*.

CHAPTER SEVENTEEN

Flint

"MY BACK HURTS just watching you." Martin Hamilton laughs, leaning on the fence between our yards.

When I returned from my disaster of a date, I changed into old clothes and got to work cutting back my plants for winter. Anything to avoid the questions I know Harrison will have once he pulls his head away from his phone long enough to really register that I'm home. I wasn't even gone a full hour. It has to be a new record for the shortest date ever.

"I don't mind it yet. I suppose I might in a few years."

"Nah, you're still a young guy. I'm sure you've got more than a few years of back-breaking work left in ya."

"Martin?" Abigail yells while jogging toward the fence.

"Oh lord …" He grumbles. "I must be in trouble for something."

"Martin, I need you to drive me to Flint's office building."

I sit back on my heels, brushing the dirt off my legs. "No one is there on Sunday," I say, narrowing my eyes a bit in confusion.

She shakes her head. "Ellen is there. I don't want her driving home. Her dad's in the hospital. I need to see if I can help her get on a plane."

"Get her a flight booked? I can do that, I've got—" Martin starts to say.

"No." Abigail shakes her head, a slight cringe of pain to her expression. "Her mom died in a plane crash. I'm going to have to give her something really strong to even get her on the plane."

Fuck. Me.

I tug off my gloves.

"Abby, you can't sedate her and put her on a commercial flight by herself. Are you going with her?" Martin says.

"I'm on call. I'll figure something out for her, but for now, I need to go get her."

"I'll handle it." I stand.

Martin and Abigail stare at me.

"You'll handle what?" Abigail asks.

"Everything." I turn and head toward the house.

They don't say another word because they know from personal experience that when I say I'll handle something, it gets handled. No questions. No hesitation.

"Boss," Amanda answers her phone on the first ring.

"I need two days. And I need you to come get Harry. I'll tell him to pack."

"What's—"

"And I need you to not ask any questions."

"I'll be there within the hour."

On my way to the stairs, I snatch Harrison's phone from him.

"Hey!" He chases me up the stairs.

"I need sixty seconds of your undivided attention." I continue to my bedroom to throw some clothes into a bag.

"Fine. What?" He plops down on my bed.

"Ellen's dad is in the hospital. I'm taking her to see him. I will be gone for two days. Amanda is coming to get you. Pack enough for two days. Don't forget clean underwear."

He knows the drill. She's watched him for me several times before when I've had other emergencies to handle.

"Is he going to die?"

"I don't know."

"Why are you taking her?"

"Because I'm connected and she needs some *special* help getting there." I hand him his phone, palm the back of his neck, and kiss his forehead. "Be good. I love you."

Ellen

LORI CALLS ME back. The hospital wouldn't tell her anything because she's not family, so I call them. It was a stroke. They're still trying to figure out the cause, and they don't know yet if he'll need surgery.

I feel numb everywhere except my stomach. There, I just feel painfully nauseous.

How did I go from having everything to having nothing? I had two parents who loved me—who loved each other. I had a husband who adored me. We had a tight circle of friends. We were adventurous. I lived a dream more grand than most ever dare to dream. In twenty-four months, I lost it all—except my dad.

After two years that nearly broke me as a person, a wife, and a friend, I gave Alex his divorce, loaded up a moving truck, and drove to Minnesota over three days.

No friends.

No family.

Just a job offer at a hospital.

It's fine. I didn't think I needed anyone until today when life kicked me on my ass, and I realized the best I could find was a colleague who could write me a prescription.

The elevator door dings. I wipe my swollen eyes, grab my purse, and sling it over my shoulder. I jolt to a halt when Flint appears at my door.

I glance at my phone. Where is she?

Keeping my head down so he doesn't have to stare at my bloodshot eyes, I murmur, "I thought you were Abigail."

Please leave. Please leave. Please. Please. Please.

His shoes come into view a few inches from mine.

"She sent you," I whisper.

"No. I sent me."

"Why?" I want to look at him, but I can't.

"Because you need to get to Massachusetts quickly and I can do that for you."

"I don't need a hero." I brush past him, taking the stairs to the main level with him right behind me. The tears come in unrelenting waves as I run toward the front doors. I don't know what I'm running from.

Flint?

Fear of getting on a plane?

Fear of losing my dad before I get to see him again?

As I push through the front door, a strangled sob breaks free, followed by two arms around my waist. Flint turns me toward him. My knees buckle, and he lifts me up like a child. I wrap my arms around his neck and drown in grief and fear.

In long, controlled strides he carries me away. I don't let

go, not even when he lifts me into the back of a vehicle. It starts to move, but he's still holding me. I don't know who's driving. I don't care.

"Open your mouth," he says.

I hiccup on my sobs as I open my eyes that are already swollen to the point of pain. "Why?"

Before I can object, he shoves a dropper into my mouth. "Yuck!"

He pulls my head into his neck and rubs my back.

Flint force feeds me this nasty liquid three more times before the vehicle stops. I'm tired … or dead. I don't know but I feel even more numb than I did before—and lifeless, yet I can hear voices, I just don't register what they're saying. When I blink open my eyes, I see a few people, and wide open space and … a small plane. Panic tries to overtake my body, but everything feels slow to react.

Just when I start to wiggle in protest, Flint shoves more nasty shit down my throat and something like earmuffs press to my ears. Muffled echoes and … Chopin's Nocturne No. 2 in E-Flat Major is all I hear. I close my eyes. My fingers feel the ivory beneath them. It's so beautiful … like I'm dancing … weightless … and that's when I see my dad. A measuring tape draped over his neck.

"Elle, bring me my pins, please."

I hand him the blue cushion and spin in circles with my red hair flowing behind me as Chopin plays from the turntable. The gentleman being fitted for a suit grins at me in the mirror.

"She's going to break all the boys' hearts," he says to my dad.

"That she is … just like her mama."

"I'm going to marry my prince, Daddy."

"Only if I deem him worthy, my little princess."

I twirl around some more. "I'm going to play music, Daddy."
"I know, darling."

I stop and watch my daddy shift the man's suit a little this way, making a mark in one place, pinning material in another place. I love watching my daddy, and I love watching the men in the mirror grin at me and smile in admiration of the suits my daddy makes for them.

"Ellen …"

Chopin. Why did Chopin stop?

"Ellen …"

I peel open my eyes.

"Drink this."

Flint scoots me off his lap and fastens my seat belt. "Here." He hands me a bottle of juice.

I look out the window of the vehicle, at first not recognizing much in the darkness, but then a few familiar buildings pass by and I know where we are—Falmouth, Massachusetts. "Oh my God. How did I get here?"

"Music therapy." Flint gives me a small smile.

I shake my head.

He shrugs, looking out his window at the road. "There may have been a few medicinal herbs involved."

He drugged me. I remember seeing that small—no, *tiny* plane. It doesn't matter. Reality of this whole situation seeps back into my mind. My dad …

"Drink." Flint nods to the juice.

Untwisting the cap, I drink it.

I don't wait for the vehicle to completely stop before jumping out with a slight wobble to my legs and rushing toward the emergency entrance.

"Jonathan Anderson."

I need a room number. The stroke unit. Anything other than that look—the one followed by she'll have a doctor come speak with me. I've been with families who get that look, get that diversion. It only ever means one thing.

The nurse gives me a room number.

Thank you, God.

It's after eight at night. The nurse finds a doctor to give me an update before they let me see him. He's asleep. I expected as much. But he's alive.

"You can't leave me, old man." I laugh with tears sliding down my cheeks as I take his hand in mine. "I was going to come see you. You didn't have to have a stroke over it."

More tears.

"I love you. I *need* you. If you leave me …" That's all I get out. It hurts too much, but I know he knows. We've never let our emotions go unspoken.

"My darling girl, the words I love you only hurt the people who refuse to set them free. So when you feel it, say it."

"But, Daddy, what if I don't mean it?"

"Feelings are our greatest compass. They will always lead you to the truth."

"I'm scared of the truth, Dad," I whisper.

When the nurse comes back in to check his vitals, I go out to the waiting room. I don't know if Flint's there. Maybe he got me to Massachusetts and turned around to fly home. In the history of long days, this is number three. The first was my mom's plane going down. The second was the day Alex went missing after the avalanche. I need this outcome to be better.

He's still here.

I stop at the entrance to the waiting room. Flint's leaning against the wall by a window, focused on the screen to his phone. He's a mess—his hair has given up on the gel, his long-sleeve shirt is wrinkled and half untucked. I think there's a hole in his jeans, and he's wearing the same sneakers he had on the day we got carried away in his greenhouse.

But ... he's here.

And as if he knows I'm standing here staring at him, he looks up.

I try to muster something resembling composure and gratitude, but it's really hard to do while my heart waits for permission to beat again—until my dad wakes up.

"Thank you." I swallow hard and rub my lips together. They're salty from being bathed in tears all day. "That's really inadequate." I grunt a painful laugh. "I don't remember everything, but I'm pretty sure you put me on a private jet. I don't know how you did it." I shake my head. "But thank you feels so pathetic."

With his brows drawn tight as if he's in his own pain, he nods slowly. "How's your dad?"

"Asleep. It was a stroke. They'll know more over the next twenty-four hours, but he doesn't need surgery. He could go home within a week."

"That's good, right?"

"Yeah. He's not out of the woods yet. But ..." I nod toward the hallway to his room. "I'm going to stay here tonight. So..." I shrug "...you're off the hook. I'll figure out a way to make it home. I'm good with trains and rental cars. I packed my stuff in boxes at your office. I'll call someone in the morning to move them out of your building and return my car to my apartment."

"You should eat something."

I shake my head. "I will, but not until tomorrow."

"Ellen?"

I turn.

"Lori." I smile before turning back to Flint. "Again, a huge, inadequate thank you. Tell Harry I'm sorry for taking you away today." I rest my hand on his arm. "Have a safe flight home."

When I turn back around, Lori pulls me in for a hug. Over her shoulder, I watch Flint leave.

I should have moved out of his office the day he asked me to leave. But I liked it there—and I liked *him*.

Flint

I GET A hotel room, take a shower, and make a few calls. By one in the morning, I still can't get to sleep, so I go back to the hospital.

Ellen's in her dad's room, but I feel the need to be near her in case she needs … anything. That realization gives me more than a moment's pause in my life. Am I here because she may need me or because I may need her?

In the waiting room, there's something resembling a sofa; basically it's three connected chairs without armrests separating them. I make it work, using my jacket as a pillow. Nurses pass through with their coffee refills. One of the florescent lights in the distance flickers every few seconds. It's just an eerie place to be—the pungent odor of disinfectants, the occasional page over an intercom, and every so often the ding of the elevator doors.

By three a.m. my eyelids begin to feel heavy. A slender figure moves in the hallway. I can't see beyond the shadows, but I recognize the messy hair. Her feet scuff along the floor, stopping every couple of steps to twist her body in one direction and then the other before stretching her arms above her head and leaning side to side, taking more steps toward the waiting room.

Just as her face comes into the light, she stops, eyes on me. Her hand covers her mouth for a few seconds.

I ease to sitting, leaning forward with my elbows resting on my knees as I rub the fatigue from my face. When I glance up, she's still there—frozen in place. Crooking my finger at her twice, she moves one hesitant foot in front of the other, inching her hand away from her mouth.

Taking her hand, I press my lips to the inside of her wrist.

She draws in a shaky breath. "You should leave," she whispers.

"Why?" I look up, my lips still savoring the warmth of her skin.

"Because if you don't, I'm going to fall in love with you."

We gaze unblinkingly at each other for a few seconds. My other hand snakes around her waist, pulling her closer. She eases onto my lap, straddling me with her knees. I thread my hands through her hair. "I'll risk it." I kiss her. She slides her arms around my neck and hums, moving her lips from my mouth to my jaw and down my neck until settling into the crook and releasing a contented sigh.

I close my eyes and let her hum me a lullaby.

CHAPTER EIGHTEEN

Ellen

I EASE OFF a sleeping Flint, grab some coffee from the cafeteria, and check on my dad. He's asleep. It's possible that he'll sleep all day. No two stroke cases are the same. The nurse doesn't expect the doctor to check in on him for another couple hours.

My phone is low battery—I am low battery. I need a shower, food, and a toothbrush. Hell, I need clothes and underwear. The original plan was for Abigail to take me home to pack. Flint must have thought the best chance of getting me on a plane was to drug me in the car and get me in the air without hesitation.

"Can you call me if he wakes before I return or if the doctor gets here early?" I ask the nurse, handing her my business card.

She nods and smiles.

It's just before six in the morning, five o'clock in Minnesota. I need to find help with my babies. They'll need food and water soon, but I don't want to call anyone quite this early.

The waiting room is minus one Flint Hopkins. Maybe he went to get coffee. Maybe I said too much and he's *gone.* I regret nothing. I took my dad's sage advice and told Flint how

I felt. So if he can't handle me falling in love with him, then he'd better run.

Before my phone completely dies, I text him.

ME: *I'm running out in quick search of a shower and food. Where are you? If you're halfway to Minnesota, thanks again.*

I press the elevator button.

"The restroom down the hall."

I grin at the voice behind me.

"Not halfway to Minnesota," he finishes as if it's an absurd assumption.

I turn and shrug. "I wouldn't blame you."

The elevator doors opens. Flint takes my hand and pulls me onto it. I like how small my hand feels in his hand. I like that he wants to hold it even while he holds and scrolls through his phone screen with his other hand.

"You have people who depend on you, so I know you can't stay. You should go home."

He keeps his eyes on his screen. "I feel like you're trying to get rid of me."

"I feel like you've taken pity on me."

"Hardly." Flint leads me off the elevator.

"Let's get a cab to my dad's place. Then we can take his car to find me a few changes of clothes and some toiletries."

"The red sedan is mine." He motions to the car out front.

"Yours?"

"Well, a rental." He opens the door for me. "We'll get you some clothes and go back to the hotel since it's close, unless you want or need to go to your dad's house right now."

I shake my head.

Within an hour, we arrive at the hotel with some necessities and takeout food, in spite of Flint's offer to take me some place nicer to eat. I just want to shower and get back to the hospital.

"I'm going to hop in the shower," I say after eating half of my sandwich. "Oh…" I turn just before the bathroom door "…I tried messaging my landlord, so if my phone rings will you answer it? The hospital could call too."

"Sure. Why did you message your landlord?"

"I need him to let someone in to feed my rats."

"I handled it." He sits back against the headboard of the bed.

"What does that mean?"

"Amanda is going to take Harrison over to feed, water, and play with your rats after school."

"She doesn't have a key."

He gives me a tight grin. "I know. If your landlord calls back, he can help them get in."

I shake my head. "You didn't know I called my landlord. How were they going to get in before I mentioned this to you just now?"

"A friend of mine was going to *get* them in."

"Pick the lock?"

"Something along those lines."

I stand idle, a little shocked. "I … I don't know if I should be grateful or pissed off."

"Let's go with grateful." He looks up from his phone, brows peaked, looking hopeful I go with the first option.

I shake my head again and drag my tired ass to the shower.

MY DAD WAKES up for less than twenty minutes today. Brain injuries require lots of sleep to heal. I know this, but it's hard to let what I *know* chase away the fear. I know the chance of dying in a plane crash is much less than dying in a car accident, but no amount of knowledge will ever ease that fear. I'm sure at least one person on the plane with my mom thought, "What are the chances of this plane going down?"

It's between one in five million and one in eleven million—yes, I've researched and obsessed over this for years. The chances of getting hit by lightning are so much better, yet I don't always stay home when it's raining. I would, had my mom died from a lightning strike.

By seven, I leave Dad's room. He opened his eyes. He recognized me. That's a blessing. His inability to speak breaks my heart, but I knew he'd most likely have a certain amount of trouble speaking for now. Still, watching him struggle, ripped my heart a bit.

"You're still here?"

Flint looks up from a magazine, not his phone. It's an odd sight, especially since it's a gossip magazine. "Did you really think I'd leave without telling you?"

I take a seat next to him. He rests his hand on my leg and leans into me, kissing the side of my head.

"Sorry, I would have been out earlier, but I just kept hoping he'd wake up again."

"You said the doctor said—"

"I know, I know … he needs sleep. I'm like a mom who wants to wake her newborn every hour to check for a pulse."

"Well, now that you're here, I will tell you that I'm leaving in the morning."

"Private jet?" I wink at him.

"Nope. I only call in that favor for others. Commercial airline for me."

"First Class?"

"Why does my flight status interest you so much?"

Running my fingers through my hair, I work out the tangles. It's been another long day, and I look it. "*You* interest me. I find you to be a very fascinating creature. I like to study your habits, your idiosyncrasies."

"I think you're delusional from sleep deprivation. I don't have idiosyncrasies."

"Delusional? No. Sleep deprived? Absolutely. And don't get me started on your idiosyncrasies." I stand. "My dad's parents will be here tomorrow. I want to go check on his place. Clean it if necessary."

"Wow, both of his parents are still alive. Where do they live?"

I hold out my hand. He takes it. And for this brief moment between breaths, my world stops long enough to think of my grandparents and the way they still hold hands. I remember my father always reached for my mom like it was just this instinct he had—an intrinsic need that never faded over time.

"They live in New Haven, but they've been out of town. They got home last night. I couldn't even contact them until this morning." He stands and shifts our hands so that our fingers interlace.

Alex rarely held my hand. He wasn't touchy-feely like that. Sex? Yes. Anything else—no. I wonder if losing his hands has put such simple things like this into perspective. He always chased the next adventure, afraid that he wouldn't conquer the world before he lost his youth. But sometimes ... we forget that the greatest experiences we have as humans are with each other.

"Let's get dinner and I'll drive you to your dad's house."

"Sounds perfect. Thank you."

"YOU SHOULD ORDER a glass of wine." Flint glances over his menu at me.

"Less than forty-eight hours ago we had a knock-down-drag-out fight in the parking lot of a restaurant. We didn't even get water served before you stormed out. Don't start this with me. I'm not in the mood." I give him a playful squint. I really don't want to revisit his issues or mine at the moment.

"I'm only suggesting you might like a glass of wine to relax after the stress you've been through."

"Thank you, but I'm good. Really."

He shrugs and goes back to studying his menu.

"Did you fight with your wife very often?" I set down my menu at the end of the table.

Flint twists his lips, eyes making one more quick survey of the menu. He sets his down on top of mine and blows a breath out of his nose. "Sure. Usually about my drinking. But sometimes we'd argue about stupid stuff."

I nod. "Alex and I never fought, not until his accident." I laugh. "I wanted to fight. He'd make me so mad sometimes, but he'd walk away or dismiss all my attempts to argue or 'discuss' with a simple 'whatever.'"

I grin. "I was so pissed off when you walked out of the restaurant on me. And when I chased after you, I expected you to get in your car and drive off. But … you lost your cool. You got in my face. And for a moment I didn't know how to respond to someone giving enough of a shit to fight it out. Then you left, and we felt over before we really had a chance to begin, but I knew you cared. You cared enough to give a shit."

Flint sips his water, eyeing me. Is he wondering if he *does* in fact give a shit? "How did you meet Alex?"

Just as I go to speak, our waiter comes back for our order. After we give it to him, I slide off my jacket and second guess saying no to a glass of wine. Talking about Alex is a conversation that requires at least a glass of wine, if not an entire bottle of vodka.

"Alex and I met in high school."

"High school sweethearts?" Flint shoots me a raised brow of surprise.

"Yes."

"That's ... sweet." He grins.

"Yes, so sweet. He *was* sweet. And outgoing. And everyone loved him. He was fun and adventurous. Our first year of college, when he asked me to marry him, I knew our life would be the grandest of all adventures."

Flint nods. "And was it?"

I drum my fingernails on the table. "Yes." I find a small smile to share in spite of the pain. "I don't regret anything. If I had it to do over again, knowing the outcome, I'd do it in a heartbeat." I laugh, shaking my head. "Wow ... I've never said that out loud. I'm not sure I've even thought those exact thoughts until now."

"How'd it end?"

I grunt. "Tragically. He tried to conquer a mountain, but the mountain won. He and his buddy got trapped in the debris of an avalanche. Alex got out but decided to go back and look for his friend. By the time he found him, his friend was dead and Alex had severe frostbite. They had to remove part of his hands. It left him with a thumb on one hand and two fingers on the other."

"I'm sorry." He frowns.

"Me too. It's interesting how our self-worth is so dependent on our capabilities—how little confidence comes from within. And I don't mean that in a judgmental way at all. I say that because I watched my husband's spirit die, leaving behind a man I don't know. And it hit me pretty hard because I thought if it could happen to him, it could happen to me.

"If someone cut off my hands, how would that affect me? And not just the physical part. How would I see myself? My purpose? My dreams? Can I be good at my job without hands? Can I be a good friend who helps someone move into their new apartment if I don't have hands? Can I be a lover to my husband if I don't have hands? So those sacred wedding vows, 'Til death do you part?' They're a little more complicated than that. I will love Alex until I die, so in that regard, I've kept my vow. The sickness and health is where it gets sticky."

"So you left?"

"No." I laugh, but it's really the most painful laugh ever. "I stuck around for two years. I would have stuck around for the 'til death do us part,' but he didn't want me there. I was a reminder of what he was, what he lost, and who he would never be. He didn't want to be touched. Not a kiss. Not a hand stroking his hair. Eventually, even a smile pissed him off. Depression turned into verbal abuse. I took all the hard licks of his words, and they bounced off this protective shield I'd built around myself, waiting for my Alex to come back to me."

"Divorce papers?"

"Yep. On our anniversary no less. Gotta hand it to him, he's always been a bit poetic with his timing. On our first anniversary after the accident, we watched our wedding video. He asked me to go get his wedding band, and before I could react, he said, 'Oh, that's right. I don't have a fucking finger to put it on. Maybe it will fit around my dick. I'm pretty sure it's atrophied from lack of use.' So I got served papers on our second anniversary, and two days later, when I refused to sign them, he had a friend come help him throw all of my stuff out onto the yard."

He flinches. "Did you sign them?"

"Ha! I hate that you have to ask that, but I know you've seen the stubborn side to me. Yes, I signed them."

"And he was calling you last week?"

"Yes. He's tried several times. I'm not going to talk to him. All the awful, cruel things he said to me finally settled into my conscience and my heart after I moved to Minnesota. I owe him nothing. His parents still live around here. I think my dad still has coffee once a month with his dad. If Alex had an emergency, my dad would've called me."

"Maybe he wants you back."

"Maybe he just needs a verbal punching bag."

The waiter brings our food, and we don't talk about Alex again.

Flint

"DID YOU GROW up in this house?" I ask, pulling into the driveway of the two-story, beachfront home with a wraparound porch. It's a great house—and far from cheap.

"No. We lived in Providence." She gets out. "Brr ..." She jogs to the porch, trying to open the door. "Of course it's locked. Come on ..."

We wind our way around to the back, lights from a string of houses reflect off the water.

"How the hell did he pass out in the yard, but all the doors to the house are locked? I'd bet money that he locked himself out." Ellen yanks on the door.

"We're locked out?" I ask.

"Here." She hands me her purse. "No." Bending down onto all fours, she crawls through a doggy door.

I chuckle, shaking my head. The porch light flicks on, and she opens the door. "Where's the dog?"

"He'll be here tomorrow. He's my grandparents' dog."

"This is quite the retirement home for a tailor." I step into a large kitchen of cherry wood, white granite, and stainless steel.

Ellen flips on a few more lights. "It's been in my dad's family for three generations. After my mom died, he moved here to renovate it ... and fish." She smiles, slipping off her jacket. "My grandparents stay here most of the summer. This is where I spent my summers when I was younger. But to answer your burning question, my great grandmother was the daughter of a wealthy man who happened to own a lot of land—the kind that was rich in petroleum. She and my great grandfather moved from Oklahoma to Providence. Shortly after my grandfather was born, they built this house."

I follow her around the main level of sprawling wood floors beneath scattered oriental rugs. She flips on the light to the master bedroom. It's immaculate.

"I'm wondering what you were worried about. This place looks spotless."

"Lori ..." She mumbles, poking her head in the adjoining bathroom. "She and Forrest look in on my dad. I bet she tidied up earlier today. I hope she didn't come across his nudie-girl magazines."

I raise a curious brow.

Ellen shrugs. "He's a guy. Don't all heterosexual men like looking at naked women?" She moves toward me in the way that I've come to expect—maybe even need.

I have no tie, but she'll find something about me that requires her little adjustments.

"I've not taken on the role as spokesman for all heterosexual men, so I'm going to decline comment."

She starts with my collar, making sure it's folded just so … then her hands slide down my shirt. "I'll rephrase, counselor. Do *you* like looking at naked women?"

Her hands ease around my waist and slide into the back pockets of my jeans, leaving her breasts pressed to my chest.

"You're grinning." She gives me a look that's both playful and challenging. "I'll take that as a yes."

My hands remain idle at my sides. If I touch her, I won't be able to stop. And as incredibly sexy as she is when she's messing with me—teasing me—I can see the wear of the past two days in her slumped posture and tired eyes.

"I'm imagining *you* naked, that's why I'm grinning."

She sucks in her upper lip, making her lower lip look pouty.

"And now I'm leaving so you can get some sleep."

Her head juts back. "Leaving? You're not staying?"

"My stuff is at the hotel, and I fly out at six in the morning, using a *commercial airline*, which means I'll need to be to the airport by four-thirty or earlier."

Taking a small step back, her hands slide out of my pockets. "You're right." She shakes her head, eyes closed. "I'm not thinking. Clearly I do need sleep."

CHAPTER NINETEEN

Ellen

I DON'T WANT him to go, but I can't ask him to stay. For everything that he's said or done that's upset me—including evicting me—he's more than made up for it by getting me here and staying for two days.

"Do you need anything else before I fly home in the morning?"

"I'm good." You. I need you before you leave. And I fear that I'll need you after you leave. But those aren't my biggest fears.

I close my eyes as he cradles my head. He does it with such tenderness, yet there's this fierce strength to his hands that makes each time he does it feel urgent—important—like he's seconds away from telling me something that will change my life.

"Call me if you need anything. Okay?"

I nod, closing my eyes because here come the tears. Fuck you, tears! You weren't invited to this going-away party.

My hands cover his as I hold in the sobs. He erases them with his thumbs and kisses my forehead.

"Why the tears, Elle?"

Elle. Don't call me Elle right now. Ellen. Ms. Rodgers. Annoying tenant. Or even Seven. But Elle feels too personal when I need to make a break.

"Are you worried about your dad?" he asks.

I'm very worried about my dad. But these tears are not his. I shake my head. "You'd better go. I told you if you stayed I would fall …" *In love.* "Now's not a good time for me to fall."

With an intense look, he nods once. "You'll be home before you know it."

I laugh, pulling away and walking away. While filling a glass with water in the kitchen, I say the words, but I don't look at him. "I won't ask my grandparents to take care of him. They're too old. My mother is dead. I am an only child." I stare out the window to the reflections dancing along the water. "This could be life-changing for him. We don't know yet. But if it is life-changing for him, it will be life-changing for me. If he can't live unassisted …"

"You will move home to take care of him."

I nod and turn to face him. "I feel like we've been trying to be *something* for weeks. And if you wouldn't have shown up with your stupid cape on, ready to walk on water for me, I would have let us die in that parking lot. I was prepared to let that happen. That's why I packed up my stuff."

Swatting more tears, I let a painful laugh escape. "But you had to put on your Superman cape, and no girl in her right mind can resist falling for the superhero. So my tears are selfishly for me because you have a son who doesn't want us together and I have a father who I know, in my intelligent therapist's mind, will need me here."

Flint rests his hands on his hips, staring at his feet. "You're going to quit your job?"

"I don't know," I whisper. "But if he needs me, then I'll

find a job here."

He rubs a frustrated hand over his face before looking at me. "It's the right choice. You do what needs to be done."

I nod.

"But ..." He closes the distance between us and presses his hand to my cheek. "Anything ... if you need absolutely anything, you call me."

What if I need you?

I force a smile as he pulls me into his body. Grabbing the collar to his shirt, I lift onto my toes, and he meets me in the middle for a heartbreaking goodbye kiss. When the desperation wears away and we come up for oxygen, I keep hold of his collar, resting my forehead against his chest.

"Tell Harry I miss him and thank him for taking care of my babies." I release him and fish my apartment keys from my purse, setting them in Flint's hand. I force my head up to meet his gaze.

Flint nods.

"I'll see you both soon, no matter what." I know it could be for a final goodbye, but I don't want to say the words quite yet. "Thank you, Flint Hopkins. Safe travels home."

His face wrinkles in pain just before he kisses me one more time. It's hard and painful, and then it's over as quickly as it began. Without looking back, he grabs his jacket and the door closes behind him.

THE NEXT MORNING I sip my coffee, waiting for the doctor to arrive, waiting for my dad to wake. With nothing better to do, I reminisce about my youth. There was a day when I lived in the moment and planned my life no further than the next great adventure with Alex. We'd hop in the car on a moment's notice with wadded clothes stuffed in a big bag, enough to get us by for a long weekend of climbing, biking, or surfing.

We slept in our little Subaru Outback almost as much as we slept in our bed. Our parents were happy and healthy. No one depended on us. We got by with working just enough to have money for play—and play we did.

No regrets.

You only live once.

Seize the moment.

Those were our mottos.

But accidents happen. Jobs turn into professions. Life starts to demand responsibility.

"Good morning." The doctor brings me back to reality.

"Good morning." I fake a smile, the one that says I'm good with being thirty-two and responsible.

He performs an exam and runs through some tests. I watch, feeling numb at the moment. Until ... my dad stirs and opens his eyes.

"Dad!" I get in his line of vision, not caring if I'm in the way of the doctor or nurse.

Jumbled sounds fall from his lips. He flinches in frustration.

I squeeze his hand, and he gives me a faint squeeze back which is good—really good. "Don't worry." I smile. "We'll find your words."

His head moves slightly in a small nod.

I step back again to let the doctor finish his exam. His words echo like I'm hearing them from the opposite end of a tunnel. I knew they were coming, but I couldn't fully imagine the anguish in my dad's eyes as he tries to process everything.

Dysphagia.

Hemiparesis.

Pain.

Spasticity.

Possibly seizures.

Impaired vision.

Incontinence.

Speech and comprehension issues.

But … here it comes …

"Good prognosis."

I smile at the doctor, but really, I'm laughing at him. The word good doesn't fit after that list of possible post-stroke conditions.

"Thank you," I say to the doctor, maintaining my smile as he nods politely before leaving the room. This painful smile is the only thing that's keeping me from falling to a million unrepairable pieces.

My dad's blue eyes focus on me. I don't know how well he's processing this. It might be a small blessing if he doesn't fully understand the possible challenges ahead of him.

I move to the side of his bed, sitting on the edge while taking his hand in mine and bringing it to my lips. "We've got this," I whisper.

Flint

"GLAD YOU MADE it safely home." Amanda greets me with a smile.

I nod. "Thanks." I shrug off my overcoat. "How's Harrison?"

"Fine. I'm sure he'll be happy about going back home after school. He's such a creature of habit."

I chuckle. "Yes, he is. Thank you for taking care of him and Ellen's—"

"Rats! Oh my gosh …" She shoots up from her desk chair, following me into my office. "At first I was like, no way am I getting near five rats, but they are so cute and smart. They play basketball. Have you seen that?"

I roll my eyes, unable to hide my grin. This conversation would bring a big smile to Ellen's face. "I haven't had much interaction with them, but they've become Harrison's new obsession. It's all he wants for Christmas."

Amanda's smile fades. "How's Elle's dad?"

"He's alive. I'm not sure what his physical or mental state will be in the coming weeks. I think he's going to require a lot of therapy and extra care." I open my computer and click on my email.

"You like her."

"We're not talking about this."

"Harrison likes her."

"Harrison doesn't like her with me." I give her a look that she needs to read as a we're-done-talking-about-this look.

"You haven't tried—"

"Amanda, I'm not discussing this with you. Ellen will most likely be moving to Cape Cod to take care of her dad. In case you're not good with measurements, that's over fifteen hundred miles from Minneapolis."

I don't need her pity look, so I wait for her to give up. After a few seconds, she goes back to her desk.

A few hours later, Harrison arrives, plopping his bag on my

desk. I set it on the floor.

"Where's Elle?" he asks.

"Nice to see you too, Harrison."

"Where is she?"

"Rhode Island."

"Did her dad die?"

"No." I type up my notes for tomorrow's deposition.

"Then why didn't she come home with you?"

"He's in the hospital. He had a stroke. She could be gone for a while."

"Are you taking me to feed her rats?"

"Yes."

"When is she coming home?"

I blow a controlled breath out of my nose. "I don't know."

"Why didn't you ask her?"

"Because she doesn't know the answer to that. It depends on her dad's recovery. Recovering from a stroke can be a slow process."

"How am I supposed to play guitar with her if she's not here?"

Pinching the bridge of my nose, I shake my head. "Maybe you can use the app she showed you."

"I don't know the name of the app. I'll call her." He pulls out his phone.

"Don't. She's most likely at the hospital. This isn't an emergency. It can wait, Harrison."

"Wait until when? Later tonight? Tomorrow? Next week?"

"Harrison!"

He frowns.

"I'm sorry …" I run my hands through my hair. "I'm tired. You're asking me questions I don't have the answers to.

Let's…" I grab my coat "…go home."

"I have stuff at Amanda's."

I rest my hand on the back of his neck, guiding him out of my office. "We'll stop and get it after we go feed the rats."

AFTER TWO HOURS in my greenhouse and another hour helping Harrison with his homework, I grab a shower and settle into my office for another hour of work.

ELLEN: *Are you asleep?*

I grin at my phone screen.

ME: *Yes*

ELLEN: *What side of the bed do you sleep on?*

ME: *The middle*

ELLEN: *What! Nobody sleeps right in the middle.*

ME: *Looks like I'm nobody*

ELLEN: *How are my babies?*

ME: *Creepy*

ME: *How is your dad?*

ELLEN: *Partial paralysis that's hopefully temporary – incontinence, speech issues … and the list goes on.*

I dig my teeth into my lower lip, staring at her text. What's the proper response to that?

ME: *I'm sorry*

A shitty, generic reply, but I don't know what to say.

ELLEN: *It's all common, we should/could see vast physical improvements in the coming weeks. Cognition, speech, and* *emotional healing can take much longer.*

ME: *How are you holding up?*

ELLEN: *OK, my grandparents are here for the emotional support I need, but they are old and slow and I love them to death. BUT their little poodle, Bungie, keeps pissing everywhere! And it takes them twenty minutes to retrieve paper towels to clean it up, so I've been doing it, I'm not too excited about taking care of my dad AND Bungie.*

ME: *There's a reason I don't have pets*

ELLEN: *I know, you're a control freak.*

I chuckle.

ME: *Organized*

ELLEN: *That's what I said.*

ME: *Harrison wants the name of that music app you showed him*

ELLEN: *Shouldn't he be in bed?*

ME: *He is. He wanted it earlier and I said he couldn't message or call you.*

ELLEN: *He can call or message me ANYTIME but I'll tell him that myself when I gift him the app so you don't misquote me ;)*

Rubbing the back of my neck, I reread her message several times. I wasn't looking for her, but I found the perfect woman to be in my son's life. But it's not going to happen. Ellen Rodgers is a missed opportunity. A close call. A what if.

ME: *Do you need anything?*

Three little dots appear. Disappear. Appear again. Disappear. But no message pops up on the screen. Maybe she's typing a long message. Maybe she keeps changing her response.

ELLEN: *Nothing that I can have.*

Cryptic.

ME: *You'll have to elaborate.*

ELLEN: *Go back to sleep, thank you for everything. XO*

ME: *Gnight*

ELLEN: *Sleep tight.*

CHAPTER TWENTY

Ellen

I T'S BEEN THREE weeks since my dad had his stroke. I've had to take personal leave from my job at the hospital and refer my other clients to another therapist in Minneapolis. He's home and making progress each day, but the recovery is slow. My days consist of taking him to therapy (speech-language, physical, occupational) and then he takes a long nap because therapy is hard work.

I do music therapy with him in the evenings, and we also use music and certain beats to work on his walking at home. My grandparents have been great about making meals. It's a fair trade for cleaning up after Bungie at least twice a day. And I know they want to be here. I see the worry in their eyes. This is their son. Things feel out of balance when a grown child needs more assistance than their parents.

It's like death. Things have a natural order. Children are not supposed to die before their parents.

I message or call Flint at least once a week to check in on my babies. They've been good about feeding them and changing their bedding/litter area once a week. And by they, I mean Harry. Flint's convinced that Harry needs to do it by himself if he ever expects to have a pet of his own. I suppose there's some logic to that.

After my dad and grandparents are tucked into their beds, I fill the upstairs bathtub with hot water and a bath bomb. It's not a huge tub, but it's quiet and all mine for the next hour until I crash for the night. I bring up my bathtub playlist on my phone and set it on the toilet seat before sinking into total bubbly bliss.

"Come to mama ..." I moan, closing my eyes, as the hot water soothes every single muscle. Paula Cole sings about "feelin' love." For one hour I get to feel carefree. For one hour I get to escape into the fantasies of my mind. For one hour I get to be naked, wet, and feeling sexy.

Even after Alex ended our life together, he still was the star of my fantasies. He may not have been touchy-feely, but the sex was always good—really good. But now I don't think of my surfer blond ex-husband. The only man I imagine touching me the way I touch myself in the depths of this hot, soapy water is a tall, well-built, dark-haired man who wears the hell out of a suit and does the most magical things with his fingers ... his lips ... and that fucking wicked tongue.

A soft moan escapes my parted lips before I trap my lower one between my teeth, sliding my middle finger between my thighs. My song cuts out once. I ignore it. Then it cuts out again.

"Nooo ..." I grab my towel and wipe my hands before snatching my phone off the toilet seat. Who the hell is inter-rupting my sacred bath time?

Flint.

He hasn't called or texted me even once since he left three weeks ago. It's been me calling or texting him. Does he know I'm touching myself thinking of him?

"Thank you for calling 1-800 TOUCH ME. How can I make your fantasies come true tonight?"

Nothing.

I hold my phone out. We're still connected.

"Sorry, I must have the wrong number. But since I do, can we think of it as a happy mistake and proceed with you fulfilling my fantasies?"

I grin. "I hate being your mistake, but I'll deal with it if you think of me as a happy mistake."

"You're in a good mood."

I hum. "Me time. Bath time."

"Fuck me ... why did you have to tell me that?"

I giggle. "Sorry. I'm not wet, naked, and touching myself thinking of a certain man in a suit. I'm covered in dog vomit and a long day's worth of sweat and grime. Better?"

"Where are you touching yourself?" he asks in a husky voice.

I bite my lips together and blow out a slow breath. This is torture. "To what do I owe the honor of you calling me?"

"Between those sexy legs of yours?"

I squeeze said sexy legs together. "Maybe."

"Jesus Christ, Elle ..."

A heavy pulse grows between my legs, just from his voice. He sounds a little pained and a lot turned on.

"I miss you," I murmur because no matter how much thoughts of Flint turn me on, I can't ignore my heart.

"Yeah ..." he says with weak defeat.

"Yeah." I mock, blowing out a short breath of disbelief. "Good to know we both know I miss you." My heart starts the familiar ache that I've tried to ignore since he left.

"What do you want me to say?"

My eyes roll to the ceiling, tears trying to fight their way to the surface. "Nothing. Why did you call?"

"Missing you won't change anything."

But it would mean everything.

"Why did you call?"

"I just wanted to see how your dad's doing? And I wanted to make sure you don't need anything?"

"He's doing. One day at a time, he's doing. As for me, I haven't had much time to think of my needs. I suppose feeling needed is enough. My dad needs me. Feeling missed is pretty fucking special too, but one out of two ain't bad."

"Elle ..."

"Don't. It's fine. I get it." I clear my throat. "Lori and Forrest are going to help out with my dad so I can take the train to Minneapolis next week. It's a day-and-a-half trip. I need to talk with the hospital and figure out what I want to do long term with my clients. Then I'll drive my car and my babies back here to Providence by Thanksgiving."

"So it's official? You're moving?"

"Yes. I refuse to put him into a care facility. He could make a full recovery, but it's going to take months ... maybe even years. He's my dad..." my voice cracks "...he's all I have."

"Let me know when your train arrives. I'll arrange to have you picked up."

"You'll *arrange* to have me picked up," I repeat more to myself than to him as I nod slowly. "I'm a big girl, Flint. I am pretty sure I can get myself from the train station to my apartment."

"Okay."

Okay. I ... I don't know what to say.

"Goodnight."

I nod, releasing the tears with one blink.

He ends the call.

"Sleep tight," I whisper to no one.

THIRTY-SIX HOURS. THAT'S how long it takes to get from Providence to Minneapolis by train. A little longer than taking a plane—*just* a little.

It's bittersweet. For thirty-six hours, someone else has taken care of my dad. For thirty-six hours I've felt my heart being pulled apart. If something happens to him, I'm back to where I started three weeks ago. I'm sure Flint would don his cape to save my day again, but I don't want that. Thirty-six hours gave me plenty of time to find empathy.

What if he cares about me even half as much as I care for him and Harry? If it's true, then I'm hurting him by moving. I don't think he will ever show me that much raw honesty and emotion. His heart is guarded—rightfully so.

Missing me won't change how he feels. Telling me won't make me stay. It's selfish of me to expect him to share anything with me. I'm leaving.

I take a cab from the train station to my house. Digging my spare key out of the pocket of my purse, I stick it in the lock, but the door is unlocked. I ease it open and listen.

Harry.

He's talking to my rats. It's their dinner time.

I set my purse on the floor. I didn't bring home any clothes, since everything at my dad's is stuff I purchased after arriving there.

"Hello?"

"Ellen?" Harry peeks his head out of the bedroom. "Why

are you here?"

I smile, walking down the hall. "I live here." But not for long. My smile falters as I meet Flint's gaze. He's leaning against the wall—in my rats' room. It's … unexpected.

"Hi," I whisper, feeling all sorts of emotions collide in my heart—pain being the strongest.

"Hey." He smiles. It's distant, forced, and gut-wrenching.

"I should have brought my guitar."

I draw in a shaky breath to even out my emotions as I pick up Lady Gaga. "Hi, baby." I kiss her. "We'll play sometime before I leave."

"You're leaving again?"

My gaze shifts from Harry to Flint. I assumed he told him. I was wrong.

Flint remains expressionless.

"Yes." I return my attention to Harry. "You know my dad had a stroke?"

Harry nods. "He didn't die."

"No. But it's going to take him a long time to fully heal, and I'm really the only family he has. His parents are still alive, but they're too old to give him the care he needs."

"Will you be back before Christmas? I asked my grandparents to get me rats for Christmas. I want to see if my rats and your rats play well together."

I look at Flint. His brow tenses.

"I'm moving to Cape Cod, Harry. It's not temporary. At least not like a few months."

"But you're coming back eventually, right? I think my dad is getting tired of driving me here to take care of your rats. Maybe we should move them to our house until you move back here."

Of course Flint's tired of dealing with my rats.

I smile at Harry. "I'm actually taking them with me."

"Oh …" His forehead wrinkles. "Come," he calls to my rats.

They scurry to their cage like Harry is their alpha. I ease Lady into the cage and give my guys all a quick pet before shutting the door.

"Come here, Harry." I walk to my room and reach into my sock drawer, pulling out three one hundred dollar bills. "This is for taking really good care of my babies."

His eyes bulge out. "Three hundred dollars?"

I rest my hand on the side of his face. He stiffens at first before relaxing a little. "Thank you, Harry." I kiss the cheek opposite of my hand, and whisper in his ear, "I'm going to miss you so much."

"You said we'd play guitars before you leave."

Releasing his face, I smile. "We will. I promise. I'll be here for a week, getting things packed."

"K." He nods. "Let's go," he says to Flint, who's watching us from the doorway to my bedroom.

Flint hands him the key fob. "I'll meet you in the car."

We stare at each other until the door shuts behind Harry.

"I'm sorry. I didn't know you hadn't told him." I slip my fingers into the front pockets of my jeans and shrug. "I think he's okay with it."

"Lucky Harrison." The muscles in his jaw tick.

"You've wanted me out of your life since day one."

"I wanted you out of my office building."

"Well…" I give him a tight-lipped smile "…I'm out."

"I can't fix this," he says with his voice so tight it feels like an elastic band ready to snap.

I shake my head. "It's not yours to fix." Turning to the side, I squeeze past him to get my purse and phone from the floor by the front door.

Flint grabs my wrist and jerks my arm until I face him. So much anger distorts his face as he presses my hand to his sternum, jaw clenched.

Blood races through my veins and my pulse pounds in my ears.

"This," he grits, pushing my hand harder against his chest like he's using it to punctuate his words. "I can't fix *this*." He hammers my hand harder to his chest one more time.

My fingers curl into his shirt, like I can grab his heart and save it. "Life is so fucking cruel," I whisper.

He cradles my head in his hands and presses his forehead to mine. "Stay."

I don't even have to blink. The tears come so fast. It's like he snapped my heart in two and I can't stop the bleeding.

"I can't." Those two words feel like razors slashing my already dying heart.

"I missed you." He rolls his forehead back and forth against mine as his grip on me tightens.

"Flint …" I sob, gripping his shirt with my other hand too. I don't want to ever let go.

"I love you," he whispers a breath before his mouth takes mine.

I kiss him and I cry.

I kiss him and I break.

I kiss him and I pretend that it matters.

But … it doesn't, so I just kiss him.

There's never a Subaru Outback, a bag stuffed with a few wadded clothes, and a great adventure waiting when you need it the most.

He breaks the kiss, breathless, searching my eyes.

I open my mouth to say something ... God, I don't know what to say. The pain has swallowed me up and left me with nothing. Not. One. Single. Word.

Say something!

He casts his gaze to the ground for a few seconds, turns, and leaves my apartment.

I WAIT IN my car until midnight; that's when the lights shut off. Buttoning my wool coat, I jump out, run across the street and up the porch steps. I pull my phone out of my pocket.

ME: *I can stay for a week*

It's windy and cold. I shiver, hugging myself while I wait for him to respond.

FLINT: *I'll take it*

ME: *Then come let me inside*

I grin. This may be the most sadistic thing I have ever done to myself. It's going to hurt so damn bad when I leave in a week, but I will regret it if I don't seize this moment, no matter how quickly it may pass.

The door eases open. I step inside, shivering. Flint's wearing only a pair of black briefs and a frown. I love every single one of his frowns. They're a silent challenge. Can I take them away? Will he give me the smile behind it? Am I worthy?

After unbuttoning my jacket and hanging it on the coat tree, I press my cold hands against his warm chest. He doesn't even flinch. Confusion etches his forehead, apprehension heavy in his eyes.

"Stop frowning, Mr. Hopkins. I'm going to fulfill all of your sexual fantasies over the next seven days."

The corner of his mouth curls into the tiniest of smiles.

Me.

He smiles for me.

I make him happy.

Another overlooked wonder of the world: bringing someone complete, intoxicating happiness. I lift onto my toes to capture those pouty lips. He picks me up, wrapping my legs around his waist, and he carries me upstairs.

"Shhh …" he says, pressing his lips to my ear as he carries me down the hall to his room. "If you don't stop humming, I'm going to have to gag you. Child in the house."

I kiss his neck.

"I feel your grin against my neck," he whispers, easing the bedroom door shut behind us and locking it.

"You love me." I smile as he lowers me to my feet.

"Lotta good it does me." Another frown.

I inch my scarf off, letting it float to the ground. "Never regret loving someone. Do it for you, not for them."

His gaze eats me up one inch at a time. And there it is … the lazy swipe of his tongue over his bottom lip. It's so fucking sexy. *He's* so fucking sexy.

I take a step back, giving him a better view as I shrug off my shirt, revealing my favorite black lace bra. "If you want to do something for the person you love…" I slide down my leggings "…open your heart to let them love you back." My hand reaches for his.

He takes it, letting me pull him to his bed.

"Sit," I whisper.

232

After a long look at my sexiest panties and bra, he folds his tall body to sit on the edge of the bed. I step between his legs. His hands inch up the back of my legs, taking their time memorizing the curve of my ass. I press my palms to his cheeks, brushing the pad of my thumb over his lower lip.

"Will you open your heart to me?"

His hands move to the clasp of my bra while his gaze remains locked to mine. "Yes."

"Good." I kiss his forehead, down his nose, and along his cheekbones. "Because I'm going to love you so hard, time won't matter." I kiss one side of his mouth as he eases my bra off. "Distance won't matter." I kiss the other side of his mouth. "All you'll feel when you take each breath..." my lips hover over his "...is my love."

For the rest of the night we pay homage to each other—physically, emotionally, spiritually. I refuse to stop until my mouth and hands have touched him everywhere and his have possessed every inch of me. I memorize the look he gets at the exact moment he loses himself to me. His back arches. My hand splays over his taut stomach muscles; my fingers curl into his tight flesh like I'm claiming him—Every. Single. Piece.

It's sensual.

It's vulnerable.

It's beautiful.

It's mine. I want that look to be mine and only mine forever.

I want to be his greatest strength—and his greatest weakness.

I want to be where he hides his lies and finds his truth.

CHAPTER TWENTY-ONE

Flint

"**Y**OU HAVE TO leave." I begrudgingly attempt to dress the naked woman sprawled out on my bed. There's bedding everywhere—pillows half on the bed, half on my night stand, my comforter on the floor at the end of the bed, blankets wadded up beside the bed, the fitted sheet pulled off two of the corners of the mattress, and the top sheet woven around said naked woman passed out on her stomach. Sweat, sex, and her fruity shampoo fight to be the dominant smell in the room.

"Elle …" I tug at the sheet, but it's all knotted. How did this happen? I grin. I know how it happened.

Her arms break free, reaching to the top of the mattress like she's getting a good stretch. But instead of relaxing, her fingers curl into the edge of my mattress like she's dangling from the roof of a tall building.

"Elle?"

"I'm not leaving," she mumbles into the mattress.

"You can't stay."

"What time is it?" She keeps her head buried.

"Four."

She grunts. "Wake me in two hours."

I sigh, running my hands through my hair that's been

234

thoroughly yanked and pulled over the past four hours. "Harry gets up at six."

"Great. I'll make everyone breakfast."

I growl in frustration. "I told him we wouldn't have sex."

"Then shame on you." Her sexy little body shakes with silent laughter.

I want to sink my teeth into the exposed curve of her ass and fuck her senseless for being so stubborn and *laughing* at my predicament. I squint, leaning a bit closer. Those might already be my teeth marks on her ass. Serves her right.

"Ellen …"

"I'm getting chilled." She turns her head to the side, blinking open one eye. "Grab a blanket and give me your naked body heat."

"You're going to have to sneak down the back stairs, *right* at six o'clock." I grab a blanket from the floor and start to slide into bed.

"Uh uh … *naked* body heat." She grins.

I slide off my briefs and cover us with the blanket. She wiggles free from the confines of the sheet and hugs me with her whole body. After shushing her humming three times, I give up and let it lull me to sleep.

BANG! BANG! BANG!

"I can't find my other sock. Why is your door locked? You never lock your door."

My eyes shoot open as I jackknife to sitting. Ellen eases to sitting next to me, rubbing her eyes.

Rattle. Rattle. Rattle.

He's already working the key from above the door into the

lock. How the hell did he get that down so fast?

"Harrison stay out—"

Light from the hallway blinds us as he stands in the open threshold, holding a single sock in his hand. Elle pulls the blanket up to cover her bare chest, but I think there's a good chance he already saw it. Maybe not. Maybe it's too dark in here.

Fuck. I hope it's too dark in here.

"Ellen?"

"Morning, Harry."

"Harrison. I'll be out in a minute. Please shut the door."

"Did you have sex with Ellen?" Harrison takes a step inside the bedroom, eyes making an inspection of the floor where I'm sure he'll find her discarded clothes and my briefs.

"Harrison, close the door, now."

He closes the door—with him still on the *inside* of the room.

"Not what I meant."

He flips on the lights. We squint again.

"For god sake, Harrison."

"Did you have sex with Ellen? You said you wouldn't have sex with Ellen. You promised you wouldn't have sex with Ellen or my teachers. I told you this would happen if you kissed her. Did you kiss her?"

He's smarter than this. He knows the answers to these questions. But when he's upset, he thinks out loud, so I let him because I'm naked under this blanket and so is she. Neither one of us can get up and cover up without leaving the other one naked. We're completely at his mercy.

"Why?"

Beneath the blanket, Ellen rests her hand on mine. She

feels his struggle. This was what I wanted to avoid.

"I told you to find your own friend. She's my friend. You don't even like her. You gave her a D—a seven—seventy percent."

Ellen's fingernails dig into my hand. How kind of him to bring up the seven.

"Harrison, get ready for school. We'll discuss this later."

"Dad, you promised—"

"Harrison! We're done. This conversation is on hold until tonight."

He grits his teeth and fists his hands as he turns toward the door. After he opens it, he turns back toward us. "Are you going to make cookies?" he asks Ellen.

I cringe. Simon and his fucking-around dad.

"Uh …" Ellen glances over at me.

"Chocolate chip. Gluten free. Dairy free."

"Harrison, out."

"When you have sex with men who have children, you're supposed to bake cookies."

Ellen stifles a laugh. "I'll have them hot out of the oven when you get home from school."

He nods stiffly and shuts the door.

I drop my head in my hands. "Fuck …"

Ellen giggles, collapsing back on the bed.

"It's not funny. Why didn't my alarm go off?" I grab my phone from the nightstand. It should have gone off. I toss it aside and nudge her leg with mine. "Get dressed. School. Work. A kid with one sock. This is going to be a long day."

Ellen rips the blanket from me and cuddles up on the one pillow still on the bed, her back to me. "I don't have anywhere I need to be for another few hours." She yawns. "Keep the noise down. I'm going back to sleep."

"What the fuck? Hello … Harrison's in the other room. He just walked in on us. Were you not paying attention?"

She tucks her knees to her chest, nuzzling her nose just under the edge of the blanket. "Not my problem. I'm off the hook with a batch of cookies."

After a few seconds of staring at her back, red hair splayed over my pillow, I realize she's serious.

"Unbelievable," I mumble on my way to get in the shower.

Closing my eyes under the stream of hot water, I think of one week with Ellen. It's not enough. All reasoning says I should not do this—I should not have said yes. She said it herself: we were over before we started. I'm delaying the inevitable. I lost one woman I loved, and I'm going to lose another. But I can't think about Heidi without thinking of all the times I wished I could have had one more day—one more week.

These are my one-more days. This is my one-more week. It won't change the future. It won't cure her dad. It won't erase fifteen hundred miles. I'd rather have her in my life for the next seven days than not. It's just that simple.

I do my usual morning grooming and pick out my suit for the day.

"Let me."

I turn toward the sleepy voice. She's so fucking beautiful in black panties and no bra, but her green scarf is draped over her shoulders covering her breasts.

"Nice scarf." I grin.

She smiles, blinking her blue eyes a few times to adjust to the closet light. Taking my suit jacket, she holds it for me to slip in my arms. After she buttons it, she adjusts my tie and grabs the lapels of my jacket.

"Flint Hopkins, you sure do look the part."

"What part is that?"

A flash of something resembling pain pulls at her brow for less than a second, but she smiles through it. "The one that got away."

Palming the back of her neck, I press my lips just below her ear, waiting until I feel her pulse. "No one's getting away for the next week," I whisper. "I'll see you later." I kiss her softly on the lips and snap the scarf off her neck, giving her a wicked grin before tossing it on the bed as I walk out of the room.

Ellen

I STAY IN Flint's bed, occasionally drifting off to sleep, occasionally shedding a few tears. In twenty-four hours he completely took my heart in the Hail Mary of all Hail Mary passes. The man who feels unworthy of true happiness laid his whole heart open for me. I'm not sure what hurt most, the desperation in his eyes when he told me he loved me or the realization on his face when it became clear that no amount of love could keep me here.

I've simply loved my father my whole life. There's nothing to contemplate.

By nine, I put on my clothes and drive home for a shower and time with my babies. After lunch I get everything settled with the hospital. I signed a contract with them, but they let me out of it, given the circumstances. I need to type out a letter to my other clients who have already been referred to another therapist temporarily. It's now permanent. But I leave that for tomorrow. I have to feed my babies and pick up ingredients for cookies.

"COOKIES." HARRISON GRINS as he comes in the back door a little before four with Flint right behind him.

"Wash your hands," Flint says.

"Yeah, yeah ..." Harrison ditches his bag and disappears into the bathroom.

"Smells good." Flint eyes me. I'm not sure if he's talking about the cookies or not. The comment fits the cookie scenario, but his eyes portray a different kind of hunger.

"Warm and moist." I wiggle my eyebrows, taking one from the cooling rack and sinking my teeth into it.

Flint gives me a look that makes everything south of my navel feel just as warm and moist. "Two," Flint warns Harry just as he starts to pile a third cookie onto a small plate.

"They're my cookies," Harry murmurs, disappearing up the stairs.

I smirk at Flint. He grabs my wrist and shoves the other half of my cookie into his mouth.

"Mmm ... you've got baking skills." He sucks each one of my fingers before releasing my wrist.

"You really need to stop acting so surprised that I have skills. And why are you here so early? It's not even five."

"Cookies." He unbuttons his overcoat.

I laugh. "Cookies? You left work early for cookies?"

"I left work early for the baker." He hangs up his wool overcoat and slips off his suit jacket, draping it over the back of the kitchen chair.

"I'm flattered." I rest my backside and my hands on the edge of the counter, admiring Sex in a Suit as he loosens his tie and unbuttons the top button of his shirt.

He halts his motions, eyes shifting to the side as he sniffs several times. "It smells like more than just cookies."

"Dinner's in the oven."

"Dinner?" He prowls toward me, caging me with his body as his hands press to the counter next to mine.

Biting my lower lip, I nod several times.

"Harrison-safe?"

I nod. "And I have tickets to the new Spiderman movie."

Flint quirks a brow. "It's a school night."

"Let's break all the rules. I'll bake muffins tomorrow and right all of the wrongs."

He slides his hand around my back and presses me to him, his lips devouring mine, his erection pressed to my belly.

I want this life.

I want Flint showing me his appreciation for baking. I want Harry grinning when he sees cookies on a cooling rack. I want passionate kisses promising long nights of being tangled in each other.

I rub my lips together when he tears his mouth from mine, both of us breathless.

He grins. "I love that you think baked goods make up for breaking the rules."

I shrug. "It's worked so far. Maybe you should take freshly baked cookies to the judge or jury on the days you have court."

"Mmm …" He takes two steps backward to distance us as the stairs creak a bit under Harry's descent.

"Can we play guitars?" Harry sets his plate on the counter.

"I don't have mine here, but we can still make music…" I

jab my thumb in the direction of the formal living room "…you have a piano."

"You play piano?" Harry looks surprised.

I laugh, giving Flint a quick glance. He's wearing his own smirk of amusement.

"Yes. I play a lot of instruments."

"Cool." Harry runs back up to his room.

"How long until dinner?" Flint looks at his watch.

"Forty-five minutes."

"I'm going to get a run in since I didn't get one this morning."

"Should I feel guilty about that?"

Harry jogs back downstairs with his guitar.

Flint winks before heading toward the stairs. "Yes, you should."

I WANT THIS life.

Playing music with Harry. Setting the dinner table for three. Seeing the look on his face when I tell him we're going to the new Spiderman movie after dinner.

We eat. Harry does his homework while Flint and I clean the kitchen, stealing sexy kisses, sharing flirty looks, and the smiles … I drown in every single one he gives me.

I want this life.

Harry plants himself in the middle at the movie. Flint rolls his eyes. I laugh. On the way home he recaps all the highlights, giving us a detailed account of the special effects.

"Bed," Flint says the second we walk in the door.

"But—"

"No buts, Harrison. Bed."

"Is Ellen staying?"

I can't read him. Is it a question of sheer curiosity or is he being challenging?

"No." I smile. "I have to tend to my babies, and I need to get some packing done."

"So no cookies tomorrow?"

Flint shakes his head, and I can't see his face, but I'm certain there's an eye roll accompanying it.

"There's six cookies left."

Harry frowns. It's so Flint.

"I'm out of here," I say on a laugh. The Hopkins boys can sort out their pouty ways without me here. "Goodnight, Harry." I wrap my arms around him, feeling him stiffen and then relax.

"Night," he mumbles.

Flint points to the stairs. "Bed."

"Okay … okay …"

I open the door and Flint follows me out, taking my hand in his. He backs me up to the driver's door of my car and envelopes me in his arms. He doesn't speak and neither do I. What could we possibly say? My life has consisted of unexpected, life-changing moments. The familiarity doesn't ease the pain, but I've learned that even when it hurts the most, something or someone comes along to take it away.

"Were you good at football?"

He chuckles, hugging me tighter. "Yes."

"I knew it."

"How many planes have you jumped out of?"

"Twenty-three."

He pulls back, giving me a questioning look.

I shrug. "Truth. It's an incredible feeling."

"Yet, you won't fly."

I shake my head. "Those twenty-three jumps were before my mom's plane crashed."

Flint nods slowly, brow drawn tight.

"I'm going to go feed my babies."

"Rats."

"Yes, my rat babies."

His hands move to my neck; they're strong, but his touch is tender as he slides them up to my face, pausing briefly to search my eyes before kissing me.

I … want … this … life …

"You're so beautiful," he whispers over my lips. "I want to be selfish with you …" He brushes his lips over mine again.

I grip his coat to steady myself.

"I…" he closes his eyes as if the pain is too great to bear "…don't deserve this." His lips ghost along my cheek, down my jaw to my ear. "But I want it so fucking bad."

I hold on, letting fate have its way.

Want.

Need.

They feed the pain. They fuel the anger. They also make us stronger when we're forced to let them go.

CHAPTER TWENTY-TWO

I CHECK IN on my dad and spend the rest of the morning packing with a little Rod Stewart singing about breaking hearts and wishing someone love. It's fitting.

"You'll like Cape Cod." I pet Mozart as he crawls through the mess on my bedroom floor and onto my lap. "Except Bungie. I'm not sure how this will go."

My phone chimes.

FLINT: *I have forty minutes for lunch. Free?*

ME: *It'll take me twenty minutes to meet you anywhere.*

FLINT: *I bet you can open your front door in under one minute.*

I set Mozart on the ground and jump up with a huge grin on my face as I weave my way through the mess to my door.

"Mr. Hopkins." I attempt to make a sexy pose. I'm not sure how sexy leggings and a bulky sweater with fuzzy socks can really be, but I'm working it.

"Ms. Rodgers." He takes two short steps before the door closes behind him and he pins me to the wall.

We turn into a flurry of hands ripping at clothes, deep kisses, playful bites, and soft moans.

Between labored breaths, I stab my hands through his hair as he licks and bites his way down my neck. "You didn't bring lunch, did you?"

"Elle ..." He hums in pleasure as his lips feather across the swell of my breasts. "*You* are lunch." Flint drops to his knees, taking my leggings and panties down with him.

My head thumps against the wall as my eyes roll back into my head.

Flint Hopkins can go all night or he can be incredibly efficient. Today he's redefining the quickie without sacrificing a bit of my pleasure—and without moving an inch past the wall adjacent to my front door. It's the crazy, spontaneous sex we should have had in his greenhouse, minus the stitches incident.

I want this life.

I want a man who can make it mean the world one minute and the next minute show me this living-in-the-moment passion that seeks nothing more than raw physical pleasure.

After he leaves me as nothing more than a pile of bones on my entry floor, Flint navigates his way into the bathroom to dispose of his condom.

"Fuck! Dammit!" He flies out of the hall bathroom with his shirt tucked halfway in and his pants still hanging open.

Perfectly ruffled. Just like I like him.

I slide on my panties and leggings, and pull on my sweater. "Let me guess ... Lady Gaga's by the sink." I grin. "Told ya she likes to watch."

Flint tucks the rest of his shirt into his pants, shaking his head. "I don't know how you live with rats."

"You make my babies sound like sewer rats from horror movies." I finish buttoning his shirt and tie his tie for him.

"Who's going to help dress me when you're gone?" He grins.

"I think we both know you do it better than anyone, but I'm sure you'll find some sexy woman who has a quiet and boring job and no pets. Harry won't like her the way he likes me, but she'll figure out that cookies get her into your bed. She'll probably buy them from a bakery because women who bake are a dying breed." I give his tie a final tug. "You have no idea how good you have it right now."

He pulls me into him, nuzzling his nose in my hair. "You're so very wrong."

"Can I get you real food?" I turn out of his hold, moving toward the fridge, anywhere to separate my heart from this long goodbye.

"I have to get back to work." He slips on his jacket.

"Work ..." I give him a stiff smile. "I need to figure that out for myself."

"Do you need money?"

I grunt a laugh. "No. I don't have any major living expenses there. At least for now."

"But if you do—"

I shake my head, knowing he's expecting me to call him.

"I have skills. I can get a job. I *want* to get a job as soon as I know my dad's doing a little better. Then we'll look for someone to care for him during the day while I work, and I can be with him in the evenings and weekends."

"Well ..." He gives me a sad smile.

"Dinner later?"

"Sure." A slow nod accompanies his sad smile.

I follow him to the door. "What's wrong?"

He opens the door and turns back to me. "Every day it's getting harder to pretend that you're not leaving indefinitely."

"It's a long goodbye."

He nods.

"Too long?"

"I…" he shakes his head "…don't know."

"It's one word. You can say it now. You can say it over the phone. You can text it." I swallow hard, trying to be strong for both of us. "Or you don't have to say it at all. It's okay to just … walk away. We've said all that has to be said, right?"

Flint

I COULD USE a drink. Ten years is a long time to feel the pain without one single thing to numb it. Have we said all there is to say? In a lifetime, will we say all there is to say?

"I won't say goodbye. And I won't walk away. But…" I clear my throat "…I'll watch you walk away."

Her blue eyes fill with tears.

"Dinner. I'll call you." I turn and go back to work because if I stay to watch her tears fall, I'll lose my fucking mind. As soon as I get in my car, I slam the palm of my hand against the steering wheel. "FUCK!" Leaning my head back, I close my eyes.

After a few minutes, I call Amanda to have her reschedule my appointments, and I find a meeting to attend. It's my first in over five years. It's hard to make sense of why the one thing that killed Heidi is the one thing I crave the most as I get ready to lose the woman I love in this present life.

"WHY ARE YOU picking me up?" Harrison asks as he gets in my car after school.

"Because you're my son."

He rolls his eyes.

Because I need to remember why I'm here. Because I need to remember why I'm doing this thing called life.

Five minutes from our house, he breaks the silence. "Simon's dad told Simon he's not getting married again. Are you going to marry Ellen?"

Maybe picking him up wasn't such a great idea.

"No."

"If you married her, would we have to move? I don't want to move."

"I'm not marrying Ellen."

"You're just having sex with her?"

"It's … complicated."

"The sex?"

"It's complicated because of the feelings. Do you really want to discuss feelings? I think that's your least favorite thing to talk about."

"But we're not moving? I don't want to move. My plants would die and so would yours."

"Ellen is moving. We are not moving."

Whisky neat. It was my go-to. But I never had an issue with beer if that's all that was available. I could drink a lot of beer. All the beer—I'd stop drinking when there was no more beer to drink. But I always had a stash of whisky at home to get me to where I needed to be to get to sleep.

"Hey, Ellen's here!" Harrison jumps out of the car before I get it completely stopped.

Why is she sitting on our porch steps, bundled up in a coat, hat, and gloves—with her guitar case?

Harrison runs around to the back door and opens it with his key. She waits on the front porch steps.

"Hey." She stands as I approach.

"Hi." Something is off. I can see it on her face. I can see it in the reddened rims of her eyes.

"You came to play?" Harrison opens the front door, grinning. I love that look that only Ellen Rodgers puts on his face.

"I did." She carries her case inside. "My guitar is cold. Will you take it upstairs and let it warm up a bit before we play?"

"Sure." Harrison takes her guitar.

"You're leaving early." I know it. I can *feel* it. It's a cloud of gloom over her.

"Tomorrow." Ellen draws in a shaky breath. "My dad fell this afternoon. He's fine, but Lori is pretty shook up because it was on her watch. So…" she takes in another slow breath, like it's all she can do to hold it together "…the moving truck is coming in the morning."

It's like I didn't go to that meeting. I want a drink so bad I can taste it in my veins.

"I wanted to play guitar with Harry one more time."

I nod, jaw clenched.

"I wanted to see you." She bites her quivering lower lip.

If I hug her, it changes nothing. If I tell her it's all going to be okay, it's a lie. If I beg her to stay, she'll leave. But if I take a drink … the pain will go away.

"I'll make dinner. Go play."

Her brow wrinkles in pain as she nods slowly before climbing the stairs to Harrison's room. I busy myself with dinner, waiting for the pain to become self-numbing the way I've had to rely on it to do for over a decade. This is my penance. This is my sentence. This is the life I chose.

A life for a life.

Harrison dominates the dinner conversation with a summary of his latest podcast on futuristic airplanes. I nod on instinct to acknowledge him, but I don't really register a word he's said. Making the occasional glance at Ellen, I'm certain she's not focusing on him either.

"Bed," I say after he's done with his story and his meal.

"It's only eight."

"Harrison ..."

He sighs.

Ellen stands. "Give me a hug. I'm leaving tomorrow."

"Where are you going?" he asks.

She smiles as I watch her eyes fill with tears. "Cape Cod."

"Oh, duh." He gives her a sheepish grin. "I knew that."

Ellen hugs him, and after a few seconds he hugs her back.

Whisky. Beer. Vodka. It doesn't matter. Anything will do at this point. I stand and grab the dirty dishes. I can't watch this. As I walk off, I hear her sob.

"Why are you crying?" Harrison asks.

She clears her throat. "I'm just ... going to miss you."

"Okay."

Okay. God ... for just one time in my life I wish I could emotionally detach myself like he can.

"Night." He goes to bed. No emotion. No tears. No regret. No *pain.*

I set the dishes in the sink. *Fuck.* I hate this.

I hear her sniffle behind me.

"Now." My pulse makes it hard to hear anything but the rush of blood through my heart. "Walk away now. Don't say anything. I ..." I grit my teeth to keep my shit together. "I lied. I don't want to *watch* you walk away."

"Flint ..."

"Go." I rest my hands on the edge of the counter and bow

my head.

Her chest presses to my back as she caresses my arm, stopping at my hand. Her fingers interlace with mine against the edge of the counter.

"Go ... please ..." My words are barely a whisper. It's all I have left.

"I lied too." She ducks under my arm and wedges herself between me and the counter, the same way she wedged her way into my life, my heart—my soul. "I need more than a goodbye."

Ellen

TEARS.

Flint Hopkins has tears bleeding down his face *for me*. The muscles in his jaw tick, and his eyes redden behind the leaky emotions. My hand inches to his face; my fingers touch the wetness on his cheeks as if I need proof that they're real.

Alex never cried for me, at least not that I ever saw. Not when my mom died. Not when I cried for the loss of his friend and his hands. Not when he ended our marriage.

I rub my wet fingertips together, still in disbelief that I matter so deeply to any man other than my father. "I want this life," I whisper. "I want you." Every piece of what gives me life feels like it's slowly dying.

"But ..." He hunches his back more until his cheek rests on the top of my head.

I rest my palms against his chest. "But ..." My eyes close.

But humans take on many forms of love, and right now my

father needs the love of his only daughter, just like Harrison needs his father's love. This just isn't our time.

But I can't make sense of it to my heart or Flint's. It just hurts.

When my gaze meets his, there's no need to say anything.

He knows.

I know.

So we say goodbye over the next few hours. It's the most painful missed opportunity. It's like trying to breathe but there's no oxygen. I will forever wear his touch on my skin as a reminder of the life I want.

In the early morning, when his breathing evens out and his hold on me relaxes, I slide out of bed before the sun and before Harrison awakes—in silence and darkness—like I was never here at all.

"I love you," I mouth, standing in the doorway to Flint's bedroom as he sleeps. "Goodbye."

I walk away, leaving him blind to my departure and deaf to my last goodbye.

Hours later, after the sun brings forth a new day, there's no call, no text. He's letting me go—as if he has a choice. As soon as the movers arrive, I give them instructions and turn in my keys to my landlord. My rats and I are on the road to Cape Cod before ten in the morning.

Someday I'm going to get to live my happily ever after. No more packing up and driving away from the man that I love. Everyone has their time. I will find mine.

CHAPTER TWENTY-THREE

Flint

"YOU LOOK LIKE hell," Amanda greets me.

"Thank you."

"It's four days until Christmas. I thought you'd have your holiday spirit by now."

I take off my overcoat and hang it on the coat tree in the corner of my office. "Nope."

"Cage called here this morning. He said you're not returning his messages. He's worried about you. I'm worried about you. When you start to ignore your only friend, it's a bit concerning."

I grunt, taking a seat and turning on my computer. "Why does everyone think Cage is my only friend? And is there a spot on my tie? Spinach between my teeth? What exactly makes me look so hellish this morning?"

Amanda turns her back to me, pounding away at the keyboard to her computer. "It's the bags under your eyes and the deepening lines on your forehead from wearing a constant scowl. Are you drinking?"

"Amanda." I snap at her with more of an edge to my voice than I intended to do.

She shrugs, still with her back to me. "I'm asking for a

friend. And that's not code. I'm literally asking for a friend—your friend. Oh … and your parents will be here tomorrow. They called me too. Did you lose your phone? And your mom said she'd call and invite Sandy since she knew you would not."

My parents and my mother-in-law. Happy fucking holidays to me.

"Can I say something as your friend?" She turns in her chair.

I glance up. "How can we be friends if I only have one friend?"

Amanda smirks. "Why don't you call her or go see her?"

"Am I supposed to know to whom you are referring?"

"I bet *Elle* would love to see you. Take Harrison to New York or Boston for New Years and then drop in to see her."

"What would be the point?" I return my attention to my computer.

"Spreading holiday cheer."

Ellen walked out a week before Thanksgiving. We haven't made any sort of contact since then. A clean break. That's what it had to be. It's like marking off days on a calendar of Ellen sobriety. I can't see her and start the whole fucking process again.

"I think I'll be plenty busy spreading holiday cheer right here."

She snorts a laugh. "Okay, Boss."

AFTER PICKING UP Harrison from school, we get groceries and head home.

"Grab the mail," I tell Harrison, pulling up next to our mailbox before pulling into the driveway.

He retrieves the wad of envelopes and advertisements, plopping them onto his lap. "Look! Elle sent me a postcard."

I glance over, sure enough, it's addressed to Harry Hopkins.

Happy Holidays! I hope you're playing lots of music this season. We miss you like crazy!

~Elle, Beethoven, Bach, Chopin, Mozart, & Lady Gaga

HE FLIPS THE postcard over. "Ha! Look at this."

It's a photo of her and her rats and they're all wearing Santa hats. She looks happy. Good for her. I swallow the fucking razor blade in my throat and pull into the garage.

"I'm going to video message her." Harrison hops out of the car, leaving a scattered mess of mail on the seat.

I change my clothes and head out to my greenhouse to make sure the temperature is staying steady. When I come back inside, Harrison's at the kitchen table eating an apple and talking to the screen of his iPad.

"Man, I can't believe you've had so much snow already. It's just cold as crap here."

I shoot him a frown for his language.

He rolls his eyes. "Sorry. It's cold as crud here. My dad just came inside and he's giving me his pissed off look because I said crap."

I wash my hands and shake my head. This kid …

"Wanna say hi to him?"

My body stiffens.

"Um … sure."

It's the first time I've heard her voice in over a month. I don't know if I can see her too.

"Look out her window. See all the snow?" Harrison brings

his iPad over, giving me no choice but to see all the snow. But all I see is her and how fucking beautiful she looks cuddled in a chair, wearing leggings and a sweatshirt, auburn hair covering her neck and chest like a scarf—and those blue eyes.

"Lot of snow," I say.

She smiles and speaks softly, "Hey, Flint."

I try to smile back, but it's hard to do.

"Happy holidays."

I nod, still searching for something to pass off as a smile.

Before I can find anything to add to my "lot of snow" comment, like, "How is your dad?" Harrison takes off with his iPad. "He hates the holidays."

"That's too bad. I love the holidays."

Of course she does. People who hum and sing all day have to love the holidays. Just like Amanda, who says fantastic all the time—holiday lover.

"I get three weeks off for break."

"That's awesome. What are you going to do?"

"Nothing. We never do anything."

He makes me sound like such a great dad. Do-nothing scrooge.

Ellen chuckles. "I'm not doing much either so don't feel too bad. But I have to go get dinner started. My grandparents went home a few weeks ago, so now I'm in charge of the meals."

"Okay. Bye." He disconnects before she says another word.

I sip my iced coffee and shake my head at him.

"What?"

"It's polite to wait until the person on the other end of the line has a chance to say goodbye too before you cut them off."

He shrugs. "Whatever."

Ellen

MY DAD GIVES me a questioning glance. His speech is still impaired, so I rely on looks and his nifty whiteboard. In the past two weeks his motor control over his right hand has improved enough to write me messages.

I grin as he reaches for his whiteboard.

"It was Harrison. I sent him a holiday card, and he just got it today."

And his dad?

"Flint. What about him?"

My dad frowns as if I should know exactly what he's asking me.

When are you going home?

"This is home. I told you."

He pushes the white rag over the board to erase his words and write new ones.

Do you love him?

"I love you." I get out of the chair and bend over, kissing him on the head.

He reaches a shaky hand for my wrist.

I sigh. This is not a conversation worth having right now.

He scribbles more words.

I don't want to be your job. A burden.

"I've already started looking for someone to take you to your appointments during the day. And I have new business cards ordered. I'm going to make house calls. What do you think about that?"

Do you love him?

"I'm not leaving you. That would mean putting you in a care facility. You won't get better there. That's where old people go to die. You're not even sixty yet."

He holds up the whiteboard again.

I sigh. "Do I love him? Yes. And I love you and my rat babies and chocolate. I've got a lot of love to give. You know what else I love? Tacos. So I'm going to make tacos for dinner."

"El … len …"

I stop, halfway to the kitchen. It still frustrates the hell out of him to try to talk. Speech therapy is his least favorite part of the day, so when he does attempt to talk, I know it's something very important to him.

Turning around, I kneel beside his chair, giving him my full attention as his hand scribbles and scribbles.

Tell him to wait for you. I'm going to get better for YOU. If you love him, don't let him get away.

I can't ask Flint to wait indefinitely for me. I won't give him false hope. "I know you're going to get better. I've made sure you have the best therapists helping you. But you won't get better if I abandon you. If I'm meant to be with Flint then …" I shrug.

Then what?

"Besides, when did you become a Flint fan? I thought you were still holding onto your far-fetched dream of Alex and me reconciling."

He erases his writing and pulls the cap off his marker.

Ron said Alex treated you badly.

I never told my father just how badly Alex treated me. It was my need to protect Alex in spite of everything he said to me, and I wanted to protect my dad too. He and Alex's dad, Ron, have been friends for many years.

I give my dad a painful smile. He wipes the board and writes again.

Don't lie to me.

"Yes. Alex said a lot of things that weren't nice. I knew it was the pain and anger talking, but ... I saw no end in sight, and he wanted me to leave. He wanted a divorce."

You deserve better.

I nod. "I do."

Don't let "better" go.

I laugh. "When you ditch the dry erase board and climb the stairs unassisted without falling, we'll talk about my love life. I'm young and incredibly good looking like my mom was." I wink at him and he grins. "So there's no need for me to tag a man like a Christmas tree. If he's here when I'm ready, then we're meant to be. If not, I'll find another one."

Another frown from my dad, but I'm fine with his frowns. It takes more facial muscles to frown than to smile, so if I upset him, it's good exercise for some of those injured nerves.

He draws a Z-shaped Christmas tree.

There are more good trees than there are good men.

I laugh. "True. I won't argue with you there."

CHAPTER TWENTY-FOUR

Flint

"RATS!" HARRISON PULLS the red bow and white blanket off the cage.

"What in God's name …" Heidi's mom, Sandy, covers her mouth with her hand.

"They're rats, Grandma. Just like Ellen has."

"Who's Ellen?"

"I told you she gave me the guitar and parachuted. She also had sex with Dad and she bakes the best chocolate chip cookies ever."

My parents cringe as Harrison spews off random facts about Ellen like it's her résumé. Sandy doesn't look too happy. I have this feeling Harrison probably mentioned the guitar and maybe the skydiving, but the sex is news to her—and not the good kind of news.

"Are they male or female?" Harrison asks.

"A word, Flint?" Sandy stands.

"Here, buddy." My dad gets on the floor by the tree with Harrison to give him the rat information.

I follow Sandy into my office.

"The only reason I gave you custody of Harrison was because I thought you were ready to be a mature father, but—"

"Whoa! *Gave* me custody? The reason I finished getting my law degree was to get him back without you airing my dirty laundry to the whole damn world. I fought for him. You did not *give* anything to me."

She steps closer, holding up her finger. "I made you fight for him to prove you had what it took. I needed to know you were in it for the long haul. I needed to know you weren't going to give up on your son, who not only needs a father but someone who can help him with his special needs—the way his *mother* would have done."

Sandy's biggest regret has always been my saving grace, even if it's all fucked-up. She encouraged Heidi to trust my judgment that night. She should not have. It's her guilt that kept me out of prison. She could have insisted they check my blood alcohol level right after the accident, but she didn't. Shock, grief, and guilt kept her from saying anything to anyone. In the meantime, the alcohol cleared my system while paramedics focused on my son and my wife.

The accident left me unscathed on the outside but dead on the inside.

She filed for custody after we buried Heidi. It was too late to prove that my alcoholism caused the accident, but it wasn't too late to save her grandson from any more grief.

I didn't even fight her; I let her take him because I was fucked-up in every way possible.

"Harrison says everything out of context. You know that."

"So you didn't have sex with this Ellen person?"

"My sex life is none of your business."

"Maybe not, but my grandson talking like he lives in a brothel is certainly my business."

"A brothel? Really?" I try not to chuckle.

"Did you tell him you had sex with this woman or did he *see* you having sex with her?"

I sigh, rubbing the back of my neck. "Her name is Ellen, not 'this woman,' and I'm not going to discuss this with you. He's *my* son. *My* responsibility. I will raise him as I see fit."

"Are you drinking again?"

"Jesus, Sandy …"

"When's the last time you were at a meeting?"

"What does it matter?"

"My daughter is dead. Whether you like it or not, I'm her voice. So you can answer my question or I can get an attorney."

"Then get an attorney."

"You killed her." Her voice breaks.

I flinch. I will never dispute that fact.

"You can't just replace her in his life."

"I'm not replacing her."

"Six years. Just wait until he's an adult. Can you do that? Can you show a little gratitude and do this for him? Can you just let him be your priority? Can you forego your physical needs and just be a dad?"

Her words are my words. They've been my thoughts of self-deprecation since Heidi died. Ellen changed that, but that doesn't matter now either. She's no longer in the picture.

"Yes."

Sandy blows out a slow breath. "Thank you." She turns and walks away.

It's hard to resent Ellen leaving me when, had she stayed, it might have caused some real problems between Sandy and me. Still, I miss her every damn day.

"Ellen, look at my rats!"

Sandy gives me a hard look as Harrison video chats with

Ellen, like I have any control over it. I give her a shrug and head to the kitchen to avoid all things Sandy and all things Ellen.

"You did good, Son." My dad pats me on the shoulder.

"How so?" I load the breakfast dishes into the dishwasher.

"The rats."

"Don't be too proud too quickly. After today, he's going to find out that they will be kept in his room and banned from every other room in the house or they're gone."

"Fair enough." Dad leans in and whispers, "They're fucking creepy."

I chuckle. "Told you."

"Everything good with Sandy?"

"Yup."

"Don't let her guilt you out of having a life beyond Harrison."

"I do that just fine on my own, Dad."

"Did you say hi to Ellen? She looks stunning today."

She looks stunning every day. "Nope."

"You should pack up the kid and go get the girl."

I grunt a laugh. "Great idea. Pack up the kid who made me promise him we would not move. And go get the girl after I just promised Sandy I'd live a celibate life for the next six years. I want to be you when I grow up, Dad. Don't think. Just do. You live in a 'fantastic' world."

"Thinking is what people do when they're not following their dreams."

"I'll stop thinking and start dreaming in six years."

"She'll be married with two kids by then." My dad fills the sink with hot soapy water. My mom has taught him well.

"Lucky for me, she's not the last female on the face of the

planet."

"Your mom and I can talk with Sandy."

I shut the dishwasher door. "Dad, let it go. The truth is, her leaving was for the best. As much as I thought for a brief moment that she could fit into our lives, the truth is it would have been extremely difficult, and I fear it would have ended in disaster."

"Wanna say Merry Christmas to Ellen?"

Dad and I turn to the iPad in Harrison's hands. *Shit.* She heard us. I can tell from the look on her face.

"Merry Christmas, Ellen." My dad smiles at her. He has no idea how well that thing picks up sound, but I do.

She forces a smile that shoves a knife straight through my heart. "Thanks, Gene."

"Merry Christmas," I say.

She barely nods at me before diverting her gaze to something else in the room around her. Technology sucks. And I'm an asshole.

Harrison runs off again.

I do the dishes with my dad, pick up the wrapping paper disaster in the family room, and escape to my office for some privacy while Harrison plays with his rats and other Christmas presents. My parents and Sandy take mid-morning naps.

After debating what good can come of calling Ellen to apologize—and deciding that nothing good can come of it—I call her anyway because all I hear in my head is her voice.

"I'm going to love you so hard, time won't matter ... distance won't matter ... all you'll feel when you take each breath ... is my love."

"Hey," she answers.

"Hi. I ... uh ... wanted to say sorry for what you heard."

"What makes you think I heard anything?"

"Ellen ..."

"It's doesn't matter. I know those words weren't meant for me. I get it."

"I didn't mean—"

She laughs. It sounds painful. "You meant it."

"I just meant ... I didn't mean anything unkind. I was just explaining ..."

"Life," she whispers. "I know."

"I don't regret anything."

"Well..." she chuckles "...we'll see about that."

"I don't." It kills me that she doesn't believe me.

"With two words, I'm going to make you regret ever meeting me."

"Elle, I won't ever regret—"

"I'm pregnant."

What?

Leaning back in my chair, I run a hand through my hair, fisting it hard to make sure I'm awake and not dreaming or hallucinating. She didn't say that. No. This can't be ... "We used—"

"Not every time."

Closing my eyes, I rub my temples. We didn't use condoms every time. There were a few times at my house—in my bed— that I simply woke up and needed to be inside of her. She blinked her tired eyes open and kissed me. Not once did she question the lack of a condom—she just moved her body slowly with mine.

"Not every time ..." I whisper.

"I wasn't going to share this today, but you called me, and then you tried to convince me that you regret nothing and ...

well … it was too much to bear. Don't let it ruin your day. I mean, I've been vomiting for the past forty-eight hours, but really, you just enjoy the holidays with your family and we'll discuss it later."

I flinch. My brain feels sluggish. It's hard to really process this. Ellen is pregnant—with my child.

"I'll fix this."

"Fix this? Really?"

I shake my head. "I mean, I'll figure this out."

"Ha! Wow … okay then. Here's the issue with that mentality, I'm not broken nor am I a puzzle you need to figure out. I'm pregnant. Period."

I sit up, resting my elbows on the desk. "You'll move back here."

"I'm not leaving my dad. You move here."

"I can't. I have my practice and there's no way Harrison will move. Move your dad here."

"So, because we were irresponsible, I have to pack up my dad in his impaired condition and move him away from his house, his parents, his doctors and therapists, his *life*? Sure, that sounds fair … oh … no … not again …" her voice mumbles.

"Ellen?"

I hear gagging and coughing and then a toilet flush.

"Shit," I whisper.

Water runs, probably from the sink. "I need to go lie down."

"Ellen …"

"Merry Christmas, Flint." She ends the call.

"THOUGHT YOU WERE dead." Cage, my "only" friend, answers

his phone.

"Might as well be."

"Drinking again?"

"No. But it's tempting. Merry Christmas."

Cage chuckles. "Thanks. You too."

"Can we do all the catching up, how's-the-family stuff later? I'm in a predicament."

"This is new, you coming to me. It must be really bad."

"A sperm got away from me."

He laughs. "Oh shit. A baby?"

"Yes, I knocked a woman up, but I'm not banging on my chest about it."

He laughs.

"It's not funny, man."

"No. I'm sure it's not to you. I was just going to say welcome to my world."

"I'd take your world over mine any day of the week and twice on Sunday."

"Harrison is a great kid."

I nod. "He is. You should hear him play the guitar. If he weren't so socially awkward, he'd sell out stadiums."

"Yeah, well ... playing to big crowds is overrated."

"That's bullshit and you know it."

"So the baby mama, was this a one-night stand."

"No."

"So what's the problem? Put a ring on her finger and sit back and enjoy the ride."

"We're not a geographic match. Circumstances have her on the East Coast where she can't leave, and I have my whole life here. Harrison made me promise we wouldn't move."

"You're coddling him. My dad never coddled me. I advise

against it."

"I'm not coddling him. He just doesn't adapt like other kids."

"Does he like this woman?"

"Ellen. Her name is Ellen."

"Aw … you do like her. You give a shit that she has a name."

"Shut up … fucker. And yes, he likes her. But as *his* friend. Not as mine. She plays guitar with him. But I'm quite certain he will not like her popping out a baby that's his half-brother or sister."

"Again, you're coddling him. I get it. He's autistic. He reacts and adapts differently, but you have to let him deal with life. You can't protect him from reality. And the realty is … you and *Ellen* are having a baby."

"Thanks for the advice. I think. Give hugs to your big-ass Monaghan clan."

"I'll do that. And Flint?"

"Yeah?"

"Congratulations."

I shake my head and disconnect the call.

CHAPTER TWENTY-FIVE

Ellen

AFTER VOMITING SIX times in one day, I start to lose my mind. I can't do this. Pregnancy hormones are the devil. I'm six weeks pregnant at most. I can't do this. My throat is raw. Every muscle in my stomach aches like I've been doing nonstop crunches. And I'm tired. So. Very. Tired.

"We'll stay a bit longer until you get to feeling better, honey," my grandma says, handing me a mug of ginger tea.

"Thank you." I curl up on the sofa with my tea.

My dad studies me, but he doesn't try to say anything or pick up his whiteboard. However, he has that look. It's the same look he used to give me when I did something wrong as a child. He rarely had to say anything; he knew if he gave me "the look" long enough, I'd fall apart in a desperate confession of all my wrong doings.

"Do you want some tea too, Dad?"

He shakes his head.

I wish he'd stop studying me.

"Tomorrow night is New Year's Eve. You should go out. Be young. Have fun." My grandma smiles.

I'm green with oily hair. There might be some vomit in my hair as well. There's over eight new inches of snow on the ground, and I haven't lived here for years. But ... bless her heart for thinking I might have some grand New Year's Eve plans.

"I think I'll save young and fun for next year. But thanks, Grandma." I sip my tea, praying it stays down.

"Your grandpa saw Ron yesterday. Alex is home for the holidays. They might stop by later today."

My dad makes a noise like he's trying to speak, but it sends him into a coughing fit instead. After he gets past it, he scribbles on his whiteboard.

He owes you an apology.

Apology or not, I don't want to see him. Not like this.

"I don't know if today is a good day to visit. I'm not feeling well. I'd hate for anyone else to get sick."

"I'm sure they won't stay long, dear. If you're not feeling well, just stay in your room. But Alex was your husband. I can't imagine him not wanting to see you. Surely he's seen you ill before."

Ill? Yes. Pregnant? No.

As a new wave of nausea hits, I set down my tea and sprint to the upstairs bathroom. A little bit of tea mixed with bile is all that comes up. Lovely. After a quick rinse of my mouth, I make my way to the bedroom and collapse onto the bed. I grab my phone and type out a text of pure raging hormones.

ME: *I hate you and this demon you put inside of me.*

A few seconds later, my phone chimes.

FLINT: *How are you?*
ME: *Fuck you.*

FLINT: *What do you need?*

I laugh. What do I need? Really?

ME: *To not be pregnant and sick.*

FLINT: *Do you mean that?*

Tears sting my eyes. Yes and no. This wasn't how I imagined my first pregnancy. I shouldn't have texted him. Feeling shitty makes it hard to think straight. I bring up my favorite classical playlist and close my eyes, praying for peace, praying for sleep.

"HEY ..."

I turn my head. It's a good dream. I'm not sick.

"Hey ... Elle ..." The voice is distant, yet familiar. I haven't heard it in my dreams for a while.

The exhaustion hasn't left my body, but I pry open my eyes anyway.

Blink. Blink. Blink.

"Heard you weren't feeling well."

I scoot myself to a sitting position. "Alex ..." My eyes go straight to his robotic-looking hands attached to his forearms and three remaining fingers.

"Pretty cool, huh?" He holds them up and wiggles the robotic fingers.

Pretty cool. Look at my new fingers. Let me mesmerize you with them so you don't think about all the terrible things I said to you and all the awful names I called you.

"Alex ..." I don't even know what to say.

He looks at me like he did before he lost his hands. It's as if those two years of hell never happened. The grudge I hold is tangible. It's a living, breathing part of who I am. And I know this anger only survives because I still love him. The memories I have of the boy I fell in love with fifteen years ago have not faded one bit. I remember the love. It was real. We were real.

The love.

The exciting life.

The heartbreak.

The tragedy.

"I'm sorry," he says, resting his hand on my leg. It's the first time he's touched me since he lost his hands.

He did the unforgivable and said the unthinkable. He broke me from the inside out and left me to pick up the pieces on my own. I'm not sure I even got all the pieces. Since that day, I've felt emotionally wrecked with uncleaned wounds and safety pins holding together my tattered heart.

Can all of that be forgiven with a simple "I'm sorry?"

"I'm going to be sick …" I leap off the bed and dash to the toilet.

There's nothing more than a trickle of bile to burn my throat, just dry heaves racking my stomach. Even my ribs hurt. I flinch at the feel of something in my hair. It's Alex's hands pulling my hair out of my face. It feels like I've waited a lifetime for his touch. The day he lost part of his hands, I knew I'd love him no matter what. I knew I'd welcome the new and forever cherish what was left of the old. But he never gave me that chance.

"Stomach flu or food poisoning?" he asks, sitting on the floor behind me, pulling me onto his lap. It's so tender. This is not the man who called me a needy cunt and threw my belongings in the yard. This is not the man who told me we died when he lost his everything. Funny … I thought I was his everything. Perspective is a sneaky little bitch.

I sigh, leaning into the familiar curves of his body. "Can you keep a secret?"

Alex chuckles a little. He used to ask me that before feeding me some exciting tidbit of information about his next big adventure or our next big adventure. We both knew I couldn't keep a secret.

"Yeah, I think I'm the only one of us who can keep a secret."

This isn't revenge, or vindictiveness, or even Karma. It's just my inability to lie to this man. Even when I should have lied to protect myself, I didn't—I couldn't. I still can't.

"I'm pregnant."

His hold on me stiffens. "Jesus ..."

"Yep." I pull away, stand, and rinse out my mouth.

Alex lumbers to his feet behind me. I look at his reflection in the bathroom mirror. He's still handsome, maybe even more so than when I last saw him. That blond surfer hair has always suited him. Tan skin. Deep sapphire eyes. He's beautiful.

"The father?"

I shrug. "It's complicated."

"That's code for he's not in the picture."

Brushing past him to the stairs, I shake my head. "No. It's not code for anything. It's just complicated."

He grabs my arm.

I whip around and narrow my eyes at his hold on me. "Let go of me," I whisper with an edge to my tone.

He releases me.

"You don't get to touch me now. Never again."

Alex holds up his new hands. "I *couldn't* touch you before. I would have, but I couldn't."

"You didn't lose all of your hands. You didn't lose your arms, your legs, your lips ... your *dick*. You sure as hell could have touched me had you *wanted* to touch me. But you didn't want to. And that's fine. I tried to put myself in your shoes. I tried to understand how you might feel like less of a man. But you wouldn't even let *me* touch *you*. And the worst part? For someone without use of their hands, you sure used me like a punching bag. Jab after jab until I was knocked out on my ass in our front yard."

He flinches. "I wasn't in a good place then, but I'm better now. I've tried calling you. I thought we could talk."

I laugh. "Good for you. I hope this 'better place' suits you, but we have nothing to talk about." I turn, making my way down the stairs.

"Ellen." Ron hugs me. "Sorry to hear you're not feeling well."

"Thank you." I pull back and fight for a smile that is one hundred percent not how I feel on the inside.

Ron eyes Alex. "You two talk?"

Alex nods, giving me a concerned look. He used to tell me, "Don't worry, Elle, I've got your back."

I think he's trying to figure out a way to have my back. He's not the man I want having my back anymore. My gaze gets stuck on his lips, the ones I've kissed so many times, but now all I can think about is the venom he spewed from them. I'm the better person, like my mom was always the better person.

On good days, I convince myself that I've forgiven Alex, but I won't ever forget, no matter how much I want to let every terrible moment vanish from my memory. They're there—painfully branded—a permanent mark.

"Ginger ale?" My grandma hands me a small glass.

"Thank you." I take it and sit in the chair next to my dad's recliner.

His inspection of me intensifies. I smile to let him know everything is fine. Even if it's not. I have to believe it will be.

"Alex is going to get back into climbing," Ron says.

My dad frowns. I reach over and squeeze his hand. He glances at me. I love how protective he is of me. It's the same reason I'm here, protecting him, making sure he's cared for and loved. That's just what family should do.

"Really?" My grandpa's bushy eyebrows jump up his forehead. "Is that possible with those kind of hands?"

Alex nods. "Yeah. Actually, if I were competing, some would say it gives me an unfair advantage. But I'm not competing. I'm just doing it because it's what I love." His attention turns to me for a brief moment.

I smile. He doesn't. That pained look lined into his forehead remains. He can be sorry and drown in regret and I can forgive him, but we're forever broken.

"He has some sponsors, so he'll get his travel and gear paid for," Ron adds.

Maybe it's a blessing at the moment that my dad can't say too much. I feel his conflict. Ron is his friend, but he can't look past what he now knows about Alex. That saddens me.

I hope I never have to deal with the physical loss Alex had. But if I ever do, I hope I can navigate it with a little more love and understanding of the people around me. That uncertainty is what prevents me from truly hating him. Destruction of self-esteem poisons everyone around you. It happened to Alex, and I think it happened to Flint to some degree. So even if I can't say the words aloud yet, I want to forgive Alex.

LATE THE NEXT morning I wake up feeling like death—I'm so weak. I can't even drag my ass out of bed. I fear I'm dehydrated. If I feel the need to vomit, it's going to land on the floor. It might be time to tell my father and my grandparents the truth. I'm supposed to be the caregiver, but I can't take my dad to his appointments, and I can't ask my grandparents to drive him, especially not in this snowy weather.

Coffee. Yuck! They're making coffee downstairs. The morning aroma I've loved for so long is now the odor that turns my stomach. The doorbell rings.

"Great …" I curl onto my side, hugging my stomach.

Alex said he would check on me today. I don't want him seeing me like this. I don't want his help. But I think I *need* it. The next thing I choke on will be my pride, but I'll swallow past it because I'm not a one-woman show anymore. I'm also responsible for the baby demon inside of me.

Even the chatter is nauseating. My grandma laughs about something, and my grandpa says the words "upstairs." Footsteps approach. I pull the blankets over my head. It's been two days since I've had a shower and I've given up on brushing my teeth. I'm a mess. There's no other way to say it.

But Alex needed help bathing and wiping his ass. I suppose this is fair.

"I smell worse than I feel. And I feel like death," I say when I hear the footsteps stop at my door.

They continue and the bed dips. This is so embarrassing. I want to stay hidden under these covers forever.

"Doctor, if you need anything, a thermometer, water, cold compresses, just let us know," my grandma calls up from downstairs.

I furrow my brow. *Doctor?* Inching the covers down like I'm scared of the boogieman, I peek to see the *doctor.* "Oh my god …" I whisper.

"God, doctor, whatever you need me to be for you," Flint grins.

I reach out a shaky hand, as if I need to make sure he's real. He snakes an arm around my back and brings me to sitting. I wrap my arms around him. If I weren't so dehydrated, there would be some serious tears.

"Are you taking good care of my baby and its mommy?"

I cough out a small sob, hugging him tighter. "No." It's the truth. Clearly he can see things are not going well.

"My baby and its mommy." My heart may explode.

"That's what I was afraid of." He pulls back to look at me.

Ugh. The view is not good. I can feel it.

"Why are you here?"

He smiles, pushing my gross, matted hair out of my face. "Elle…" he leans in, pressing a kiss to my forehead as his hand cups the back of my neck "…you know why I'm here."

"I smell."

With his lips still pressed to my forehead, he chuckles. "Perhaps."

"I need a shower, but I'm too weak."

"That's why Dr. Hopkins is here." He stands, shrugging off his suit jacket.

"You're wearing a suit?"

He loosens his tie. "I had to look the part."

As crappy as I feel, I can't help but smile. Dang! My teeth are fuzzy. So gross.

"Give me a sec …" He goes across the hall into the bathroom and starts the water.

I ease my legs over the edge of the bed, grimacing at the mix of nausea and lightheadedness overtaking my body.

"Where do you think you're going?" He kneels on the floor in front of me and unzips a bag that bears resemblance to an old leather doctor's bag.

"Not far," I murmur.

"Open." He holds out a dropper.

I shake my head.

"Open," he says with a bit more authority.

"I will vomit it right back up on you."

"I'll take my chances. Now open."

I open with a half cringe.

Yuck! "Nasty!"

He smirks. Screwing the dropper lid back onto the bottle. "Yes. Now drink." He hands me a bottle of some sort of liquid.

My nose wrinkles again.

He sighs. "Just do what I say, okay?"

I'm not vomiting *yet*, so I drink the liquid. It's like a flavored water. Not terrible.

Flint pulls up his shirt sleeve and glances at his watch. "Another dropper full in twenty minutes." He stands and unbuttons his white shirt.

I stare at his bare torso.

He grins. "See, feeling better already."

My gaze shoots up to his. He winks. Arrogant ass.

He neatly lays his shirt on the bed and unfastens his pants.

My gaze goes from his to the door. "What are you doing?"

"Stripping. I'm not bathing you while wearing a wool suit."

"The door is open, what are you—"

"I'm not too worried about the two elderly people downstairs who took fifteen minutes to get to the door, or your father in his physically impaired state. Nice guy, by the way. He already complimented my suit."

"He wrote nice suit on his whiteboard?"

"No." He pulls off his briefs too.

Well, damn …

"He said, 'Nice suit.' It was a little choppy, but that's what he said." Flint grabs the hem to my shirt and pulls it off. "Arms around my neck, baby."

Baby?

I lean forward and wrap my arms around his neck. He lifts my ass just enough to slide off my pajama bottoms and panties. With one easy motion, he picks me up and carries me to the bathroom, kicking the door shut behind us.

"Toilet?"

I shake my head.

He eases me to standing and gives me a frown. "You're way too dehydrated."

I nod.

Flint shuts off the water and steps into the bathtub. Then he helps me in before sitting down and guiding me to sit between his legs with my back to his chest. He wastes no time before washing my hair. His fingers massaging my scalp feel incredible. I'm pretty sure I hum an entire symphony.

After he gently and thoroughly washes me from head to toe, he leans back and folds me in his arms with his right hand splayed over my tummy. It covers my whole abdomen right now. "I want you." He kisses my head.

I blink my eyes open, but I don't respond.

"And I want this baby." He kisses my head again.

I slide my hand over his and interlace our fingers. I don't know how this will ever work out without huge sacrifices, but I refuse to worry about it in this moment—a moment that feels so perfect until the bathroom door opens.

"Ellen? Oh!" My grandma jumps, her hand covering her heart.

I hope it's still beating.

"Dr. Hopkins ... well, I ... I just wanted to see how things were going."

I cringe, biting my lower lip, but Flint doesn't even flinch, not one single muscle of his flexes a centimeter.

"We're just finishing up a round of hydrotherapy. We'll be out in a few minutes. If you wouldn't mind, Ellen could use some broth soup if you have any."

"Hydrotherapy ..." She nods slowly. "Broth soup ... yes, I can do that."

"Thank you."

She eases the door shut.

I let go of his hand and slide my entire body under the water because ... Kill. Me. Now. He grabs my arms and pulls me up again, handing me a towel to wipe my face.

"The *most* embarrassing moment of my life."

Flint chuckles. "I thought it went quite well."

CHAPTER TWENTY-SIX

Flint

"I THINK BRUSHING your teeth three times is enough."

Leaned against the doorway to the bathroom, I watch Ellen spit out a wad of foam, gagging a bit each time. Something tells me blowjobs will be out of the picture for a long time. It's pathetic my mind even goes there, but it does.

"Never underestimate the power of clean teeth." She sets her toothbrush by the sink and turns toward me. "I'm weak, but I don't feel like vomiting. That's good, right?"

I smile, pulling her into my chest. "Never underestimate the power of herbs. But we need to get some food in you. We'll start with broth."

She grabs my tie as I start to step into the hallway. I've missed her hands on me like this. "Where's Harrison?"

"New York with my parents. They're going to watch the ball drop tonight."

She lights up, still pale as a fucking ghost, but her eyes have some sparkle. "Do they know?"

Sucking my lower lip between my teeth, I shake my head. "I haven't figured out the logistics of this yet. I'm still trying to figure out how to bring another child into my life without sacrificing the relationship I have with the one I already have."

She frowns as if it's her fault she's pregnant. "And you're trying to figure out how to bridge the fifteen hundred mile gap between your two children."

I frame her face and brush my lips over hers, inhaling her minty breath. "I'm trying to figure out how to bridge the fifteen hundred mile gap between *us*."

"Speaking of us. How's this going to go down?" She nods toward the stairs.

"They like me. All of them. Your grandfather said it's so rare to find doctors who make house calls these days, and your dad smiled. I think he's impressed not only with my suit but also with my bedside manner."

"Bedside manner?" She quirks a brow. "You sent me a bottle of personal lubricant. My dad thinks it was a watch. He was pissed you didn't get it engraved!"

I chuckle. God, I love this woman. And there it is—the truth. I love her and it hurts like hell to not know how to be with her. I grin to hide my concern. "Such a wasted purchase on my part. By the time we explored *that* territory, you were plenty lubed all on your own."

Her jaw plummets to the ground.

I pinch her cheeks. "There's my girl. Finally, a little color in your face. Shall we go eat?"

As expected, Grandma eyes me with suspicion. The mood here has changed. I no longer feel like the hero doctor who makes house calls. I feel like the teacher who just got caught with his hand up a student's skirt.

"How was your *hydrotherapy*, sweetie?" Ellen's grandma sets a bowl of broth at the table and eases into the chair next to her.

Ellen smiles, giving me a quick glance. "Grandma, Dr. Hopkins is not really a doctor. His name is Flint. I told you about him and his son Harry. Remember?"

Grandma looks at me. I give her a wink, sitting across from Ellen.

"Oh, why did you say you were a doctor?"

"I didn't. I said I was here to take care of Ellen. You inferred doctor from that. I didn't argue."

Ellen sips her soup and wipes her mouth with a napkin. "Flint is an attorney. He's good with word manipulation." She smirks before taking another sip of soup.

"Samuel, he's not a doctor." Grandma calls like she wants the neighbors to hear too. "Hydrotherapy is not a real thing. It's just a perversion."

"A what?" Samuel either lacks good hearing or needs to turn the TV volume down. It's pretty loud.

"El-len …" Ellen's dad calls her name.

She eases up from the table and sits on the arm of his recliner.

"Fl-int?"

"Yes. He's the guy I told you about."

"Love … him …"

My favorite blue eyes shift to meet my gaze, and she nods, giving her attention back to her dad. "Yes. I love him."

I want to pound my chest. The last time I felt like this was the day Harrison came into this world.

Her dad grabs a whiteboard from the end table and writes on it. She reads it, giving me another smile.

"His parents are in New York with Harrison. Flint came to spend New Year's Eve with me."

I guess we're not sharing the baby news yet. It's a relief since I'm not sure what I'm doing here, except taking care of a sick woman and unborn child. I still don't know how I'm going to explain this to Harrison without blowing up his world.

Harrison doesn't like it when I change his sheets or rearrange the furniture in the family room. A baby and a possible relocation will completely overwhelm him. Cage is right, I coddle him. But killing his mother buys him more than the average amount of coddling. Killing his mother means I owe him a life that doesn't involve turning his world upside down.

"I'm feeling better, Dad. Flint's not a doctor, but he's really knowledgeable about herbs. In fact, after your stroke, he used herbs to get me on a plane. When he's not being completely obnoxious, he's pretty *fantastic*."

I narrow my eyes at her. *Fantastic.*

Ellen

"WELL …" I lie on my bed that Flint just stripped to wash my sheets. His household domestic skills are quite impressive. "I think my dad likes you, even though you're not a doctor." I grin. "But I'm pretty sure my grandpa still thinks you're a doctor." Flint lies beside me, holding my hand. "But my grandma … a hundred bucks says she's on her iPad right now doing an internet search on hydrotherapy."

He turns toward me, resting his head on his hand. "And how are you feeling?"

"Like a new woman. I'm still pooped and I haven't done anything, but I don't feel nauseous. You and your contraband herbs are my magical unicorns." I yawn. "But I do need a nap. Why don't you let my babies out of their cage so they can come cuddle with us for a nap?"

Flint turns his head, giving my babies a look. I doubt it's a favorable look. "Maybe we wait until tomorrow or the next day when I leave."

When he leaves. Of course he's leaving. My brain knows this, but my heart won't come down from the incredible high over him being here and confessing that he wants me and this baby.

"What's the plan, Flint? I know you well enough to know that you have a plan. Even if you aren't sure how you're going to execute it … you have a plan. You wouldn't have come here without a plan."

His forehead wrinkles with deep lines of thought as he reaches over and curls my hair behind my ear. "What if I told you I don't have a plan? What if I told you I booked this trip last minute after you texted me yesterday about not wanting to be pregnant?"

"Flint, I didn't mean—"

He shakes his head. "I know you didn't mean it—at least, I do now. All I knew at the time was you were feeling bad and you have no one to take care of you. So, I just reacted. No grand plan."

No grand plan. I let that sink in for a few moments. "It's early. I could miscarry. You just never—"

"Jesus, Elle …" He grimaces.

I rest my hand on his chest. "I don't want to, I'm just being realistic. I could miscarry. I've never been pregnant before. I don't know how this will go. But I know a lot of women who have had multiple miscarriages. All I'm saying is that I don't want you to stress out over this right now. You could go home and tell Harry, and if he doesn't react well, you'll have put a strain on that relationship over something that may never happen."

"Something that may never happen?"

I nod.

He sits up, hunched over the side of the bed, fisting his hair. "I need some air. I'll be back later."

"Air?" I sit up as he walks away. "It's cold and snowy outside."

He continues out of the bedroom and down the stairs without responding. I flop back onto the bed and try to get some sleep, but after long minutes of incessant thoughts, I sit up. Throwing on some warmer clothes and boots, I tiptoe downstairs and try not to announce my departure as I escape out the back door.

"Dang! It's cold." I pull my hat down over my ears better and cinch my scarf tighter. There's a rental car in the driveway, so he didn't go far. I follow the footprints in the snow to the dock where Flint stands with his back to me.

"It's cold. Go back inside," he says without turning.

"You're upset. Why are you upset?" I stay a few feet behind to give him some space.

"I'm not upset. I'm just trying to figure out everything."

"Were you not listening? I told you it's too early to stress over figuring any of this out."

He turns. Cheeks rosy from the icy air. Jaw set as if it's frozen in place. "You miscarry. Then what?" His shoulders lift toward his ears.

"Then …" I shake my head. "Nothing."

"Nothing," he repeats with a breath of cynical laughter. "I go back to my life and you go back to yours?"

I cringe, turning my body to guard my face from the wind.

I'm not sure which is more chilling, the frigid wind or his words. "I … I don't know. Maybe."

"Maybe." He nods slowly with an indiscernible expression. "And if you don't have a miscarriage?"

"Then we figure it out."

The warm air condensing from his exhales floats over his shoulder, proof that he's here. I still can't believe it.

How ridiculous of me to think that, even for one second. Of course he's here. When I break—he picks me up.

"Let's go inside. I don't want you in the cold any longer." He wraps his arm around my shoulders and guides me into the house.

"Oh shit." I stop, looking up at the back door and the man opening it to go inside like he lives here.

"Who's that?"

"Alex."

"Your ex?"

"Yes. He's here visiting his parents for the holidays."

"And how do you know that?"

I continue toward the door. "They stopped by yesterday."

"I see."

"There she is. Where did you go?" my grandma asks as we step inside from the freezing cold.

"Just to get a few minutes of fresh air." I smile, shifting my gaze to Alex, but he's not looking at me.

"Who's your friend?" he asks as if we're still together and he's curious about this man behind me.

"Alex, this is Flint. Flint, this is Alex."

Alex doesn't offer his hand, but maybe it would be weird since his are kind of robotic. I don't know what the protocol is on that. "How do you know my Ellen?"

My Ellen? Since when? I narrow my eyes at Alex, but he's still not looking at me.

"I wasn't aware that she'd been chipped and registered to a specific owner—like a dog."

I snort at Flint's response.

"Sorry." Alex gives me a brief glance. "Habit. I feel like we've been together forever."

Except for the two years you treated me like shit and the year since our divorce. But who's counting.

Alex steps toward me, giving me that look of adoration that he used to give me, as he lifts his arm up, touching my cheek with his cold, prosthetic fingers.

I stiffen as Flint's hand wraps around Alex's forearm, pulling it away from my face. "But just to be clear … *if* any man were going to put something inside of Ellen and lay claim to her … it would be me."

Just to be clear … I just fell in love with Flint Hopkins *again*.

From the kitchen table, my dad and grandparents look on with confusion while Alex's face alights with realization as he jerks his arm from Flint's grasp. Flint steps between me and Alex like he's protecting me. He doesn't need to protect me from Alex, not anymore. But seriously, I love this man so damn hard right now.

Alex takes a step back. He's athletic, lithe but strong, like most good surfers and climbers. But my ex-football-playing baby daddy probably packs a bigger punch.

"So you're the responsible one who put her in this *situation*. How kind of you," Alex says.

"What situation?" Grandma asks.

I move around Flint, giving my best fuck-you look to Alex.

"There's no situation, Grandma. I'm good, Alex. Thanks for stopping by to check on me."

Alex stares at Flint. I'm afraid to turn around to see the look on *his* face.

"Call me if you need me." A smug smile crawls up Alex's face. The only thing he loves more than knowing my secret is knowing Flint knows that he knows. "Like if things get too complicated."

"I don't anticipate that." I give him a tight smile.

Alex nods slowly. "Have a happy New Year." He turns and gives a polite nod to my dad and grandparents.

I watch him all the way to the door. When it shuts behind him, I turn toward Flint. He's wearing his special unreadable expression, but the vibe I'm picking up is that he's upset. At Alex? At me?

I don't know.

"El-len?"

"Yes, Dad?" I smile at him.

He gives me a look that's much easier to decipher. It's the look that will make me confess if I don't get out of here soon. All these years later, and even after suffering a stroke, he still has that look.

"Do you need something? If not, I'm going to go get ready to take you to your appointments."

Dad continues to stare at me. Nope. I'm not going to let him break me. Not right now. "Okay, give me twenty minutes." Without glancing back at Flint, I climb the stairs, but I feel the heat from his body right behind me. Maybe it's not his body, maybe it's his anger.

"You're mad, but I'm not sure why." I turn the second I step foot into my bedroom.

He towers over me in our customary toe-to-toe stance. "Your dad doesn't know about the baby?"

I shake my head.

"Your grandparents don't know about the baby?"

Another head shake.

"But your fucking ex-husband knows about the baby?"

My chin drops, gaze to the floor. "He was here. I threw up. It just ..." I shake my head. "I don't know. It came out. I felt like hell. I was mad at you and mad at the world because feeling like that makes you hate life a little."

"Why were you mad at me?"

I look up. "Because you are partly to blame for this pregnancy, and when I was bent over the toilet dry-heaving until every single muscle burned, it wasn't your hands pulling my hair out of my face, it was his. And that pissed me off. It pissed me off that you weren't here. It pissed me off that he *was* here. And I ..." I sigh. "I needed to tell someone."

"I hate that he touched you. I hate that it was his fucking hands that pulled your hair back. I hate that I wasn't here."

I nod. "I know."

The pain intensifies in his face. It hurts to imagine what's going through his mind.

"My dad has his therapy appointments. Are you coming with us?"

He pulls me into his chest. "Yes."

FLINT DRIVES US through the snow-covered roads to my dad's appointments. Flint makes dinner for my family. Flint dazzles all of us with his knowledge of—everything. Flint helps get my dad ready for bed so I can rest.

He reminds me why I so easily fell hard for him, long before I admitted it to him. Long before I admitted it to myself.

This man didn't come here to just take care of me, he came here to take care of what means the most to me. Those who love you the most, will cherish what you cherish. They'll nurture what makes you—you.

I grab a glass of water and turn off the lights before heading upstairs to bed. Flint's making my bed like there's going to be a military inspection. I don't think he ironed the sheets, but I can't say for sure. I don't see a single wrinkle in the perfectly turned down bed. Speaking of perfect ... the sculpted man stuffing the pillows into pillowcases and wearing only partially unfastened pants makes me feel something in my tummy besides nausea. "I'm not going to let you leave."

Flint smooths out the downturned sheet once more. "Yeah?" He takes my glass of water and sets it on the night table.

"Yeah." I press my hands to his chest, letting my fingers trace each muscle. "If it's a boy..." I whisper "...I hope he looks just like you."

His fingers find their way through my hair, until he's holding my head, tipping it back until my gaze finds his. "And if it's a girl?"

I smile. "I hope she brings you to your knees every day."

"Like her mom?"

Mom. No words can describe how that makes me feel. My life started over after the divorce. My dreams vanished. I've been waiting for life to show me where I fit in again. *Mom.*

I want *this* life.

"Do I bring you to your knees?"

Flint pulls me to the bed and guides me to sit on the edge.

He kneels on the floor between my legs, wrapping his arms around my waist as his cheek rests on my chest next to my heart. "More than anyone."

My fingers trace the hard lines of his bare back as I think about Harry's mom. "Surely not more than *anyone*."

He shifts his head so his lips press to my sternum. "Anyone," he whispers.

Sliding my hands to his head, I slowly fist his hair and drop my chin until my lips press to his head.

I want this life.

I want this man.

Do I want the impossible?

CHAPTER TWENTY-SEVEN

Flint

I WAKE BREATHLESS with this woman in my arms—and my child. Sweat beads along my brow from a nightmare.

We were in the delivery room and Heidi was at the door shaking her head. She mouthed "Penance" just before fading away like a ghost. Ellen gave one more hard push. The doctor announced it was a girl. I kissed her until her lips fell limp against mine. Machines started beeping. Everyone scrambled. The doctor said, "We're losing her."

In a blink, I was standing over Ellen's grave holding our baby.

"Mmm …" She hums, her ass pressed to my morning erection. "I like where your hand is," she murmurs as her hand covers mine over her belly. "Happy New Year."

"Happy New Year. How are you feeling?"

"So so. A little queasy."

"Food and more contraband herbs for you." I sit up and reach for her water and the glass tincture bottle.

She giggles. "Is it pot? Are you giving me marijuana?"

"The correct name is cannabis. Open."

She sits up, giving me the hairy eyeball. "So that's a yes?"

"Open." I hold up the dropper.

"Flint …"

"Elle, open."

"Not until you tell me."

"It's not a yes."

"So it's a no?"

"Open."

"Tell me!"

"I make my own tinctures. Marijuana is illegal to grow in Minnesota."

On a stubborn sigh, she opens her mouth. I squirt in a full dropper.

"Yuck!"

I hand her the water. "Drink. And let's get you some food."

"You're evading my question. I need to hear, 'Ellen, I'm not giving your baby marijuana tincture.'"

I slip on sweatpants and a tee. "*Our* baby."

"Our baby. You have to tell me how you got into growing everything, making your own tinctures. It doesn't fit the football player, the sports agent, the attorney."

I shrug. "I've always liked botany. In school, it grabbed me. I know I give Harrison a hard time about his obsession with science or music, but I was the kid obsessed with collecting seeds and growing anything I could wherever I could find the space. Just wait … at some point my parents will tell the story of carrots growing in the middle of our front yard."

Ellen grins. "Yet, you're an attorney."

"Yeah, well, people rarely do what they love. We do what seems smart at the time. I loved football too, but when that didn't work out, I did what seemed smart."

"I love hearing about young Flint." She smiles and stretches, arching her back. I focus on her nipples pressed to her nightshirt.

"Whatcha looking at?"

My gaze snaps to hers.

Busted.

"I'll make you your ginger tea. Do you want a piece of toast and eggs or oatmeal?" I tug on my sweatpants and pull my shirt down as low as it will go.

"Shhh ... hear that?" She presses her finger to her lips.

I listen and shake my head. "I don't hear anything."

"Exactly." She sits up on her knees and shrugs off her nightshirt.

"Elle—"

"Shhh ..." She shakes her head. "You know what else can ease nausea?" She walks on her knees toward the edge of the bed. "Endorphins. Wanna help release some endorphins in my body?"

"Ellen. We're not ... fuck ..." I suck in a hard breath as her hand dives into the front of my pants.

She strokes me. "I'll take this as a yes."

"You need food." I grimace as she tightens her grip and slides her thumb over the head of my cock.

"Then you'd better see how fast you can give me a rush of those nausea-relieving endorphins." Grabbing the neck of my shirt, she jerks me toward her until I'm bent down close to her face. Her lips brush my ear. "How fast can you make me come, Mr. Hopkins?"

"I'm trying to be a gentleman with you. I'm here to take care of you." I grab her wrist, but I can't bring myself to force her to stop.

"Take a five minute timeout from being a gentleman." Her teeth sink into my earlobe as she works my sweatpants and briefs past my hips.

"Your rats are watching."

She smirks, jerking her hand up my length a few times. "Just Gaga."

"Five minutes?"

Ellen nods. I love her messy red hair, those eyes … the freckles. She's the fucking package of all packages.

I kiss her hard until she moans, making long strokes with my tongue. She tugs at my shirt. I pull away and shrug it off before pinning her to the bed. "Move your panties to the side," I whisper in her ear.

"Yesss!" She slides the crotch of her panties to the side, closes her eyes, and lets me give her all the endorphins.

I remind myself that she wants this.

I'm not an inconsiderate man simply getting off at the first chance.

Her rats are not watching me—judging me. Except Gaga. The ugliest one of the bunch.

"Right there …" Ellen's pelvis lifts from the bed, reaching for more.

I kiss her and slide my hand between us. She cries into my mouth then jerks her head to the side. "I'm coming …"

Good for her. I want to. I really do, but I can't reach an orgasm with images in my mind of a hairless rat watching my naked ass.

Now it's just awkward. I'm not wearing a condom. She'll know if I simply quit and don't orgasm. But I fear I could break her pelvis if I keep pounding into her while trying to focus on her sexy tits or how warm and tight she feels around me instead of images of Gaga with her freaky little hands gripping the cage as she just *stares* with her black, beady eyes and pointy snout.

My five minutes are about up. Ellen digs her nails into the muscles of my ass, urging me on.

Fucking rats!

I stop. There's no point in continuing.

"What are you doing?" she asks, a little breathless.

I pull out and roll onto my back, sliding up my briefs and sweatpants. "You beat me to the finish." I stare at the ceiling with my hand splayed over my chest. "You needed the endorphins, and now you need some food since I gave you those herbs."

The bed vibrates as she laughs. "I *beat* you to the finish? Since when is sex a race with winners and losers?"

"Since you got pregnant and now your needs trump mine."

"Oh my gosh!" She sits up, holding her nightshirt to her chest. "You've had sex since ..." Her head shakes as if she needs to rattle out the words instead of speaking them. "Since we were together before Thanksgiving. You ... you've had *adult companionship* haven't you?"

"What?" I sit up just enough to lean back on my elbows. "What are you talking about?"

"It's the only explanation for pity sex."

"Pity sex?" I try not to laugh, but this is the craziest thing I've ever heard.

"Yes. Pity sex." She crawls off the bed and pulls her nightshirt back on over her head like she's angry at it too. "It's what you give to someone who you deem desperate after you've had your fill."

"My fill of what?"

"Sex! Are you not listening?"

So. Fucking. Much. That's how much I love this fiery little

woman stomping her feet and fisting her hands.

"You think I've been off getting 'my fill' of sex since you moved here?" I laugh.

She stabs a finger toward me. "Don't you dare laugh at me."

"I'm not laughing. I'm—"

"You're laughing." She marches out of the room, slamming the bathroom door behind her.

Okay, I'm laughing a little bit. I knock on the door.

"Go away."

I turn the handle. It's not locked.

"Gaga …" I step in and shut the door behind me.

Narrowed eyes look at my reflection in the mirror. "What?"

"I couldn't stop thinking about Lady Gaga watching us. That's why I didn't finish."

"Bullshit."

"Turn around."

She shakes her head.

"Turn. Around."

On a sigh, she turns, leaning against the vanity. "What are you doing?"

"Taking five more minutes to prove a point." I squat down in front of her, pulling off her panties.

"Flint—"

I hold a shushing finger to my lips a second before shoving my sweatpants and briefs down my legs. Her gaze drifts to my erection because it's pretty much a constant when I'm with her.

"I haven't been with anyone but you since the day you walked into my life." I lift her up onto the vanity.

"Flint—"

"Shhh …" I kiss her while wedging myself between her

legs.

She sucks in a quick breath as I push into her. My hand finds her breast as I find a rhythm.

"Race you to the finish," I whisper in her ear.

Elle's lips press to my neck, pulling into a grin. I show her how much I love her. How much I've missed her. How much I crave every inch of her. And then I beat her to the finish, pulling her across the line just after me.

With her arms draped over my shoulders, she collapses into my chest. And because this is my life with Ellen Rodgers, the unlocked door behind me opens while I'm still balls deep.

"Grandma!" Ellen shrieks.

"Oh … dear." She clears her throat.

I glance up at her reflection in the mirror, but she's staring at my bare ass like fucking Lady Gaga.

"Your grandpa is using one bathroom downstairs and your dad is in the other. I really need to relieve my old bladder." She continues to focus on my ass.

"Thirty seconds, Grandma. Just shut the door. Okay?" Ellen buries her face in my neck.

"Oh … okay." She backs out and shuts the door.

"Oh my god …" Ellen whispers.

I chuckle, pulling out and easing her to her feet.

"Turn around."

I raise a brow as she lifts the toilet lid.

"Just do it," she says with exasperation.

I pull up my pants and turn my back to her while she pees … and hums. She slips back on her panties and washes her hands. We both stare at the door for a few seconds, readying ourselves for Grandma on the other side.

Ellen takes a deep breath and opens the door. Grandma

smiles as we squeeze past her.

"What kind of therapy was that, *Dr. Hopkins*?"

She's good.

I grin. "Just good ole sexual healing."

Grandma purses her lips to keep from grinning and shakes her head at me before shutting the door.

"I feel very close to your grandma."

Ellen pulls on her robe, still red from nose to toe. "You're going to give her a heart attack."

"I'm going to start locking that bathroom door. She just doesn't look like the stairs are her thing." I lean against the doorframe. "Yet, she seems to navigate them just fine when she senses we're naked in the bathroom."

Ellen rolls her eyes and fists my shirt while she gently taps her forehead against my chest. "It's something with my dad's family. A sixth sense. I didn't tell my dad about my *situation*, but I have this feeling he knows."

"You should tell him. Do you want me to tell him?"

She glances up. "No. Do you want me to tell Harry?"

"Yes."

"Sure." A laugh escapes at the end of her single word.

I don't smile. I don't blink.

"You're joking."

I shake my head.

"You want me to tell Harry that you got me..." she lowers her voice "...pregnant?"

"No. I want you to word it more like this, 'Harry, I got a little carried away and now I'm pregnant and your dad is my baby's daddy too. Please don't blame him.'"

She opens her mouth to speak, just as my new ass admirer comes out of the bathroom.

"What can I get you two mischievous kids for breakfast?"

"Don't worry about it, Grandma. I'll be down in just a minute to make something."

"Okey dokey."

Ellen loses the smile as she returns her attention to me. "You want me to throw myself under the bus to save you?"

"You walk on water in his eyes. I'm not sure he's truly capable of getting upset with you, especially if you make cookies."

Her lips purse to the side. I'm not sure if I should cover my junk or run.

She shrugs. "Fine."

"Fine?"

"I'll tell him."

"You will?"

"Yes. But not for a couple more months. If I miscarry, it's all for nothing."

I swore after Heidi died I'd never let another woman tear my heart out. Yet, here I am, letting this woman do exactly that.

"Let's go eat." I turn before she can see how much her words slay me.

CHAPTER TWENTY-EIGHT

Ellen

I WATCH HIM pack his bag. Why does he have to leave? I know the answer, but my heart still asks the question.

"I hope Harry loved New York City."

"My dad texted me a picture of him in Times Square." He holds up his phone for me to see.

"That's a big smile."

"Yeah." Flint stares at the photo for a few more seconds.

"You miss him."

"I do. Some days I can't wait to distance myself from him, but after a while, I miss his constant nagging and incessant talking about random stuff."

And that's why he has to leave. I may feel this need for him to stay, but only one of his children really needs him at the moment, and it's not the one in my womb.

"So it's weird that we never really discussed a plan. Do we have one?"

He zips his bag and slips on his winter coat. "I'm taking your lead on this, which seems to be a wait-and-see. So I guess we'll wait a few months to see if you're still pregnant."

I flinch. "That's a little abrasive."

"No more so than your comments."

"What comments?"

"The reminders that you could miscarry. The 'all for noth-ing' comment. I get the impression that we are one hundred percent contingent on this child coming into the world."

"Well …" I say slowly. "Are we not? I left. You never con-tacted me until Harry and I were video chatting on Christmas—over a month after I left Minneapolis. Then you called me because you felt guilty about something you said to your dad. And you only showed up here because you thought I didn't want this baby. What's changed?"

"Everything!" He bites his lips together, hands on his hips as he looks up at the ceiling. "Don't you get it? I'm not going to move Heaven and Earth to make this work and then scrap it all if you miscarry our child. For me, this is no longer about the baby."

Everything inside of me tingles with emotion.

I want this life.

"You're going to move Heaven and Earth for me?"

He blows a cynical laugh out of his nose. "Is that so hard to believe?"

Yes. Men love me when it's convenient. When life is good. When they have two good hands. There's nothing convenient about us. When Harry finds out, life might not feel so good. And Flint didn't lose his hands, he lost something—someone—so much greater.

Yet he's here for *me*.

"Do it," I whisper. "Move Heaven and Earth."

A painful smile pulls at his mouth. I hug him, fighting the emotions that come with goodbyes, fighting the emotions that come with loving someone so completely.

"Heaven and Earth," he says, kissing the top of my head.

FLINT THANKS MY family, giving an extra-long hug to my grandma. I'm not sure, but I think she gives his ass a soft pat, however, I catch it just as he releases her, so I can't say for sure.

"No need to walk me out. Stay inside where it's warm."

I slip on my jacket and hat. "Not happening. Be thankful if you don't see me chasing after your rental car like a dog."

"Stubborn." He shakes his head and opens the door for me. We stand by the door to his car.

"I'm going to cry my normal tears, multiplied by one thousand because … pregnancy hormones."

"Crying's not necessary—oh, Elle." He pulls me in for a hug as I blink out the first round of tears and sob at the same time.

I knew it would hit me hard when it came time to say the words.

"There's s-so m-much I want to s-say."

He hugs me tightly, kissing my forehead. "Then say it."

I shake my head, fighting back more sobs. "It's st-stupid."

"It's not stupid. Just say it."

I take a few seconds to reel in the burst of emotions so I can get all the words out before falling apart again. "I love you, so don't die in a plane crash. Don't change your mind. Don't sleep with another woman. Don't think about me getting fat or getting stretch marks. Don't ruin your relationship with Harry to be with me. But *be* with me. Gah! I know that sounds impossible. But …"

He kisses me. And kisses me. And kisses me until I could faint. "Heaven and Earth," he whispers over my tear-stained face.

I nod and sniffle. "God … you sure do look the part, Flint

Hopkins." I grab the top to his jacket because he doesn't have lapels to hold.

He grins. "What part is that?"

"My man, of course."

"I like that part." He kisses just the tip of my cold nose and opens the door.

"I love you."

He slides into the seat and starts the car. "I love you too. Take care of my baby and her mommy."

I lift my shoulders to hide from the wind. "Her?"

His lips purse as he nods. "Just a feeling."

"Bye," I whisper just before shutting his door. I watch him pull out, but I don't chase after him. Harry needs him. And I love Harry. That's what's going to keep me going while Flint, god of my world, moves universes to be with me.

Flint

THE QUIET HUM of the plane mixed with the impossible decisions on my conscience makes my eyelids heavy. There's nothing more exhausting than the unsolvable.

"You haven't said much about Ellen." My dad nudges my arm. "You two figure your shit out?"

I grunt, shaking my head.

"How's her dad?"

"Better. But far from healed."

"And Ellen? How is she?"

I glance across the aisle to my mom reading a book and Harrison, on the other side of her, leaned against the window of the plane, sleeping.

"Pregnant," I say in a voice just above a whisper.

"What?"

I give him a long sideways glance. He heard me.

After a few seconds, he blows out a slow breath. "It's yours?"

"Dad ..."

He holds up his hands. "I had to ask."

I get it. It's the same question I would ask anyone else in my shoes.

"Should I be concerned that you're on a plane going in the opposite direction of where she's at?"

"She can't leave her dad. I can't leave my life in Minneapolis. The odds of this working are stacked against us, but I'm going to make it happen." I'm going to move Heaven and Earth. "I'm not sure what the biggest obstacle will be, her dad or Harrison."

"Don't complicate this. Get her ass back home—with you—ASAP."

I laugh. "You make it sound so simple."

"It goes like this ... 'Harrison, Ellen's pregnant with my baby. You're going to be a big brother. She's moving in and so is her dad. He'll use my office for a bedroom until we build an addition to the back of the house for him.'"

"That's insane."

"Which part?"

I shake my head. "All of it."

"Pull your head out of your stubborn ass and do what needs to be done."

"I can't just ask her dad to move."

"Does he know about the baby?"

I shrug. "I don't think so ... maybe. Ellen thinks he suspects something."

"He will move for her. He will move for the baby. You can get him new doctors and therapists in Minneapolis."

Rubbing my chin, I stare out my window into the dark starless night. We must be getting close to landing, I can see some lights below.

"I wanted to tell Harrison about the accident before I brought someone else into our lives."

"Then tell him."

"He'll hate me. I don't want that environment for Ellen or her dad."

"Then don't tell him."

"It's not that easy."

"Is your need to tell him for your sake or for his? Because I don't really see how this benefits him. It just feels like you need to clear your conscience."

Could it be that simple? Can I not tell him? Can I move Ellen and her dad here? Whether I deserve it or not, can I have a second chance?

"YOU'RE HOME," ELLEN answers her phone.

"Did I wake you?" I sit on the edge of my bed, tired from the long day of travel.

"No. Just playing with my babies."

"Can you start referring to them as rats, since you do have an actual baby now?"

"I will not, but thanks for the suggestion."

"Are you taking the herbs I left you?"

"The liquid weed? Yes."

"It's not weed."

"Sorry. Cannabis."

I chuckle.

"How's Harry?"

"Good. I think New York was a little overwhelming for him. He was pretty excited to get back to his rats. I think you and Harrison officially have Amanda sold on rats for pets."

"They're the best."

"They're not."

"Agree to disagree."

I grin. I'm sure she has them running all over her bed right now. "Have you told your dad about the baby?"

"No. I dodged him as much as I could today. I know he suspects something."

"Tell him."

"What?"

"Or I will tell him if you want me to do it."

"No. Harry may take the news better from me, but I guarantee you my dad will not take it better from you."

"Then tell him tomorrow. I can't have you fifteen hundred miles away from me."

"Does this mean you have a plan?"

"Yes. You and your dad move here. He can use my office as a bedroom until I have an addition built for him to the back."

"You're asking my father and me to move in with you and Harry?"

"Asking? Not really. I'm just telling you my plan."

She laughs. "He's recovering from a stroke. His doctors and therapists are here."

"He'll find new ones here."

"This is his home."

"You are his home."

"His parents—"

I sigh. "His parents. His boat. His friends. His favorite coffee joint. His collection of nudie girl magazines .... I get it. It's all there. But you are having *my* child, and I need you here, which means he needs to be here too. Tell him you're pregnant and let him make the decision. Don't underestimate his commitment to your happiness."

"Do you think we should wait a month or two?"

"No."

"I could—"

"You could miscarry. I get that too. I'm not asking you to move here to have a baby with me. I want *you* ... period. Get that through your stubborn head."

She whispers something.

"What did you say?"

"Nothing."

"No. Tell me."

"I said I want this life."

I let her words hold the space between us for a few seconds. "This life? With me?"

"Yes," she whispers.

"Then take it. I'm giving it to you. I'm moving Heaven and Earth. Just take it. Tell your dad. Pack a bag and I'll send a moving company to pack the rest. I'll arrange transportation. I'll find your dad the best doctors and therapists around here." I rub the back of my neck. It's tense with guilt and worry. Guilt that I don't deserve this. Worry that the laws of the universe will figure it out and take away what I haven't earned so that all can be right, just, and balanced again.

"Give me a month."

I shake my head even though she can't see me. "I'll give you a week."

"A week? I can't be ready to leave in a week."

"Then you don't have the right people."

"The right people?"

"Yes. Successful people surround themselves with the right people."

"Like your lubricant messenger?"

I smirk. "Exactly. I'll loan you my people. One week. Now get some sleep and share the good news with your dad in the morning."

After a few seconds of silence, I glance at my phone to see if we've been cut off.

"Elle?"

"Yes," she chokes out.

"Are you crying?"

"No."

"You are. Why are you crying?"

"Gah … nothing. Hormones. And you said tell my dad 'the good news,' which means you think …"

"I think this baby is pretty damn good news."

"I love you," she murmurs.

I didn't see this coming. In a little over three months, my life has transformed into this existence I never imagined. On my road to sobriety, there were many days I thought about ending everything. I thought Harrison would be better off without me. Sandy could raise him. My debts to this life would be paid.

And I wouldn't have been a father to Harrison.

I wouldn't have met Ellen Rodgers.

And I wouldn't be getting a second chance to bring a child into this world and do it right.

I'm going to fucking. Do. It. Right.

CHAPTER TWENTY-NINE

Ellen

FIFTEEN MINUTES MIGHT be a bit long to stand at the top of the stairs, biting my nails. This gives me flashbacks to my childhood. I'd hide in my room after doing something wrong and stew over it at the top of the stairs until I finally got the courage to make the walk of shame down to the living room to confess my sins.

I'm an adult.

I did nothing "wrong."

I'm pregnant … with no husband … and no job. So what?

I chew my fingernails some more. This is a brand new habit for me. It's rather disgusting, but I can't stop.

"You've got this," I whisper to myself as I take the first step toward eternal damnation. That might be a bit extreme, but I've never had the dear-daddy-I'm-pregnant speech. It's terrifying, even at thirty-two.

"Just you … and me," he says.

I grin as I look down at my dad in his recliner. "Did you just hear yourself? Four words, no stuttering. Barely a pause."

"Yes," he says with a resolute nod and a slight smirk stealing his expression.

"I'm not going to lie. I'll miss Grandma and Grandpa, but

I'm not going to miss Bungie."

"You miss Fl-int?" He cringes at his slight stumble.

"So much. That's what I need to talk to you about." I take a deep breath and hold it until I just can't hold it any longer. Here goes everything … "I'm pregnant."

Two unruly eyebrows shoot up my dad's forehead. I may have been wrong. Maybe he didn't suspect anything more than the feeling that I had *something* to tell him.

"Go be with … him."

I shake my head. "Not without you."

He shakes his head. "M-my home is here."

"I won't leave without you. The speech this morning is blowing my mind, really. And your mobility is getting stronger every day. I think you will make a full recovery. I really do. But until then, I will *not* leave you."

"Elle—"

"No." I hunch down in front of him, resting my hands on his knees. "It's more than your health, Dad. I'm your only child, and I'm getting ready to have a baby. A *baby*, Dad." I smile and it feels so good to not only want this life, but to know that it's possible … I can hardly breathe.

"Your first grandchild…" I give him a sly grin "…except for your five grand rat babies."

He shakes his head.

"I want you to be part of this. I don't want to worry about not getting the shot to send you photos of first smiles and first steps. I want you to be there." I squeeze his hand. "Mom would want you to be there too."

After long moments of concerned looks and a few failed attempts at saying something that I know is just another argument, he gives me one slow nod. "A baby."

I bite my lower lip as tears burn my eyes. "A baby," I whisper.

Flint

"YOU TOOK HARRISON to New York City for New Years. Wherever did you get that brilliant idea?" Amanda asks when I arrive at the office.

"Technically, my parents took him. I sort of dropped everyone off." I hang up my overcoat. "And I think my mouthy, occasionally useful secretary may have suggested it."

"Dropped everyone off?" She swivels in her chair, eyeing me with suspicion as I take a seat at my desk.

I can't put off the inevitable. "I'm going to tell you something. You're going to nod once, turn around, and get to work. No questions. No suggestions. No I-told-you-so's or anything like that. Okay?"

Her jaw unhinges as she gasps. It's not the response I anticipated. Is she offended?

"Oh my god! You're confessing to my brilliance. You're getting ready to acknowledge that I'm more than just a hot piece of ass guarding your door. Swearing me to silence is just cruel. It's like taking a child to an amusement park and telling them they can't ride the rides. Just ... cruel. So before I start my vow of silence, let me just say how proud I am of you for doing whatever it is you have done. And I'm here for you if *you* have any more questions for me."

She draws in one more deep breath before continuing her theatrics. "And finally ... I told you so." With a twist of her wrist at her lips, she signals that her lips are locked.

I'm already regretting this. "Ellen and her father are moving here in one week."

Amanda nods slowly, eyes squinted a bit.

"They will live at my house."

Her eyes widen a fraction, lips twist to keep from speaking.

"Ellen is pregnant."

Her eyes open even more. I'm not sure, but I think she's holding her breath.

"With my child."

Amanda's hand flies to her mouth to muffle her scream. Her eyes are the size of saucers.

"Harrison doesn't know yet. I need you to turn around and call the baker who made his birthday cake. Order six dozen cookies for me to pick up this afternoon."

She's in shock. I think.

"Breathe."

Amanda blows out a quick breath.

"Now…" I wave my hand "…turn around. This conversation is over."

For the remainder of the day she shoots me desperate looks, silently begging me to let her speak about the forbidden topic. I ignore her. On my way out, she grabs my wrist as I pass her desk.

I turn, peaking an eyebrow.

"Congratulations." She gives me a heartfelt smile.

I feel every bit of her sincerity. "Thank you."

I TAKE THE cookies home and put all six dozen on plates scattered around the kitchen before picking up Harrison from his friend's house. When we walk through the back door, he stops so fast, I run into his back.

"Whoa! What is this?"

I step around him, shrugging off my coat. "Cookies."

"Duh. Why?" He grabs one and shoves half of it in his mouth.

I shrug, taking one and shoving half of it into my mouth. He watches me with suspicion.

"Ellen's moving back to Minneapolis."

Harrison crams the rest of the cookie into his mouth while his gaze moves around the kitchen counter filled with plates of cookies. There's a fifty-fifty chance of him piecing this together. But I think, as he meets my gaze, he's figured it out.

"You want to have sex with her." He makes another inspection of the sea of cookies. "I think you want to have *a lot* of sex with her."

I laugh. He's not entirely wrong.

"I've invited Ellen and her dad to come live with us."

"What? Why?"

"She needs to help him, so she can't leave him behind. And I want her here because …" I pause to think of which direction to take this first. "I love her."

His head jerks back, brow furrowed. "You love her?"

"Yes. I do."

After a few more seconds, the shock wears off and his face relaxes. "For how long?"

"Well, her dad will stay with us for as long as he needs help. I don't know how long that will be."

"And Ellen?"

"She's …" I have this child who takes everything at face value. If I say forever and anything happens, then I'm a liar.

"Ellen is pregnant. You're going to be a big brother."

His head jerks back again. "Uh …" He laughs, picking up another cookie. "No thank you. Hayes' mom just had a baby. He said it sucks. Everything is about the baby. They even expect him to help change diapers. And he said all the baby does is cry. Hayes has to use earplugs and a noise machine to sleep at night. The baby pukes milk everywhere, and Hayes can't practice his trombone when the baby is sleeping."

Kids share too much. I regret encouraging Harrison to make friends.

"I'm trying to be considerate about this. I know you don't love change. But sometimes things happen in life that we don't plan on, and we're forced to adapt or accept them. I didn't plan on raising you by myself, but it happened. I didn't plan on falling in love with Ellen, but it happened. I didn't plan on you wanting pet rats, but it happened."

I throw that into play so he's reminded how I bent to accept something he wanted when I did *not* want rats. It's unlikely that he'll take that into consideration, but I have to exhaust all possibilities to make my case.

"Did Elle plan on getting pregnant?"

This kid …

"I'm sure at some point, but this is a bit earlier than either one of us planned. But it's not a bad thing. She wants this baby and so do I. And we hope that you will eventually grow to accept this baby as your brother or sister."

"I don't want a sister."

I chuckle. "*Again* … adapt. Accept. We don't get to choose whether it's a boy or girl."

He piles two more cookies onto his palm and heads toward the stairs.

"Harrison?"

"I need some time to think about this before I say for sure yes or no."

Pinching the bridge of my nose, I shake my head.

CHAPTER THIRTY

Ellen

I NEED PEOPLE. Maybe not a guy who delivers lubricant on the weekend, but people who transport pregnant women, stroke survivors, five rats, and a large moving truck fifteen hundred miles without a bump in the road. I want those people.

We leave most of my dad's stuff behind. He thinks the day will come that he returns to Cape Cod and his boat. As much as I want him to be close to me and this baby, part of me hopes that he finds his way back to the place I know he loves best.

One day at a time.

Flint stands on the front porch, bundled in a winter coat and hat, as we pull into the driveway just before dinner time. It's been a long three-day drive, taking lots of stops for my small bladder and my dad's old prostate. The hotels Flint booked us were top-notch, but nothing beats the sight of our new home.

I get my window seat.

I get the guy.

I get the boy I adore.

I get the life I want.

"Well, aren't you a sight for sore eyes." Flint holds out his hand to help me out of the car. The driveway has a light layer of snow on it from recent flurries.

I ease out and throw my arms around his neck as soon as I find my footing. "I can't believe we're doing this," I whisper in his ear before my lips find his.

He kisses me and grins. "Sadly, I think those are the words that are still going through Harrison's mind."

The driver helps my dad out, but he's pretty good on his own.

"Come on, it's cold out here." Flint takes my hand. "Mr. Anderson, how was the trip?"

"You're opening your home up to me, I think Jon works." My dad winks at Flint.

Yeah, they're going to get along just fine.

"You're speaking quite well."

Dad nods. "Days of being stuck in the car with a bossy therapist."

I laugh. Things started to click, and in a matter of days his fragmented speech flowed into full sentences.

"Harrison, come down here, please," Flint calls as I take my dad's coat and hang it up on the coat tree.

Derek, the guy who drove us in my car, and Greg, the guy who drove the moving truck, unload everything, including my rats.

"Jon, this will be your room until the addition is complete." Flint leads us to his office.

My cheeks heat just being in here. Flint's gaze makes a leisurely stroll down my body, letting me know I'm not the only one thinking about what happened in here.

"The stairs." Dad nods.

"They go to the master bedroom."

Dad's attention turns to me. "I can keep an … an eye on you two."

Please don't.

I smile. "It's a little late for that."

Flint raises his eyebrows, but he doesn't say anything. Not even the slightest apology to my father for knocking up his daughter.

"Hey."

I turn. "Harry." Before he can protest, I hug him. "I've missed you."

I release him. He has a forced smile and conflict flashes across his face. We're infringing on his territory.

"This is my dad, Jon. Dad, this is Harrison or Harry."

Flint rolls his eyes. I grin, coveting the fact that I'm the chosen one he lets call him Harry.

"Good to meet you." My dad holds out his arm.

Harry stares at Dad's hand. Flint nudges him, and Harry shakes my dad's hand.

"Hello."

"Harrison, take Ellen and Jon to the kitchen. Offer them a drink or a snack while I talk to the movers."

"Where are your rats?"

Of course that's first on his mind. "They set the cage inside the door. It's covered with a blanket."

Harry nods and we follow him to the kitchen.

We are home.

WE GET ALL of my dad's stuff unpacked and him settled in his room for the night. He's pretty excited about the TV on the wall opposite his bed. Harrison acquaints all of the rats, insisting they stay in his room, to which Flint doesn't argue one bit. Shocking.

"I'm going to go shut off the lights downstairs." Flint nods toward the stairway as I sit on the floor with Harry, playing with the rats.

"Okay."

We've had a good evening. Dinner was an interesting dynamic. To my surprise, and I think to Flint's too, Harry took a huge interest in my dad's stroke. How he felt. What he remembers. Is it weird to think he could have died? *All* the questions. My dad answered every single one.

"Every four weeks I will visit my midwife and she'll check on the baby. Would you like to come with me sometime? You might be able to hear the heartbeat."

He shrugs.

I want to push it. I want him to feel included. I want him to *want* this baby too. But … I let it go for now.

"Do you want to put them to bed? Or do you want me to do it?"

"I will." He keeps his focus on them. He's been a bit more quiet around me than he was before Flint told him about the baby.

I stand, bending over to kiss him on the head. "Goodnight, Mr. Harrison Hopkins."

All of the boxes with my name on them and my travel suitcase are in the spare bedroom. I ease open the door to Flint's room. It's dark except for a sliver of light under the bathroom door.

"My dad changed the sheets in your room." Harry startles me. He flips on the light to the hall bathroom.

"My room?"

He nods toward the guest room with my boxes stacked along the end of the bed.

I smile. "Okay. Thanks."

Harry shuts the door and turns on the shower.

Opting to stay in neutral territory, since in the past six hours I haven't managed to embrace their home as mine yet, I flip on the light to the guest bedroom and shut the door. It's a great room too—a window seat, a walk-in closet, and a queen bed. I find the box with my pajamas and change into them.

Harry takes the world's longest shower, so I use the downstairs bathroom to brush my teeth and wash my face, taking the opportunity to check in on my dad one more time, but he's asleep.

"Crap!" I jump when I turn the corner at the top of the stairs, running into bare-chested Flint. "You scared me."

He inspects my toothbrush and toothpaste in one hand and bottle of facial wash in the other. "I heard humming. What are you doing?"

I stare at his wet hair and just how low his jogging shorts hang on his hips. "Brushing my teeth and washing my face. Harry is still in the shower, so I used the downstairs bathroom."

"Harrison recently discovered how fun his dick can be, and my water bill has doubled."

"How fun his—oh!" My eyes widen. "No."

"Yes." He smirks. "Now follow me."

I follow him into his room and beyond to the en suite bathroom. He flips on the light. "This is *our* bathroom." He takes everything from my hands and sets it onto the counter by the sink. "Okay?"

I rub my lips together, nodding slowly. "Harry said you

changed the sheets on the guest bed for me, and all of my boxes are in there."

He leans back against the vanity, crossing his arms over his chest. "You think I want to be roommates with you?"

He's so damn cocky.

"There's no reason why you wouldn't. I'm a wonderful roommate."

"You're not. You're messy, noisy, and you have rats."

I cross my arms over my chest, matching his stance. "Well, you have OCD, a perpetual frown, and you're completely irresponsible when it comes to birth control."

Flint grins just to prove me wrong about the perpetual frown.

"This is weird." I laugh. "We're having a baby. You've seen me at my worst. My grandma caught us naked in the bathtub and having sex on the vanity. Harry caught us in bed. Your dad caught us in the closet. Abigail saw the embarrassing aftermath of the greenhouse incident. We've already survived all the awkward there is to survive, yet I feel very awkward and shy right now."

He crooks a finger at me. I erase the three feet between us and find my favorite spot wrapped in his arms. Just like that, I feel less awkward.

"I understand." He kisses the top of my head. "We really need to stop hiding in the closet and start using locks on doors."

I giggle. "That wasn't exactly my point."

Flint grabs my ass, giving it a firm squeeze while he buries his face in my hair, working his lips past my ear to my neck. He inhales deeply and exhales a low growl like an animal pleased by my scent.

I love this life.

"This is your bedroom and bathroom. Downstairs is your kitchen and living area. The front door and entry closet are yours. The driveway. The garage. The trees. The grass beneath the snow. It's all yours." His lips and tongue tease my neck. "*I'm* yours."

Yep … so much love for this life.

CHAPTER THIRTY-ONE

Ellen

TWENTY-FIVE WEEKS

WE'RE TWO WEEKS away from summer break, four weeks away from the official start of summer, and fifteen weeks from my due date.

I love this life.

"Elle?" Flint calls my name.

"Upstairs."

"That's my girl," he says as his voice draws nearer. "What are you doing?"

I crawl to the side of Harry's bed, reaching for more stuff he has shoved beneath it. "I'm not cleaning it. I know he doesn't like anyone messing with his stuff, but he has too many dirty clothes everywhere. I thought he might like to have some clean laundry. He's always complaining about missing socks."

"Leave it. I have less than an hour before I have to go back to work. Is your dad at Martin's?"

"Golfing." I'm still in awe. He says his shot is not perfect, but the fact that my dad is golfing less than six months after his stroke just blows my mind.

"Tick tock, baby."

"Just a second." I wrinkle my nose, tossing several washcloths into the laundry basket. "Why does he have so many washcloths under his bed? They're not really wet, they're just a little crusty in areas. I'd say he's using them to blow his nose, but they kind of smell."

Flint chuckles. "He's definitely blowing something in them, just not snot."

I use the side of the bed to climb to my feet, rubbing my lower back a bit. "What are you talking about?"

"Same reason he takes long showers. Now wash your hands and get your ass in the bedroom."

"Long showers ... wash my—ew!" I cringe, holding my hands out from my body, fingers stiff. "Semen? That's semen on those washcloths?"

"Hence the smell." He grins as I hurry past him to the bathroom, surgically scrubbing my hands with hot water and lots of soap.

"Boys are gross. That is just *gross!*"

"Forty-seven minutes, Elle. Let's go," he scolds me, while loosening his tie and unbuttoning his shirt.

We didn't have sex at night until the addition at the back of the house for my dad was complete. Apparently, I'm too loud during sex, which didn't work with an open stairwell between our bedroom and Flint's office where my dad slept. So Flint hired someone to take my dad to his appointments so we could have sex over Flint's lunch break. And when my dad no longer required long days of therapy, Flint introduced my dad to Martin, and now they are buddies who just so happen to hang out during the middle of the day.

Coincidence? I don't think so.

"I thought the nooners would stop when my dad's new room was finished." I follow Flint into the bedroom.

He's already naked from the waist up.

"Yeah, well ..." He pulls my tee over my head and unhooks my bra. "That's before I discovered you have such a dirty mouth during sex. It's so fucking hot. And the only time I get you completely uncensored is over the noon hour when we're all alone."

"I don't have a dirty mouth."

He ducks down, sucking in my nipple until I feel it between my legs. Every part of my body is hypersensitive and so responsive at this point in my pregnancy. I feel good. And horny. So horny. "Fuck me ..." I close my eyes, threading my fingers through his hair.

He chuckles, lapping his tongue over the bite marks. "So dirty."

I love this part. Mr. Tick Tock Hurry Up drops to his knees before me. I think he'd forego his own orgasm if he had to choose between it and this moment. It's my favorite moment too.

"Hey, baby," he whispers over my belly just before pressing his lips to my little bump, hands on my hips.

Tears fill my eyes today, the way they did yesterday, and the day before that—the way they have since the first time he did this so many months ago.

"It's me, your dad." Another kiss to my belly. "You're loved." Another kiss. "You're wanted." Another kiss. "You're the best thing that's happened to me in twelve years." Another kiss before his voice lowers even more.

Here it comes ...

"Be nice to your mommy. She's the second best thing that's happened to me in twelve years." Dark eyes meet mine as his lips stay pressed to my belly.

I feel loved. *I* feel wanted. I feel like someone moved Heaven and Earth for me.

He slides down my leggings and panties. I suck in a breath as a shiver jolts up the entire length of my body from his fingertips ghosting along the back of my bare legs.

His touch has had this effect on me since the first time his hand touched mine. At the time I thought it was this craving for *any* touch after feeling starved of that kind of affection for so long. I was wrong.

It's Flint.

It's his touch.

It's me.

It's how he reacts to my touch.

It's us.

We're that moment of light and whisper of hope that sprouts from the barren ground after the end of the world. It's not him. It's not me. It's *us*. We defy the laws of existence. We are forgiveness and redemption. What we have is not a victory against all odds, it's the inevitable.

Just as his mouth moves toward my legs, I shake my hand and give him the same crooked finger he likes to give me. He gives me a questioning look but obeys, standing to his full height. I back him up to the bed, working on removing his pants and briefs.

He steps out of them and sits on the bed.

"I hate how we got here." I crawl up onto his lap, standing tall on my knees, looking down on him.

His brow draws tight as he palms my backside. We don't pretend my life with Alex didn't happen. We don't pretend Flint didn't kill Heidi. The pain of our pasts keeps us grounded, focused, and living in gratitude.

"But I'm glad we made it." I kiss him, and he guides me onto him, both of us letting go of a moan.

Sometimes I like our quick and dirty-talking nooners. And sometimes I like this position where we stare into each other's eyes and spend our lunch time falling in love all over again.

We kiss. His hand kneads my breast before sliding between us, his thumb making circles on my clit. I can't see past the little bump between us, but I love, *love* watching his face as he watches his hand. His tongue makes a lazy swipe along his lower lip, eyelids heavy with lust like he doesn't know what he wants more—to touch me there or taste me there.

I lean forward and suck in that bottom lip of his, and then I slide my tongue into his mouth. He moans, moving both of his hands back to my hips.

"Flint ..." I curl my fingers into his back as this builds into something stronger and erratic. Our breaths quicken.

"Elle ..." His grip on my hips tightens, and he slams me onto him as his hips rock up into me. "You're so fucking beautiful."

Our mouths crash together again seconds before we fall apart. I love being in Flint's world. It's tragic. It's complicated. It's filled with obstacles. But ...

It's passionate.

It's addictive.

It's the deepest kind of love.

It's *everything*.

His forehead falls to my shoulder and my body collapses into his. "I love you."

When the tick tock of responsibility approaches, we make our way to the bathroom and piece ourselves back together. Like every day, I button his shirt, tie his tie, and help him into his suit jacket.

"Well, I have to wash some spank rags." I give his tie one final adjustment.

He chuckles. "Diapers, spank rags, underwear when they have a million accidents during potty training ... spit up ..." He shrugs. "Cleaning up bodily fluids is ninety percent of parenting."

"And the other ten percent?"

"Finding ten minutes of alone time to have sex with your husband." He grins. In a flash it fades, just like the color from his face.

My eyebrows ease up my forehead as I bite my lower lip and nod. It's funny how we've not breached this topic. I never feel like it's my place to bring it up. Even my dad has managed to not ask Flint if he plans on making an honest woman out of me.

"I see. Well..." I tug on his lapels "...I hope my baby daddy doesn't get too jealous when I sneak off for ten minutes to have sex with my *husband*." I can't resist tightening his tie just a little more, like a noose. "First I need to find this husband. Maybe Amanda can find a good match for me. I have a thing for guys with wavy red hair. Blue-collar workers. Pet lovers. Pickup drivers. Soccer players instead of American football."

We have a silent stare off. I wish I could read his mind, but he's not giving me a single clue. Not one single tell.

Finally, his lips twist and he nods once. "I'll give Amanda your wish list."

I smooth my hand down his tie. "You do that."

His hands claim my head just before he plants a no-question-who-owns-me kiss on my mouth. "Use the sanitary cycle on those washcloths," he whispers over my lips before disappearing out the door.

CHAPTER THIRTY-TWO

Flint

THIRTY-FIVE WEEKS

ELLE'S MISERABLE IN the dead of summer. Harrison's showing anxiety as we turn the spare bedroom into a nursery. It's as if he thought we were joking about the baby until I assembled the crib. Even after seeing the 3D ultrasound, which he thought was extremely cool, he hasn't shown signs of reality setting in, but the crib—the physical change in his surroundings—has caused a flare up in his attitude and anxiety.

An unexpected surprise to this new life of ours has been Jon. He's almost made a complete recovery, and he loves working in the garden with me. "Ellen wants me to stay, but I'm better. I don't need her to take care of me. She's going to have her hands full. You guys need to settle into your own routine." He tugs at the weeds that popped up overnight.

"Who would help me in the yard?" I glance over at him with a grin.

"I'm sure you'd manage. I'm itching to get out on my boat, but I won't leave until the baby gets here."

I shake my head. "She's not going to like it."

"What if you hinted that it might be best if I weren't here all the time?"

Ten weeks ago I fucked up and said the word husband and we haven't mentioned it since then, but I see the looks she gives me. "She's hormonal. Hot. And sometimes I think she wants to rip my nuts off. I'd rather not be the one to suggest you leave. Five more weeks. Just ride it out. She might feel differently after the baby's here demanding so much of her time."

Jon tosses a handful of weeds into the bucket and wipes his brow with his sleeve. "I shouldn't have made you those suits."

"Those are the best-fitting suits I have ever owned. Why would you say that?"

"She thinks we bonded over that."

I laugh, but it's true. I fell in love with Jonathan after he hand made me three suits.

"Now she'll never believe you want me to leave. She'll think I need to stay for you just as much as her."

"I do love those suits."

"Which one does Ellen like best?"

I don't even have to think about it. "Classic black with a vest. She has a thing for three-piece suits."

Jon nods. "She has good taste. Now, that's the one you need to wear when you marry her."

I still, planted on my hands and knees, sweat dripping down my face and arms.

"Don't act surprised. Did you really think I was going to let you bring a child into this world with *my* only child and not make her your wife first?"

I sit back on my heels and grab my water bottle, taking a long drink before screwing the cap back on and tossing it aside.

"What color shirt and tie?"

Jon smiles.

ELLE HAS A late appointment. Right after I hired someone to take Jon to his therapy appointments, she started seeing clients again at their homes, just like her father suggested. She still gives me the hairy eyeball when she visits me at work and sees the sign for my new tenant, a tutoring service. I can't lie. I prefer her making noise on top of me in bed than above me at work.

This is the perfect time to talk with Harrison alone. I glance in his room, but he's not there.

"What the hell, Harrison? Get those rats out of the crib!"

He shrugs. "They like it in here."

"I will kill every single one if you don't get them out of here now."

"Elle will kill you if you kill her babies." Harrison huffs as he sets them on the floor and says, "Cage." They all scurry back to his room and get in their cage.

I don't want to admit that I'm counting down the days in their three-year life expectancy, but I most certainly am.

"I'm going to ask Ellen to marry me. Are you good with that?" There's no beating around the bush with him. I've discovered the direct approach is best.

Harrison locks the door to the cage. "Why? What's the point? Does that make her my mom?"

"No. It makes her my wife. And your stepmom, I suppose, but you don't have to think of her any differently than you do now."

"Then why marry her?"

"I love her and it's the right thing to do."

"Why is it the right thing to do? If you were going to get married, shouldn't you have done it before she got pregnant?

Before she moved in here?"

"Yes. I should have married her before she got pregnant. Yes, I should have done it before asking her to move in with us. But to be honest, after your mom died, I didn't think I'd ever get married again. I didn't think I'd have any more children. Ellen and this baby have taken me by surprise, and I'm still struggling to do the right thing."

"Grandma was pissed off when she found out about the baby. She's not going to like you getting married."

"Sandy is upset because your mom died. I'm not sure she'll ever completely stop grieving her loss. But if she needs to be pissed off at me to deal with her grief, then I'll take it."

"It's stupid for her to be pissed off at you. It's not your fault Mom died."

This is it. Right here. Right now. There may never be a better opportunity to tell Harrison the truth. I know nothing good can come of it for his life, but I'm so tired of carrying this secret around. The guilt that it *was* my fault is enough to last a lifetime. The guilt of him not knowing is enough to last more than one lifetime.

"I want to talk about your mom's death."

Harrison plops down on his window seat. "What about it?"

I grab my vibrating phone out of my pocket. "Just a second, buddy." I answer it. "Flint Hopkins."

"Mr. Hopkins, my name is Laurel. I'm a nurse at Methodist Hospital. Your name is listed as Ellen Rodgers' emergency contact. She's been in a car accident."

And. My. Whole. Fucking. World. Ends.

Ellen

THERE WAS CHOPIN and heavy evening traffic. The first made the second bearable. I turned off the main road to take a longer but less congested way home. I saw the bend in the road, headlights, and then nothing. Every day really is a miracle. We dodge a million chances at death for one chance to live. The odds are not in our favor.

My name. Lots of people and echoed voices. Lights. Beeping. My name again. Baby ... someone said baby. My baby? She's a girl. I didn't think I wanted to know, but when we had the 3D ultrasound, I couldn't resist. Flint was right.

My stomach feels tight and there's pain in my lower back. And my head hurts. I feel my pulse in my head. It's angry. Why is my pulse angry with me?

"The father is here. Let's get her prepped for OR Two."

Whose father? My father? My baby's father?

"I'm here." Something warm touches my forehead.

I open my eyes again. Flint. He's wearing a blue gown and a cap like a doctor going into surgery. *OR Two.* He's not a doctor.

"What are you doing?" I say in a weak voice. Or at least it feels weak. I feel weak ... and my back hurts, but not as much as my head.

"You're going to have a C-section. I'll be with you the whole time."

"No." That's not the plan. I have a midwife. We're having a natural birth. We did the 3D ultrasound when they were concerned about the baby's growth, but everything was fine.

"You were in an accident. You're fine. The baby is fine. But your water broke and she needs to come out now. She'll be fine."

Who is this guy? My Flint speaks with confidence and authority. This imposter speaks with a shaky voice, like every other word is broken.

I don't like this. Why are his eyes red?

"I'm scared," I whisper.

His brows come together in an anguished expression. "Don't be scared." He kisses my forehead.

C-section. It's too early. Her little lungs aren't ready. Her immune system isn't mature. I close my eyes and wait because I don't feel anything. The back pain is gone. I don't feel her.

Beeping. Voices. Lights. Flint.

"Ellen, say hi to your daughter."

I open my eyes as a nurse holds my tiny little girl beside my head for two seconds before whisking her off in the other direction. She's too small. She's not crying.

"Is she breathing?"

No one answers me. Flint's head is turned, looking in the direction of our baby.

"Flint?" I say louder, aching with desperation.

He jerks his attention back to me.

"Is she breathing?"

"Mom needs an update," the doctor calls from just in front of me.

And then there's this faint squeak, but I hear it and tears spring free.

"She's five pounds three ounces and breathing on her own," the nurse says.

Flint kisses me again, and I die a little seeing the unshed tears in his eyes. "She's fine, Elle."

"You stay with her."

"Elle—"

"Don't take your eyes off her. Promise me."

I can't worry about the conflict on his face. She's my priority, and until I can be there with her, I need him to be her advocate.

He nods.

CHAPTER THIRTY-THREE

Flint

ARIA MEANS MELODY in English. It's also the name of our daughter who I have not taken my eyes off of since they moved her from the OR to the NICU. She's doing well, and they don't anticipate her being here long.

Jon and Harrison are with Ellen, and my parents will catch a flight here first thing in the morning. I've called a friend of mine to find out everything he can about the accident. In the meantime, it's just me and Aria, the nurses monitoring her, and the other preemies in the NICU.

"Your wife is out of recovery and in her room. In another hour they're going to try and bring her down here to see Aria."

I nod at the nurse without taking my eyes off my tiny daughter in the incubator. Thankfully, she's not as tiny as some of the other babies in here. And she's breathing on her own with just a little bit of oxygen. Aria is already kicking ass in the NICU. I can tell she's going to be beautiful like her mom and no-nonsense like her dad.

The hour disappears before I realize it, probably because I could stare at her all day. I remember this same sentiment when Harrison was born; it's feeling drugged with disbelief that this tiny human came to life because one night I physically lost myself in the body of a woman.

And there she is … that woman. I smile.

"Hey," Ellen whispers as the nurse wheels her into the NICU.

I stand and go to her, my fingers finding their way through her hair to hold her head while I kiss her. "She's so perfect," I murmur over her lips. "Just like you. Thank you for being so strong and amazing."

Ellen smiles, pale and tired, eyes red with tears, a Band-Aid where she has a small cut from the accident. Thankfully no concussion. "They said I can try to feed her."

I nod, moving out of the way to make room for the wheelchair. The nurse helps Ellen get Aria situated. Elle grimaces a little, I assume from the pain she's probably still in from the C-section. After several attempts, Aria latches on for a few suckles before drifting off to sleep. The nurse assures her it will get better, but Aria will probably take most of her milk from a bottle until she can stay awake long enough to nurse longer. She praises our little girl for already having the suck-swallow-breathe reflex.

Ellen pumps her breasts and gives her a bottle, Aria's tiny diaper clad body pressed to Elle's bare chest. She's going to be a great mom, and I think I knew it the first time I watched her interact with Harrison.

While the nurse helps Ellen and Aria, I step out of the NICU and turn on my phone. A message from my friend pops up on my screen.

Male - 27 - DOA - thrown from car. BAC .17 - Hope Ellen and the baby are okay. Let me know if there is anything else you need.

I stumble back until my back hits the wall. My lungs can't find any oxygen. My phone falls from my hand.

"Flint?"

"Dad?"

I blink several times until Jon and Harrison come into view.

Harrison picks up my phone. "'Male – 27 – DOA – thrown from car. BAC .17 – Hope Ellen and the baby are okay. Let me know if there is anything else you need.' Who's Ben? What's DOA and BAC?"

Jon takes the phone from Harrison. I can't fucking move. This can't be happening.

"Dead on arrival." Jon gives me a sympathetic look, but not the kind that says he knows about Heidi—the kind that says how lucky his daughter and granddaughter are to be alive. "Ellen was hit by a drunk driver. The driver died."

I lived. Heidi died.

"If he was drinking and driving then he deserved to die," Harrison says.

Jon nods. Holding out my phone to me. "I don't know if he deserved to die, but if someone had to die tonight, I'm just glad it was him and not my girls. Right?" He rests his fatherly hand on my shoulder, just like my dad would do.

I nod.

I lived. Heidi died. The wrong person died. The wrong person lived.

"How's Aria?"

Heidi died. She died on the night I was supposed to give her another baby.

"Flint?"

I shake my head. "Yeah?"

Jon narrows his eyes. "Are you okay?"

I nod on impulse. I'm so fucking not okay.

"How's Aria?"

"Sh-she's perfect."

"Do you need me? Or would you rather I take Harrison home? It's almost midnight."

"Take me home," Harrison says.

Jon laughs. "Okay, buddy. Flint, sure you're okay?"

I nod again.

"Call if anything changes. We'll be back in the morning."

Another nod.

Ellen

I STAY WITH Aria until I just can't keep my eyes open any longer. The nurse takes me back to my room, but I can't find Flint. He said he'd stay with our baby girl. Where is he? The nurse promises to message him and have him come see me, but I fall asleep before he comes to my room.

Several times during the night I wake when they come to check on me. Flint never shows up. I wake early in the morning feeling like death. Every part of my body aches, but nothing more than my arms that ache to hold Aria. After they check my incision and my bleeding and I eat something, they take me to the NICU.

No Flint.

Why did he leave our baby? Where is he?

"Good morning," the NICU nurse whispers. "Ready to work some more on breastfeeding?"

I nod and smile at my little girl in spite of the pain in my chest for her missing daddy. I work on feeding her, pumping, and giving her a bottle until they drag me out to go back to my room for the doctor to do his exam. Everything looks good. They want me to try to walk around today. The thought alone exhausts me.

"The more blood we can get flowing to all parts of your body, the faster you will recover, and Aria needs you strong and healthy for her." The nurse gives me an encouraging smile.

I sigh and ease my feet over the side of the bed. "You don't play fair." I smirk at her efforts to use Aria to motivate me.

"No marathons or heavy lifting, but gentle movements are good for you."

I walk to the bathroom, pee, and walk back without passing out, but by the time I reach the bed, I'm exhausted.

"Knock knock."

"Dad." I smile. "And Mr. Harrison." I wait, leaning my head to the side to see the door. "Where's your dad?"

Harry shrugs.

"I took Harry home last night. Flint stayed. Maybe we crossed paths this morning. He probably needed a shower." My dad looks down at his phone. "I'll message him."

"I haven't seen him. I don't think he was here last night."

"He was distracted when we saw him. It was late. Long day." My dad slides his phone back into his pocket and sits next to me on the bed, squeezing my hand. "I'm so glad you and Aria are okay."

"The driver died," Harry says.

"What?"

My dad frowns. "The guy who hit you. He died at the scene."

"Drunk driver." Harry looks at the monitors above my bed.

"What?" I whisper.

"He deserved to die," Harry adds without a shred of emotion.

My heart feels like it's being squeezed to death. "Does Flint know?"

Dad nods.

"I …" I shake my head. "I have to get back to the NICU. I need you to find Flint for me as soon as possible."

"Maybe he's at the airport. His parents were flying in this morning."

I nod. "Maybe. But please keep trying to get hold of him for me, okay?"

"Okay."

I reach over and tug at Harry's arm. He jumps like usual then settles into my touch. "Do you want to meet your baby sister?"

He shrugs. I'll take the lack of a solid no as a yes or at least a maybe. I'll take anything anyone will give me to keep my mind off the fact that Flint is missing. I know it has everything to do with the cause of my accident.

Past colliding with present. His son showing no empathy—no forgiveness. It's been the nightmare that Flint's been running from for over ten years.

CHAPTER THIRTY-FOUR

I T'S BEEN FOUR days. No Flint, in spite of his dad looking everywhere.

The doctor discharged me this morning, but I won't leave Aria. Then there's Harry … he breaks my heart. I can tell he's starting to worry about his dad. What will he do when he finds out that Flint's running from him? From the truth. From ten years of pacing the gates of Hell.

"She likes that," the nurse whispers as I hum one of the many lullabies I sang to Aria in the womb.

With a smile, I nod while feeding Aria. I sing and hum to her all the time, watching the monitors to make sure she's never overstimulated.

After she's done feeding, I let the nurse examine her while I use the bathroom. When I come out, another nurse stops me.

"Is your husband feeling better?" the nurse asks.

I bite my tongue from saying that he's not my husband. "Feeling better?"

"It's heartbreaking to see him at night watching you and Aria from the window." She nods to the window opposite of where I hold Aria. "I told him to go in, but he said he's fighting a cold."

"When's the last time you saw him?"

She shrugs. "Last night. He's been here every night. Just … standing there for hours."

I nod slowly, biting my lips together. Tears burn my eyes. Of course he's watching over us. He's always there watching … protecting. He's my superhero fighting his mortality.

"Elle."

I turn. "Camilla." I smile.

She holds up her phone.

FLINT: *I'm safe. Don't worry. Tell Elle I'm sorry.*

More tears sting my eyes. "Where's Harry?"

"Gene needed coffee. They'll be here soon."

"We're here." Gene holds up his coffee as they walk down the hall toward us.

I blink back my tears and find the perfect smile for Harry. "Are you ready to be Aria's music therapist today?"

"I'm not a music therapist. You just told me to bring my guitar." He holds up the case.

I nod toward the entrance. "Let's play her a lullaby. You're going to let your fingers whisper to the strings."

He stares at me expressionless. "O … K."

I bring her to my chest, letting my heart start the rhythm of the song. "What's your favorite lullaby, Harry?" I whisper. "Play it."

He shakes his head. "I can't."

"You can. Let your fingers translate what's in your head." He can do this. He's just *that* gifted. And the wonder of it all is that he doesn't see it yet.

His brow tenses; a few seconds later his fingers do exactly what I told them to do … they whisper to the strings. He plays "You Are My Sunshine."

It's my turn to save Flint. I'm going to piece his world back together. He just needs to hold on. He needs to give me a chance, the one thing Alex never did.

AFTER ARIA'S NEXT feeding, I ask Camilla to sit with her while I take Harry to the cafeteria for lunch.

"You walk really slow."

I laugh as we step onto the elevator. "I'm still sore from the accident, and I have an incision on my abdomen from the C-section. Everything's a little sore when I move, so I move slowly."

"They cut her out of you?"

"Yes."

"My mom pushed me out. My dad has a video of it. He had me watch it once. It's pretty gross."

We get some food. Harry sticks with a bowl of fruit. He seems lost when Flint's not around to tell him what's safe to eat.

"After your mom died, you lived with your grandma. Did you ever wonder about your dad?"

Harry chews a piece of cantaloupe and shrugs. "He was sick."

"Is that what she told you?"

He nods.

"But then you ended up living with your dad again."

"He got better."

"Did anyone ever tell you what kind of sickness he had?" I blow on my hot soup.

"What do you mean?"

"There are a lot of different illnesses: cancer, heart disease, diabetes."

"No. My grandma just said he was sick, and maybe I could

see him if he got better."

I stare at my soup. It must have been difficult to explain this to a young child. "Well, here's the truth about illnesses or diseases, most of them are preventable through better choices. Diet, exercise, abstaining from drug and alcohol use. But a lot of these things are addictive. You probably know that tobacco, like cigarettes, are addictive, but so are unhealthy foods. Too much fat can lead to heart disease. Too much sugar can lead to obesity and diabetes. And the more we eat these foods, the more our bodies crave them. Food can be just as addictive and harmful as any drug."

"My dad thinks I'm addicted to sugar. That's why he limits it."

I smile. "But you like sugar, right?"

He nods.

"When there's a plate of cookies in front of you, is it hard to resist eating them?"

"Yeah."

"It's because the feeling you get when you're eating them is a drug. Just like someone who inhales the nicotine of a cigarette, they get this good feeling in their body. But these feelings are temporary, so to keep the feeling alive, we need more and more. More sugar. More nicotine. More fat. More salty chips."

"You're not making cookies anymore, are you?"

I laugh a little. "I'll make you cookies as long as you can control how many you eat. But if you start to get shaky and moody, or you start to gain an unhealthy amount of weight, then I'll have to stop baking cookies."

Taking a deep breath, I move forward. "You know your dad doesn't drink alcohol, right?"

"Yeah. He says it's not healthy. He's a health freak."

"Well, a lot of health freaks are recovering addicts. Maybe they almost died of a heart attack. Maybe they got diabetes after gaining lots of weight. And they had to choose between living or letting their addiction kill them. And your dad many years ago was addicted to alcohol."

"What?"

"That illness he had, the one that kept him away from you when you lived with your grandma? It's called alcoholism. He couldn't just have one drink. He lost control with alcohol."

"It's not a real illness."

"It is, Harry. And there are a lot of people with this illness. There are a lot of people who die from this."

"But my dad didn't die. He quit."

"Correct. But most people don't quit their addiction until they die *or* something life-changing happens to them. Usually a near-death experience, like someone who changes their diet after they survive a heart attack that could have killed them. Some people call this a coming to Jesus moment."

"I don't believe in God. There's no real proof."

I grin. "It's a saying. It's something bad that happens and then everything in your life changes forever. Your dad had one of these moments, and that's what made him stop drinking."

"I don't understand."

"Your dad didn't believe he was an alcoholic until something bad happened because he drank too much."

"What happened?"

I'm here. I've walked him this far. Maybe Flint's walked him this far before too. Right to the edge. The moment of truth. But it's stuck in my throat, strangling me because I know if I say the words everything will change. I don't want Harry to hate his father. I don't want Flint to hate me. But this family of ours is cracked and vulnerable because of this secret.

Maybe everything has to break before it can truly be fixed.

"The night your mom died in the car accident, your dad was driving."

"It was raining. The roads were slick. They've told me this story before."

I don't know. I never asked if it really was raining. Maybe it was. It doesn't matter.

"But no one told you that your dad had been drinking that night. No one told you that he was intoxicated, and that's what caused the accident. Because it's hard for an adult to understand and accept something so tragic, but it's unimaginable to expect a child to understand."

"I hate when they serve watermelon that's basically rind. Look, it's clear. No color. No flavor."

Oh, Harry ...

"Your dad hasn't been around because he knows you think the guy who caused my accident deserved to die—because he'd been drinking. *I'm* telling you this so you know. He needs for you to know. But I don't think he expects you to forgive him. It wouldn't be fair to ask that of you."

"Grandpa found this donut place that has gluten-free donuts without dairy, but I'm not supposed to tell my dad."

I slide my soup aside and fold my hands on the table. "Remember that photo I had of the guy, Alex, jumping out of a plane? The one I told you climbed Mt. Everest?"

Harry glances up. "Yeah."

"He got stuck in an avalanche, and by the time they rescued him, his hands had severe frostbite. They had to remove his hands. Alex was my husband. But after he lost his hands, he treated me badly. The things he did and said to me were, in many ways, unforgivable. We divorced. But I kept telling myself I forgave him. I thought if you truly love someone, nothing should be unforgivable."

I blink several times to keep the tears in check. "But if I'm honest, I don't know if I'll ever completely forgive him. I will love him forever. Emotions are ours. They are intimate and personal. And they shouldn't be right or wrong. No one should tell you what to feel, who to love, or how to live." I reach across the table and cover his hand with mine.

He curls it into a fist, but he doesn't pull away.

"Your dad just needs you to know. That's all. And now you do." I ease out of the chair and grab my tray.

"If Aria died, would you forgive the driver that hit your car?" Harrison's gaze meets mine.

I hurt for him so damn bad right now. Of course Flint hasn't told him. Who turns their child's world upside down on purpose?

"No," I whisper. "But that man wasn't my father."

CHAPTER THIRTY-FIVE

Flint

"**Y**OU'RE A HARD man to find."

I look up from the table as the sax player narrates my grief in song. "Who helped you?"

My dad inspects the tumbler of whisky next to my half-empty glass of water. Concern etches his already wrinkled forehead. "Cage."

I nod.

He takes a seat across from me, eyeing the glass. "Jameson?"

"Monkey Shoulder."

"How appropriate." He chuckles. "It's been a week. Aria gets to go home in two days. She's gaining weight and maintaining body temperature."

I nod.

"Have you held your daughter yet?"

Swallowing hard, I shake my head.

"I have. She's a little miracle."

My jaw clenches. I know she's a miracle. I know what time she usually wakes during the night. I know how long she nurses from Elle and that she prefers the right breast over the left.

"This is your life, Flint. Get in the game or quit, but don't sit on the bench watching everyone around you live your dream."

When I don't look at him or acknowledge him in any way, he stands and rests his finger on the rim of the whisky tumbler. "I don't have to ask if you've taken a drink. I know the man you are today."

He tips the tumbler on its side, sending the gold liquid spilling off the opposite end of the table. "And Harrison knows about Heidi. Ellen told him." He hands me a folded piece of paper. "She asked me to give this to you."

I stare at it for a few seconds before taking it. Dad turns and walks out the door.

I always loved music. My piano teacher was my mentor. She lived two blocks away from us, a retired professor from Juilliard. I was her only student. She taught me because my dad made suits for her husband. Her name was Ethyl—the name you said we would NOT name our daughter. (I forgive you.) My junior year of high school she was hit by a drunk driver. She spent three months in the ICU. They said she'd never walk again.

My mom took me to visit her at the hospital every week. One of her therapists was a music therapist. I'd never heard of such a profession. Over the following eighteen months, I witnessed a miracle. Ethyl surpassed every goal the doctors said she would never achieve.

She walked again. Talked again. And played the piano again. Every therapist played a role in her recovery, but Ethyl said music healed her. That's when I knew what I wanted to do with my life.

BUT ... are you ready for the good part? Because

there's always a good part. Of everything Ethyl accomplished in her life, by far the greatest, most admirable thing she ever did was forgive the man who drove the car that almost ended her life.

Heaven and Earth, Flint …

I'm going to love you so hard, time won't matter. Distance won't matter. All you'll feel when you take each breath … is my love.

Elle

I CHECK OUT of my hotel room and go to the hospital just before midnight. Ellen should be feeding Aria soon. I can't hear her, but I know she's humming to our daughter. I just know.

"Feeling better, Mr. Hopkins?"

I turn toward the same nurse I've seen off and on for the past week. "I think so."

"Good to hear."

I stand in my spot for almost forty-five minutes, failing to find the courage to go inside. And as if she knows, Ellen straightens her back and twists her body to glance over her shoulder at me.

A second chance has never looked so beautiful.

I wash my hands and put on a gown, keeping my eyes on her the whole time. The automatic door slides open. She smiles as tears race down her face. I stop in front of her, aching to touch her, aching to touch my daughter.

"I want this life too," I whisper.

Elle blinks out more tears, her smile reaching the corners of her eyes. "I think it's going to be a good one." She eases to her feet. "Sit down, Daddy."

I sit in the rocking chair; it's warm from her body.

"Meet the girl who's going to bring you to your knees."

I grin as Elle hands Aria to me.

God ... she's so perfect. And so is our daughter.

WHEN ELLEN WAKES a little before seven in the morning to feed Aria again, I slip out and go home to take care of unfinished business.

My dad greets me, shuffling from the coffee pot to the kitchen table. "Getting in the game?"

I shut the door and set my bag down. "If coach will still let me play."

He nods toward the stairs. "Coach is upstairs feeding his rats breakfast."

I nod, making my way to the stairs.

"Son?"

"Yeah?" I look back at my dad.

"Do you realize you have eight rats living with you?"

I chuckle. "I haven't counted them recently, but that sounds about right." I take one step at a time, preparing myself for the unexpected. "Hey ..." I step inside Harrison's room and shut the door behind me, leaning back against it with my hands shoved into the front pockets of my jeans.

"Hey," he says without looking up at me.

"How's the rat pack?"

"You just call them that because you don't care enough to memorize their names," he murmurs.

"Wolfgang Amadeus Mozart, Johann Sebastian Bach, Ludwig Van Beethoven, Frédérick Chopin, Stefani Joanne Angelina Germanotta, aka Lady Gaga, and your three guitarists—Jimi Hendrix, John Frusciante, and Carlos Santana."

"Lucky guess."

I grin. "Probably."

"You want to know what you can do to make it okay that you killed my mom. Don't you?"

I flinch. Here comes a shitload of the unexpected. I brace for impact but speak my peace first. There are a few things he needs to know. "Nothing can make it okay. Not a million 'I'm sorry's,' not all the money in the world, or all the cookies from your favorite bakery."

"I'm ready for an electric guitar. A new one. The nicest one money can buy."

"Harrison, I just said—"

"What?" he says with an edge while ushering the rats back into their cage and shutting the door. "A new guitar is too much to give me in exchange for me forgiving you?" Pushing to standing, he kicks at a pile of dirty clothes on the floor, crosses his arms over his chest, and paces in front of the window.

"I'm not asking for your forgiveness. I just want you to know that I'm truly sorry, and there's not a day that goes by that I don't wish it would have been me who died in that accident."

"Fine. Great. Whatever."

"Harrison—"

"If you're not going to buy me the fucking guitar, then get out of here!"

"Harrison, that's enough."

"What? You can kill someone, but I can't say fuck?" He balls his hands, arms shaking. "Fuck! Fuck! Fuck! Fuck! FUUUCK!"

I draw in a controlled breath. "I'll give you some time alone."

"Great. More time alone. Maybe we watch more videos with my mom in them. Maybe you give me more framed pictures of her." He picks up the photo next to his bed, the one where Heidi's crossing the finish line, and he heaves it at me, missing me by a good three feet. It shatters against the wall. "Then what? All this *fucking* time spent in the past like you're so *fucking* worried I'm going to *fucking* forget her! Newsflash! I DON'T FUCKING REMEMBER HER!" He pulls at his hair. When he opens his eyes, they're red and filled with tears.

I don't remember the last time I saw Harrison cry. And when I blink, releasing my own emotions, I wonder if he's thinking the same thing about me.

He falls to his knees, still fisting his hair as his voice shatters like the glass frame. "I d-don't remember h-her." He sobs.

I step over the mess on the floor to get to the other side of the bed. Hunching down in front of him, I pull him into me, falling backward under the weight of him when he surrenders. And for the next few minutes, I hold my child, gently rocking him, feeling his pain and bleeding more of my own.

He doesn't know how to forgive me for taking something—someone—that doesn't exist in his mind. I get it. I finally *fucking* get it.

"THINGS GOT A little loud." My dad cringes as I walk into the kitchen.

"Flint." My mom hugs me. It's the first time she's seen me since they arrived last week. "I'm so glad you're okay."

"Thanks, Mom."

She gets me a coffee, and I sit at the table with them.

"The boy likes the word *fuck*." My dad eyes me, sipping his coffee.

"And he uses it with surprising accuracy."

"You two are terrible." My mom shakes her head.

I rub my hand down my face, blowing out a long breath. "I have to find some humor in this situation before it kills both of us."

"He doesn't remember Heidi." Mom frowns.

"No. He doesn't. I always just assumed. Hell, I think Sandy always assumed."

"I think he should talk to someone. Maybe a psychiatrist." Mom says.

I nod. "Maybe."

"Maybe you should too."

I grunt. "Probably."

"What's he doing now?"

"Playing his guitar. He doesn't want to talk anymore. And if Elle were here, she'd tell us to leave him be. So …"

"Leave him be," my parents say in unison.

"Where's Jon?"

"Breakfast with Martin, and then they were going by the hospital," Dad says.

"I need to get back there." I stand, taking my coffee mug to the sink.

Dad clears his throat. "The woman, the feisty redhead?"

I grin with my back to him. "What about her?"

"I know she's just a seven, but you're not getting any younger. Maybe think about asking her if she'd like to take your last name."

I chuckle while nodding.

2 days later …

"WHERE'S MY DAD and your parents?" Ellen asks when Harrison and I walk into the NICU carrying Aria's car seat.

After his breakdown, we didn't say anymore. I followed his lead of pretending it never happened. He knows my secret and I know his. I can't bring Heidi back to life, and Harrison can't find his memories of her. So … we let her rest in peace.

"They thought it should just be the three of us bringing her home." I kiss Ellen and then Aria on her warm, fuzzy peach head.

"Home." Elle sighs and smiles. "That sounds amazing." She puts Aria in her seat.

"She looks too small for it." Harrison frowns.

"She is a little peanut," Elle says in her mommy voice.

I carry Aria in her seat to the car parked at the entrance while Elle and Harrison walk in front of us.

Elle hums.

Harrison shakes his head.

She nudges his arm.

He shakes his head some more.

She wraps her arm around his shoulders.

He doesn't fight her.

She kisses the side of his head.

I fall deeper in love with her.

She whispers "I love you" to him.

He mumbles, "Love you too."

And for the first time in a decade, I know we're going to be okay.

"I'll sit in back with her," Elle says to Harrison after I latch Aria's seat into the base.

"No. I want to sit in back with her."

Elle's head jerks back a bit as a smile climbs up her face. "You *want* to, huh?"

He shrugs. "Yeah ... whatever. It's fine."

"Okay."

I close the door after Harrison gets in next to Aria, and I open the door for Ellen. "Let's go home." Before she gets in, I pull her into my arms, cupping the back of her head while I press my lips to her forehead.

"I love you, Flint Hopkins," she whispers.

I nod, keeping my lips pressed to her head, too choked with emotion to say anything.

After we get buckled up, I take my whole *fucking* world home.

Sober.

Two hands on the wheel.

Driving like an old lady.

"When are you going to give her the ring?" Harrison asks.

"Give who a ring?" Elle asks.

"You," Harrison says.

"What ring?" She looks over at me.

I keep both eyes on the road.

"The diamond one he stuck in his pocket before he left home."

"Little shit," I mumble.

"Diamond ring, huh? How many carats? Seven?"

I ignore her. I ignore both of them.

Several minutes later, Mr. Delayed Response says, "Ha! That was funny. Seven. She said that because you called her a seven. Seventy percent. You gave Elle a D. Remember that?"

Elle covers her mouth to contain her laughter.

"I remember. Thanks, Harrison."

"Just ask her."

Ellen rests her hand behind my head, tickling the nape of my neck. "Just ask me."

"Fine. Will you marry me?"

"What do you think, Harry? Should I say yes?"

I roll my eyes. They're making a mockery out of my proposal.

"Yeah. I think he spent a lot of money on the ring. It's pretty big."

Elle shrugs. "Okay. I'll marry you."

I try to keep from grinning, but it's a futile attempt.

A couple blocks from our house, Harry leans closer to Aria's seat and he hums "You Are My Sunshine."

"He likes that song," Ellen whispers. "Did you used to sing it to him when he was younger?"

I shake my head. Making a quick glance in the review mirror, I meet Harrison's gaze.

Heidi's eyes. Heidi's nose. Heidi's smile.

He remembers the song she sang to him. He remembers her even if he doesn't realize it.

I love him beyond words.

EPILOGUE

Flint

Five years—Dozens of Cookies—A New Baby Brother—And Thirteen Rats Later ...

"I SHOULD HAVE brought Harrison here by myself." I sigh, carrying my sleeping five-year-old across campus, messy red hair tangled around my neck like a scarf. I'm sweating. She's dead weight and way too much body heat for August.

"This is a big deal. We all want to be here." Elle walks with an exaggerated bounce to her step as nine-month-old Isaac starts to fuss.

He wants out to crawl around. It's been a long trip. All of our trips are long since we *drive* everywhere. I've not given up hope of getting her on a plane without having to knock her out with my concoctions.

One day soon. I hope.

"You don't have to go up with me," Harrison says as we approach the entrance.

Of course. We drove twenty-one hours to walk this far in the heat for a simple "Goodbye, see you at Thanksgiving."

"Call often. Study hard. Find a nice girl, but not until your senior year. And remember you are here to learn, but along the way lots of students will learn from you too. Be kind. Be gracious. Be happy." Elle hugs Harrison.

He hugs her back without hesitation. "Bye, buddy." He hugs Isaac too.

"Call every couple of weeks. Study harder than you think you need to. I'm not paying for you to fail. Find a nice girl to take your virginity so you can focus on your studies instead of your blue balls. Remember you are here to succeed and other students will feel threatened by you. Ignore them. Be strong. Be cool. Be responsible and wear a condom." I hug Harrison as he rolls his eyes.

"Harry …" Aria wakes, rubbing her eyes.

"Hey, Sunshine." He takes her from me.

Thank God!

"I'll miss you. But stay out of my room."

She nods, looking at him like he's her idol. "Bye." She puckers her lips.

He wrinkles his nose and goes to kiss her on the cheek. And like always, she finds a way to land her puckered lips on his. Harrison wipes it off.

She giggles.

He sets her down and hikes his bag and guitar over his shoulder.

"The rest of your stuff should arrive this afternoon," I say. "And don't forget to call Grandma Sandy. She'll want to know you're settled into your dorm."

He nods. "Bye."

As soon as he turns, a lady with a name tag hanging from a lanyard smiles at him. "Welcome to Juilliard. Can I help you find where you're going?"

WE GRAB LUNCH and finish our four hour drive—which takes us five—to Cape Cod.

"Boat! Papa! I want to ride the boat." Aria jumps out and runs toward Jon as he makes his way up the hill from the dock.

He opens his arms, always smitten with his favorite granddaughter. The only person she has wrapped around her little finger tighter than me is him.

"Two weeks." Elle grins, nuzzling her nose into Isaac's chubby neck. "Two whole weeks in Cape Cod. Mama's gonna get a massage and pedicure. Yay me!"

I glance over my shoulder to make sure Jon and Aria are still out of earshot. "Daddy's going to get laid. A lot. While Papa and his younger girlfriend take Aria and Issac to the beach. Yay me!"

Ellen gives me her best hairy eyeball.

"It's hot out. Let's go inside. Cora made lemonade and iced tea."

"How is Cora?" Ellen asks without trying to sound catty.

When she hired Cora to do some light house work for Jon after both of his parents passed away, she didn't expect Cora to keep his bed warm as well—especially since she's only five years older than Ellen.

"Oh, she's good. Keeps me young."

Ellen frowns at me as we follow him into the house.

"And you say I frown. Be happy for him."

"You're such a guy."

I am. Cora's a little too fake for my taste. And by fake, I mean her perky double D tits. But if Jon has a heart attack and dies with his face nestled between them, we'll have to believe he died a happy man.

"Elle! Flint!" Cora bounces those big boobs in our direction.

Elle hugs Isaac to her to avoid the full-on boob hug. Then she quickly passes him to me before Cora hugs me.

Well played, dear.

Elle smirks.

"Hand him over." Cora takes Isaac from me and snatches the diaper bag from Elle's shoulder. "I'll give him a diaper change and find a healthy snack for Aria. You two head upstairs and get settled in. Enjoy a little alone time before dinner." She winks.

I like Cora. I don't see what Elle's issue is with her.

"No. They're going out." Jon winks at Cora.

"Oh! Yes. We're watching the kids while you two have a night out alone."

"Alone?" I raise a brow. "What's that?"

Elle can't hide her smile. She knows it's true.

"Flint, come with me." My dad nods toward the master bedroom.

"And you come with me." Cora grabs Elle's arm and drags her upstairs.

Ellen

"WHAT DO YOU think?" Cora opens the bedroom door.

There's a dress draped across the bed. It was my mom's. A simple strapless black dress with a delicate cream ribbon tied around the waist. I remember trying it on when I turned eighteen, but my mom was bustier than me. It's always been a timeless dress. And I haven't seen it in years, but it's still my favorite.

"Your dad went through some of your mom's stuff that was packed away in the attic. He said you always loved this, but it was a little too big. I told him he should alter it for you. He didn't have your measurements, but I think it might fit okay now. Do you want to try it on?"

I feather my fingers along the silk ribbon. "Yes," I murmur.

"Wonderful! I'll plug in my curling iron and do your hair and makeup."

I take Issac and feed him while Cora grabs my bags from the car. Then Aria plays with him on the bedroom floor while Cora makes me feel like a princess.

"You're good at this."

She smiles. "I worked at a salon for ten years. There." She gives my curls a light misting of hair spray. "Let's get you into the dress."

I step into it and she zips the back. It hugs my curves perfectly. I close my eyes and remember how my mom looked in it—how my dad looked at her when she wore it.

"Beautiful." Cora presses her hand to her chest.

"Thank you," I say. And I mean it sincerely. Maybe she's exactly what my dad needs in his life right now. Cora doesn't have to be my mom. I'm not Heidi.

"You're welcome." She picks up Isaac.

"There's a bottle in the diaper bag."

She nods. "I already put it in the fridge."

"Mommy beautiful."

I look down at Aria. "Thank you, sweetie."

I like this life. A lot.

"Coming?" My dad calls from downstairs.

I ease my way down the stairs in the heels Cora got for me

that are a good inch higher than what I usually wear.

Flint's jaw unhinges as he takes a few steps backward like he's losing his balance. "Leaving me speechless, Elle."

I grin. We didn't have a wedding. Neither one of us wanted it. We both did the wedding thing the first time. Instead, I slid on his ring and I took his last name in front of a judge.

But right now I feel like a bride walking down the aisle.

"On a scale of one to ten, how speechless?"

He takes my hands and brings them to his shoulders and slides his hands around my waist. "Infinity. Just like my love for you."

I step back just enough to admire his new three-piece suit, much like the one he wore when we got married. A Jonathan Samuel Anderson original. But my dad used a different material this time, maybe more silk with fine pinstripes—and a sexy red tie.

I yank that tie several times until he smiles so big my heart wants to burst because … this life … it's mine.

After I deem the knot to look as perfect as my man, I grab his lapels and pull him a little closer.

"Flint Hopkins, you sure do look the part."

Out of the corner of my eye, I see my dad smile. It's a lot of joy with a sliver of sadness.

"What part is that, my beautiful wife?"

"My husband, of course."

The End

ACKNOWLEDGMENTS

A heartfelt thank you to the usual suspects …

Tim, Logan, Carter, and Asher—my favorite guys.

Leslie, Kambra, Sherri, and Shauna—my unicorns.

Max—my smart-ass editor. ;)

Monique, Kambra, Leslie, Shauna, Allison—the polishing crew, aka proofreaders.

Jenn Beach—personal assistant, graphics genius, and gate-keeper to my sanity.

Jenn and Sarah with Social Butterfly PR—My best find of 2017. You both rock!

Sarah Hansen, Okay Creations—book cover guru.

Regina Wamba, MaeIDesign & Photography—It's like you read my mind when you took the cover photo!

Paul with BB eBooks—I don't know how you do it so well and so quickly, but you are amazing!

Readers—author friends, bloggers, Jonesies, and every single person who reads my words.

ALSO BY JEWEL E. ANN

Jack & Jill Series
End of Day
Middle of Knight
Dawn of Forever

Holding You Series
Holding You
Releasing Me

Standalone Novels
Idle Bloom
Only Trick
Undeniably You
One
Scarlet Stone
When Life Happened

jeweleann.com

Stay informed of new releases, sales, and exclusive stories:
Monthly Mailing List
www.jeweleann.com/free-booksubscribe

ABOUT THE AUTHOR

Jewel is a free-spirited romance junkie with a quirky sense of humor.

With 10 years of flossing lectures under her belt, she took early retirement from her dental hygiene career to stay home with her three awesome boys and manage the family business.

After her best friend of nearly 30 years suggested a few books from the Contemporary Romance genre, Jewel was hooked. Devouring two and three books a week but still craving more, she decided to practice sustainable reading, AKA writing.

When she's not donning her cape and saving the planet one tree at a time, she enjoys yoga with friends, good food with family, rock climbing with her kids, watching How I Met Your Mother reruns, and of course...heart-wrenching, tear-jerking, panty-scorching novels.

Made in the USA
Lexington, KY
06 May 2018